THANESMAN

By
V. A. Boston

Botulf's Stone Press
2025

THANESMAN

First Printing: March 2025

ISBN 978-1-7342521-2-5

Botulf's Stone Press

To my husband. You make me laugh, for which I can't be thankful enough.

Contents

8

Prologue

"Idiot kids," grumbled Thaellas as he shut the mess cabin door behind him. The nine-tailed cat would come lashing with the morning. He'd told the recent recruits time and again never to get drunk while on the ship, and to never take even a sip of drink while up North. But they were new to trading in this part of the world, and they were young. The young rarely learned without experience. Unfortunately, experience here often meant death. Yes, there was good money in trading what warmer countries considered mundane for the ornate trinkets of the half-human barbarians of the cold North, especially after recent colonial exploits, the establishment of new trade routes, and an increase in long-distance travel had generated a growing interest for the foreign and the strange among various nobilities, but it was still dangerous to do business with the very people who had been constantly harassing northern borders all across the Holy Empire for the last ten or more centuries.

To an extent, Thaellas was glad the cold came so hard and fast to the lands north of the Ostran Sea, just as he was grateful for the biting wind that drowned out the ruckus below deck as he stomped up the stairs. Pausing at the last steps, he pulled down his fur hat, even though it couldn't go any lower, and wrapped his scarf over his nose and mouth a couple times before tying it in place. Yet the air still caught him off guard as he emerged from below deck into the wind. An Ithaenian man is made for warmer weather, not the icy autumn nights of the barbarian north.

Blackness surrounded them. On most nights, the stars and moon shown with eerie, silver light across the narrow strips of grassland bordering the river in which they were anchored, framed by dense, untamed forests and tall, rocky mountains, the favored haunts of monsters and the fae. However, clouds covered the sky tonight, and a light snow had begun to fall, hiding even the plain in darkness. Even that thought made the man shiver. A man of ports and seas and open air, Thaellas had always associated enclosed spaces with entrapment. He didn't like cities–too many people in too little space–and only stayed long at any one place to winter. Even so, he would take a crowded city to this Northern wilderness and its inhabitants, especially the half-fae-half-human barbarian tribes that infested the hills, forests, and mountains in most of the Northlands.

At the ship's stern, a lantern glowed gold upon a shivering sentry, a winter-primed rifle lying across his lap. Thaellas called out, "Any sign of trouble?"

"N-n-no, captain. Nothin' tonight," replied the sentry. "Not even a river sprite, much less a mixed-blood."

"Won't see many more naiads this time of year," said Thaellas, sitting down on a nearby bench. "See that frost on the edge of the river, once that starts up, they go into hiding. I wonder if some fairy folk hibernate, like the bears up here and the like. As for the rendeilxue, well, you never know with them. If they were human, I'd say they'd be crazy to be out on a night like this, but with that fairy blood of theirs," he shrugged, "never know what to expect of them. If only iron worked on them like it does the rest of the fae. But it doesn't, the bastards."

"I-I s-s-see, s-s-sir. V-v-very t-t-true, s-s-sir."

Beneath his scarf, Thaellas grinned to himself. Here was another young man–what was his name? He was Aurelan... ah, right, Mauranius–a youth more willing to work than most of his fellows, but who still didn't know Thaellas could recognize an exaggerated stutter anywhere. He kept that to himself for now and simply said, "Get down below deck, Mauranius. I'll take the next shift. Get some food and drink in you, but not too much of either. I'm a bit short-handed at the moment, and I'm sure you can guess why. But if you keep up the good work, I won't bleed your back and kick you off the ship at the next port like the rest of your peers. Got it?"

The young man beamed, his stutter mysteriously vanishing as he said, "Yes, sir! Thank you, captain, sir!"

Laughing quietly, Thaellas accepted the sentry's rifle and watched him disappear below deck before looking out into the blackness. The snow continued to fall. From the lamplight, he could see a little past the riverbank, where a layer of white was gradually growing. By morning, the grass would probably be covered, and by tomorrow afternoon, it would be half-gone again, the air still a little too warm during the day to protect the snow from the sun, even if the earth was ready for winter. After checking that the rifle was ready in case of trouble, he dug into his pocket and pulled out a wooden pipe and tobacco box. Thaellas didn't usually smoke this late at night or while on guard duty, but the alien cold and silence and the sharp smell of snow made him crave the familiar comfort. Lighting a match took some time due to the wind, but eventually he had the leaves lit and the mouth of the pipe slipped between the layers of scarf.

Much time passed, made more bearable by the pleasurable taste and smell of tobacco and the feel of the pipe between his teeth. The snow was getting heavy, now, and Thaellas worried they might have to delay departure tomorrow. He never sailed at night in the Northlands. The water was too rocky, there were too many shallow areas, and with the added danger of ice and snow… he hoped to God he hadn't delayed their return too late this year. He was just considering finding someone to take over as sentry so he could pull aside his navigator to discuss plans for the morning when hints of sound drifted out from the shore, causing his arms to automatically lift the rifle toward the darkness.

At first, he thought he might have been mistaken, hoped it, even. Then came a voice, faint on the wind and weak, and two figures suddenly appeared within the curve of snow tinted gold from the lantern light. A pair of rendeilxue, one dragging the other along by an arm draped over his shoulder. The one being dragged appeared unconscious, and the man carrying him looked wan and pale as he stumbled out of the darkness through the snow, yelling hoarsely for help in strongly accented but still understandable Ithaenian.

Thaellas gaped at them, still unsure if he was seeing truth or an illusion. Then the walking man saw him. Their eyes met, and there was no denying the reality of those frantic, fevered, and determined eyes. A moment later, those eyes rolled back, and their owner groaned and collapsed. From reflex alone, the ship man jumped up to help the figures now slowly disappearing beneath the falling snow, but when the man's mind caught up with his body, he paused. These were not humans. They were rendeilxue. For all he knew, this was a trap to lure him and his crew off the ship before raiders snuck aboard to gut the ship, kill the crew, and steal his goods. Such a thing had happened to a fellow merchant, an acquaintance who had dropped his guard at the wrong moment and washed up on shore with the ruins of his boat down where the river met the Ostran Sea, the only witness a member of the crew who had come ashore with him and died a few days later. What if this was a similar trick? If they were pure-blooded fae, Thaellas would assume so, but….

Thaellas cursed their half-human blood as he ran below deck.

A few minutes later, he and a few of the sober men rowed the dinghy to shore. When they reached the unconscious figures, snow sticking to their wool cloaks, Thaellas scanned the blackness for signs of ambush, rifle held at the ready, and then paused again as he looked down at the rendeilxue. As seen before, there were two, their clothing hard-worn and half-frozen, both looking sickly and underfed. One man was taller and more physically robust—almost human even, in his breadth of body compared to the fae-like litheness typical of his race—while the other looked more like a waif than a man. But Thaellas felt sure that the thin, stick-of-a-man was the one who had called out to him while carrying his companion. Perhaps he was mistaken?

"Sir?" Mauranius shouted over the wind.

Thaellas shook the thoughts from his mind. Now was the time for action. With as much speed as care would permit, the merchant crew got the two strangers onboard the ship and changed into spare clothes, Thaellas snapping out a few choice insults along the way as the men stopped to stare at the veins visible on the rendeilxue's backs in the tree-like patterns that marked every member of their race. Soon they were both bundled up and laid to bed within Thaellas's own cabin. Both ran high fevers, their pointed ears and youthful faces an odd, olive brown due to their inhuman blood, and they both shivered horribly despite the multiple blankets. Makeshift bandages wrapped around ugly, infected wounds were changed, and the ship's physician somehow managed to get some water and medicinal broths down their throats. He shook his head in doubt that either one would last till morning. They were too weak, he said, and had signs of frostbite. Not bad enough to cause permanent damage, but still evidence of the conditions they had been enduring. Even if they survived the night, they probably wouldn't live long enough to get proper treatment. However, in the face of Thaellas's protests, the doctor agreed to do what he could but would make no promises of success. Thanking him curtly, Thaellas dismissed the doctor so the man could go make the necessary preparations for the all-night vigil he would now have to keep.

Thaellas released the other men to their respective tasks, having already decided to stay up and help the doctor himself. Once alone, he settled into a chair by his cot, now occupied by the smaller of the two rendeilxue for the purely practical reason that the other was too tall for it. Rubbing his hands across his face and through his hair, the Ithaenian merchant released a long, loud sigh. He knew the doctor was right. These two were in bad shape. Very bad. He shouldn't get his hopes up. By all rights, he shouldn't even be disturbed by the diagnosis. He didn't know these men. No. They weren't even men, only half. And yet, he had still taken them under his care. Against all his reason told him, even though they were only half-human, he cared about them now and didn't want to fail in the responsibility he had taken on.

A low groan pulled him from his thoughts to the patient lying beside him. The figure moaned again and slowly opened his pale blue eyes in a half-focused stare. Thaellas jumped to his feet, and the eyes sluggishly strayed to him. The wind-chapped lips parted, moving wordlessly before their owner croaked out, "H-help."

Kneeling down to better hear the weak voice, Thaellas said, "Yes. Don't worry. We're here to help you. You're safe now."

The eyes stared at him without comprehension, and Thaellas wondered if the mind behind them even understood him. After all, just because Thaellas had picked up a few rendeilxue words after years of working up and down the river, trading with the different tribes, that didn't mean he knew the language. Maybe it was the same for this pale-eye half-man.

After a moment more, the rendeilxue repeated, "Help… help."

"Yes. We're here to help," Thaellas said again, more slowly this time.

Suddenly, the rendeilxue's eyes widened, and Thaellas saw fear in the unfocused gaze. To his shock, the sick man tried to get up. Thaellas protested, insisting that the man, who looked ready to keel over dead at any moment, lie back down, but he seemed determined to not just sit up but stand. Between shivering breaths, he muttered, "R-Restag… help… Restag…."

"Restag? Is that your friend? He's here, too. Look," said Thaellas. He took the sick man by his shoulders, turning and supporting him so he could see his companion sleeping on a pallet on the floor. Immediately, the worry left the rendeilxue's face, and Thaellas nearly dropped him as he suddenly went limp. Once lowered to the bed, the man then reached within his shirt, and again he looked afraid as he mumbled, "B-bag?"

"If you mean the bag you had hanging from your neck, here you go," said Thaellas, picking out the item from the disordered pile of the men's meager possessions. He handed the small bag to the rendeilxue, saying, "Had to take it off, since it's cold and wet. A bit heavy, too, not the kind of thing a sick man should be wearing, let me tell you."

Even if the barbarian had understood that string of words, he completely ignored them as he struggled to open the little drawstring bag. Eventually, Thaellas took it and opened it for him, dumping the single item inside into the sick man's palm. It was a ring. Beautifully crafted, even when compared to other pieces Thaellas had procured from the preternaturally skilled metalworkers of the northern rendeilxue, made of thin wires of pure gold twined together into a delicate band that wound around the finger and then around a large disk imprinted with an intricately designed and stylised animal—a ram, he thought—and a circle of rendeilxue runes. A seal ring, Thaellas realized with a start. Holding out the ring, the barbarian said, "Th-Thenika… take… Aleu…kus… give… A…leu…."

The hand fell, and the ring clinking to the cabin floor as Thaellas stared pale-faced at the once again sleeping form that breathed raggedly before erupting in a fit of wet coughs. The horrible sound unnerved Thaellas, who could only look helplessly on. Thankfully, the physician returned moments later, taking over and directing Thaellas until the fit passed and the sick man settled back into fevered sleep. While the physician began unpacking his supplies, Thaellas picked up the ring. He stared at it till the physician called his attention again, shakily dropping the item into his pocket.

Thenika. That was the capital of Thaellas's homeland, Ithaenia, currently ruled by King Aleukus III, a name no rendeilxue barbarian, to his knowledge, even cared to know. But this one did, and he had a seal ring, another anachronism among a people that barely used their writing system for more than keeping inventories. One of those facts was odd enough. Both together….

As the night and battle against death dragged on, Thaellas prayed to God the physician's prediction would prove wrong.

15

PART 1
THE
NORTHLANDS

Chapter 1

"Thane's thunder, Witheric! A dragon would envy such a hoard as this!"

Witheric Iron-Brow, High Thane of the Asgradi, looked up from the map he was copying to see his chief companion maneuvering around tables draped in parchment and stacks of leather-bound sheets. He smiled apologetically when the warrior's scabbard caught on a table's leg as he stepped between it and a pile of tomes topped with trinkets, jerking him to a stop. "It has overflowed the dam, hasn't it?" Witheric said.

The warrior snorted. "It has drowned the town. Were these scribblings gold, we'd be burned to ash by now, if not by dragons than by all the other tribes."

"So I have doomed us by both water and fire, have I, Restag Far-Sighted? It is good these are not earthly gold then," said the thane, smiling at the man's grimace. Restag knew what was coming next, but so long as his friend voiced his objections, Witheric would respond as he did now. "No, these are more than gold. They are star-gold! The gold of the gods to match and surpass the Eisenband itself," he said, tapping the runic ring around his forehead.

Gathering a pile of loose parchments that had slipped to the floor, Restag evened their edges as best he could and placed them back on the table, saying, "Don't let the Council hear you say such a thing. Were you not High Thane, you could be justly slain for calling the marks of mere men the works of gods."

"Were you not Thanesman, I would not have said it," replied Witheric. Satisfaction beat in the young thane's chest as the hints of a proud smile showed on his friend's face.

Finally reaching the table at which Witheric worked, Restag looked down with disapproval at the map, the land already drawn and inked and now in the process of being labeled not with the foreign letters of the original but with Asgradi runes of Witheric's own translation. "More of the red-bloods' work? Do you really believe the land to submit more to human eyes than to your own?"

"The Ithaenians have been refining their maps of the lands along the river, including our own, for centuries. Why should I not trust their work over one that is drawn today and tomorrow used to kindle a fire or to craft a shield?" replied the thane.

"And all this… whatever it is," said Restag, motioning to the stacks and piles around the room.

"It's called paper, Restag, as you well know, and since you are so forgetful today, those are called books," responded Witheric.

Snorting again, Restag said, "Scraps. Scraps of strange leaf covered with scribbles and good leather wasted."

Witheric eyed the pile of "scraps" and "wasted leather" the warrior had so carefully stacked behind him but said nothing. Returning to the map he was inking, the High Thane said, "What do you need from me, Restag?"

"Nothing," replied Restag, regaining Witheric's attention. "However, I received something for you from those returning from trading with the red-bloods. I thought you might want it as soon as possible."

The map was forgotten as Restag pulled from his pouch a small, folded paper kept closed by a wax seal bearing the image of a ring of leaves surrounding a large man standing over a lion. Crying out excitedly, Witheric snatched the letter away and quickly opened it, slowly reading and trying to understand the contents. Eventually, he moved to a stack of rolled parchments and searched through their notes to translate some words he recognized but whose meaning escaped him. In his haste, the young thane missed the warm smile that came to his friend's face, which soon disappeared again beneath the stern mask. After a little while, Restag said, "Another message from your human scribbler?"

"From the Ithaenian king, Restag. King Aleukus of Ithaenia," said Witheric, not looking up from his notes. He smiled. "He… I think he says they are doing well, that the harvests were good and the waters peaceful. In response to my question, he says his son is getting stronger, that he tried… tried to hold… I think it says 'sword.' Restag, come look at it and tell me if you think it says 'sword' here."

When he looked up to his friend, the warrior was bent over the map, carefully inking in the runes sketched across the surface. Eyes still focused on the task, Restag replied, "You know I cannot read those human scribblings. You are one of the only Asgradi among the Eisensaet who even bothers with learning the human's boneless speech, let alone its twisted writing."

Smiling despite the harsh words, Witheric said, "Then maybe I shall be the first of our people to inscribe a bond-bone with them."

Looking up briefly, Restag said, "I thought humans used this paper-leaf for their bond-runes, not bones or even wood. Their word must be easily broken to use a thing so easily destroyed. How can a bond that cannot even withstand the rain and mists of summer withstand the ice and snow of winter?"

Witheric frowned deeply. "You do not trust the humans to keep their word."

"I do not trust any who can so easily give their words away to people who cannot even read them," he replied.

Witheric sighed. Though at times frustrating, his friend's bluntness was why Witheric had named Restag his Thanesman, despite the Council's desire for the position to be filled by someone older and less willing to entertaining the High Thane's oddities. The tall, sinewy man before him also stood among the Eisensaet tribe's best warriors and was therefore highly respected by both warriors and thralls. Then there was his fae-gift. He alone was truly Far-Sighted among the living of his clan, able to see not just beyond an ordinary man's abilities–beyond stone and hill, across rivers and lakes and seas, and through the shadows of the forest–but even into the minds and hearts of men. No one else of his clan currently held the fae-gift so strong, not even the High Elder, who shared the warrior's blood. As such, none could reasonably question Restag's right to stand beside the High Thane as his right hand and chief retainer. However, many on the Council still did, Witheric knew, and he worried for his outspoken friend. Even the High Thane could not command the Council of High Elders in all things and was required to at least heed the rune-readers' advice, however much he disagreed with it. If only they knew how much Restag did check his master's fancies, perhaps they would not... no. That was not the true cause of their doubt. The true reason, he knew, was that Restag was his Thanesman, and a Thanesman of such power and respect beside a thane like himself would never sit well with the current High Council. If he were more to their liking, then maybe....

Letting out another sigh, Witheric said, "Perhaps you're right and the word of most humans is weak. But the word of King Aleukus is a straight-shafted spear, true in its purpose and aim, and binding as an iron chain."

Restag grunted skeptically. "Perhaps. But tell me, why would a human king, one with such apparent wealth and stature, receive and send…."

"Friend-speech?"

"Trinket-speech with the ruler of a small tribe such as ours. High Thane you may be in blood and title, but few recognize it beyond the safety of the old songs. Why should this King Aleukus take such interest in a gleam-less crown fallen from its once high throne seven-hundred years passed?"

Witheric opened his mouth to answer, but nothing came to mind. Eventually, he could only lay the letter on the table beside him, lean against the wood, and say, "I don't know."

His eyes searched the floorboards, tracing the whorls and lines of the wood's grain as if they were a river that could carry him to the answer. When they led him nowhere, he removed the band of iron from his brow, turning it in his hands, examining the ancient runes that told the story and purpose of the crown's fashioning, the origin of his people and his blood right as High Thane over all Asgradi. Bitterness welled in his chest, an emotion he could not quite hide as he said, "I expect it is hard to believe. As hard to believe for you as it is for many of our own people to believe I am a thane worth serving."

Restag once again glanced up, taking stock of his lord and friend. It was true that Witheric Iron-Brow, first son of Witheow Wolf's-Arm and heir to his father's crown, was not the image of the High Thanes of legend. Since infancy, he had been small and thin, even for their people, and often sickly. He had his father's hair, the color of fresh straw, but his restless, pale blue eyes indicated a mind more like his mother's, who had died of grief soon after the loss of her husband and their second son a few years before to the endless blood wars of the Asgradi tribes, leaving Witheric as the last of his family line. Yes, there were others who carried within their veins the blood of High Thane due to past marriages within the tribe, but he alone remained directly of the Sons of the High Thanes and the true heir to the Eisenband. The Council of High Elders, whose role was to advise the thane and aid him in ruling and meeting out judgments, had at first appeared to accept that truth, but only up until the new high thane had declared his intentions to cease invading the territories of other tribes, instead focusing on their own lands and trying to establish some form of peace with the peoples around them.

For a thousand generations, the wearer of the Eisenband had ruled over all the Asgradi tribes. From the Great Sea in the north to the islands known as the

Dragon's Spine in the west to the southern Halls of Getergrad, the great dwarf kingdom and former border of the human lands, the High Thane had ruled as rune-speaker, ring-giver, and bond-carver. Then, seven-hundred years ago, it all fell apart. How was not remembered. There were hints in songs and poems of oath-breakers and thane-slayers, but little more. For centuries now, the high thane and those clans closest to him, the tribe of the Eisensaet, had been at war with the other tribes. War that, over time, had gradually chipped away at the high thane's reach like water to a stone until all that remained was that small collection of families who remained loyal to the Band and its bearer.

Like most of his forefathers, Witheow Wolf's-Arm had carried on the campaign and had even significantly expanded their borders for the first time in generations, though the peoples remained unsubdued. The high elders had seen hope for continued conquest in the thane's second son and had counseled the thane to make the boy his heir, only to be thwarted when those very wars claimed their greatest warlord in living memory and that very son they had placed their hopes upon. Despair seized the Eisensaet. What could they hope for from the first son, one who shared his father's temperament as little as he did his stature?

Then the Leikgaard tribe from the south, one of the enemies with whom the Eisensaet shared a blood-debt as wide and as deep as the Great Sea, seeing the turmoil of the lost thane as a chance to finally destroy what they called the evil of the Eisenband, attacked. With no other choice, the Eisensaet gathered their men and marched out under the command of their new High Thane. He was not a man unfamiliar with war, having accompanied his father before and watched over many battles, but never had he entered the field himself nor spilt a drop of blood. Their doom seemed assured. Yet it did not come. For, so the common man said, the gods still knew the brow that bore the Band and came to his aid, revealing to him the secret words and paths to rout the enemy. Under the arms and eyes of Restag Far-Sighted, spear-man and chosen Thanesman of the new ruler, and the gods'-speech of Witheric Iron-Brow, High Thane, the hated and deceitful Leikgaard were driven back, a victory that promised many more to come under the new ruler.

The Council remained skeptical, but as other battles arose and the young thane's plans found victory again and again by the hands of his thanesman, their hopes rekindled, plans of conquest again filling their hall. But when they brought these plans to the young thane, he rejected them at once. They appealed to him again and again, but every time they were denied, so they began to spread seeds of doubt against the young thane among the people, leveraging his youth and weakness against him to hinder his purposes until they could work their will over his own. Perhaps if the Leikgaard had not attacked so soon as they did and the Council had brought doubts against the young thane from the start, the attempt would have had a stronger impact. However, it was too late. Men had witnessed victories over old foes. Mothers had seen their sons and husbands return home on their own feet. Already, some among the people called him Witheric Dar's-Mouth. The Council's working was not without fruit, and much skepticism remained against the young thane, but to their frustration, with each victory the fear and despair among the people following the death of Witheow lessened, and doubts in his older son diminished. Then there was the ongoing threat of war. To again change the ring-giving hands, the Elders at last saw, was foolish in the face of the blood-debts they and the High Thanes had bought for centuries. And so, they shrank away from visions of glory regained, contenting themselves with regaining first their dignity and influence with the thane himself.

Or so was Restag's interpretation of the three years since Witheric's crowning, one that informed his understanding of the thane, not yet twenty-five, who bore the heaviness in his eyes of a man twice his years. But the image passed, replaced by sorrow as Witheric turned the Band in his hands, absently caressing the runes and said, "I am not the thane they wanted."

Looking back to the map and slowly tracing Witheric's straight, clear runes with the reed pen, Restag responded with a measured voice, "You are respected by your people."

"By some. Others, like the Council, wanted a warlord, like my father. Like my brother," said Witheric.

"Your brother could not have inherited the throne. He did not possess the Gift of High Thanes," said Restag.

Witheric shook his head. "He could have if the Elders had chosen a bride who did from among the Eisensaet. They could have placed her on the throne as a proxy while Ultheow ruled in truth. It has been done before."

"Not to the pleasure of any, whether warrior or thrall," countered Restag. "And not when a true son with the Gift lived. To place one of indirect lineage, a thanesbride even, upon the throne for even a short span has only been done when necessity outweighed shame, to preserve the true bloodline of the High Thane."

"Then it is to my fortune that my brother joined Valaka's hunt before someone could create such a state, is it not?" said Witheric with a grimace. "Or else another arm would be raising the sword over our shield-men and another voice leading the war cry. A stronger one."

"You are a good commander," said Restag.

"Yes, but a poor fighter, and you know which the Council values more," returned Witheric. "Every victory is a chance to count the dead, and every loss a chance to say how my father would have turned the tide."

Restag paused. "Not all of the Council."

"No… not all," said Witheric. "But enough, and even among them, few are willing to counter the High Elder besides yourself."

That was true enough. It didn't help that the head of the Council was a kinsman of Restag and one also gifted with powerful Farsight. He could not see into the hearts and minds of men as could Restag, but he could certainly speak his way in through the secrets his Sight could uncover from beneath the blankets of a man's bed, behind the sacred walls of his home, or in the meeting of two when no third should be present. He had a serpent's hold on the Council. They both knew it. Restag said, "It does not help when you speak of forming bone-bonds with the other tribes on the promise not to claim what the Elders see as our birthright."

"Birthright?" Witheric said with a hint of scorn. "What right has a man to claim another who is not his own? They are their own people, with their own laws and thanes and ways. Why should I be their thane when they are not of my people and I am not of theirs? Why should I slay my own people so as to take and rule another?"

"And this, too, Witheric," said Restag, finishing a label. "This odd speech and refusal to begin the battle, the insistence on defending your own lands and people without expanding them, all these thoughts and more which you have gained from the humans' writings, these are not our people's words or thoughts, and the Council rightly distrusts them. Some even say you steal from them the glory of the Final Battle of the Asgrada at the End of All Things with this refusal to seek war."

"Let war come to us, if Valaka so wishes to test the blood of our men," said Witheric, the process of debate exciting his spirit. "Yes, let it come rather than be sought, that we may add the weight of home to our shields and the fire of the hearth to our war cries and so build a bulwark for men's valor so that none shall run but shall show his spirit worthy of Final Glory and so gain Valaka's favor. As for all other times, between those tests of courage, the King of War and his half-god daughters are not the only weighers of the scale, or else why keep men beyond their strength of arm or teach our women beauty of craft or our bards grace of speech or anything beyond the use of shield and blade?"

"You have been lying awake till your candle dies again, haven't you?"

Witheric laughed self-effacingly. "If only just till then, my friend. I know the Elders dislike my reading of the human elders and song-speakers, but they are right, Restag. The histories give strength to them."

"Their histories. Ones which only you can read, for only you among us have been sneaking out to follow the trade parties, to meet the red-bloods at their sword-ships, to learn the humans' boneless speech and their bending runes and to use the wealth of your forefathers to obtain leaves covered in the stuff and maps that show our land's smallness in a way the Council would refuse to believe. Then, you have our craftsmen make for you a ring after the humans' design so you can send sealed papers after the humans' fashion and in the dark-haired humans' runes in hopes to form a bond with their king. You wonder that the Council should question your judgment?"

"No," said Witheric after a long pause. "No. I don't."

He fell back into silence and once again began turning the Band slowly in his hands. At last, he said in a much quieter voice, "Do you, also, doubt my judgment? Or perhaps my sanity?"

"Neither," said Restag with such immediacy it surprised the young thane. Without looking up from the map, the Thanesman continued, "As to your judgment, it is solid. The dark-haired are powerful among the humans, and of great wealth, eager to trade us weapons and food and many useful things for trinkets. To form a bond with them could bring our people much wealth in addition to the presence of a powerful sword-brother, which could then make the other tribes hesitate before drawing their swords against us and could perhaps be used to leverage a peace-bond with them. No. I do not doubt your judgment, nor your sanity, Dar's-Mouth. I doubt the assumptions on which your judgment is based."

Witheric stared in admiration at his friend. He had never spoken his full thoughts to Restag. Bits and pieces, yes, but never the full sequence, the ideas and possibilities still too uncertain and fluid for him to speak them. Yet here they were, so simply said. Here was the future he so greatly desired. But there was more to his thoughts, which Restag's pause showed he suspected and which Witheric provided, saying, "You always get straight to the true matter in hand, don't you, Thanesman? Yes. That is the issue. I said before that Aleukus's words are a spear and a chain, but there are two edges to any blade. Yes, they are a spear, but will they be the spear with which to defend our walls or the stake on which we are impaled? They are a chain, but will they be the bond of brotherhood or the bond of thralls? Even if he proves true and the bond is made, will that be enough? The blood of our kin and our enemies have mingled and soaked this land and fed the grass and the trees and the beasts on which we feed for so many cycles of the seasons, can such a blood-debt be forgotten? Put before us like the corpse it is and allowed a proper funeral, to burn away with the bier? Can such a thing be? Yes, these are true questions to which I do not have answers, only hopes and assumptions."

Following another thoughtful pause, the young thane scoffed bitterly, his eyes hard and cold as he stared at the Band in his hands. No longer trying to contain his emotions, he said, "And what of their assumer? Not the thane his father was, nor his father's father, nor his father's father's father. Not the man who can stand strong, with bones of iron, against his enemies and their swords or who commands silence and respect by his mere presence. But a small, weak man who should have been left to die as an infant but for false hopes–a portent perhaps?– and who would not have been made thane but by the accident of his blood and the death of those more worthy. 'Heir to the Eisenband'? 'Iron-Brow'? Ha! Only if iron is as fragile as clay."

The anger passed, and the young thane smiled mockingly at himself and said, "I am not the thane they want, Restag, nor probably the thane they need."

At last, Restag lowered the reed pen and moved around the table with the unfinished map to stand before his friend. Without bothering to ask, he took the band from Witheric's hands and placed it back on the thane's head. Looking into the ice-blue eyes that now stared at him in confusion, the Thanesman said, his voice gentle but firm, "Your bones may not be iron as your father's were, but your will is, and your blood is fire. An alliance with a human king? A peace-bond with our fellow tribes? The burial of blood-debts? Who even among your forefathers has burned with such ambition? Ambition not even your first father held when Dar sent down the star-iron to forge the Band and gave birth to the blood of High Thanes. Ambition worthy of the old songs. Those who say otherwise are fools."

Despite himself, Witheric grinned. "You, a mere spear-man, presume to call the Council of High Elders fools?"

"I presume to speak the truth," he replied.

"As Thanesman? Or as friend?," asked Witheric.

"Are they mismatched?" said Restag.

No. Not with you, thought the thane, picking the letter back up and smiling to himself. He perused the contents again, making sure he understood them correctly, and then pulled out from a stack on the table a clean piece of parchment. By the time he had laid it out on the table, Restag had brought over the pen and ink well from the unfinished map and placed them before the thane as he unrolled his notes and considered his reply. Before he began setting the words in place, however, he said to his friend, "I want this taken to the Ithaenians at daybreak tomorrow, before they leave."

"Yes, Thane Dar's-Mouth."

Trying to glare at Restag, Witheric said, "And stop that nonsense. You know as well as I do that it is not the gods speaking through me that has won us battles, but simply a bit of knowledge, much planning, your own quick thinking, and perhaps the favor of Valaka and his Valaki. If I could hear the gods' voices, all would be so much easier."

He fell silent for a moment, then said, "I will do it, Restag. I still cannot be sure I'm what our people need, but I will try. And I will try how I see best."

"Yes, my thane," said Restag, removing some of the unused items and stacking papers and books out of the way. Once he was done, he prepared to leave his master to his work while he returned to his own, but he took a moment to say, "Even if it is the wrong choice, even if it is not what we need, you have my blade, Witheric."

Glancing up from his letter, the young thane smiled broadly and said, "Thank you, Restag Thanesman. That is all I need."

Chapter 2

Restag nearly tore the curtain off the entrance to the High Council's Hall as he stormed in, his voice like a crack of thunder as he bellowed, "What is this false play?"

Around the long room sat twelve men, each man the representative from one of the founding families that made up the Eisensaet tribe. Terror filled half the faces, and most of the others looked away. Only one met the thanesman's eyes, smiling in that disarming way Restag so despised as he gestured around them, saying, "Restag Thanesman, my kinsman, it is good that you are here. I had forgotten to summon you. But now we can hold a proper vote, can we not, my brothers?"

"What vote? Answer me, Ecthar!" Restag snapped.

The face and posture of Ecthar Far-Sighted, High Elder of the Council, remained placid as he tapped his fingers against the rim of the Eisenband sitting on his lap. The elder replied with seeming confusion, "What else but the election of a new High Thane?"

Though he had expected the answer, to hear it so calmly stated flared Restag's fury, his flushed face contorting briefly before he pulled himself together. He knew this man, knew he had intentionally replied in the way that would most stoke the thanesman's ire, and Restag wanted to give that snake the least amount of pleasure he could. Gritting his teeth, Restag said, "There is no need, High Elder Ecthar. We have a High Thane. We do not need another."

Shaking his head regrettably, the older Asgradi said, "But he has disappeared, vanished from his bed in the middle of the night."

"It is not even midday. So few hours cannot merit this action. And would you, a keeper of the old ways, presume to name a new High Thane without the counsel and acknowledgement of the Lady of Alfmere? And what of the Foul Beast? Would you weaken its chains and tempt their breaking by allowing a false Thane's brow to claim the Band?"

"What place has an elf mystic in the rule of the Asgradi?" replied the elder. "None in the lesser tribes, let alone the tribe of High Thanes. Her counsel and acceptance is a mere formality. Thane Witheric himself was named without seeking first her words due to the peril of that moment, and only several months later, when more peaceful days allowed it, was the pilgrimage made to the lake to receive the Great Lady's blessing upon the new thane. Surely now, with winter fast approaching and so long a trip and the threat of snow and ice any day now, surely such practical circumstances permit the suspension of ceremony. Regarding the Beast, as Thane Witheric's pitiful display during his ceremony did not rouse the creature to action, I cannot but suspect the Fell Shadow has faded after so many thane-worthy strikes of Dir's heavenly fire during the countless prior crownings."

Restag seethed at the blatant disregard for one of their people's most sacred rituals and at the smiles several elders hid or barely restrained at the slighting of his friend and master, but before he could object, Ecthar continued, "As for the missing thane, yes, it is but a few hours since the discovery, but not, so far as we know, the event. And such a violent one, if the signs were read right. It is fortunate the Lady Eathir happened to be ill and absent from their bed that night. I take it, Thanesman, that you have yet to recover the body?"

What body? Restag said to himself. Yes, there were signs of struggle, but little blood or any indications of mortal injury. "No, but–"

"Ah, then that settles the matter," the elder said, looking sorrowfully to his fellow council members. "After all, though we are in the season of rest from war, we cannot afford to leave the throne empty and the Eisenband unclaimed. We cannot afford to give our enemies another chance to attack us as they did three years ago, and with the marriage to Eathir Thanesbride so far fruitless…. Do not be so worried, Thanesman. It may be only temporary. Should Thane Witheric be found, then of course the Band shall be returned to his rightful brow. But until then, we must have someone on the throne, someone to guide us and command our warriors until the High Thane's whereabouts are revealed."

Blood boiling and darkening his face, Restag growled, "What vile of venom you spit today, High Elder."

The elder's mask slipped, and his words hardened as he said, "Watch your tongue, Thanesman. The High Council is decided, and not even you can stand against it. You are oath-bound."

"I am oath-bound to the High Thane, not to the Council," he retorted. "I owe you nothing, especially when you are so quick to abandon your thane."

Another crack briefly showed, but the high elder reigned it in, returning to a calm face and voice as he said, "Do you call us oath-breakers, Restag Far-Sighted?"

"I spoke no such claim. That accusation is self-named," he returned, and the older Asgradi's face twitched. Suspicions that had been growing since Eathir woke him in the early morning at finding Witheric gone gained greater purchase in the Thanesman's mind. He had fought against them, for they were grave, the gravest of their people, and not ones to bring against the esteemed High Elder without proof. But having witnessed his speech and actions....

Restag knew the insult he was about to levy, the implication of the act he was about to commit, but he needed to know. Gripping the pommel of his sword, he took a brief breath and plunged into the high elder's mind. He felt the surge of heat from his fae blood as he drew upon its magic, all other feeling drowning beneath that heat. Sound disappeared, and his vision darkened for a moment before he found himself standing within a room much like the High Council's hall, only draped in woven gold, talismans and engraved metal decorating the pillars and beams. At the head of the room was a dais of equally engraved stone, and sitting upon the dais was a gold-leaf chair occupied by Ecthar himself. The man looked out into the room with a straight stare, unable to perceive Restag's visual and auditory presence. However, when he spoke, the thanesman knew his act had been expected and noticed.

"You should not speak so boldly, Restag. Thanesman you may be now, but only until the Band is bestowed upon another," said the image of Ecthar's mind.

Restag did not answer. Anything he said would be with his physical lips for all to hear, and he had no desire to speak before the Council when his own eyes and ears would not witness their response. With the passing of a thought, Restag crossed the room, intent on exploring the deeper rooms and paths of the high elder's mind. However, the voice again caught him before he could leave.

"You will not find him here, Restag."

Restag looked again at the figure on the throne. A narrow smile stretched across his face as Ecthar's mental image said, "I do not know exactly where he is or what has happened to him. Nor does any here. And there is no point in consulting a Troth-Seer. He shall See only truth in my speech. Witheric is gone, Restag."

Restag pulled his vision back to the physical world around him. Ecthar's smile had taken a condescending turn, as if looking at a child, but the rest of the council still refused to look him in the eye. They knew what he had done and what he suspected. They knew it to be true, but they would not say or do anything. Focusing in particular on the few members who usually took a moderate or supportive position toward their thane, Restag saw the deep shame they held in their silence. What did Ecthar have over them to reduce them to spineless worms? It hardly mattered, he decided, turning from them with such clear contempt they shrank further into themselves and the shadows of the room. Without another word, the thanesman marched toward the exit.

"Where do you go, Thanesman?" said Ecthar, a sneer entering his voice. "You are needed here to tip the scales in case of an even vote. Or do you forfeit?"

You know my vote, snake, Restag said to himself, but he did not speak it out loud and simply left the room. With quick steps, he crossed the fortress town, passing children and farm animals running through the streets and the sounds of shuttles on looms, food cooking, and daily chores from the homes around him. A few women gave worried glances at the young man's back, whispering concern for the thane. Men watched him in wordless understanding. None called out to him. They had seen his countenance as he approached the Elder's Hall. They knew not to stop him.

Once inside the Iron Hall, ancient home of the High Thane, Restag went to his room, pulled out a pair of large satchels, and began filling them with clothes and equipment. From the wall, he grabbed his winged spear and strapped his shield across his back over his wool cloak. He then went to grab similar items from the high thane's chamber, including Witheric's gun, a strange, human-made weapon, and its accessories, and food from the larder. Afterwards, he entered Witheric's study at the back corner of the Hall, heading directly for the map the young thane had finished inking only days before. Maps were not of great concern for him with his Sight, but habit had made even him feel uneasy without one. Next, he dug through the papers, locating a few detailed maps of smaller areas, again with Witheric's translations written across the landscape. All these he rolled tightly together, stuffing them into a waterproof storage tube of human design. For all he might distrust them, Restag appreciated the practicality of many human goods. Finally, he uncovered the small chest Witheric kept beneath the floorboards by his writing table and pulled out the spare key his master had given him, carefully turning the key and fiddling with the mechanisms of the lock so as to undo the spell craft that guarded the contents. Inside were a few trinkets, including a small piece of braided hair, the brooches worn by the thane's father and brother as they went out to their last battle, and the silver hairpin the previous thanesbride had worn, a gift from her husband on their wedding day and her most treasured possession even after grief destroyed her will to live. The last item in the chest was Witheric's seal ring, a thing Restag still did not understand but which he sensed might be better to bring than to leave. All these things he threw into a drawstring bag and tucked into his shirt. With one last look around the room, at the piles of fragile books and papers and maps and drawings and the smell of ink and parchment that had come in his mind to mean "Witheric," and which he knew would be no more than ashes in the hands of another, he left.

He found himself stopped not far down the passageway, however, by a young woman, her golden hair pulled back into a thick braid and her usually bright eyes shadowed with worry. Though he knew he had little time, Restag approached the young woman, who said in a soft voice, "Restag, what is happening? They are already saying… Witheric, he isn't… is he…."

She then noticed the satchels and the gun he carried, and her eyes filled with fear. To see such an expression on her caused Restag's chest to tighten again with anger at those who were the cause. Lowering his voice but keeping a firm tone, he said, "I am going to find him, Eathir. I will find him and bring him back. This I swear."

Eathir nodded, but she did not speak, and her expression remained tense. Unsure what else to do, Restag knelt before her, took her hand, kissed it, and pressed it against his brow, sealing his oath, and said, "I swear it. Upon my name as thanesman, I will find him, and I will bring him back, if I can. However, if we do not return before the first snows fall, or you fear those who wish to place a false thane upon the Iron Throne, go to my family. My father and brother will protect their Thanesbride, even from the Elder of our clan. Not all of us have lost sight of our true oath-bond."

At that, Eathir's gaze softened, and she raised him and returned the ritual of an oath-bond to him. She then said, "And I shall await your return. So, too, do I swear. No other man shall I know, for I am Thanesbride. I shall die before swearing fealty or marriage vows to any but my true thane. This shall I carve into bone and wear over my heart, and if I should break it, may I be broken in like manner."

For a moment, a fierceness filled her, one which but a few years ago had been unknown to her face but which she had learned as she held her own battles against those who opposed her husband. It did not last, however, and her eyes again brimmed with tears as she whispered, "Bring him back, Restag. Please."

"As you command, my Thanesbride," said Restag. He took her hands in a firm but gentle grip and then, releasing her, left her without another word, feeling her eyes linger on him before she, too, turned away, and her swift steps continued down the hall in the direction of the thane's chamber.

With even faster, but no less measured, steps than before, he crossed the Hall and stepped out into the cold, late autumn air, his purpose decided and mind focused.

"Where do you go, Restag Far-Sighted?"

Restag barely stopped at the oily voice, fully intending to simply march around the high elder standing on the steps leading back down into the town. As he did, however, Ecthar grabbed his arm with surprising strength and spoke again. "Don't be a fool, Restag. You are Thanesman. Our people need you here, to guide and defend them, not chasing mists and seeking dewdrops at midday."

Restag glared at the high elder, not bothering to conceal the hatred in his eyes and voice as he said, "I will not stand beside cowards and thane-slayers!"

"It is well that you held some murkiness in your words to the Council. Those are grave accusations, Restag," said Ecthar. "And false ones. I am no thane-slayer."

"No," said Restag, breaking free of the older man's grip. "You are too clever for that. You would have someone else's hands do the deed so you can flick lies off your adder's tongue before the troth-seers and have your venom confirmed in the presence of witnesses. But I am not fooled, Ecthar. After I take care of the one who did this—"

"Witheric is alive," said the elder, catching Restag off-guard. His stomach twisted, and anger flared at the sneer on the other man's face. Ecthar knew he had him, just as Restag knew he could not give up this lead. Without ceremony or care for the other man's comfort, Restag gripped his arm and pulled him inside the Hall and back into Witheric's study, where they were unlikely to be disturbed. Ecthar glared in blatant revulsion at the papers and books piled around him but wisely held his tongue.

"Where is he?" demanded Restag, tightening his grip so that the elder winced.

Dropping all pretense of cordiality, Ecthar hissed, "Unhand me, shield-man. I am High Elder, not some thrall. Yes, you can search my mind, but I know how to make my mind a maze, full of secret paths and false ways, and I do not think you have time to waste traveling them to find your answers."

Roughly, Restag released the man, who took his time rubbing the area he had held, which rather than goading him to impatience, gave Restag the time to gather himself together again, much to the disappointment of the elder. At last, the thanesman said, his voice sharp and level as a well-made blade, "Where is he, Ecthar? You say he's alive. If I find you are lying...."

"Do not take me for a fool, Restag Far-Sighted," snapped the high elder. "I know better than to buy a blood-debt from you. Nor am I foolish enough to call down the gods' wrath for being a thane or kin-slayer. The boy is alive and, for the moment, safe. Not that he should be. Restag, see sense on this matter. The boy is a fool, one chasing the death of his own house. He cannot lead the Eisensaet. He cannot bring us back to our rightful place among the Asgradi. Though you call him High Thane, he is neither high in his ideals nor a thane capable of leading our people. It is best that he simply disappear. Yes, it is a shame to bestow the Eisenband to one of thinner blood and right, but it is for the best of our people. Surely you, a shield-man of my blood, who entered the battlefield before most boys are considered men, know the threat we face, the swords and spears we have at our throats from all sides. Surely you know—"

"Where is he, Ecthar?" repeated Restag.

Sighing audibly, Ecthar said, "I speak truth when I say I do not know where he is, but I can take you to one who does. But you are a fool should you choose to follow him. No. More than a fool. You would call ruin upon yourself."

Ecthar paused, giving the other man a meaningful look. Without hesitation, Restag said, "I am Thanesman."

At once, the placid expression fell over Ecthar's face again. "If that is your answer," he said, leaving the room and motioning for Restag to follow.

Chapter 3

They did not pass through the center of the village again but made their way along the edge of the wall to exit through a small wicket gate out onto the tall, layered outcrop from which the walled town overlooked the farms below and the rolling hills, vast forest, and the blue haze of mountains to the east and north. The trees were stripped of their leaves for the year, making the glitter of sunlight upon the River Reinor barely visible between the bare branches. Despite the urgency of the situation, Restag could not help the tightening of his throat as his eyes passed fleetingly over the image, and it was only the presence of his current task that kept him from pausing to look out upon the landscape he had known since infancy, had looked upon from his mother's arms, and then his father's shoulders, and then his father's side, had gazed upon countless times as Dar rose from his sleep to chase away his jealous sister, Dir, and reclaim the world again for the living. The land that he felt was part of him, the stones his bones, the earth his flesh, the many and hidden streams his blood, the settlement upon and around the hill his heart. And it was only with great effort that he kept his emotions hidden as he turned away from it all to follow the man slipping away to the steep, narrow path that ran as a crack between the rocks, hidden from any angle but above and therefore a way used often for entering or leaving the town without being seen from the surrounding country.

They followed the path to its end, Ecthar pausing to use his Sight to look past the stone and all around them to ensure they were neither observed nor followed. Once satisfied, he again motioned to Restag and began traveling along the edge of the hill. They came to a crevice in the rock, and if Ecthar had told him to enter, Restag would have refused unless the other went first with his own spear at his back. However, the high elder did so on his own. With his senses aware and his spear hand ready to act, Restag cautiously followed. In front of him, the older man constantly glanced around, his own shoulders tense, as they passed through the narrow gap in the rocks to a small space where the stones rose in a jagged ring around them. Wordlessly, the elder dug a flask from his belt pouch, approached one of the walls, and poured the contents onto a small bowl on a jutting rock until the liquid overflowed and ran down the stone to the ground. Hastily, he backed away and watched. Restag remained just outside the circle, spear ready. Stillness fell over them, broken only by the sharp call of a crow as it passed overhead. Restag crept just past the opening, unsure what Ecthar had done or if he should just kill the man and leave.

"About time you got out of the way."

Ecthar jumped, and Restag instinctively swung the spear around, the hard wood striking the stone wall with enough force that the rebound knocked him back a couple steps. Reclaiming his footing, he brought the spear down into an attack stance, the tip pointed to the small Asgradi who now filled the crevice, smiling till his teeth showed, malicious laughter in his eyes.

Swearing profanely, Ecthar snapped, "What was that for?"

The little man looked to the elder and grinned contemptuously at the man, saying, "So you're the contact. Nothing much. It's just a lot more fun to let your prey walk right past you before stabbing them in the back. Much more interesting."

It took a moment for Restag to fully take in the little man—to notice his unkempt braids and ornamented beard, his many engraved trinkets and rings, his worn boots and filthy skin, and above all the ugly brand burned into his cheek and from which ran rune-like tattoos that made Restag's skin crawl—but the moment he did, fury flushed his face, and his eyes locked on Ecthar even as the spear remained pointed at the strange man. "Halsk take you, Ecthar!" he snarled. "An Oathless! You bought the service of an Oathless!"

The elder's face turned stoney as he returned the warrior's gaze. "I did what I must," he said.

"But they are murderers! Kin-slayers! Thane-slayers! Swearers of false oaths with no loyalty but to themselves and to their purses!"

"They are men willing to do what must be done," replied Ecthar calmly.

There were very few men Restag hated, and even those he did he still respected, whether for the man's abilities or his cunning or his status. For the first time in his twenty-seven years, Restag now looked upon a man whom he both reviled and had drained every drop of respect he had once held toward him. Restag looked away, unable to stand the sight of the creature his kinsman had become.

The Oathless leaned lazily against the rock wall, staring at Restag with a bored expression. Looking over the thanesman's shoulder, he said, "So he's the one I need to take?"

Ecthar replied, "Yes. This is Restag Thanesman." The Oathless's gaze sharpened, and his body tensed as he focused again on the shield-man. Ecthar continued, "He wishes to go with his master. Fulfill this task, and when you and your sword-brother return, you shall have your reward."

A mocking grin flickered across the little man's face at the term "sword-brother," but it soon disappeared again, replaced by a critical eye and a quick, sweeping gaze at the warrior. He seemed hesitant for a moment, but in the end, he pushed off from the wall, turned away, and called behind him, "Follow me, Thanesman."

As Restag left, Ecthar spoke once more, and though the tone indicated the words were directed at the Oathless, Restag felt Ecthar's eyes upon his back as he said, "I shall watch for your return."

Restag refused to acknowledge the words or their speaker. It was the last and greatest insult he could pay him.

Unlike Ecthar, the Oathless did not bother with secrecy but walked with confidence out into the full light of day. The mercenary kept a quick pace, one which any but one seasoned to long and hard travel, as all Asgradi warriors were, would struggle to keep. They passed through the hills and beneath the edges of the surrounding forest. Once hidden within the trees, the Oathless slowed his pace, taking a leisurely stride only just ahead of Restag. Off-handedly, he said, "So, are the stories true? Are you really able to see into a man's soul?"

Restag did not answer. When the little man prodded again, the thanesman said flatly, "Take me to my thane, Halsk-worm. I need no companionship from you, and you shall receive none from me."

The little man's eyes narrowed. "I don't like you, Thanesman," he said.

"You do not need to," replied Restag. Muttered curses followed, which Restag pretended to ignore. He knew, however, that his bluntness had been foolish, considering the nature of the man with whom he currently traveled.

He used his Sight to catch a glimpse of the man's soul. Only a glimpse. He could afford neither to stop nor to risk tripping over or walking into something as his eyes and ears left his immediate surroundings, which might alert the Oathless to his actions. A glimpse was all he could afford, but that glimpse of malice and ill intent drenching the man's thoughts was more than enough.

A few hours later, they came to the remains of a stone building. The sun had begun to set, strengthening the forest's shadows. Restag had seen the building before on hunting trips into the forest, though he had never bothered to investigate it. It was a human structure, though its purpose, whether as a fortress or a house or a temple, had been long lost. Moss and lichen covered the stones. Grass grew thick and tall, hiding the remnants of stone floors. Most of the wood was long-rotted, the windows empty and the walls crumbling. With caution, Restag followed the Oathless into the shadowed remains of a tower, climbing up not with the stairs, which were no longer extant, but over a pile of rubble that built a sort of pathway up to what had once been the second floor, judging by the windows in the surrounding walls, where all paths ceased. Following a sharp whistle from the outlaw, a thin rope ladder rolled over the side of the highest floor, granting access to the top of the tower.

The Oathless stepped aside, motioning with mocking courtesy toward the ladder. Restag stared suspiciously at the ropes. There were too many options for what could be done during the vulnerability of the climb, whether he or the Oathless went first. Risking a pause, his blood flared as he snuck into the man's thoughts again, seeing nearly at once the image of his own throat being cut from behind the moment they both reached the top. Restag came back to himself just in time to hear the mercenary say, "Well? You going up first, or me?"

After quickly deciding the doom he knew was better than the one he did not, Restag took the ropes and began to climb, his spear in hand making it a bit difficult, the Oathless not far behind. His thoughts raced with each rung, trying to think of some way to escape the situation. By the time he reached the top, he had a plan. Not a very good plan, but hopefully good enough to buy some time to better assess the situation and gain some advantage.

Restag peered over the edge of the patched, wooden floor to the area beyond. It was a somewhat small space, perhaps half the size of the Elders' Hall. Large gaps in the wall allowed a wide view of the land around them, but enough remained to provide an area of wind cover, which had been supplemented with what looked to be oiled deer skins to form a sheltered section on the floor's far side. Nearby stood another man bearing the brand of an Oathless, though he appeared much more nervous than his companion and had not added decorative runes to his brand. Behind him, leaning against the ruins of the wall and looking absently out into the distant landscape, sat Witheric. A few bruises showed on his face, and he wore nothing more than a night shirt, but he was alive. In the surge of relief, Restag nearly cried out to him, but the Oathless below him interrupted his thoughts, shouting, "Hey! Keep going!"

The sharp command broke whatever mire had claimed the young thane's mind, and he looked toward the ladder, gasping as he saw his friend's face over the edge. He blanched, rising shakily, his eyes wide as he said almost despondently, "R-Restag... why are you–"

"I said move it, Halsk take you!"

Restag gave Witheric a pointed look but did not wait to see his response before pulling himself up.

"About ti–" began the Oathless, but his words were cut off as Restag spun around and shoved his boot into the man's face, not quite knocking him off the ladder. In nearly the same movement, the warrior brought his spear around and sliced across the taunt ropes, cutting the chords enough that the mercenary's weight snapped the remainder, dropping the ladder and its stunned climber two stories and hopefully killing him, but even if it had not, it would at least hurt. More importantly, it evened Restag's odds.

Spinning around to face his remaining opponent, his spear raised, Restag flinched as his eyes met nothing but the sight of Witheric standing alone. He was sure....

"He's a Sight-Bender!" shouted Witheric.

Restag quickly moved away from the hole in the tower floor, cursing under his breath. Although he could see through stone and into a man's mind, even his Sight could not see through gifts of that kind. Moments later, vile oaths came from one of the gaps in the wall, followed by the first Oathless somehow pulling himself over the stone, his nose bleeding beneath his enraged eyes. He had kicked off his shoes, despite the cold, and he cursed again at the chilled stones as he drew a short sword. The thanesman held his spear ready, wishing he had the time to remove his shield, hackles raised as he tried to hear for his hidden enemy while keeping an eye on the one charging toward him, blade swinging. It was a clumsy move, and one that would have been easy to parry, but as he raised his spear to deflect the blow, a sharp stab struck his side. The chain mail beneath stopped the blow from digging deep, saving his life, but it off-balanced him enough to allow the sword to swing down at him unhindered. He dodged, the blade barely missing his exposed head.

He swung his spear in the direction from which the stab had come, but his enemy had moved. Restag disliked using his Sight in a fight. The mental energy required to activate the magic long enough to be useful, but short enough to keep track of his surroundings, and the speed of thought required to process the information made it more practical to simply use his ordinary eyes, instincts, and trained reflexes. Usually. Flaring his fairy blood, he managed with several quick reaches of his Sight to locate the direction of his invisible enemy's mind. He did not know the distance and could not risk reading the man's thoughts, but the knowledge did let him maneuver in another direction as he avoided and knocked aside the swinging sword. He managed to do the same for the next few strikes, but it was difficult. He could already feel the mental strain, and his enemies still managed a few glancing blows that bruised and drew blood.

From behind them, Witheric watched helplessly, cursing his lack of weapon and physical weakness, wondering if the best he could do was not get in his friend's way. Then he saw a flicker in the air and the hints of movement on the floor, a scuff in the grime covering the wood, where there appeared to be nothing. Without further thought, he charged for it, slamming into the unseen man and sending them both to the ground. The Oathless cried out, his illusion breaking in his surprise, and Witheric wrapped his arms around him, clinging to the man's waist from behind. Suddenly, he felt pain in his arm as the bandit stabbed him with a knife. Biting back a cry, the thane grabbed the wrist of the enemy's striking arm, the knife still in his other arm. Clenching his teeth, Witheric flared his blood.

Restag heard the cry behind him right before blocking another attack. Seeing an opening, he kicked his opponent, knocking him away. When he turned around, Restag saw, to his horror, Witheric engaged with the second Oathless, a knife buried deep into his arm, clinging to the man's waist and wrist and lightning crawling along his skin and up the knife into the other man. The Oathless screamed and spasmed and kicked, trying to get loose. Rushing to his master's aid, he cried for Witheric to release him. Witheric obeyed, and the Oathless tried to stumble to his feet, his limbs jerking beyond his control, only to fall to a thrust from Restag's spear. With one enemy subdued, Restag turned again to the first Oathless only to see him vault over the side of the tower. Crying out in anger, Restag ran to the edge, but when he looked over, he saw the

Oathless running down the sheer side of the wall as if it were the earth below, the tips of the Blood Mark visible on his neck shimmering bright gold in the dimming light. Almost on instinct, Restag raised his spear and threw it, straight down at the enemy. However, his aim was off, and the weapon did not strike him beneath the glowing Mark but merely lodged itself into the retreating man's shoulder. It was still enough, however, to knock him off the wall and send him plummeting down into the forest.

Though he wanted to immediately pursue the man and confirm his enemy's death, when Restag turned around, his attention was immediately drawn to Witheric lying on the cold stone, the knife still in his arm. Fear gripped him, and he rushed to his friend's side, calling to him. Even before he reached him, Witheric released a large breath and a grunt of pain. Feeling his legs grow weak with relief, Restag knelt beside Witheric, asking, "Are you all right?"

Witheric met his eyes and smiled weakly, saying, "Just… tired. And hurting, but mostly tired. Too much magic."

Restag nodded. "Can you sit up?"

"I think so," answered Witheric, wincing in pain as he tried to move. "With a bit of help."

As Restag helped his friend up, they heard a miserable groan. It was the Sight-Bender. Restag immediately reached for his sword, but when he saw the dimness in the man's eyes, he knew the Oathless would prove no danger and relaxed his grip. A thought then struck him, and he rose and approached the dying man.

"What are you doing?" asked Witheric.

"Checking something," said Restag, reaching out his hand to grip the man's face as the light faded from his eyes. He didn't have much time. Using the physical touch to ease his entry and strengthen the connection, Restag dove into the man's mind. It was a jumble of memories and thoughts racing together and over each other, and Restag hurried to sort through the mire until he saw what he was looking for. He watched the memory play out, his blood further heating with anger before all suddenly went dark and he found himself staring at a corpse. Releasing his hold on the lifeless face, Restag spat out a string of profanities to the gods.

Witheric waited until his friend reclaimed himself before asking, "What did you see?"

The young thane suspected the answer, but it still stung as Restag snapped,

"Ecthar met with this one here, promising wealth from your family's coffers to have you stolen away and thrown out into the wilderness on the eve of winter without even a pair of boots. That viper! He planned a way for you to die such that he could easily lie to even a Troth-Seer to hide his deed."

Restag watched as the truth settled painfully into his master's mind, swearing curses against the High Elder in his thoughts. He had not told Witheric the rest, how Ecthar had told the Oathless to wait for him the next day in that narrow split of rock, how he would signal to them should he fail to persuade a certain man to give up on the missing thane and how they were to take that man to his master and do with them both as they saw fit. That part he kept to himself, where it could not harm his friend.

After a long stretch of silence, Witheric whispered, "What do we do now?"

Restag faced his friend and master, the uncertainty he saw softening his anger. Looking around them and then at Witheric's bleeding arm and cold-reddened fingers and feet, he said, "First, we must dress you in something warm and tend your wounds."

Shaking his head, Witheric said, "No! You are more wounded than I am!"

As if the words broke a spell, Restag suddenly felt the pain from multiple bruises and cuts across his body. Witheric was probably right, but Restag responded, "I am not near-naked and half-frozen. I brought some of your clothing with me. Change into them, and then we can argue about whose wounds weigh more."

A strong shiver passed through Witheric, so he reluctantly agreed. Because Restag refused to remove the knife before they had something to wrap around the wound, as well as due to the pain of lifting his arm, the thane needed help pulling off the bloodied nightshirt. After wrapping himself in a wool cloak, he then watched in irritation as the thanesman tore off parts of the shirt to use as bandages, realizing too late that he had been tricked into being treated first. Soon after, he was pulling warm clothes over his bandaged arm and buckling on his gun belt while Restag dug through one of the packs. Pulling out a rope, the thanesman said, "I'm going to get some wood for a fire. Stay here."

"What? No! I can look for wood. You need to address your own wounds," said Witheric, shoving his feet into boots taken from the dead Oathless. They were a bit big, but warm and welcome in the evening air.

Restag shook his head. "You cannot climb easily with that arm, or carry much. The light is almost gone, as well."

"And you should not be climbing with open wounds, especially not when you might run into that other Oathless," countered Witheric, feeling a touch of pride as Restag's silence confirmed he had correctly guessed the man's second, hidden purpose. He continued, "There is still a bit of light left, and there are no clouds to cover the moon. Let me take care of the worst wounds before you go. Do not argue with me, thanesman. I will command you if I need to."

Sighing, Restag dropped the rope and handed Witheric the cleaned knife and the remains of the nightshirt so he could finish cutting it up while Restag removed his clothes and mail. Most of the cuts proved shallow, but the shield-man now carried several large bruises, and there were a few gashes that worried Witheric as he cleaned and bandaged them.

Before long, darkness fell, and with it the temperature, their breath showing in the light of a large fire anytime they turned away from its heat. Before gathering the wood for that fire, Restag had made a quick search for the missing Oathless, but while he found the broken shaft of his spear and blood on the grass, he did not find a body. There was enough blood, however, that he did not feel concerned about any attacks that night and had quickly gathered up a bundle of sticks and a few small logs and sent them up to Witheric before climbing back up the rope, pulling it up with him.

From his pack, Restag extracted some cheese, biscuits, and dried meat, which Witheric accepted eagerly, having not eaten all day. "You really thought of everything," he said between bites.

"Except your boots and some bandages," said Restag as he sat with his own dinner.

Witheric smiled slightly. "Yes. How could you forget those? Your thoughts must have been full to the brim."

"Hm," was all the reply he got. Witheric watched his friend, trying to read the thoughts on that calm face. As he started on his food again, he said almost casually, "What shall we do now?"

Restag took the time to take another bite before saying, "First, make it through the night. Tomorrow morning, I want to make another search for the missing Oathless. After that? I am not sure. We could go back, of course. We know who planned your kidnap and murder. We could call for a trial of the High Council. Ecthar could just claim I was lying about what I saw, of course, but we could easily demand he be tried before a Troth-Seer. It would be a dragon's trial, but if we ask the right questions, maybe we can catch him in a lie. Then even the secrets he holds over the other elders would not be enough to spare him the death due to an oath-breaker."

Witheric stared incredulously at his friend. It took him a few moments before he could say, "You do not mean that, Restag. You would not have packed all of this if you really expected us to just go home."

A long pause followed. Finally, Restag, his voice tired and tinted with a mix of emotions that Witheric could not decipher but which gave him sorrow, said, "No. I do not. Ecthar's hold on the Council is too strong. He might even have a hold on the Troth-Seers. Perhaps not a complete one, but still enough of one that he knew he would be named true of speech. No. If we return right now, I expect we will be killed before we can call for a trial. That is, if he lets us return. He shall be carefully watching for us, ready to send someone to finish us if he catches us with his Sight."

Heavy silence fell upon them once again, each man lost in thoughts of the truth of that statement and the reality of all that was lost by it. After a long, painful pause, Witheric left his own sorrows to look again to his friend. A new ache formed in his chest, and he said, "Restag, why are you here? Why did you come for me?"

Restag turned to face him, whatever other emotions he held hidden behind the sudden conviction he now showed in his steady eyes as he simply said, "I am Thanesman."

Rather than bring encouragement as had been intended, grief overcame Witheric as the words pierced him. He stared blankly into the fire and then buried his face in his hands and moaned miserably. Restag came to his side, worry creasing his brow. "Witheric? Witheric, what is it? Your wound, is it—"

The high thane shook his head, his voice trembling as he said, "No. That is not…. Oh, my friend, I have ruined you!"

"Stop that, right now!" said Restag, frightened now by Witheric's despair. He had only seen this once before, when the young man lost his family and the weight of High Thane fell so suddenly upon him. It was the most terrifying time in Restag's memory. If not for the immediate necessity for the young thane to act in defense of his people, he was not sure when his friend would have emerged from that grief. Now Restag faced it again, and he did not know what to do. Unable to think of anything else, Restag said, "It is not your doing, Witheric."

But the young thane replied, "Yes it is! This happened because I am thane.

Because I am not strong enough! If you were not my Thanesman, you wouldn't… you wouldn't be…."

"Witheric, stop!" Restag snapped fiercely, making his friend's eyes jump to his. Forcing his anger down again, he continued, "It was my choice. Not yours. I could have abandoned you. As you said, I knew there would be no return if I came here to find you. But I did come. I chose this." He gestured around them and paused, letting the words sink in before lowering his voice to say, "I swore an oath to you, Witheric, and I intend to keep it."

Those last words hit the young thane like a slap to his face, shaking him from the dark claws that had been digging themselves into his heart. Taking a few breaths to calm himself further and wiping away the tears that had started to fall, he faced the other man and said, "As did I, Thanesman. I swore, as your thane, to protect and lead you. I gave you my oath-bond, and I do not intend to break it."

"Good," said Restag, fear and tension leaving him like a shadow lifted. Returning to his dinner, he said, "Since we cannot go back, where should we go? Wherever you decide, I shall follow."

That was the question, wasn't it? Witheric fell into his thoughts as he, too, continued his dinner. As Restag said, they could not go back. Unfortunately, there weren't many places they could go forward to, either. The Eisensaet had been at war for so long, trying to reclaim control of the other Asgradi, that Witheric had no doubt the other tribes would turn them away to face winter's wrath should their identities be revealed if they didn't just kill them on the spot. No. Seeking the aid of the other tribes was out of the question. He had heard that there was a kingdom to the south ruled by an Asgradi king, one which was far enough that they had not fought each other for several generations and powerful enough that none of the other tribes bothered attacking it. Perhaps the grudge between their people had eased enough that they would be willing to shelter them. Though based on the rumors he had heard, they were highly territorial, averse to any outsiders entering their lands, even fellow Asgradi. Such a people held little hope to them, but where else–

"Oh!"

Witheric jumped at Restag's exclamation. Looking at his friend, he saw him dig through his shirt and pull out a drawstring bag, tossing it over as he said, "I forgot about this."

The thane dropped his food to catch the bag, which was heavier than he had expected. Undoing the drawstring, he emptied the contents and stared at them in disbelief. Gaping at Restag, he said, "You forgot bandages and boots, but you thought to grab these?"

Restag shrugged and went back to eating. Witheric stared in amazement at the collection of things in his palm. Precious things. Things he had never expected to see again. Quietly, solemnly, he put each item back into the bag, all but the ring, whose gold surface shone like the fire it reflected. An idea was forming, and he turned it over in his mind as he turned the ring over in his hand. Finally, a smile forming on his lips, he said, "We shall go south, to Ithaenia."

Witheric laughed at the look on Restag's face. Clearly, the warrior hadn't even considered such a possibility. "You disapprove, my friend? Do not worry. King Aleukus will welcome us. Maybe he would even be willing to help us return home, come spring. Trust me, Restag. You will see."

The thanesman's scowl did not change, but he replied, "I will go where you decide, High Thane. If you say you wish to go to the dark-haired humans, I shall make sure you get there."

Witheric smiled warmly at his friend. "Thank you, Thanesman."

Restag did not reply, so Witheric simply dropped the ring back into the bag, tucked the bag into his shirt, and returned to his meal with the knowledge that he would sleep soundly that night.

Chapter 4

The next day dawned cold. With only their wool cloaks, their clothes, and the meager remains of their fire to keep them warm, the two exiles were more than eager to get down into the forest, where they would not be so exposed and could get their bodies moving. It took some effort getting them both down, as soreness from their injuries had settled in overnight, but they were traveling through the forest in the direction of the Reinor River, munching on more biscuits and meat strips, soon after daybreak. They had decided to travel through the forest near the river, following the water south. They had debated leaving the trees when they reached the narrow grasslands that stood on either side of the river, to make use of the warm sunlight and the river's resources, but the lack of cover when so many tribes, all of them hostile, used that same river was too great a danger. They made little progress that day, due mostly to Witheric's unfamiliarity with prolonged foot travel forcing them to rest often, during which Restag checked for signs of pursuit or unfriendly Asgradi. Though he saw nothing, he remained on guard throughout that day and the next, only reducing the frequency of his surveys when it became clear to him that Ecthar had not sent anyone after them. There were still the dangers of other Asgradi, the possible return of the missing Oathless, and the general dangers of traveling through the wild, but at least one concern could be released.

On the morning of the third day, Restag opened his eyes to find Witheric awake before him, heating breakfast over a small fire. Though he did not have much endurance, often riding a pony to keep up with his men whenever they set out for battle, Witheric had always been one of the first to adjust to camp life, rising naturally before the sun and eagerly taking on a multitude of small tasks. It had become a source of good natured teasing directed toward the thane, calling him the camp mother, which he always played along with and so had earned the fondness of many of his men. Meanwhile Restag was the camp father, dealing out punishments any time someone tried to perform some mischief or another while simultaneously taking on more tasks than any one man knew about. As the thane and his man ate that morning, Witheric wondered what would become of those warriors now, having lost their guiding hand, Restag, how many would die under their Elders' choice of the usurper, and what other consequences might follow that he could not foresee.

He pulled out his trinket bag, removing from it the two brooches. They were of iron, beautifully engraved with runes and shapes curling around the central animals, a crouching she-wolf for his father's and a leaping buck for his brother's, tokens of the beasts whose virtues they embodied. Witheric had one of his own bearing a horned ram, which had been the source of the design for his signet ring, but it had been left behind, forgotten and still pinned to the ceremonial cloak he wore when not on the battlefield. He ran his fingers over the engravings, tracing the protective runes, before finally pinning his father's brooch to his cloak. The other he held out to Restag, saying, "Wear this. You haven't worn your family's raven since becoming my thanesman, and it invokes the Valaki's protection."

Restag stared at the token, his thoughts hidden from his face. "It was your brother's."

"And he will not be using it," replied Witheric.

Looking to his master, Restag said, "And you?"

Witheric pointed to his father's brooch. "It bears a she-wolf. Of course the Valaki will give aid to their own mounts. The runes call upon Dar himself, as well, calling for protection against the tricks and distractions of Dir."

Restag looked back to the brooch, his hand straying to his sword hilt where had once rested a token bearing his family's crest, a raven with bright eyes of glass, which he had left behind years ago, along with his loyalties to his family to serve the high thane and all the Eisensaet. In the end, he shook his head, saying, "It is a token of the blood of High Thanes. It is not for me to claim."

Though he disagreed with his friend's reasoning, Witheric nodded in understanding and tucked the item away.

Later that same day, Restag noticed signs of other travelers along their path. The marks in the earth were slight, the ground too hard from lack of recent rain and the frozen nights to retain much, and could have been from an Asgradi or some other creature that haunted the forest. They were too vague to tell. When Restag searched with his Sight, he saw nothing, but he and Witheric picked up their pace for the rest of the day, their eyes open for any further signs. A couple days later, more tracks were found, these much clearer than the last, and more numerous. Restag suspected it might be a hunting party, though what kind of creature they pursued could not be discerned, nor was it clear if these tracks were related to the ones found earlier and, therefore, if the pair was wandering in the same area as the larger group. Still Restag could see no other Asgradi or sizable creatures nearby, not even after following the direction of the tracks until he lost them a few miles away, and the forest was too vast for him to quickly search around every tree and under every bush. After a brief discussion, they decided to continue as they had for most of the day, where they would have plenty of cover, but then to leave the forest around sundown to continue a bit farther at night with the moonlight and river to guide them, allowing them to cover more ground and, if they were indeed still around, to hopefully pass the hunters as they slept.

For Witheric's sake, they kept a lighter pace for the rest of the daylight hours, and when the first signs of twilight colored the sky, they cautiously slipped out of the trees and into the grasslands. They approached the river at an angle so as to make progress even as they covered the mile between the forest and the river, and by the time they reached the waterfront, Dir hung high overhead, shining her influence over the land. Sharp shadows lay everywhere, and the river and knee-high grass looked edged with silver. The ground was smoother here, without tree roots, sticks, and bushes underfoot, and the walking was easier. A few hours and some miles later, they found a bank hidden by one of the occasional rises in the land and decided to settle there for the night, where no one could see them from their side of the river.

As Restag refilled their water skins, Witheric gingerly dipped his feet into the water, flinching and then shivering as the icy water ran around his ankles. Restag said, "More blisters?"

"One or two," said Witheric between chattering teeth. "Having shoes too big for your feet does not help. But at least my toes aren't freezing."

"I apologize," said Restag. "If I had noticed they hadn't taken your boots, I would have grabbed them. I would offer you mine, but...."

Witheric chuckled. "I could fit my whole body into those giant's shoes of yours. Then you would have to carry me, and how would we get anywhere with that weight on your shoulders? No. I shall walk another day."

And another, and another, and Dar knew how many till they reached Ithaenia, or more specifically Thenika, the Seat City of King Aleukus. Perhaps they could convince Roth to lend them some of his seven league boots or to guide them on a fairy way, not that they had anything to use to bargain with the nomadic god.

As Witheric wrapped his cold, wet feet in the edge of his cloak to dry them, Restag said, "I'm sorry I forgot the bandages. If you do need me to carry you, I shall be willing."

The thane gave him a side-eyed look. "I am not clay-footed, Restag. I can walk."

Restag's face shifted just slightly to show his surprise. He turned away, watching the river's slow movement for a spell before saying, "Forgive me, my thane. I was thinking of other things and said too much."

That was odd, thought Witheric. Restag rarely apologized for anything he said. In fact, he had been unusually apologetic in general the last few days. Witheric watched his friend, the man's face impassive. Restag was not a man prone to joviality and rarely showed strong emotion unless angered or especially disturbed. However, he was honest. He might not smile or laugh much or openly, but Witheric could usually tell when his friend was happy. Same with sorrow. Like most Asgradi men, he was not one to weep in the presence of others, but there was usually an air about him and a way his brow creased and eyes shone that spoke his feelings. Now, he felt closed off. His true feelings locked away for reasons unknown.

Was he worried? Afraid? Or… perhaps he was grieving? Mourning the loss of his home and his family and his friends and his life. Perhaps it was because this was the undercurrent of Witheric's thoughts and feelings, which came and went throughout the day and tinged everything with a sting of sorrow, but it felt right. And it hurt. He felt that pain up until he fell asleep, curled up in his cloak and listening to the flow of water washing away his thoughts.

A strange sound woke Witheric that night. Strange, but ethereally beautiful. Like what moonlight or hoarfrost might sound like if it had a voice. He turned over. No. Not hoarfrost. It was too warm, though it still held that tinge of sadness that brought to mind the ice crystals climbing across his window in midwinter, like a thousand, tiny birds frozen mid-flight. He sat up, rubbing the sleep from his eyes. The moon still stood high in the night sky, and his breath made silver clouds as he listened to the strange sound, which he finally recognized as singing. Turning to where he knew his friend had lain down, Witheric said, "Do you hear that?"

But Restag was gone. Witheric scrambled to his feet, eyes searching, and almost at once saw his friend walking upriver. Hastily grabbing the travel bag and shield his friend had left, he raced after him, calling, "Restag! Where are you– that's not the right–Restag!"

However, Restag did not respond, and when Witheric caught up to him, he felt his blood chill as he stared into the dazed eyes of his friend. Then Restag turned toward the river, and Witheric saw that the place where they now stood sloped gently down so that the river lapped rhythmically over the rocky bank. All the while, the song continued, ringing through the night to the rhythm of the water. Dropping his luggage, Witheric grabbed at Restag as the larger man steadily approached the river.

"Stop, Restag! Stop! You can't–you'll freeze! Restag!"

Witheric pulled back and dug his heels into the grass. It did little good. Restag was a shield-man, large and strong, and Witheric did not have the raw power to hold him back, even without the enchantment drawing them closer and closer to the water's edge. As they left the grass for the pebbled bank, the small rocks slipped under Witheric's feet, causing him to trip more than once, but he held on even as Restag's boots began slowly parting the water. Deeper and deeper he went. His ankles disappeared, and then his knees, then his waist, Witheric gasping as the icy water forced the air from his lungs.

Once more, he tried to call his friend out of the spell, but his voice was weak and broken from his chattering teeth and the cold pressing against his lungs. The thanesman continued onward, the river now reaching his chest and, soon, Witheric's chin. It was then that Witheric saw it, the glowing eyes watching them just above the water's surface, rising just a little more to reveal the smiling face of the water sprite, her long hair hanging wet against her head as her song passed through her bloodless blue lips and pike-like teeth. Restag finally stopped, his gaze unfocused and body rigid. Meanwhile, the sprite began approaching, her song turning playful as she reached out her webbed hands. Stiffly, Restag followed suit, reaching out to her as if to a lover.

Witheric's mind raced. He knew what would come next. He had never seen it himself, but he had heard stories, both ancient and recent, of the water woman who lulled men into the water with her song, releasing the spell with a kiss as she dragged the man under so she could feel him thrash as he drowned. He had to do something, anything to stop her before she grabbed them and her fae strength overpowered them. But what? He knew iron to be fae-bane, but even if he could load the iron shots into his gun in time, his flint and powder were soaked by now. What could he–

Then he remembered Restag's shield. He had picked it up earlier, but only that and his friend's bag. He had not seen Restag's sword. His iron sword. With numbed hands, Witheric groped around in the water, hoping and praying to the gods that he hadn't simply missed it, that his friend's vigilance had ruled that night. His fingers touched on something colder even than the water, something rounded and attached to what felt like a pole: the pommel and handle of a sword. Gripping the handle, Witheric pulled out the blade, the motion exhausting for his chilled body and tight lungs. The sprite was close now, nearly within reach, the iron blade heavy both from its own weight and the cold and current of the river. Witheric released Restag, grabbed the blade with both hands, and heaved it clear of the water just as the sprite reached out to take his friend, nearly laughing as she sang sweetly, alluringly, causing the warrior to lean in toward her. Witheric let the sword drop, the blade's weight pulling his stiffened limbs down hard onto the water, causing a splash that stung as the cold water hit his cheeks. Above it all, he heard a horrified and satisfying scream pierce his ears.

When the last of the waves settled, he saw the river sprite screeching and hissing furiously, holding one arm underwater, the shimmering gold of fae blood shining even beneath the dark water. At the same time, Restag started awake, gasping as he suddenly felt the cold, his mind suddenly clear of the muddiness. He had a moment to register Witheric standing nearby before a strong grip suddenly pulled him underwater. He tried to pull away as the river filled his nose and mouth, but he was too cold and the water too deep. His legs and arms had no strength. He also could not see much, the water black save for the pair of glowing orbs watching him and the shimmering lines trailing out beside them. Then he heard the sound of something plunging under the water. The orbs widened, and he heard a scream and hiss as the golden lines began curling out in another place, then turning into a cloud as the powerful grip suddenly released him and another, this one much weaker than the first, tried to pull him up.

Planting his feet on the riverbed, he stood, breaking the surface with such force he nearly stumbled back. Immediately, he began coughing both from the water his body wanted to expel and from the cold air hitting his throat, tightening it. At the same time, that weak grip pulled him back, his unstable feet following the pull into increasingly shallow water. As he reached where the river rose only to his knees, whoever was pulling him tripped, releasing him as the grip's owner fell back with a splash, Restag following close behind as his weakened body dropped him waist-deep into the river, coughing and spitting out water. Not long after, he saw Witheric stagger to his feet beside him, dragging a sword with one hand and trying to support Restag with the other. Both men heaved against the current's pull, stumbling the last few yards onto the pebbled bank and then to the grass, where they collapsed from exhaustion, Restag still coughing up water. The water sprite's screams continued at a maddening pitch and volume for a few moments more before finally dying out with a grievous, heart-wrenching moan, leaving the two men alone in the still, autumn night, hearing only the river and their own heavy breathing.

After a while, Restag, shivering badly in the cold, managed to say, "W-w-what ha-hap-p-p-ened?"

"Water sp-sprite," answered Witheric. Dragging the sword forward along the grass, he said, "St-stab-b-bed it."

And hopefully killed it, thought Restag, feeling a new wave of weariness. He was so tired, his limbs heavier than a dead horse. He wanted nothing more than to sleep away the weariness and the cold and the pain in his chest and limbs. Sleep as if the world would pass away, leaving him to feel nothing but the warmth of his own dreams. However, when he saw the blue shade of Witheric's lips and his pale face, Restag realized he couldn't sleep. Not yet. To sleep now would likely be death from the cold for them both. With a deep heave and groan, he pushed himself up. He helped Witheric do the same, sheathed his sword, stumbled over to his discarded shield and travel pack, and supported the shivering thane back across the mile of grassland to the treeline. He hardly remembered them gathering the firewood, his conscious mind barely present as his years of wilderness experience and will to live remembered for him. He did recall staring at the pile of wood, wondering why it wasn't burning as he shivered uncontrollably, as well as the lightning dancing between Witheric's fingers and over the wood, soon lighting the dry sticks. He also had a vague sense of warmth and the smell of smoke as he curled up in his wet cloak and fell asleep.

They both slept late into the next day, Witheric waking with a high fever. Restag hurt everywhere, and some of his wounds had reopened from his efforts the night before. With whatever movements his stiff and pain-filled body allowed, he rebuilt the fire and tended to his master, trying to keep him warm. He removed both their cloaks and their wet clothes, changing himself and Witheric into some of his own spares, as the thane's had all been soaked by the river. For that day and the next, they stayed in place, Witheric's fever breaking the afternoon of the second day. He was still too weak to walk, though, and Restag was still too sore to have much will for hard travel.

As they ate dinner that night, both still dressed in Restag's clothes but now bundled in their dried cloaks, the thanesman said to his friend, "You saved my life twice that night. First with the sprite, and then by having enough of a mind still to light the fire. Three times if you count the fight with the Oathless. Thank you, Witheric."

Smiling sheepishly, Witheric held up his hand, letting sparks jump between his fingers. "I cannot call down Dar's thunder like Father could, but at least I don't need a tinderbox."

Restag released a short laugh. Looking out over the grasslands, he said, "I suggest we stay away from the river for now, at least until the first ice-cover sends the sprites into hiding."

"Agreed." Witheric shivered. Looking at his friend's profile in the dimming light, he said, "Hey, Restag...."

"Yes?"

"You have terrible taste in women."

"Shut up!" said Restag, tossing a dried shirt at his laughing friend while holding back his own smile. After a moment of thought, he then said, "I do wonder, though, why weren't you affected? I have never heard of a man being unmoved by a sprite's song."

Witheric frowned and began fiddling absently with his brooch. "I don't know. To say I was 'unmoved' does not quite hit the mark. It was beautiful. I recall half-dreams and thinking it beautiful, but I do not know why the snare didn't catch. Why you but not me? It seems backwards, so why...." His eyes widened and darted down to the metal clasp between his fingers. He gasped, "Of course! The brooch! Father's brooch is iron. It must have acted as a talisman against the fae's song!"

Restag turned the idea over in his mind but ended up shaking his head. "No.

It still isn't clear to me. I'm wearing chain mail, and my sword, also, is iron. If it was the iron brooch that warded off the magic, then why was I still ensnared?"

"But your mail is steel, not pure iron, and your sword was sheathed," countered Witheric. "Iron must be bared to show its teeth, and when mixed with lesser metals, it loses influence. The thinner its purity, the weaker its power."

"'Clear-speech from Dar's mouth,' if I ever heard it," said Restag, nodding and grinning ever so slightly as Witheric caught his friend's reference to the nickname and grimaced. Soon, though, Restag's eyes grew troubled. "Does this mean I will need to walk with my sword unsheathed? That is ill-fated, calling for trouble."

"That won't be necessary," said Witheric, reaching into his pack and pulling out his drawstring bag. "After all, I still have a second brooch."

Restag stared at the metal, the conflict not leaving his eyes. Eventually, he shook his head again, saying, "No. I can't. For a mere Thanesman to wear the token of the High Thanes, it is crooked."

"Oh for the love of— Restag, I am High Thane. I am Bread-Giver, Ring-Giver. It is my right to give what gifts I see fit to those I see fitting of them," said Witheric, to which Restag could give no objection. What the thane said was simply true. To continue to deny him would be to deny his thane-ship. Even so, Restag looked troubled as he nodded his acceptance. Sighing in exasperation, Witheric rose, pulling out the brooch. Standing over his friend, he said, "Very well, Thanesman Restag Far-Sighted. If you stand iron-willed against my gift, then hand me your sword."

Utterly confused, Restag obeyed only to jump to his feet in shock as Witheric used the blade to slice open his right hand. "What are you–!"

The thane silenced his thanesman by holding out the blade to him, saying, "And now you, with the other edge."

Restag stared at his master in near disbelief. "Witheric... you can't... I'm not...." He stared into his friend's eyes, seeing the decisive fire within them. He wanted to obey, to listen to his friend, to listen to his master. However.... With a painful sigh, he reached up and placed a hand over his friend's that held the sword, lowering the blade. Looking Witheric in the eye, he said, "I shall receive your gift, High Thane, and with many thanks. But I... I cannot become your blood brother, Witheric. I cannot join your house."

The fire in Witheric's eyes died, replaced by immense hurt that stabbed Restag's heart. In a confused voice, Witheric said, "Why? Restag, we have fought and lost and won battle after battle together. Now, we have shed blood for each other, and shed the blood of our enemies for the other. I owe you my life, and you yours to me. You, and only you, searched me out and found me and came with me into this place, where we are without home or hearth or family. You, and only you, have always been by my side. Of anyone I know, you are worthy of it. You are worthy to be of the House of High Thanes."

"Because I don't want it!" said Restag, trying to sort out his own feelings at that moment. He paused, piecing together his thoughts, before saying, "Witheric, I am honored that you should wish to give me this. I can't… I do not have the speech to name it truly or give form to it. But I… I am Thanesman, Witheric. Thanesman, not thane. Please. I shall accept your gift. I shall accept whatever you give me, do whatever else you ask of me, go wherever you send or take me. But please, if you have spoken true-speech just now, if those are your true heart-thoughts, then grant me this boon. Only this. Do not make me take this bond, Witheric."

Restag's throat tightened as Witheric's face fell, and the sword with it, the heavy blade landing on the forest floor with a dull thud. Gripping his bleeding hand at his side, the green blood shadowed black against the firelight, Witheric said, "I grant you your boon, Thanesman."

Breathing out his relief, Restag said, "Thank you, High Thane. Your gift is accepted with many thanks. Now, let me see your hand."

In the silence that followed, the two knelt together by the fire, Restag cleaning the gash and then carefully wrapping it in a small strip cut from the corner of one of his shirts. Once the binding was finished, Witheric stared at it, cradling it in his hand before whispering, "Restag, I'm… I am sorry."

Pausing as he rolled up his shirts, Restag said, "You are tired, and you have just gotten over a fever. By the way, are you sure you don't want me to use more of this for your feet?"

Witheric shook his head. "I can walk."

Seeing his friend and master bent like a withered plant made Restag uneasy. Though they had known each other all their lives, both from growing up in the same town and the close relationship between their families, they had rarely disagreed like this before. Small arguments here and there, or Restag pushing back on Witheric's ideas, or something of the like, but something like this… it was almost like seeing his closest friend and sword-brother reveal himself to be in fact a stranger. Restag knew how to act with Witheric. He did not know how to act with this new, strange man he had just seen.

Unable to think of what else to do, Restag held out his hand. "Were you not bestowing on me a token of your favor, my thane?"

Smiling, but with the pain still in his eyes, Witheric handed over the brooch. According to the rightful ways, he was supposed to put it on his friend, as the thane bestowing the gift, but he was glad that Restag did not insist on the tradition just then. He did not much feel himself worthy of his thanesman at that moment.

After clipping the brooch to his cloak, Restag bowed, saying, "I, your unworthy servant, accept this thane's-gift with many thanks and only hope to someday prove myself worthy of it."

Smiling sadly, Witheric shook his head resignedly at his mulish friend. How could he, Witheric High Thane, ever deserve to have such a Thanesman? Oh, how the gods shrouded themselves in their secret ways and wove the threads of fate beyond man's sight. He kept these musing to himself, knowing what kinds of answers the proud thanesman would give and how untrue they would be. Out loud, he said, "Get some sleep, Thanesman. You have toiled when you should have rested for your thane's sake. Now, your thane orders you to bed, to be ready for the toils of Dar's-hours."

Restag bowed again. "Yes, my thane."

Chapter 5

The next few days were, indeed, toilsome. Restag still ached from his wounds, and though Witheric had recovered from his fever and the cut to his hand was healing well, the stab wound in his right arm began hurting again. They had not changed the bandages for days, due to their low supplies and health. When they removed the cloth to examine the wound, the scabs pulled away painfully, and it reeked of infection. Restag's spare shirt was soon torn and wrapped around Witheric's arm and its owner's own wounds, along with a simple salve made from foraged herbs. Witheric had also found, to both of their concern, that when he was tying on Restag's bandages, his injured hand's grip was weaker and shakier than before. Whether that had come before or after the infection, or even if it was a result of his self-inflicted wound, neither knew. He tried to recall if the shakiness had been present before their confrontation with the water sprite, but all he could remember was pain and exhaustion.

Added to that, and unbeknownst to Witheric, ever since tending to Witheric after the attack, Restag felt weaker and feverish, though never enough for his friend to notice. When he was searching for herbs for Witheric's arm, he had found a few to reduce his fever, at least during the day. At night, however, when the effects wore off, he tossed and turned restlessly with fever, and he woke up feeling as if he had barely slept at all. He knew, at some point, he would have to tell his friend, but for now, the thanesman kept the pain to himself, unwilling to add another worry to the long list they shared.

Chief among those being the discovery of tracks much like they had seen before their ill-fated visit to the Reinor. It seemed that they were, indeed, traveling along the hunters' trail. What was worse, the tracks they found now were clearly fresh and they discovered the identity of the hunted.

Witheric stared, wide-eyed and pale at the three, long claw marks in the trunk of a thick oak, along with a forth mark at the back, the gashes reaching multiple rings-deep into the wood. Similar marks could be seen on other trees, as well as signs of wanton destruction across the earth and undergrowth, such as branches as thick as Witheric's arms brutally snapped off their trees and brush ripped up from the roots. Witheric breathed out the words, "Halsk spare us! They're hunting a wudwyrm!"

Restag nodded, clenching his fists to stop their trembling. No wonder he hadn't been able to find out what the hunters were pursuing. He had been focusing on the ground while what they had been tracking had been traveling through the treetops. Searching now through the leafless branches, he said, "It must be a boon-hunt, probably for a thane's son."

"Why, by all that in Dar's domain, would a thane risk his son hunting a creature straight from Halsk?" gasped Witheric.

Finding nothing with his Sight and feeling only dread for it, Restag said, "I can only speak from hear-say, but if what I say is true-speech, it is not the father but the son who buys the risk. Among some of the tribes, if a son of lesser right desires to be thane, he may request a boon-hunt to prove himself worthy of the thanes-seat. He presents the trial to his father, and if the trial is deemed thane-worthy, he is given the chance to prove that the fates stand with him, not his brother."

"But to hunt a wudwyrm for something like your father's seat, one would have to be possessed by the Fae Madness!"

"Perhaps, or perhaps it is only madness to those who never wanted such a thing," said Restag, and Witheric flushed with shame, for he understood the double meaning of Restag's words. Eventually, the shield-man sighed and said, "We mustn't stay here. We are where we are, and they are where they are, and may we two never meet."

Witheric nodded mutely as he followed his friend.

They traveled swiftly and wordlessly the rest of that morning and into the early afternoon. The air grew colder, and the wind brushed dried leaves around their legs like the scratching of claws on rock. Or scales on scales. They shared the thought, but neither dared speak it, for fear that in naming the thing they might summon it. Afternoon came, and the sky clouded over, draping the air itself in a dull gray. Witheric began shivering terribly, prompting Restag to ask, "What is it? Is your fever...?"

Witheric shook his head. "Something else," he said. "Something in the air, it isn't quite right."

The words made the hair on the back of Restag's neck prickle, and he looked around, focusing his senses on the world around them. Witheric was right. There was a strange energy to the air, something akin to the air around Witheric when he used his fairy blood, something like…. Restag's eyes darted to the trees, searching the dead boughs. There was magic in the air, powerful magic. Of what kind, he didn't know, but he knew it was there, drifting through the air like smoke, trying to ensnare them. Even so, he did not see anything in the trees above them. He was considering using his Sight when, out of the corner of his eye, a thick branch moved as if blown by the wind. In the wrong direction. He had just enough time to warn Witheric before the branch suddenly leapt from the tree, landing where the two had just been standing in a hissing, growling mass of scales and claws and fangs.

It was small for a wudwyrm, stretching nearly twice Witheric's height as it uncoiled itself to loom over the men on its two back feet, its barbed tail adding another full-grown man's length. It was young—the two, claw-tipped wings not yet full-span and webbed—which meant the creature had to travel either on the forest floor or through the treetops, using its ridged, bark-like scales to blend into the branches. It also meant that its fangs still dripped the corrosive poison it had used as an infant to escape its shell and would use as protection until its magic grew powerful enough to generate the legendary fire of its dragon cousins. Even as a youth, the creature was an apex predator, only naturally vulnerable to its own kind and Asgradi of high enough skill in large enough numbers, and after over a week of interruptions in its hunting, it was hungry.

Restag knew they did not stand a chance fighting the creature. They were both weak and tired, Witheric recovering from sickness and Restag perhaps falling into it. Their only hope was escape, and what a dim hope it was. Still, he quickly unstrapped his shield and took out his sword. They may not be able to kill the wyrm, but if they could at least injure it, slow down its pursuit of them, perhaps—

He did not get to finish the thought as all his faculties focused on the monster as it lunged at him. He dodged to the side, barely avoiding fangs as long as his arm as the creature's foreclaws slammed down onto the ground, raking up dirt and roots and rocks and the head snapped at him. Witheric then called out a warning, and Restag managed to bring his shield up just in time to guard against the tail that suddenly appeared beside him. The force of the blow knocked him back, and he heard the terrible sound of the barbed tip scraping against the iron bolts and plates on his shield. He had only just returned to his feet when a clawed wing appeared over him, dropping down with what felt like the force and weight of a house beam falling from the rafters. The shield's wood cracked under the force, and pain shot up Restag's arm. Still, the barrier held, though he doubted it would last another blow.

The wudwyrm didn't let him find out. Irritated by the shield that had now twice prevented its kill, the creature did not bother with using its claws but instead took the shield in its jaws, letting its poison rot the wood in its mouth. Restag grunted in pain as some poison leaked through the wood onto his arm, burning through his clothes in an instant to begin working on his skin. Cutting away the leather bindings with his sword, he jerked back his arm and rolled away moments before the shield shattered, poison spittle raining down onto the ground where he had just been and making smoking holes in the dead earth.

Restag held his arm close to his body, the pain burning through his senses and clouding his thoughts. He didn't dare look at it, not yet. Instead, he took a stance, sword ready. The beast turned to him, its yellow eyes keen and angry, focused on the sword. It had seen them before, been bitten by them, and hated them. It growled in its throat. Taking advantage of the creature's pause, Restag used his magic, jumping into the wyrm's mind. If it had been a dragon, perhaps it could have helped, but this irrational relative to those primordial monsters acted only on instinct, like any other beast, and its instincts said to kill.

The wyrm still crouched, staring at Restag's sword as he quickly pulled his vision back, fighting despair. What could he even do now, with one arm too injured to use and only a sword between him and over ten feet of armored death? Even injuring it enough to escape seemed impossible now. He began circling the creature, trying to see some option somewhere as the monster's head followed him, snarling.

Suddenly, the air shook with a loud crack, and the wudwyrm roared, stumbled for a moment, and spun around, revealing to Restag a small puncture wound in the creature's thigh. Just managing to dodge the tail as it whipped over him, he glanced past the creature to see Witheric crouched a short distance away, hands quivering as he aimed his gun, thumbed back the lever, and pulled the trigger, sending another crack into the air, Restag flinching at the sound. This shot, however, went wide, as the gun recoiled sharply in the owner's weakened grip, sending the shot through the wyrm's still-useless webbing rather than someplace more impactful. Even so, the creature hissed angrily and thrust out its neck to bite, but not before Witheric managed one more straying shot.

Using the wyrm's distracted attention, Restag rushed forward, getting a quick swipe at the already wounded thigh as he did. His sword barely bit, but it was enough to interfere with the wyrm's attack and let Witheric scramble out of its immediate reach. Continuing his dash, Restag sheathed his sword and intercepted and grabbed his friend, running from the monster and pulling Witheric stumbling after him. Neither bothered to look behind them as they ran, but they heard the wudwyrm's destructive pursuit. It roared, the sound deafening even as a youngling.

After the echo of the wyrm-cry died away, a new sound arose, both wonderful and terrifying. A high, rhythmic sound, followed by voices and cries maddening in their ecstasy. Forms appeared between the trees, closing in with exclamations of recognition and discovery and a desire for violent death. Neither Witheric nor Restag knew the number of the hunting party, drawn to their prey by the gunshots and wyrm-cries, nor did they see who it was who ran toward the monster from which they fled. They only ran, knowing with certainty that their lives depended on it. Briefly, the thought slipped into Restag's mind that he was a coward. That he, like any Asgradi shield-man worth his blade, should be adding his own war cry to the others, not running from the battlefield like a startled hare. However, Witheric's wheezing breath behind him and the thin wrist encompassed by his hand overcame his warrior's honor. No. This was not his fight, not his trial. They would only be in the way. Nor could they afford to buy the risk of recognition from hot-blooded warriors drunk on the thirst for blood. So they ran, ran until even the echoes of battle were far behind them, till Dir rose high and strong over the skeleton trees, turning trunk and branch to black shadow and pure white bone, till, at last, Witheric could go no farther.

With a crash, he fell, too winded even to cry out. Restag, his grip lost by the sudden collapse, stumbled forward another few steps before stopping to turn around. Breathing heavily, he staggered back to his master's heaving form, his legs giving out part way back as the excitement-driven strength drained away. Witheric, too exhausted for fortitude, wept quietly to himself from the pain and relief. Meanwhile, Restag stared up at the moon, feeling as if the clouds that filled his vision were not his own huffing breath but steam rising from his burning muscles and sweating skin. Then came the pain. Feverish pain that spread from his arm with such intensity he doubled up, biting his good arm till he drew blood to muffle the agonized scream. At some point, he blacked out, and when he awoke, Witheric sat beside his prone form, trying to wrap his throbbing arm in the last of their fresh bandages with cold, trembling hands.

Restag watched him absently for a while then croaked, "Put on some mittens."

Witheric shook his head. "I can't tie it if I do."

"...Woe or weal?"

Laughing sardonically, the thane said, "It probably feels worse than it looks, though that is no honey-speech…. It is… Halsk's hounds snapped, but you slipped between their jaws. They have left their mark, but I think you shall hold a shield again, my friend."

Releasing a long, heavy breath, Restag gasped, "Thanks be to Svanril!"

Again, Witheric laughed, though this time it was a softer, more natural sound. He said, "Her father counts no new shield-men among his war-reapers tonight. Not from us, at least."

Not yet, anyway, thought Restag, shivering in the hoarfrost-light. Despite the pain and weariness pulling his body to the earth like an anchor, as soon as Witheric tied off the bandage and began searching his travel sack for mittens, Restag forced himself up. Witheric did not waste time or energy protesting, instead helping his friend to stand so they could find kindling and clear a space for a fire. Neither man had the stomach to eat that night, so they simply took turns slowly sipping from a water skin, curled up close to the fire, and fell asleep.

One of the first thoughts to cross both men's minds the next morning was the fact that they were utterly lost. They did not know which direction they had run the night before or how far. They knew they must go east to reach the river, but the pain throbbing up his arm and the way it worsened his existing fever prevented the shieldless shield-man from focusing enough to activate his Sight. Pulling out the large map, they estimated their location and searched through Restag's collection of local maps to find one that might tell them something of the land, but there were no distinguishing landmarks besides tall oak and ash trees splintering the gray sky. In the end, they simply chose a direction, hoping to find elevated ground from which to either place their position on the map or see the Reinor.

It was slow going for the wounded men. Witheric had reloaded his gun but had lost much confidence in his ability to use the weapon after his unsteady hand had caused him to take so long to aim his one good shot the day before. If he had only been faster, perhaps Restag's arm... he shoved the thought away. Until they reached a shelter, they had not left the battlegrounds, and he was High Thane. He must not lose heart. Not while he still had one man who followed him.

After wandering for hours through the endless mass of wood and dead leaf, they stumbled upon a house sitting in a small clearing. It was shocking in its suddenness. The two men had neither seen nor smelled the wisps they now saw rising from the smoke-hole of the building that seemed to just appear from between the trees. A hushed argument ensued, with Restag saying they did not know if the owner was friend or foe while Witheric, noticing his friend's sweating brow and heavy breathing, insisted they at least investigate. A few heated moments later, Restag finally agreed on the condition that he take a look around before they got any nearer, to which Witheric readily agreed. Soon after, Restag reluctantly reported that it seemed an ordinary house. He had seen only one person, a young woman sweeping up leaves at the back of the house, too focused on her task to notice him. He still did not wish to approach, but Witheric was more than satisfied.

They decided it best to go around to the back of the house and approach in view of its owner, so as not to startle her. As they neared the back corner, still traveling through the trees, the woman Restag had seen rounded the corner. She was a pretty girl, her dark, waist-long hair braided away from her plump, youthful face and bright green eyes. She was dressed in a simple hangerock dress and carried her broom lightly as she quietly hummed to herself. For a moment, she did not notice them. Then, her eyes happened in their direction, and she gasped. Witheric rushed out of the treeline, though remained a good distance, reassuring her that they intended no harm.

"We're lost, you see, and my friend, he's terribly hurt!" he said.

The girl looked to Restag, and her surprise turned to concern. "Oh dear!" she gasped. "How ill you look! Yes, please, come in. Come in. I don't have much, but perhaps... anyway, I won't know till I get a proper look. Come."

She turned toward the front of the house, Witheric starting after her until he noticed Restag's absence. Looking back, he saw unease on his friend's face.

When asked about it, Restag's eyes darted toward the girl disappearing around to the front of the house, and said quietly, "I don't like it, Witheric. Something feels... odd. Bent, though I don't....."

Witheric frowned. He supposed it was a little strange to just stumble across a house in the forest, and there was something about it all that made his skin itch, but did not events such as this happen in the old stories all the time? Unexpectedly coming upon a house of hospitality in a hostile land? Could it not be the work of the gods, providing for them in their need? Before he could pose the questions, the girl peered around from the front of the house, asking if they were alright.

"Yes, we're fine," Witheric replied. "My friend is just…."

Just what? What could he say that would not insult their hostess. However, the girl smiled sympathetically and nodded, as if understanding. Turning back to Restag, he said, "Come on. We agreed, didn't we? Didn't you say it seemed ordinary enough?"

Unwillingly, Restag nodded and, encouraged by his friend and the now questioning look from the girl his way, he stepped into the clearing. He shivered, though if from his fever or his unease, he could not be sure. As he approached the front of the house with Witheric, that unease did not lift. There really was something odd about this place. It looked entirely ordinary, but he sensed something out of place, though he could not discern what. His gut and the tightness in his chest, however, told him it was, so he rested his hand on the pommel of his sword as they entered the longhouse after the girl.

It was a clean house, neatly kept, the hearth lit with a small pot hanging above it, earthen floor bare of clutter, unused candles sitting in their candlesticks, and a sleeping bench sitting neatly draped in blankets against the wall with a few storage chests beneath it. Against the opposite wall were some tables, on which sat tools and herbs for cooking, pots and a small cauldron stored beneath them, and at the back sat two doors, one of which the woman opened to reveal a larder and the other which Restag deduced to be a closet based on the space remaining in the house. There was little decoration on the walls, and no sign of another inhabitant. Overall, it was a small, cozy, but lonely looking house.

Looking over her shoulder from the larder, the young woman said, "Hang your cloaks on the pegs by the door. I have some pallets under the bed you can use to rest. Would you travelers like a drink? Some wine, perhaps?"

To Restag's relief, Witheric replied, "Your generosity is overwhelming, woods-maid, but I'm afraid we have no time for a long stay. Only tended hurts and directions are needed."

"Oh, yes, of course, and that shall come, but please, there is no harm in a sit and a meal, is there? I should be loath to learn you did not reach your aim for want of food and rest. And it shall cheer your spirits, which is quite a boon for the battered body," replied the girl, pulling from the larder some aromatic cheese and a few small rolls and smiling softly at her guests.

Witheric glanced at Restag, who said, "My thoughts remain unchanged, but I shall leave the decision to you."

After another moment's hesitation, Witheric unpinned his cloak and hung it as directed, Restag following his lead. Soon, the forest girl had them sitting on the bench, apologizing she had so little to offer as she ladled them both a small cup of dark drink from the pot over the hearth fire. Restag sipped it carefully, the liquid thick and warm and tasting of cinnamon and cloves and citrus and the smell bringing to mind memories of long, winter nights back in the Iron Hall of High Thanes, memories intoxicating in their comfort. Another sip came, as did like memories, and another, and another. Then Restag heard voices and realized Witheric and the girl were speaking. She was cutting up herbs on the table, and he was leaning against the wall nearby. The exiled thane had not looked so pleased since they had left, and as the young woman chuckled at something he said that Restag did not catch, he understood why. He wondered, the thought almost lethargic as it slid across his mind, how he had not noticed just how pretty she was. Yes, he would have admitted her pretty if asked from the first, but it had somehow not settled in how her hair shone and her eyes danced, how charming were her little gestures and the curve of her lips and the dimples of her cheeks when she smiled. It had not struck him at the start, but watching the two now, he understood, and he felt his cheeks heat from both wine and jealousy as he did. Why should Witheric be the one given her attention? Had they not come here for his sake, to tend to him? Yet there they were, ignoring him and his pain, twittering to each other like birds in spring. Why should Witheric be the one? After all, he–

Restag's inner complaints cut off as Witheric suddenly slid to the floor and lay there, immobile. With a sobering chill, Restag realized that his friend had not been leaning against the wall in ease but for support. He tried to jump up to help his friend, but the moment he stood, his legs gave out, and he crumbled to the ground, his mind and vision foggy. From across the room, though it sounded a much farther distance than he knew it to be, he heard the girl say, "Come now, don't move around like that. A burn from a wudwyrm's poison is no wound to take lightly."

He wanted to ask how she knew about his injury, despite having never looked at it. He wanted to ask what was wrong with Witheric, and what was wrong with him. But his lips would not move, and his tongue felt weak as the world came in and out of focus. As it did, the young woman continued, "What you need is rest. Lots and lots of rest. No use fighting it. This is my domain, and you hung your shield by the door of your own will, twice-lost-shield-man. Rest now."

When Restag woke later to Witheric's concerned voice, it was so dark he thought himself blind. However, then he saw the slight crack of a door, through which came a sliver of light. He sat up with the grogginess of one who has slept but without refreshment, groaning, "Where are we? What happened?"

"In a closet, I think," said Witheric, his voice miserably sheepish. "Well, friend, you were right, yet again. It would seem we were enthralled by a spell. The wine must have been a witch's brew!"

"Maybe," said Restag. Then recalling the iron broach attached to his cloak hanging by the door, he said, "Or perhaps it simply strengthened the magic's hold. I don't suppose it matters either way, though."

"No," sighed Witheric. "No. I suppose not. So, now what? I tried the door, but it must also be enchanted. I tried to force it open, but it is like hitting a mountain and hoping it will move."

Before Restag could answer, there was the sound of a catch, followed by a panel sliding back, letting in a brief stream of dim light before a face filled it. It was a horrible, wrinkled face covered in veins spreading across the skin like dark green roots. Bright, golden eyes glowed slightly in the dark. The face's thin lips pulled back into a smile, and a voice, unmistakably female but also so old it sounded covered in dust, said, "Did the children have a good nap?"

Witheric glared indignantly at the old woman, snapping, "What are your purposes, hag?"

"Hag?" said the old lady, breaking out into laughter that sounded like the crackle of old parchment. "Yes. I suppose I am a hag. You forget, sometimes, when you have lived on the edge of Faerie for so long, the names given you. Safer that way. Hm… but I do like 'hag.' I think I'll keep it for a while."

Forcing himself to his feet, grunting in pain as he put weight on his injured arm, Restag reached for his sword and found it missing. The witch grinned toothily at him, saying, "A Dar's-word for you two boys: remember your stories.

Never enter a woman's house in the middle of the woods. She may just be a witch. And never, ever relinquish your iron, especially of your own will. Oh, and don't let anyone take your weapon. That's a silly thing for a shield-man to do."

Flushing angrily, Restag clenched his good fist and said, "You were asked a question, Witch. What are your purposes? If you mention the stories, then should I think you wish to eat us?"

Witheric paled, but the hag laughed again, saying "Such ill-speech for a child. Your mother must weep for that tongue of yours." The flush deepened across Restag's cheeks, reaching his ears and down his neck. The witch went on, "But that's a man for you. Always thinking with his stomach! You are right, though. It's been quite a while since I've had the taste of fae-blood, even if it's only half the potency. It will be quite welcome, this time of year."

"But-but aren't you an Asgradi, too?" said Witheric. "Your face… aren't those…."

The hag answered, "Ah, yes. Well, that was a long time ago. Back when I did not need my fae-gift to fish for pretty little boys who love a pretty little face."

So, thought Restag, that explained the strange feeling from earlier. As only half-fae, iron did not stop or weaken an Asgradi's magic, but it did react to it, often generating discomfort or something like an itch for the wearer. It was why the Asgradi had long used steel for their metal armor, rather than iron. Iron rings or plates became a distraction whenever the wearer used or was hit by another's magic, and a moment's distraction could mean death in battle. This witch could probably sight-bend or weave some other cunning through which Restag's Sight could not penetrate. When they had entered into her spell's influence, the broaches had sensed the fae magic, but he and Witheric had not listened and instead walked right into the snare.

Witheric, having come to a similar conclusion as Restag, looked apologetically to his friend, who shook his head. They shared the blame for this doom, to some extent. The thane knew, though, that his share was the greater, as was his duty to free them from the noose. To the hag, he said, "Is… is there no way to sway you against eating us?"

The hag looked at him like he was an idiot, but after her eyes scanned them, they narrowed, and her said thoughtfully, "You do look rather more like bones than flesh. Of course, I could just plump you up a bit…. Or, if you have something, some token or treasure that I deem worth your worn bone-houses, perhaps I may take that than use up my larders feeding two grown men."

Hope pulsed within Witheric, and he said excitedly, "What about the broaches? We don't have much of value, but–"

"Bah!" said the hag, swatting the idea away. "I'm a witch! What use have I for iron? Besides, didn't I just tell you that's a fool's deed? Do you have sieves for ears, you hollow-head! No, no. Iron is no good. I need something more. Something useful. Something… precious, something that holds a piece of you worth keeping."

A shiver ran down Witheric's spine as he realized the witch was not truly looking at him. Her eyes were focused on his torso, right where the little draw-string bag carrying fragments of home brushed against his chest beneath his shirt. With shaking hands, he reached into his tunic and pulled it out, slipping the contents out onto his hand. The witch's eyes gleamed greedily.

Restag, meanwhile, said, "Witheric! What are you–"

"Stay out of this, Restag," said Witheric, not looking away from the hag. "This is thanes-work. Not yours."

Restag fell silent, his emotions falling behind a mask.

The witch stared for a long while at the small pile in Witheric's hand. Finally, she said, "The ring means nothing to me. Yes, it is gold, and gold has its uses, but few of value to me. The hair, on the other hand…."

A pang filled Witheric's throat, his eyes darting to the small, braided lock. Memories rose, clear as the days they occurred, his throat tightening as he said, "It… it belonged to my wife."

"Ah," said the witch, nodding in understanding. "She is a pretty woman, I see."

"Yes," said Witheric, his voice distant as he drifted back, back into the sea of memories like a ship with neither anchor nor sails. He recalled their childhood, the timid, summer-blue eyes and freckled face, the long, blond braid bouncing behind her like a chain of gold as she shyly ran after them in their play, the slender form that suddenly obtained a grace he had never known in her or anyone else. He remembered the day she gave him the braid, slipping it into his hand one night following an unexpected kiss in the deepening shadows between houses. He remembered the fear he felt, soon after, when he approached his father to ask permission to marry her, the fear that he would be rejected or that perhaps his younger brother, the favored son, might have already made such a request. He had not. She was of a good family, with reasonable strength in their gift, and the boon was readily granted. He remembered going to her house the next morning to tell his intentions to her father, the smell of freshly baled hay blowing through the village and the sound of the blacksmith's hammer ringing earlier than usual. He remembered the pride that filled her father's face and the joy that blossomed on hers. He remembered their wedding, the bridal crown upon her head and the way her hair looked like a veil trailing beneath it against the black and white and red of her embroidered gown, the way she cried as he took her hand and led her away and the utter happiness of their wedding night.

He remembered those few months, happier than he had ever been, at last knowing what it meant to live and enjoy living. And he remembered the long winter that year, and the plague that took so many, nearly including her. He remembered how his father had placed his hand upon his shoulder one cold night, when she came closest to death, how when he turned his weeping eyes to the man he saw neither disappointment nor contempt, only pity and understanding. It was one of the few moments his father had ever shown him true compassion, and it was to be the last. For he died the following spring, along with Witheric's brother after being ambushed in the heat of battle. Next was his mother, and then came the thane's seat and all the weight of the Eisenband. All to bear with an aching soul. Without her, he wondered if he could have borne it.

"Eathir," he whispered. "She is… like her namesake. Eathir, River of the Moon, Dir's River, the thick band of stars that stretch across the night sky, filling the darkness with light and beauty beyond the bounds of words."

"Oh? A song-speaker, are you?" said the witch, though her old voice did not sound quite so harsh. "Yes. She is beautiful. More than songs can speak. Yes. It is Eathir I want."

Witheric's attention returned like a bow string released from full draw. He could hardly breathe as he forced out the words, "Very well."

"Witheric!" Restag snapped, yanking the other man's arm, his face white with fury. "You-You can't… that's not…."

Witheric winced as Restag's hold tightened when words failed. However, the pain in his arm almost felt good compared to what rested in his throat and chest and heart. Yet, in the end, he looked his friend in the eye and said, "What then, Restag? What have you to offer? Or is holding onto memories more important than life in the present? You may as well hold onto the dead at the cost of the living."

Sorrow, no, grief fell over Restag's countenance, and his hand fell limply as his face shut itself behind the mask, and he stepped back. The hag looked delighted, as if ready to squeeze through the little window to grab her prize.

"Give it!" she said. "Give it here! Hair from a lost beloved, such a prize. Such a prize! Give it!"

Witheric put his mother's pin and his signet ring back in the bag, wrapped his fingers tightly around the small braid one last time, and began holding it out to her withered hand snaking through the little window when Restag's voice jumped between them.

"Hold!" he said. The shield-man's eyes were dark and cold in the dim light as he glared at the witch, a stare made all the harsher by his otherwise placid face. She cringed. The thanesman's voice was hard as he said, "Open the door first. Open it and let us out. And if you try any false turns afterwards, you will beg for Halsk's hounds before I finish with you."

The witch's reaching hand jerked back through the window with a hiss. Her eyes narrowed and she bared her few, jagged teeth, but in the end the latch lifted and the door opened. Witheric smiled his thanks to his friend and stepped through. However, when Restag tried to follow, the door slammed shut again. Restag shouted and tried to grab the witch through the window, but she scurried away, screeching, "Not fair! Not fair to get one and lose two! See? Not false. The false are you who want to take two but only give one. That is ill-doings, little High Thane. Ill-doings. May Wyrdi take you for ill-doings, for a High Thane trying to cheat an old woman!"

A flow of curses sounded from the closet, followed by several loud thumps and even more profanities and calling for damnation upon the witch. From her distance, she laughed her dry, crackled laugh and said, "Careful, child. Do not hit too hard or you'll undo all the work I did on that arm of yours. Nasty, nasty work. Surprised you didn't lose it to the hounds. There, that's better. You see? I did as I promised. Can't do anything about the scars, but you can use it. No use eating a useless thing, now is there?"

Restag glowered at the old woman. It was true. He hadn't realized in the moment how much better his arm felt, nor the new bandages wrapped skilfully around it, but that did little to ingratiate to him the ugly form just out of reach.

Recovering her composure, the witch pretended to swat away the glare and said, "Bah! Such shifty blood. Cold when thinking and hot when acting, and nary the twain shall meet. You must be favored by Svanril, Halsk take her. A little hesitation wouldn't hurt, you know. Like your thane."

Looking now to Witheric, who watched the exchange with a troubled brow and wide, uncertain eyes, cooled Restag's temper. The witch nodded and said, "Good. That's better. Now then, little High Thane, give me the braid and then run along."

"What? No!" cried Witheric, holding the precious item close. "I'm not leaving without Re- my thanesman."

Clicking her tongue, the witch said, "Almost let me catch a name there, didn't you? Quick learner, boy. In any case, I already told you, it would be a cheat for you to take two but only give one."

Reaching back into his bag, Witheric pulled out the hairpin, saying, "You didn't say this was useless earlier. Would it be enough?"

The witch looked over the ornament, but eventually said, "No. It is silver, yes, which is of great use for one of Dir, but it has not the ties and tangles of heart-felt loss from him for it to be a fair trade. Even when laying aside my treating his wound."

A touch of despair crept into Witheric's heart and settled there, gradually growing as he tried to think of something else, something to save his friend, but he could think of nothing. Then the witch spoke again, her voice almost lilting as she said, "However...."

Both men's eyes focused on the witch, who feigned indecision before carrying on. "Yes, yes I think I can. How about, little thane, you give me the hairpin for yourself and the braid for your friend?"

Witheric blinked in confusion. Hadn't she just said Restag's cost was greater because of her treating him? Granted, her value did not seem based on anything like material or artistry or anything like that, but how could a small braid....

He looked to Restag, and the terrible answer revealed itself. His friend's mask had fallen, unveiling a face drained of color, sickly in its dread and fear and shame. It was a face Witheric had never seen before on his friend. Had he–

Swallowing back the question now haunting his mind, Witheric said, "I'll... Very well. I agree to your trade, Witch."

The hag practically danced in her glee, her laughter sending shivers up and down his spine as she tittered dryly, the sound like a snake's rattle. To take his mind off the happy, malicious creature, as well as the more dreadful thoughts wrapping around him, he looked to his mother's hairpin, taking in the details one last time. It had been a gift from his father on their wedding night, a masterful work that would earn even an elf or dwarf's admiration, shaped into a running horse of pure silver that seemed almost alive in its curves and wild eyes and mane. He remembered her wearing it everyday. If, in truth, she had not, the woman in his memories still did, incomplete without that regal, leaping beast taming her long, brown hair. The only time he recalled it missing was in those last few weeks, her hair draped over her face as she mourned and slowly withered away, pushing away all but her remaining son, not even bothering with the simplest tasks such as holding a brush as she stared blankly at the pin, dying as it slipped from her fingers to the floor. The deaths of his father and brother had been hard and aching, but his mother almost broke him. Such a senseless death, such a preventable death, and yet he'd been unable to stop it. The hollowness it had left had nearly collapsed him inward, like a rotted roof, and only the support beams of his duties, his wife, and his thanesman had kept him up.

Now, he handed that hairpin over, almost seeing the threads of love and pain and loss and hurt that tied it to him snap as the witch took it. Next was the braid. As Restag had done before, he insisted on his friend's release before handing it over. This time, though, the hag shook her head.

"No. If I do, he'll kill me. I am no false-trader, little thane. You shall have your friend back, and your possessions, too, worthless as they are to me, but I must have the token first."

Witheric hesitated, curiosity coming to mind, and he said, "Why? I don't mean why do I need to give it to you first. I mean… why didn't you just ask for them both this way in the first place? Or even more, just take them while we slept?"

The witch turned a golden eye to the young man, its depths canny and versed in roads he could never know. She said, "The sacrifice must be made willingly, High Thane, and the pain felt in order to hold its greatest power."

His breath hitched, and he paused before saying, "Yes, I think I understand."

Without another word on either side, he handed over the braid.

They never quite knew how they came to be back in the forest, walking with their gear reclaimed, the moon shining over their silent march. When Restag tried to recall it later, he could not bring the images to mind. All he knew was that he had been locked up, watching his friend give away two of his most precious treasures, and the next moment the two of them were free, the witch's house gone, as if it had never been.

The night wore on, the clouds gone and the moon sinking low in the sky, neither man feeling tired, until, suddenly, they stood on the edge of the forest, the grasslands lining the Reinor river stretching out before them. In the cold, quiet wind, Witheric whispered, "Restag, please, tell me honestly. About Eathir, do you… are you…."

Restag did not meet his friend and master's eyes as he said, "She chose you."

He then turned away, following the treeline south, Witheric following silently after him.

Over the next couple weeks, the world around them grew colder and colder. The wind picked up, and clouds hid the sky nearly every day. They kept along the treeline, unsure between the forest and the river which held the greater danger. Food grew scarce. Restag tried to hunt, making a makeshift sling from some of their makeshift bandages, but the birds were hidden away, as were most other small game, leaving the snare traps he began setting up every night empty come morning. They had no arrows to hunt the occasional deer they heard bound between the trees. Restag did make a javelin from a fallen branch, which, after making sure the river had frosted at the edges and sent its fae inhabitants into hiding, did catch them a couple fish. However, they were small things, and catching them took too long for him to do every day.

After the first week, Witheric realized that Restag was not eating as much, giving him the greater portion of food or the larger fish. The thane protested, but Restag brushed away the concern, saying he was the stronger of the two and did not need as much. Of course Witheric pushed back, trying to say it should be kept even, but Restag refused to let him handle or even see the food stocks, declaring it "beneath a high thane's notice" and unintentionally increasing that same thane's concern.

For Restag's part, he saw how Witheric was falling ill again. His friend's eyes told of his lack of sleep, and the thane could do nothing to hide his fevered shivering. The herbs Restag had gathered were soon gone, and any replacements were dead on the frozen ground. Despite the thane's best efforts, their pace slowed. Every time Witheric apologized, Restag denied any wrong, secretly grateful himself as his own symptoms began to worsen without the medication.

At last, the day came when Witheric collapsed. He managed to push himself back up, but the fall had triggered something in his body, something which his mind had been fighting for the past few days and that demanded he go no further. But he knew he had to. It was getting dark, and the air smelled of coming snow. They needed shelter, or something they could turn into one. His dazed eyes scanned the world, trying in the growing shadows to make out something suitable for their survival.

Then, he saw it. At first, he thought it a trick of his eyes. In the distance, somewhere down the nearly flat riverbank, was a light. It was far, no larger than the hole from a needle to his eyes, but it was a sign of someone else, perhaps someone with shelter. Perhaps it was another Asgradi tribe. Perhaps it was another deceit of Faerie, but as he shivered from another snow-scented gust of wind, Witheric was willing to risk another wudwyrm for a place to weather out the coming snow. He turned to Restag, preparing his counter arguments as he pointed to the light. But when he looked, his friend was not beside him. Panic heated the young thane's blood, and he called out to his Thanesman as his wide eyes whipped around, finally seeing the form of his friend several yards behind him, leaning against a tree.

With a cry, he ran back, reaching his friend to find him barely conscious, sweat heavy on his brow and his breathing labored. Wiser now from the witch's work, Witheric said, "How long?"

Restag shook his head, though the action was barely visible, it was so slight. Angry now, Witheric demanded, "How long have you been sick, Restag Thanesman!"

The Thanesman's eyes cracked open, their gaze unfocused. After a few moments of silence, Restag breathed out, "About three weeks."

His own illness nearly forgotten, Witheric yelled, "Three weeks? Three weeks ill, and you never told me. Hid it from me! You fought a wudwyrm, dragged me at Roth's-pace through the forest, supported me, deprived yourself of food, all while you were sick, and you hid it from me!"

Witheric's anger subsided, and hurt slid in its place. Much softer now, he said, "What else, are you hiding from me, Restag? What else have you been hiding from me, all these weeks or months or years?"

If Restag was willing to answer, Witheric could not know it. The man leaned against the tree, looking and sounding as if drawing breath was a struggle on its own, let alone speaking. At this rate, he might die. The thought jolted Witheric from his own hurt, and he hurried to take Restag's arm and drape it over his shoulders, pulling at him to shift his weight from the tree. Restag tried to shake his head, to object, but Witheric hissed, "Stop it! I don't have the strength for you to dig in your hooves, you ass!"

Apparently, neither did Restag, for his struggle ceased, and he let himself be slowly led forward as Witheric turned from the forest and made as straight a line as he could for the distant light just as the first few snowflakes began to fall. He cursed under his breath but continued moving away from any semblance of shelter onto the barren plain.

At this point, he didn't care even if that light was another hag's hut. It was unlikely to be Asgradi, he concluded, since no right-minded Asgradi would be wandering away from the trees the shelter they provided this late into the year, but even if it was his worst enemies, he didn't care. Whoever or whatever it was, it was something or someone else out in this cold, and that meant the chance for help. It was a gamble, and based on his last one, it did not seem Wyrdi was much on his side, but he saw no other choice and stumbled on, half-dragging his much taller friend's half-conscious body.

As they went, the snowfall began to thicken and pile up. The world was now nearly black, save for that single light in the distance. He hoped he didn't end up toppling them both into the river in the darkness. Neither could afford wet clothes in addition to everything else.

A little while later, Witheric suddenly felt immense weight on one shoulder that yanked him down into the unseen snow. Restag had fainted. Witheric didn't need to see him to know. The snow continued to fall. Tears of anger and despair fell from Witheric's face, the streaks they made on his cheeks freezing painfully in the cold.

Why hadn't he noticed his friend's condition? He had, his conscience told him. He had known something was wrong for a while. However, he had always explained it away, ascribing it to the shield-man's injuries or exhaustion or to some other cause. Anything to not admit his friend was ill, weak, in need of support the thane feared he would be unable to provide. Every time Restag seemed to be better, Witheric had relaxed, let himself believe it had just been a passing spell. And look where it had led him, trapped in utter darkness, unable even to see his dying friend beside him, and the sky providing the burial shroud. Why had he ignored the needs of his man? Why had he–Witheric son of Witheow, High Thane of Eisensaet–let his Thanesman carry all the weight?

Wiping the tears away, he felt around till he located Restag's arm again, forcing them both up, going on not because he hoped to reach safety. Not because he thought they would live through the night or even the next few steps. He pressed on only because he knew he had to.

The blackness persisted around them, the wind and snow swallowing sound, even the sound of his own steps and Restag's legs dragging behind them. His sense of touch disappeared, numbed by the air seeping through their soaked clothes and the wind against his face. Still he dragged them on, more, now, from sheer stubborn will than any clear thought or desire or reason. Moving just because he still could.

Then, another sound snuck through the wailing wind. A sound almost like the echo of a laugh. As if in the literal blink of an eye, with almost the same suddenness as the appearance of the witch's house, a shape materialized in the abyss, made visible by what he now saw was a single lantern glowing gold in the black, revealing the dark silhouette of a small ship. A human ship. Witheric nearly wept at the sight of it. From the hearth of his body, dimming embers glowed as a new breath fed them, encouraged them to keep alight that small flame, the burning will to live. He groped about his fading mind, seeking in the shadows the human words he had learned over the years, looking for one with any use. He found it, and his numbed lips formed the word as his tightened throat let out the yell that struggled through the muffled air. Again, he called, and again, and again. And with each call, the light came closer until, suddenly, he stepped through that final wall of darkness, and his foot appeared within the edges of that little sun shining through the glass. It was as if he stood in the first of days, when Dar was born, emerging with such brilliant light his mother had to throw him away and his father had placed him in the sky to keep him from burning them to death. So did the light feel to him as he stepped into it, sympathizing with those parents of the king of gods.

He forced himself to look at it, to look into that burning, blinding power and straight into the dark eyes of a single human standing on the deck, looking down at them. Their eyes locked, and Witheric willed to speak, to beg the man to help them. Instead, everything went black.

PART 2
THE SHIELD
MAIDEN OF
THENIKA

Chapter 6

Restag regained full consciousness to a strangely colored sky. He had held similar, hazy visions as he drifted near wakefulness only to be pulled back into a sea of sleep for only Dar knew how long, but this newest vision was much clearer. The sky was almost yellow, with clouds the color of goat's milk reaching in odd lines toward a larger cloud in the center, and they were all strangely shadowed and angled in appearance. It was that last detail that finally brought the realization that he looked not at the sky but at a high, unusually bright ceiling. In fact, the whole room was bright, and he had to close his eyes again as a headache started behind his eyes, causing him to grunt in pain. When he opened them again a moment later, a dark form loomed over him.

Reflexively, he jolted up, grabbing at the form. Then, he was falling, hitting the floor and pulling whatever he had grabbed down with him with a yelp. There was a brief struggle, but soon, he had the form pinned to the ground, only realizing afterwards that it was a young woman. However, she was not like any woman he had met before. She was broader, for one, not the thin, delicate creatures he knew, but more muscular, her face rounder. Her hair, which was braided tightly against her head, was dark brown, like the coat of a bay horse, a color uncommon but not unknown among his people, as were her brown eyes. Her darker skin tone, however, was foreign to his people, as was the pink flush to her face and the large red mark on one side where he had knocked her against something during their struggle. Those dark eyes flashed angrily at him, and words that reminded him of a horse's hooves over stone snapped from her lips, striking sharply against his ears. Words he did not know. Human words.

Startled, his gaze raced around the room. It was enormous, perhaps the length of the Iron Hall's throne room, but wider. The walls were a calming off-white with dark, wood trimming and white-painted arches on the ceiling. Beds and small tables and seats, enough to fit more than one family, lined the walls, and the light broke in through small windows spaced above their sight-line on either side of the room, a large curtain at the end covering what he assumed to be another window, based on the light lining it. Any other details were lost on him for the moment, for as his eyes turned to the back of the room, they fell on the next bed over, where Witheric slept. Crying out, Restag released his hold and tried to stand only for his strength to suddenly empty from his limbs, and he fell as his legs gave out under him, followed by a large door from the front of the room bursting open, lightly armored men in strange, matching robes rushing in, drawing their swords as they called out in their sharp tongue.

Meanwhile, Korena Iegam, the woman Restag had wrestled, cursed under her breath before rolling to her knees and shouting to the guards, "Halt! You're going to frighten him and drive him to recklessness!"

The guards stopped mid-step. One looked at her with discomfiture and said, "B-but, Miss Iegam, I-we thought we heard you cry out, and then shouting, and soon after, there was another shout, and-and...."

Korena looked at the man flatly, and he blushed. "If you heard all that you should have come in earlier," said the look, but out loud she simply sighed. She understood the guards' hesitation. Few of the palace guard knew how to interact with a rendeilxue, and the stories surrounding them did not help with confronting the very real threat of super-human, magical powers. Still, what use were guards who didn't guard?

Turning back to the rendeilxue, she softened her voice and said, "I apologize for startling you. Are you–"

Another curse nearly escaped her lips as she saw the thin, dark tips of the half-fairy's Mark that crept like tree roots just over his shoulder and were visible due to the loose shirt collar shift from a black-ish green to shimmering veins of gold beneath his skin. He was using his magic. Hastily, she reached out and took his sleeveless arm. The moment her skin touched his, the golden light vanished, and he looked to her with a start. Before he could pull away, however, Korena wrapped her arms around his, saying in a low voice, "Calm down! No magic. If they see anything strange, they might hurt you. Now, let me help you. Come on. On your feet."

Restag understood none of this. However, he was too disoriented and weak to resist as the human woman helped him stand. Recovering himself, he tried again to use his Gift, but he couldn't. More than that, an uncanny emptiness beat through his heart and out through the rest of his body, through his very veins. He never would have thought his half-fairy blood had a sensible feeling to it, or that magic possessed something resembling life, but now he did, and its absence frightened him. His eyes latched onto the woman. She had done something. When she had touched him, she had done something to him. For a moment, he thought to break free of this witch-woman, to take hold of her again and demand she undo what she had done, but the hiss and clink of a sword being returned to its sheath and his own need for the woman's support to even stand outweighed such thoughts for now. He may not understand their words, but he understood a sword well enough, as well as what it meant to confront two armed men in a state like his current one. No. For now, he would wait, see their next moves and divine their abilities and intentions.

Much to his surprise, the woman led him slowly around to the other side of Witheric's bed and helped him sit on a small stool beside his master. He glared at her suspiciously, but then turned his attention to Witheric. His master was gaunt, his skin pale and sweaty.and breath heavy. But he was alive. Somehow, they were both alive. Against his better judgment, Restag let himself feel relief, and as he did, the woman let go. Instantly, his blood came to life again. He tried not to show his surprise. He had shown too much already. But the immediacy of it confirmed his thoughts toward the woman. She had been the cause, and as she took a couple steps back, he was determined she never would be again.

Korena addressed the guards again, saying, "What do you stand there? Someone must inform the king that one of his guests has awoken! Also, get the doctor. He should be in his workroom preparing medicine."

As the guards saluted and one ran off, she said to the rendeilxue, "And you? Are you in need of anything? Food? Water?"

However, the strange man simply sat and stared at his companion, his face now a mask with only his eyes showing the deep concern and trouble he felt. According to the report from Thaellas the merchant, who had picked them up three or four days upriver from the delta on the northern end of the Ostran Sea a couple weeks back, one of the only things the still-sleeping rendeilxue had said was the larger one's name. What was it again? Regard? Rotag? Resig? Something like that. Based on the way he had dropped everything at the sight of the sleeping man and had not relaxed till seated beside him, they were clearly friends. Close friends, probably, and to see a friend in such a state....

"Water, then," said Korena, only half to the man. She went to a nearby table on which sat a pitcher, returning with a small cup and offering it to him. "Here. Drink. I expect you are dehydrated. I know I often am after sleeping."

Finally, the rendeilxue's eyes shifted toward her, though his face did not. His gaze darted down to the cup, his eyes narrowing. Oh, for the love of–did he think she was trying to poison him? Although, thinking of how they had started off just now, he didn't exactly have much reason to trust her. Sighing, Korena took a sip, holding the cup back out to him as she said, "See? Just water."

The man's eyes remained suspicious, but after a quick glance at the guard who still remained in the room, he accepted the cup, took a sip, and then downed the whole thing in one gulp, shoving it back as if trying to neither take his eyes off the armed guard nor touch her. Which was probably the case.

She pulled over a chair, making sure as his body tensed and eyes focused on her again to stay just out of arm's reach. A few feet away, the remaining guard tightly gripped the pommel of his sword. After motioning for the guard to stand down, she turned to the rendeilxue again and smiled in a friendly manner. Taking her best posture, hands folded on her lap and legs close together as if she wore a skirt rather than her trousered uniform, she said, "I apologize for earlier. I did not mean to startle you. I'm all for putting it behind us if you are. My name is Korena Iegam. And you are?"

She held out a hand, inviting him to speak. He did not. But he did turn to look at her in full, his large, focused eyes drifting over her, measuring her up, before finally returning again to her face and locking onto hers. Deep, blue eyes with a green tint that brought to mind the teal waters of the Ostran Sea under the summer sun. Eyes that revealed what the rest of his expression hid: a passionate soul, steady and enduring as the waves' beat against the land. Then those eyes blinked and looked away, trouble clouding their natural clarity like a cloud of sand from a dropped anchor. As they left her, Korena felt a peculiar tension leave her, though she heard and felt its echo beating in her ears.

For his part, Restag did not understand what was going on. Where were they? How had they gotten here? Who were these humans? Were they friend, or foe? And, most of all, who was this strange woman against whom his fae-gift faltered? He had tried, just now, to enter into her soul, hoping to read her intentions and glean answers to his questions, but he could not. It was as if the moment his power touched upon her mind, it crumbled away and fell asleep, only waking again when he pulled back. For a moment, he had worried his gift might truly be lost or somehow broken, but he had entered the soldier's soul easily enough, seeing there fear and indecision, as well as the foolish imaginings that ran through the man's thoughts like a herd of frightened deer of Restag displaying fae-gifts the warrior wasn't even sure existed. It seemed his magic was neither bent nor broken, only failing in the face of this woman.

"You know," said Korena, disturbing Restag's thoughts, "I am surprised you're able to move around so well. After so long on bedrest, I would think you would be having a harder time of it. Perhaps it is your fairy blood?"

What was this human saying? And why did she keep trying to speak with him. Was she simply cracked in the head? She was certainly dressed oddly enough. In that dark, sleeveless, high-necked jacket and matching trousers that cut off just below her knees, he might think she was a man were it not for her obvious, female attributes. She was nearly tall as a man, too, with arms, legs, and torso notably thicker than any other woman he had met. If her appearance could be so off-balance, perhaps her mind was, as well. It was the only judgment he could arrive at that made any sense.

Unaware of the insulting conclusion Restag had reached, the human woman prattled on, saying empty sounds in her boneless speech. Stones sliding down a cliffside held greater meaning to him than whatever words were clattering out of her mouth. Finally, he could stand no more. He held up a hand and was relieved to see that her intelligence at least permitted her to understand that gesture. In a flat, deliberate tone, he said, "I do not know your hoof-beat tongue, human. Reign it in, and leave me be."

Korena listened to the guttural language first with confusion and then with an understanding that made her blush. Not from understanding the words, but from her own mistake. She had heard that the other rendeilxue understood and spoke a bit of Ithaenian, so she had assumed.... Her cheeks burned as she realized the fool she had just made of herself while Restag turned away again to watch his master, satisfied with the return to silence.

It was, however, a short-lived silence, for mere minutes later, many voices and sounds came from beyond the door at the far end of the room. The door opened, and several guards filed in, spreading out to line the room with spears and swords. Restag jumped up, nearly knocking over the stool, and reflexively reached for his sword only to be reminded he wore nothing but a loose-fitting, sleeveless shirt and baggy trousers, not even a belt. In short bursts, he jumped from soul to soul, finding a similar unease as he had seen in the first guard, but without the fear. There did not, though, appear to be any intention to attack him or the sleeping Witheric, not without provocation. From her own chair, the woman rose, bowing with surprising beauty, like a stalk of wheat to the wind, as a man entered the room, the band of gold around his head telling Restag the man's identity and reason for the additional spear-men.

Just behind the king, almost stepping on the hem of his robes, followed a little man, back just a bit too curved as he puffed out his chest. The little man smiled to himself as they entered, that smile growing to be just a bit too long as his dark, little eyes found the woman bowing beside Restag. He almost waved at her, caught himself, and then pretended nothing had happened, though his bright red cheeks betrayed his thoughts and focus. Glancing sideways, Restag saw on the woman's face the most wooden expression he had ever witnessed. When the king finally spoke, however, her expression softened, though her body had become as a well-crafted pillar, her hands still held as if resting on her lap.

Korena bowed again, saying, "My king, welcome. Your guest awakens. I have sent for the doctor. I am surprised he is not with you."

Smiling apologetically, the king replied, "Yes, I met the man you sent and have rerouted him to my wife's chamber."

"The queen? Is she—and the baby?"

With a light chuckle, he replied, "Rather straight to the point, are you not, Miss Korena Iegam? No, no, do not blush. You have done no wrong. The queen is fine. It is only that her morning sickness has been especially wearisome, so she wished for something to help her. Nothing to worry about."

Korena couldn't help the small sigh of relief that escaped her. "I see. I am glad."

Suddenly, the little man stepped out from behind the king, smiling adoringly as he said, "Oh, Miss Korena, you truly are—" He gasped, his face paling. With a yelp, he dashed forward, stopping just short of touching Korena. His head came only just over her shoulder. With a look of horror, he said, "What are these scrapes on your lovely face, milady, and this unsightly splotch of red! Who has dared harm you!"

An idea struck the little man, and he whirled to face the rendeilxue, growling, "Was it you, Barbarian?"

The rendeilxue's eyes barely took notice of the little man, his expression remaining impassive in the face of the heated address, as if he hadn't even noticed it, before looking right back to the king. Korena forced back a smile as the man right in front of her turned bright red. She took a half-step back before saying, "I am perfectly fine, Sir Ortheus. In fact, I hadn't even realized the injuries were there, they hurt so little. And there is no need to assign blame. I fell earlier. It might have happened then."

"Might?" said Ortheus, narrowing his eyes. "As in, there 'might' have been another cause? And, pray tell, what 'might' that other cause be?"

Barely stopping herself as she began to roll her eyes, she said, "Sir Ortheus, I hardly think this is the time to–"

Raising his voice, Ortheus said, "Yes, yes, well, I think–"

A non-discrete cough cut the little man off, who then turned to look shame-faced at his king. The king stared down blandly at the little man, saying, "Sir Ortheus Meathorsis, I believe I brought you here to perform a task for me?"

Korena had never known a person could turn so deep a red. With a pitiful, squeaky cough, Ortheus straightened himself, took a clumsy military stance, and said, "Right, my king. O-of course."

While Ortheus could not see her, Korena smiled her thanks, which the king acknowledged with a discrete nod. Ortheus, meanwhile, attempted to put on an air of dignity and turned again to face the rendeilxue. Restag then had the distinct displeasure of hearing his own tongue gutted as Ortheus said in something resembling Asgradi, "Good friend-greeting to you, up-river sword-man. Be in awe. You stand here, in-room with Thane Aleukus, thane of Ithaenia. Be knowing of your lowness!"

For a moment, Restag could not even answer, his mind still trying to process what had just been said and wondering if the horrendous speech and accent he had just heard was an intended insult or just lack of ability. He quickly decided it best to place the question to the side for now and focus on the content, which, from the arrogant tone and clearly insulting final statement, was not much better. King Aleukus! The man bearing the crown was King Aleukus of Ithaenia? The straight-speaking man so trusted by Witheric? The man they had traveled Halsk's roads to reach? This man, who, by his kings-man's witness, spoke to a Thanesman of the High Thane as if he were a mere thrall? Restag clenched his teeth, grinding back the anger and humiliation just served to his master.

His blue eyes looked fiercely to the king, to his black, curly hair and beard, to his gold band around his brow, to the robes embroidered with gold and intricate designs and even studded with thumb-sized jewels, and then they paused on the man's warmly dark eyes that studied Restag with an intelligent, curious light. A light so very different from what he would have expected from the introduction he had just heard. Deciding to give Witheric's judgment the greater weight over this servant's impression, the thanesman worked to harness his anger. He dared not enter into this king's mind or those of his retainers now that he knew their status, not without Witheric's allowance or some suspicion of imminent threat. Such an act would be an outright rebuke of his thane's trustworthiness, of Witheric himself, and such a dishonoring act was not to be done in the presence of a foreign court. However, he remained wary and ready to react at the slightest warning.

Addressing the king directly, Restag gestured around them and said, "Thenika?"

The irritating mouse-like man began squeaking something, but the king silenced him. He reached into his robes, pulling out a little bag, and removed from it Witheric's signet ring. He held it out to Restag, saying something in a deep, hearth-fire voice. The mouse-man seemed hesitant to translate it, but with another look from his king, he said, "Thane Aleukus of Ithaenia friend-greets ab… Above-Thane Witheric and friend of Above-Thane to house to Thenika. He…," the little man whined something to the king, who responded firmly. A look of despondency came across the translator's face as he said, "He, Thane Aleukus, only wish to ahead of coming be told so to give good friend-greeting."

Restag again met the eyes of the smiling king. There was no guile in those eyes, no mockery, only an honesty Restag rarely saw in a man without his Sight. The eyes of a man whose word might just be straight as a well-made spear and binding as an iron chain. Squaring himself to them, he tried to bow only to have a dizzy spell nearly send him to the floor. He was saved by a strong hand catching him, one which also caused an eerie silence in himself that made him instinctively pull away, nearly losing his balance again.

Korena glared at Ortheus, who was smirking at the rendeilxue, and snapped, "Stop sniggering like a school child, and someone come help me!"

The smile vanished from the little man's face, and he shrank away while one of the king's guards handed his spear to his fellow and took the woman's place, saying, "What do you need, Miss?"

"Just hold him there," she said, pulling her own chair over and turning it so the rendeilxue could take hold of the chair's back as support. A strange, perhaps inquisitive look passed through the half-fae's eyes, though its exact meaning was lost on Korena, who could only smile reassuringly.

"Are you all right, sword-man?" asked Aleukus, Ortheus translating. "Is it perhaps your fever returning?"

Restag considered his answer. There was no point in trying to hide his physical weakness, so he said, "No. I have but been ill and asleep for a long time, I think. But it shall pass. My many thanks to you for your care of me." Then, before the translator had even finished that portion, Restag used the chair to stand straight-backed and then bow at the waist, saying, "Many thanks, as well, for your welcome, High Thane Aleukus of Ithaenia. My master, regrettably, still sleeps, but know that I, Restag-Thanesman of High Thane Witheric of the Eisenband, speak both our true-hearts when I say I am beyond the boundaries of words to thank you for your greetings to my master."

For some reason, Restag's response irritated the mangled-tongued little king's-man. Restag knew it had been simple and inelegant, but it was the best he could do. He did not have Witheric's gift for song-speech.

"Well? What did he say?" demanded Aleukus, making the translator flinch. Aleukus forced back a sigh. He had known bringing Ortheus would be a mistake, but he had been caught off guard by the rendeilxue's timing and had accepted the man's offer in order to save time. He made a note to see if his younger brother, who worked much more with the rendeilxue in and outside the city, if he had anyone he recommended. In the meantime, he said, "Come now, Sir Meathorsis, must I ask again?"

After coughing to buy himself a moment more, the translator squeaked, "He... um... they clearly speak a dialect with which I am not familiar. You see, I know the dialect of the more southern tribes and, by Your Majesty's own description, they are from quite far north, so it is clearly a situation quite beyond my own powers to prepare for and not at all my...." The king's stare silenced him, and he gave another false cough before saying, "Um... I think he's saying thank you and that his name is Restag, Sire, as you know. Restag-Somethingorother."

Nodding, the king said, "Good. King Witheric had mentioned his chief advisor by name in his letters. It is good to finally meet the man himself."

Noticing a derisive sneer come over Ortheus's features, Aleukus said, "Did you have something else to say, Meathorsis?"

"Oh, no, nothing much, Your Majesty," said the little man with a contemptuous glance toward the rendeilxue. "Only I think you ascribe far too much ability and intellect to this upper-thane, or whatever he calls himself, and his people. Chief advisor? They are barbarians, Your Majesty. I would be surprised to find them capable of recognizing the concept of advice, let alone having anyone capable of giving it."

Korena flushed with anger. She had interacted with more rendeilxue than most, including the Asgradi, and while she still knew very little of them and their culture, she knew "unintelligent" to be a grossly inaccurate assessment. As a man from a near-identical family situation as her own, Ortheus should know this, as well. Before she could respond, however, King Aleukus said with an edge to his tone, "I understand your thoughts, Ortheus Meathorsis, but I would not be so quick to make assumptions. Especially when this 'upper-thane' you presume to look down upon has demonstrated in his letters to me a capability of learning another's language at least on the same level as your own. If even a barbarian of questionable intellect and ability can teach himself understandable Ithaenian, I cannot help but wonder what that says about you."

Sounds from the hallway interrupted Ortheus's sputtering, and the door was opened to allow the palace's primary physician and alchemist, Paskhalon, into the room, a large medicine box in his hand and a look of disapproval fixing one-by-one on each guard standing around the room. His cool, gray eyes then found Restag, and he spared only a brief glance and bow to the king as he approached, saying, "I did not give approval for your retinue to barge in and disturb the sanctuary of my infirmary, Your Majesty."

King Aleukus's brow twitched, and Korena bit her lower lip. Though she knew it would end peacefully, as it always did, she had never liked being in the room with both the king and physician present. Paskhalon had a habit of skirting the edges of etiquette. She had never seen him push so far as to undermine Aleukus's status as king, but if rumors of his and the king's long history were to be believed, this was a learned skill.

Standing as tall as he could so that his superiority in height was evident to all, including the doctor, Aleukus said, "My men are always present when I welcome visiting nobility."

"Yes, I know," replied the doctor, placing his medicine box on the table by Restag's emptied bed. He eyed the rendeilxue, who watched him back with a suspicious eye. Paskhalon raised his brow at the man, crossed his arms, and said, "What? If you have something to say, say it. I don't have all day."

"Actually, he can't understand you, doctor, so you're wasting your day and your breath on him right now," said Ortheus with a malicious smirk.

Sparing the little man no more than a glance, Paskhalon said, "You brought this little sot with you?"

Ortheus flushed, and he squeaked, "I'm not a sot! I've hardly had a drink in my life!"

"Who said you were drunk on drink?" said the doctor.

"That is literally what being drunk means," said Ortheus. "'Drunk' as in the past tense of 'drink,' or in other uses referring to someone who had consumed copious amounts of alcohol to the point of impaired judgment. Furthermore–"

However, the doctor was already finished with the topic and turned back to the king, saying, "Well, then, if it pleases your majesty, would you mind clearing my work space so that I might do my job?"

A tense pause later, Aleukus said, "I'm leaving one guard in here and another two as sentries outside."

The doctor was already looking through his medicine box again and said, almost lazily, "If you must. Oh, but take the Dampener girl with you while I conduct the examination. I doubt her services will be needed, and indeed may put my patient on edge."

Korena nodded. "Yes, sir. I shall wait outside the door for when you are done or if you need me."

"Very good. That is, if your Majesty permits it."

"I do," said Aleukus. "I am also leaving Ortheus here to help you."

Both men looked with disbelief at the king, the translator with horror and the doctor with disgust. When Ortheus tried to protest, however, Aleukus motioned for silence and said, "For the moment, Ortheus is the only man on hand who speaks conversational Asgradi. I trust you won't skewer him with a scalpel, Paskhalon? And you, Ortheus, if I find you have said or done anything to deserve a scalping, including to our guest here, do not think it shall go unaddressed. Do you both understand? Good. Now, Miss Iegam, let us leave the men to their respective tasks."

Korena almost felt sorry for Ortheus as she heard him whimper, probably due to a glare from Paskhalon as they left the room, all but one of the guards following them out. Just before leaving, she did take one last look behind her to find those green-blue eyes staring at them intently, her heart skipping a beat from their intensity, before the door closed behind them. While Aleukus dismissed all but a few of his guards and chose the sentries, she tried to calm her rattled nerves.

"I apologize for the position I have placed you in, Miss Iegam," said Aleukus, interrupting her efforts. "If I'd had anyone else on hand who could translate...."

Korena smiled understandingly. House Iegam of Thenika had an unusual relationship with its royal house. As one of the original and more powerful of the families whose blood could dampen or even nullify fae magic, including a rendeilxue's, the Iegams had always been closely tied to the king and his guards. However, they were one of the founding lines of either Ithaenia or Thenika itself and so were not officially a noble house. As such, they were somewhat outsiders to both the ordinary man and the aristocracy, seen as either useful tools, a necessary evil, or almost friends, depending on who wore the crown. With some of the stories Korena had heard growing up, she was grateful to be serving Aleukus and quite willing to overlook many faults and mistakes from the man.

"You have done no wrong, my king, so no forgiveness is necessary. All fault is on Ortheus's head. I have already turned down his request for marriage more than once, but he seems to think that so long as he flatters me with looks and words and gifts that I will eventually say yes. It has gotten worse since Aristi left like he did and the future lordship was given to Ortheus, but it is nothing I'm not used to or incapable of withstanding," she said. She then frowned and continued, "I am actually more worried about him as the translator. Did you see how the rendeilxue looked after he announced you? I'm pretty sure Ortheus improvised at the end and said something foolish that he thought superior to your own words."

With an exasperated sigh, the king said, "Yes, I expect he did. Sometimes I cannot help but wonder if he's for or against me."

"Neither. He is simply for himself. Even Paskhalon is better than he. At least he has enough sense not to undermine the man he respects."

The king chuckled. "There are times, Korena Iegam, when it seems as if Aristi has not left. I am sorry nothing came of you two. It would have been interesting, to say the least."

Korena flushed, glancing at the guards who were pretending not to hear. Looking away, she said, "There was nothing that could come of it. What could happen when the other man sees you as a sister, and not as a woman? Besides, after he dropped his position in your court to pursue his own goals, any chance for a union disappeared. Father would never sanction marriage to someone he sees as perfectly willing and capable of abandoning his responsibilities to his king and disgracing his family, no matter how powerful his abilities."

"And yet," said Aleukus, with a knowing grin, "I cannot help but think your father's objections could hardly stop you, should you make up your mind otherwise about the issue."

Again feeling self-conscious about the guards nearby, she said, "Maybe. But I don't suppose we shall ever know."

"No. I suppose not. Well, that is enough gossip for one morning. After I check on my wife, I shall see if I can catch my brother to ask for recommended translators, see if I can find someone more tolerable and less likely to sour our international relations, intentionally or not," said Aleukus, receiving a smile both thankful and amused from the young woman.

By the time the night-shift came to replace her, Korena was ready to punch Ortheus herself. The king, as promised, had sent a replacement a few hours later. However, Ortheus had refused to leave, claiming he must remain for Korena's sake because he did not trust someone from the palace to protect her after they had let her get injured earlier. Thankfully, the rendeilxue Restag did not seem to be an especially talkative type, being quite content to sit beside his sleeping master in silence or to help Paskhalon feed and tend to the sick patient. That meant there were few chances for Ortheus to anger the man, which made her job as magic-nullifier easy, but that also meant Ortheus could ignore his own job and direct his attention to her. She would have preferred another fight with the rendeilxue to the torture of the small man's endless chatter about things she cared nothing about but which he seemed to assume all must find interesting or important simply because he did. Eventually, self-interest overrode good manners, and she tuned him out to turn her thoughts to the problem of bridging the gap with the rendeilxue until relief finally came with the end of her shift, and she slipped out with mutual nod of farewell with Paskhalon before Ortheus noticed her replacements' arrival, leaving the man to brief them alone.

As she sat at the dining table the next morning, drinking her after-breakfast tea before heading to the palace, she considered her options for the whole situation, but each led to a dead end. She was still lost in thought when another's voice entered the room, saying, "Your tea looks cold."

Looking up from the cool cup on its saucer, she saw her older brother, Karas, approaching her. He had the lopsided smile he always wore when trying not to show he was troubled. After turning down the seat one of their servants pulled out for him near the head of the table, he sat down beside her, and taking one of the bread slices and, with a mournful comment about the time of year and the way the Lesser Fast deprived his bread of butter, he slathered the bread's surface with enough preserves to make Korena feel sick looking at. Before taking a bite, he asked, "We finished work late last night. How is his Highness? I heard one of the king's… unusual guests woke up. It must have been frightful." He tapped his cheek in the place where Korena had seen the large bruise on her face in the mirror that had formed overnight.

Despite the churning in her stomach, Korena smiled. "Welcome back, Brother. Mother has already informed nearly everyone in all the other families multiple times about how Father so easily prevented the assassination. It has become almost unbearable. As for myself, the bruise is the worst of it. The rendeilxue who has awoken is very well-behaved."

"A well-behaved barbarian?" said Karas, amused. "I shall have to see this for myself at some point. Even so, I hear you returned in a black mood. If the barbarian half-man was not the issue…?"

"…Ortheus," she said, Karas's face scrunching up instantly. She went on, "His Grace did not have anyone else on hand when the rendeilxue woke up who spoke Asgradi."

A maid entered with a new cup, placed it before Karas, and poured him some tea, offering to refill Korena's cup. She declined, instead moving the honey bowl in her brother's direction before he asked, "Any chance of someone else being there to translate today?"

Korena sighed. "Yes, but of course Ortheus shall come up with some excuse to be there as well, as he did yesterday. Of course, if I told the king, he could intervene, but I don't wish to bother His Grace with such a petty issue, not with Prince Aganectus's recent report. I assume Father was sent a copy already?"

Drizzling honey into his tea, Karas said, "Yes. I am glad I don't qualify for the city guard branch of our blood's uses. The chaos just seems to worsen every year, especially in the barbarian camps outside the walls. They just can't behave themselves, especially when the ships are coming in for the winter. The damage to this year's cargo, the math is beginning to worry me. I wish the guard was better at calming conflict rather than just stomping all over everything and increasing the costs."

"Maybe you should be a guard. You might help with diplomacy, and you can dampen magic well enough," countered Korena.

Karas smiled sadly. "Not well enough for Father's standards. No. My prospects in the active side of the family business are not exactly good. Even Ortheus is stronger than I am. I shall simply marry a hopefully pretty and amiable girl from an acceptable family, inherit the family headship, and deal with all the stuffy politicians, merchants, and the like who seem incapable of cleaning up their own messes and just want to complain about how we didn't protect their lives and fortunes well enough and leave being a human shield against magic fireballs and the like to nullifiers like yourself." He set down his cup and leaned back in his chair, thoughtfully tapping his fingers against the armrests. After a few moments, he said, "Say, why don't you ask Nursie?"

"Ask her what?" said Korena.

"About being your translator," replied Karas. "Isn't her family from some northern tribe that fled this way to avoid destruction in the whole civil war thing they have going on up there?"

Korena's jaw nearly dropped. How could she have forgotten? Friathri, the family's nursemaid, was an Asgradi herself. Even if her dialect was different than Restag's, surely she would be able to help! Jumping up to hug her brother and nearly knocking over the chair, Korena cried, "Oh, thank you, Karas! Thank you! You always know how to fix my problems, don't you? I love you!"

The young man laughed nervously, saying, "Glad to know you do now, since I'm not so sure you will in a moment or two."

Pulling away, Korena again saw the troubled look in Karas's eyes. "What is it?"

After reaching for his cup again to delay answering, Karas replied, "Father wants to see you. It might not be bad, of course. You're his favorite, being the strongest in the family and all, but still. He wants to see you before you leave today."

Korena felt her stomach twist into knots. She should have expected it, since much had occurred since he and her brother had departed for a job two months back. They had returned a week ago and had since been swamped with writing reports, filing paperwork, managing receipts, and whatever else happened on that side of the business, and she had hoped her father would be too tired to demand to see her for at least another day or two.

She took one large drink to finish off her cup and pushed her chair in, saying, "Might as well get it over with, then."

"Hey, Rena," said Karas, making her pause. Mimicking the action, he said, "Smile. You're prettier when you do."

Giving her brother a small grin, she turned, thinking that if she could smile with their father she would.

Outside her father's study, she straightened out any wrinkles, real or imagined, from her uniform and checked that the padded silk was properly buttoned and her gun belt and revolver were neatly positioned so as to be both functional and aesthetically arranged. An Iegam must be the example in all things with regards to his uniform. She tweaked a few things here and there, took a deep breath, and knocked. A deep voice from beyond the polished door beckoned her in.

Kairon Iegam sat at his desk with an air and posture worthy of royalty. His study was immaculate, the books flush against the edge of the shelf and organized to a level of detail surpassed only by the city's libraries. His entire form, from his, dark, slicked back hair to the soles of his polished boots, spoke control and measure and order, and many among his peers knew of how he had refused to adopt the spreading trend toward fountain-ink pens because of the rhythm in the writing process that was lost without an ink well, the rhythm Korena now heard and saw as her father moved his pen across a sheet of paper. Korena softly closed the door behind her, stepping lightly till she stood in silent parade rest before the large, oak desk while the man before her continued writing. It did not matter that she needed to leave soon to be on time for her shift. Kairon Iegam did not wait on any but the king and noble heads; you waited on him. Likely because of the nature of her job, however, she only had to wait for him to finish his current page before he wiped clean his pen and placed it gently on its resting spot. As he did, the man's voice rumbled out, "I heard His Majesty received some unusual guests while I was gone."

He looked to Korena, giving her permission to speak. She nodded. "Yes, Father. Two rendeilxue, both terribly ill upon arrival, one identified by a signet ring on his person as a Thane Witheric of the Asgradi. The second has since awoken and confirmed his suspected identity as the thane's chief retainer and counselor, Restag."

"And the king personally asked you to be one of their regular guards?"

Korena nodded again, waiting for her father's signal to continue. "We do not know their abilities, nor were we certain of their identities until Restag awoke, so His Majesty requested the two strongest Dampeners among his guard to take shifts chaperoning them, both as a precautionary measure against magic use and as reassurance to the ordinary guards. Due to the superior strength of our family's blood, I have been assigned the day hours."

As she knew it would, that last statement brought a proud glint to her father's eyes. Crossing his fingers on the desk, the man before her said, "Very good. It would seem you are proving beneficial to the king and a proper representative of your family name, Korena. Yes, very good. And I assume I do not have to remind you of the importance of not bringing shame to that family name?"

"No, Father," she said, perhaps a little sharply, resulting in a twitch in her father's brow. Pulling back her emotions, she said, "You have been vigilant in your reminders, including the day you departed for your most recent assignment. Two months is too short a time for me to forget such a consistent lesson."

Kairon's dark eyes narrowed, his own voice dangerously flat as he said, "And yet, it seems a lesson never enough said, especially when accounting for the amount of time you spent with Karas's former friend."

Karas and Aristi were still friends, she said to herself. They still sent each other letters and met together outside the family grounds when they were both available, even inside from time to time, though Kairon pretended that they didn't. Korena felt sure that the only reason this was tolerated was the fact that House Meathorsis had never officially disowned their first son, so to outright forbid him from the house would be an insult to the other family, one of the few as old and respected as House Iegam and therefore both its chief ally and rival, depending on the circumstance. Even so, her father still had not forgiven the young master Aristi, who had practically held a position of adopted son to the household and who many had assumed would later become the family's son-in-law. And who, a few years ago, had suddenly abandoned his position as a rapidly advancing palace guard, with the potential of entering the king's personal retinue before the age of thirty, saying he was bored and wanted to pursue a more challenging lifestyle. The decision had utterly baffled and rocked the small circle of anti-magic families like Korena's, known as the Blood Houses, embarrassing his entire house and, by close association, hers. The fact that her brother had maintained his friendship with the wayward Aristi had caused quite some tension between father and son for the first year, which then turned into a coldness between them that she feared would never be repaired.

Because she knew her brother would bear the brunt of her father's ire should she push against him on the matter of Aristi, rather than condemn of a man she still cared for, she simply stared ahead and responded indifferently, "I shall endeavor to do my work and serve the king to the best of my ability."

She knew her father had caught the evasive nature of her response. However, he said nothing more on the subject. He dismissed her with a wave of his hand, and it was a struggle to hide her desire to be gone as soon as possible in her step. The moment she closed the door, she walked a ways down to hall and leaned against the wall to take a few breaths and calm her anger. It was a frequent occurrence after speaking with her father. Soon after, she was jogging down to the servants' quarters, more than ready to leave the walls of that house.

When Korena opened the door to the palace infirmary, the first thing she noticed was the palpable hostility in the air. It was enough to make even Friathri, born to a warrior family and the tumult of constant war, flinch as she followed her mistress into the room. The second was the dangerous scowl on Restag's face and the form of Ortheus sitting in the back corner, as far away from the rendeilxue as possible. Skirting the edge of the room, Korena approached Paskhalon, who sat at that room's work desk taking notes, and whispered, "What happened?"

The doctor gave the rendeilxue woman behind Korena a look that might have been curiosity, though his tone did not show it, as he said, "The idiot said something that angered the rendeilxue. He then shouted something back, and the child's been sulking in the corner, muttering to himself ever since. Don't ask me what. I don't know, and I don't care to, so don't bother telling me."

"Thank you, doctor," said Korena. Paskhalon nodded in response and then went right back to his work. Meanwhile, Korena continued down the room, heading for the little man in the corner. As she approached, she picked out petty curses and muttered insults, before gently greeting him.

Ortheus had been so lost in his thoughts he jumped from the greeting. "Oh, Korena, my angel! You're here. I-I'm so, that is, I'm glad you've arrived. Did that doctor already tell you about why I'm over here? Of course he did. He never knows when to stay out of someone else's business and keep his mouth shut. But anyway, can you believe it? And I was just trying to help. You know, make the barbarian feel welcome. I just knew he must be bored sitting there all morning, doing nothing, so I thought I'd start his education on the greatness of Thenika, and you know what he did? He got mad at me! Yelled at me! Just for trying to help! He should be feeling grateful, but no. He decided to be an ignorant, bumpkin jerk, instead. Ha! Fine, then. I won't help him anymore. He can go fall off the walls. See if I care!"

Inwardly, Korena thanked the irritated rendeilxue. She had been unsure how to best convince the proud and pettily vindictive Ortheus to give up his role as translator, and here was the answer. "Then I suppose you had better go find someone who will appreciate your help."

Ortheus blinked in apparent incomprehension. This had not been the sympathetic, comforting response he had expected. "B-b-but, Miss Korena, milady, who will translate for you, then?" he asked.

Motioning to Friathri, who curtsied, Korena responded, "Oh, that won't be an issue. As you can see, I brought a family servant who is, herself, a rendeilxue and native speaker of their language. I am sure she can manage the job, and, really, it's much more proper for me, a woman, to be accompanied by another woman rather than surrounded by men. Don't you agree?"

The little man's mouth dropped, but when he had no answer forthcoming, Korena took his arm in hers and began leading him to the door, saying, "Since my maid can act as my translator, that frees you up to find work somewhere else. Somewhere that doesn't involve a rendeilxue warrior who is clearly a bad sort to anger and who is, also, clearly angry at you."

"B-but… but…."

Korena opened the door, guided the man out, and said to the guards, "Could one of you find something productive for Ortheus to do? Preferably something where he shall receive the appreciation proper to his efforts. Thank you!"

The dazed man was still trying to form a response as one of the guards led him down the hallway and Korena closed the door. When she turned back around, she saw Paskhalon looking at her, one eyebrow raised. "Impressive," he said, "if unnecessarily tactful."

Korena let out a small laugh only to swallow it as she noticed Restag's eyes focused on her. She felt her cheeks color. He had bathed sometime between her departure the day before and now and changed into a clean shirt, one that hid the scars covering his arms, except the burn marks on his left hand that she knew reached up to his elbow. He looked better than the day before, if still disheveled, what with his long, unruly hair, like a pile of freshly gathered wheat waiting to be sheafed. Chiding herself for such thoughts and blushing like she was only just past girlhood, she approached the occupied bed and its attendant. The bedside had been cleared of unnecessary furniture, so she brought a chair over again, Friathri following suit with a stool. Both sat down near the bed, staying out of arm's reach of the rendeilxue warrior.

Restag had watched the exchange between the woman and Ortheus with great interest, revising his opinion of her intelligence and sanity as the scene played out. He had suspected his conclusion to be erroneous the day before, but as she had barely spoken the rest of her time there, and never to him, he had had no way to confirm those suspicions until that moment. She had also surprised him by the other woman who accompanied her. This second woman was clearly Asgradi, though she wore a sleeveless linen dress and wool shawl that did not match her heritage. Her exact age could not be known on sight, as the Asgradi's fairy blood kept their features largely unchanged from around their thirty-fifth year until they neared their hundredth. However, he could guess her to be well-past childbearing. She carried herself with the air of an elder, and there were subtle signs around her eyes, hands, and hips that spoke of many years lived and worked. To his eyes, she appeared almost grandmotherly as she said, "Does your thane bear this day well, Restag Thanesman?"

The Asgradi woman's accent was unfamiliar to Restag, and a bit difficult to understand, indicating that her dialect probably originated in one of the tribes farther west or south than he was used to dealing, but anything was better than the barrage of incompetence he had endured over the last day. Speaking with deliberate annunciation, he replied, "He sleeps still. An uneasy sleep it is, as well. However, he does not appear to approach Halsk's gates."

The Asgradi woman nodded and spoke to the human, who smiled pleasantly in response, an expression that made her almost pretty, if still on the plump side. The human then spoke, following which the Asgradi said, "My mistress says she is glad to hear of your thane's improvement and offers her peace-sorrows for what ill-speech was pressed upon you by the little man."

"Mistress!" cried Restag, the human woman showing surprise at his outburst.

The Asgradi, on the other hand, had apparently expected his reaction and calmly said, "Yes. My name, good thanesman, is Friathri Soothe-Speech, and I have served House Iegam of the Blood-Houses since my maidenhood, when my family came here from the north to escape Halsk's Gates."

"Blood-Houses? That is an ill name," said Restag, eyeing the human woman with a mix of curiosity and unease, which the human mirrored.

Friathri bowed slightly. "Such is Dar-Speech, even among the humans. To their kind, as well, it is seen as both weal and woe, for those who live within these houses hold trickles of the blood of the Gift-Sleepers, or as some call them, the Gift-Slayers."

"What!" snapped Restag, nearly falling back as he recoiled and slapping away the human's hand when she tried to help him. For that brief moment of contact, he felt it, the vanishing of his magic, a sensation he now understood. The Gift-Sleepers were a legend among the Asgradi, an ill name used to frighten children. It was said that they were immune to magic, that it could neither harm nor influence them, and that at their touch one's gift was either weakened or slain until such contact was broken. The stories said the family blood had long been drained, the line destroyed centuries before, during the rule of the Eisensaet. And yet, rumors persisted that traces remained, occasionally revealing itself, as it did now in the worst way possible. Clenching his fists, Restag spat, "How can an Asgradi serve such a master? A human who taints the Asgradi blood! And what blood! How can one pledge to serve such a master? The Valaki do not serve the Midrad, let alone the Halskrad!"

Korena watched as a green tint came to Friathri's face. Between the sudden shouting and her own maid's reaction, she began to be afraid. Trying to keep her voice level, she said, "Friathri, what happened? What did he say?"

The indecision in the older woman's blue eyes was clear. She said, "It is probably best you do not know. It would only make you angry."

After a moment's thought, Korena said, "No. I think I should. If there's something I said or did that made him angry, I should know it."

With an angry sigh, the Asgradi woman said, "Very well."

She paused to put together the right phrasing and replied, "In essence, he that said for me, an Asgradi, to serve a human of your particular household, it is as if the demigoddess Valaki, wolf-riding shield-maidens in the Asgradi pantheon, were to serve the denizens of Hell."

Korena paled and then flushed a deep, furious red. Holding her back straight and still as a sword blade, she said, "Well, then tell him that I'm not an ill-tempered, uncouth barbarian who twice needed that denizen even to stand not two days ago!"

Friathri stared wide-eyed at her mistress and, for a moment, looked as if she might refuse. In the end, however, she gave in to the young woman's fierce gaze, repeating the essence of her response. Restag's own face flushed a deep, olive-green. His voice held a deadly edge to it as he began to respond, his voice rising as he went, heating Korena's blood, though she did not know the meaning of the words being thrown at her. A retort formed in her throat, and it was crawling its way to her mouth when, suddenly, a loud bang sounded behind them, startling everyone. All turned and flinched at the venomous glare from Paskhalon, his face pale and body quivering.

The man's voice seethed as he said, "This is an infirmary, a sanctuary for the sick and injured, and if you can't shut up and honor that, then get out!"

As if to emphasize the point, Witheric groaned in his sleep. Restag looked guiltily at his master. Korena, too, blushed, wilting. She looked at the man across from her, at the scowl he wore, one even worse than Ortheus had given him, and she wanted to cry from the blow to her pride and the resultant shame. A touch on her leg brought her attention back to Friathri, who said gently, "Let me speak to him. I shall see if I can calm him."

Swallowing the lump in her throat, Korena said, "Okay. And could you… could you tell him I apologize… for using his health as a weapon. And for calling him an uncouth barbarian. It was wrong. Please tell him I am sorry for it. Only… please don't use your gift to soothe him. I don't… I mean.…"

The older woman smiled softly and patted the younger's cheek. Keeping one hand over her mistress's as a sign of her acceptance of the young woman's request, she repeated her mistress's words. Restag briefly glanced at her, and Korena felt the contempt that glance contained.

Restag's voice was a low growl as he said to Friathri, "You ask a high task, Soothe-Speech. The spears she has flung cannot be called back, and their damage not so easily tended."

"She understands as much, thanesman. She is no child. However, may I call to mind who threw the first dart? And at one toward whom you owe no little boon," said Friathri, posture straight, her tone no longer that of a servant but of an elder.

Restag stiffened. "How mean you?"

The older woman kept her tone, the elder's assumption of attention, as she said, "It in part through her vigilance that you and your thane still draw breath. When few others dared, she remained beside you, helping the plague-banisher in his craft. You owe her at least half a life's debt, for both you and your master."

Friathri could not have chosen a better direction from which to break through Restag's wall, and she knew it. Horror, both at what he owed and to whom he owed it, drained his otherwise firm face. At last, he returned his gaze to the human. Her eyes met his, warm eyes wet with barely controlled emotion and a face too much like his own people's brimming with honesty. Witheric's defense of humankind and praise for their apparent virtues came to him.

But she was not human! She was something even lower than that, some creature that had emerged from Halsk and the distant echoes of half-forgotten legends to haunt the living. He knew her to be something contemptible, something worthy of his hatred. And yet, somehow, looking into that face with his master's words within his mind, he could not do it. Against his better judgment, he could not see her as anything more than a human girl, and while he could dislike her, he could not hate her. The realization bothered him. Perhaps the High Elder and the Council had spoken some truth in their resistance to Witheric's interest in humans, if the result should be an inability to hate that which deserves nothing else.

Friathri's voice came again, commanding his attention. "Also," said the woman, "I remind you, she is my mistress. Do not think that though I have lived long among the humans or that because her blood is the lowest of her kind's that my loyalty is less than our people's laws demand. Though it may not be so strong as it would be to my own people, she and her family still hold my oath-bond, and I will not accept further insult to her and leave it unavenged."

Restag nodded in understanding, the thought of what he had and would have done in the face of lesser insults to his master, especially if by one who owed him a life-debt, revealing what sort of meaning lay behind the woman's word-veil. Hesitantly, his mind still trying to grasp the full nature of all these things rolling out before him, revealing a path he did not know how to walk and feeling forms of weakness he had not faced for a long time, he said, "Tell your mistress I, too, am regretful for my own strikes. They were... disgraceful of me." A thought struck him that made his skin nearly dark as tree bark. "And that... she said nothing false. Her words were Dar's own."

Friathri caught her breath at the label, one of the highest in their language, her eyes suddenly searching for any sign of mockery. Instead, she saw the pain of honesty. Once the woman was satisfied that his words were genuine, she spoke to her mistress. The change in the young woman was incredible. She immediately locked gazes with him, eyes wide. They still held tears, which at last escaped to streak reddened cheeks. Her lips moved from a slight gape to a smile that softened every feature and seemed to summon light to her eyes. It was a face disturbingly Asgradian in its beauty, and he was relieved when it vanished a moment later as she wiped away the tears.

She cleared her throat and began speaking again, Friathri translating, "My mistress says that, if you are willing, she wishes to bury past grief and rebuild your relationship upon a new foundation."

An uncanny feeling came over Restag at the similarity of these words to ones he had said in response to Witheric on a day that now seemed so long ago, words of encouragement and hope. Trying to push away the thought and what such a meeting of words might mean, he nodded. The human grinned and began to reach out her hand only to suddenly pull it back, digging into a pocket to pull out a glove. She pulled it on and held out her hand again, Friathri saying, "She says her name is Korena of House Iegam and that she sees good to come of this meeting."

Restag stared at the outstretched hand quizzically, finally reaching out to mirror the gesture. To his surprise, she suddenly grabbed his hand in her gloved one and managed to shake it up and down a few times before he jerked it free, nearly pulling her from her seat as he did. Rather than being upset, however, she laughed. And to the sound of her lovely laugh and Paskhalon's chiding, he wondered what he had just done.

Chapter 7

Over a week passed in relative peace. Witheric's fever spiked again, but Paskhalon soon had it back down, and the "little lord" slept without the dreams that had previously sent him writhing. The doctor had been unable to identify the disease, believing it to be a strain of sickness that was either largely confined to the north or, perhaps, might be a sickness particular to the Fae and so not found among the human patients and studies with which he was familiar. In either case, he found himself experimenting with medicinal mixtures in addition to the tried and true remedies that had kept the illness in check so far. When he questioned Restag, the thanesman could only shake his head, saying they usually relied on those gifted with healing power or wise in the ways of herbs. He, himself, knew very little.

Korena couldn't help pity the thanesman as she sat before her mirror, Friathri brushing her hair in preparation to braid it tightly against her head. Though he often remained calm in appearance, she so often noticed the uncertainty and fear hiding just behind his eyes. Fear that was being fed by him spending all day in the infirmary, reinforcing a sense of helplessness. He had even refused to move into a guest room a few halls down, though Aleukus kept it prepared should the rendeilxue change his mind. It made her sigh in frustration just thinking about it.

Behind her, Friathri grinned and said, "That is the fifth time this morning, Miss. Something troubles you?"

"The thanesman," said Korena. She could not bring herself to speak his given name, a gesture too intimate for their acquaintance, but according to Friathri, to call him "sir" or "mr" would imply him to be his own master, something his Asgradi sensibilities would find insulting, so she had settled for his title, the closest he had given to a surname. She continued, "He's going to ruin himself, sitting in the sick bay, staring at his master all day."

Nodding, Friathri said, "He is an excellent thanesman. The Asgradi tribes, as you know, have many differences, but among what we share is loyalty as our chief virtue, loyalty to the thane superseding all. The thanesman embodies that virtue to the people, swearing an oath of fealty to his thane above all other ties till one of them should die or his oath-bond be released."

Korena frowned. She wasn't so sure she liked that. Yes, she could see much to admire in the idea and probably much that was good, but based on what she had seen so far, she questioned the overall fruit it produced. Outwardly, however, all she said was, "I still think it's unhealthy for him to stay in that one room all day, barely getting sunlight or moving around. How is he going to regain his strength?"

"Hold your head still, Miss, or your braid shall be crooked," said Frithri. "I did not contradict your opinion. I think you are likely right, but what can be done? He is determined to do all he can for his master."

An idea came to Korena, one she liked the more she thought of it. Looking up to her maid, she said, "Friathri, I think I'd like something besides a braid today, and a change of clothes. Oh, and can you call for Casselus? We're changing today's plans."

Restag brushed aside the curtain at the back of the infirmary, revealing a large glass pane, beyond which sat a series of walking paths that he assumed were much more beautiful in earlier times of the year than they were now, with only a few ever-green bushes and trees here and there showing that life existed beyond the glass. He had been told that there was a hall close to the infirmary that led outside and that the window was often opened to let in air and light during the warmer times of the year. However, touching or even standing near the glass at that moment revealed the world outside to be too cold for the sick. Nothing like up north, but still cold, so for the time being, the window stayed closed and behind the thick curtain for the sake of preserving heat. Restag let the curtain fall into place behind him, shutting out the world in the closest thing to solitude he dared pursue. Most days, he waited till either later in the day, using the moment to stretch his cramped legs, or in the early morning right after waking, watching the sun rise over what he assumed to be neighboring buildings while one or both of his guards dozed. Today, in fact, was the second time he had found himself drawn to that makeshift space.

The human named Korena was late. Paskhalon had already dismissed the night guards. Though he savored the silence and solitude that had so far followed, he had already begun adjusting to the routine change of guards and the two women's presence throughout the day, so the unexpected and unexplained change disturbed him. And so he had sought the window space, where he now leaned against the glass, letting the familiar cold seep into his body, sorting through his concerns.

Witheric had slept peacefully that night, in no small part thanks to the potion-mixer Paskhalon. The Asgradi woman, Friathri, had explained the irritable man's craft was not potions as Restag knew them, the blending of herbs and items and magic, both spoken and runic, but rather what humans called "alchemy"–the purification and mixing and preparing of plants, metals, and other materials to more fully utilize their natural influences and powers. To Restag, however, it still appeared as magic, and he marveled at the results it produced. By now, he also knew it was all that stood between Witheric and Halsk's Gates, alongside the exiled thane's will to live. An iron will Restag knew quite well and which he prayed to Dar would hold without snapping.

He was still swirling within these troubled thoughts when the infirmary door slammed open, Paskhalon responding sharply. Curious, he began to moved back the curtain only to have it suddenly pulled aside, revealing a human woman that, after a moment of confusion, he was shocked to recognize as Korena. But not the one he knew.

One of the things he had learned in the past week was that, contrary to his initial impressions, Korena was physically healthy by female human standards. Before waking up in Thenika, he had only seen human men, and that rarely. He had never made the connection that, just as a healthy human man would be generally thicker than his own people, so it was with their women, and he had begun to recognize from the reactions of his other guards that Korena was admired for her appearance. With her armored vest and loose leggings, however, he had held a somewhat masculine image of her, one that did not match with the creature who now stood before him.

The young woman he now saw wore a long, pleated dress of white cotton, gathered at the waist by a braided belt. Around her neckline and over her shoulders lay more of the dress's fabric, layered over itself to form a wide cowl collar. What looked like a decorative wool shawl was draped over one arm. Her hair, rather than being braided such that its texture could be barely seen and its length was unknown, had been gathered behind her head, held in place by gold-laced ribbon, the loose ends of that hair dropping in tight ringlets past her shoulders. She had also made up her face, some kind of paste or powder hiding the lingering signs of bruising, and her eyes and lips lined with color, both of which brought out the warm brown of her eyes. All together, if he had seen her from a distance, he would have denied she was the same person. But up close, such a thing was not possible, despite the extent of the transformation.

Then she smiled, the red curve of her lips adding to the dancing light in her eyes. She said something he could not understand, wrapped her arms in the shawl, and grabbed his arm, pulling him from the window, through the room, and out the door before he had the chance to think.

As they passed him, Korena said to Paskhalon, "I'm borrowing your patient."

To which the physician waved her away like a pest, saying to her departing back, "If you must" before returning to his work.

Once outside, Korena handed the stunned thanesman to a couple of guards, who continued leading him down the hallway. Finally recovering, the rendeilxue began resisting, shouting something Friathri translated as a request to know what was going on, though Korena expected he had said it in a much more colorful way than Friathri's translation.

Korena replied, "I'm taking you out to see the town."

The pronouncement did not sit well with the thanesman who, despite at least three weeks of muscle atrophy, managed to break free of one escort's grip and stop the other's progress to snap his refusal to the young woman. Calling for the guards to stop and crossing her arms, Korena met the thanesman's gaze, raised an eyebrow, and said, "Consider this, Thanesman. What would your master like better right after waking up from weeks of sleep and sickness: to hear you talk about sitting around all day, doing practically nothing, or an eyewitness account of the place you two risked your lives to reach?"

To her amusement, the rendeilxue glared at her. He knew what she was doing, she realized, knew that she was using his own loyalty against him. However, in the end, he grudgingly shook off the second guard and willingly continued the way they were going, growling out a question about her plans. Korena increased her pace to walk beside him, the guards and Friathri a half-step behind them, and said, "First, we must get you cleaned up. It has been days since you've washed properly, and we also can't have you going about dressed like that." She motioned to the simple tunic, trousers, and boots that had been returned to him, the only set that had survived washing. "You'll draw enough attention just by being a rendeilxue. Dressing like one in these streets is just asking for trouble."

After Friathri translated her words, Korena was pleasantly surprised to see Restag nod without complaint. She expected the older, Asgradi woman had supplemented her words with some reasoning or phrasing more compatible with the man. When they came to the door to Restag's guest room, Korena dismissed the guards and opened the door to a small sitting room, across which approached an older man dressed in garments somewhat similar to her own, though without the accents and quality that indicated her position. The man bowed at the waist and then let his eyes wander over to Restag, saying, "Is this the young man we must prepare? Hm... I'm not too sure anything we have prepared will quite fit his physique, but I shall see what I can do."

"Thank you, Casselus. I'm sure whatever you have will do just fine." said Korena to her family's head servant, letting Friathri lead the thanesman inside, the rendeilxue man suddenly alert, eyes darting around the room in a mix of surprised interest and wariness. She continued, "Just... be careful with him. He has a bit of a temper, and he's stronger than he looks."

"I have worked with many rendeilxue over the years, Miss, most of them Asgradi like himself. I know how to handle them," said Casselus with a reassuring smile. The man motioned to a side door, saying, "Come then, good Thanesman. My men have already drawn a bath and prepared your clothes."

Restag glanced over his shoulder at Korena as he was pulled toward the door leading to the bedroom and, through that, to the private bath, though the exact meaning of the look escaped her. Before she had a chance to study it, the trio disappeared into the next room. With nothing to do now but wait, Korena made herself comfortable on one of the room's sofas, humming to herself and fiddling with her dress to pass the time. It felt like forever since she had worn a simple dress like this. She had even worn her uniform to the divine liturgy a few days ago, a private affair arranged by King Aleukus for her and Paskhalon's convenience. Sure, it hadn't actually been that long, only about a month, as her now daily guard duties had only begun with the arrival of the thane and his man. However, it was still a relief to actually dress up again. To actually feel pretty again, rather than relying on her biased older brother's words.

She knew how much her palace uniform meant to her father, just as she knew that, despite her lack of combat talent, it had been assumed that she would follow the family trade and be at least a for-hire body guard due to the strength of her power. All the hours of hand-to-hand training, the shouted corrections and discouraging string of failures and losses, all the frustration vented on targets at the shooting range and on her morning and evening runs, all the years wearing dresses to official functions one moment and padded vests made of bullet-resistant silk the next, all to bring her here, to a position she had filled when a close friend abandoned his post. A position she had never even wanted.

Better here, though, than at home.

Korena clenched her skirt as the thought flew unbidden through her mind. She brushed it away as she brushed out the self-made wrinkle. Having too much time sitting by herself was proving quite bad for her spirits, so she rose and began walking laps around the room, the movement helping to calm her agitated thoughts. Around her fifth or sixth lap, she suddenly heard shouting from beyond the wall separating the sitting room from the bed and wash rooms. Giving into her curiosity, she moved toward the door, placing an ear against the wood. As suspected, it was Restag's voice, followed a moment later by Friathri's, the woman's in that firm, no-nonsense tone that had been one of Korena's childhood fears. Soon after, she heard footsteps, and she hurried back to the sofa, sitting just in time for the older woman to emerge from the room, carrying Restag's clothes.

"Is everything all right? I heard shouting," Korena asked.

Friathri huffed, saying, "Yes, it is fine. Only the boy is being stubborn about having that unruly hair of his trimmed. Not even given a real cut, just a trim. Says he doesn't want to have blades anywhere near his face. Hmph. Good thing he hasn't grown his beard yet. Imagine the fuss that would have brought about."

Now that Korena thought of it, she hadn't even seen a whisker on either the thane or thanesman, despite weeks of lying in bed sick and over a week since Restag's waking without sight or sign of a razor. So many of the men around her, outside her more traditional family, were shaving their faces clean, so she hadn't thought anything of it. But now, she realized it was odd. She asked, "How old would you guess he is then, since he hasn't grown any facial hair yet?"

"Oh, surely under thirty, for sure," said Friathri. "That is when a rendeilxue man's beard usually begins coming in. As for the other direction, he could be as young as fifteen."

Fifteen! thought Korena. Had she been arguing so much with someone six years her junior!

Friathri continued, "I would guess, though, just based on his position, that he's in his mid-twenties. To give anyone younger than twenty years the title of Thanesman would be a farce rather than an honor, and he wears his status with too much pride for me to think that likely."

Korena relaxed. So a peer, or perhaps a little older. At least she hadn't made quite so big a fool of herself, then. Wishing to move away from that train of thought, she said, "Is it unusual for someone so young to be named thanesman?"

"Oh, yes," said Friathri without hesitation. "Most men never receive such an honor, for there is only one for each thane, and even those who do rarely before their thirty-fifth year. To be thanesman is to have the thane's complete trust and enough prowess on the battlefield to hold the other men's respect, if not admiration. After all, it is the role of the thanesman to serve, guide, and protect the thane, to be his spear and shield and the example to follow. He is the tribe's champion. The local hero, in a sense."

So why, wondered Korena, had the thane and thanesman been driven from their tribe? Hadn't Friathri said earlier that day that Restag was an excellent example of a thanesman? How had such a man, who must have been highly respected, and the master who was supposedly the spoke to which the tribe's loyalty was connected, sent into exile? When Restag had first revealed their banishment to Friathri, the woman had gasped in disbelief. Of course, it had to be true, as the pair was here, not with their tribe, and the situation was far too shameful to be admitted if it were false. However, Restag refused to say much more, only indicating that they had been betrayed and had fled south after an attempt on Witheric's life to hopefully find help in the human king the young thane had been corresponding with for around the past year or so.

Unaware of her mistress's troubled thoughts, Friathri went on, "I'm not too surprised, though, to be honest. Even after all that time wasting away in bed, he is strong enough already to walk on his own, so he must have been strong beforehand. He recovers quickly, as well. A good quality for a shield-man. For all those flashes of temper we've seen, he appears to be a quick learner and very reasonable young man. And, based on his blood-mark alone, very powerful."

Korena nodded. During her time helping Paskhalon tend to the rendeilxue, she had seen the iconic markings on both men's backs: the visible veins of green so dark as to be almost black spreading out like tree roots or branches from the men's spines up and down their backs, in Restag's case reaching to the base of his neck and halfway over his shoulders. The "blood-marks" that revealed the thickness of fairy blood within a rendeilxue and, therefore, the power of his gift and which shifted to a shimmering gold as he activated the magic coursing through that same blood. Even without that witness, though, she would have known by way of her own power. She had been told a rendeilxue's blood had a certain presence or "life" to it, one that the owner might not notice for its familiarity, a presence that was stronger the more powerful the blood. Therefore, when that presence suddenly disappeared, it was often a shock to the owner of that blood the first time its absence was felt. The stronger the blood, the greater the shock. Restag still flinched anytime her skin happened to brush against his.

"What did you say to calm him down?" Korena asked.

Friathri eyed the young woman suspiciously, Korena realizing that she had just revealed her eavesdropping. However, the older woman simply said, "I reminded him that he is a guest of King Aleukus and that he must present himself in a way that will not disturb Ithaenian sensibilities. As any thanesman worth his shield, he is quite conscientious of the respective duties required by proper hospitality, such as the duty of a good guest being to give as little trouble or disrespect to his host as is morally possible, and how his public conduct reflects on his master. He quieted down quite quickly after that."

Their conversation was then interrupted by a cough from the direction of the door. Casselus stood in the threshold. With a quick bow, he said, "The young man is ready for your inspection, Miss Iegam."

When Korena followed the manservant next door, she had to admit to herself that she had not expected the rendeilxue to clean up quite so well. He still looked thin, of course, but the loose, sleeveless chiton, which was, admittedly, just a little short, filled him out a bit as it fell on him and gathered around the belt, the scars on his exposed arms giving a fierceness to the bulkier appearance. The winter version of the garment, which on most men would land mid-shin, came to just below the knees on the rendeilxue's tall form. Most notable, though, was his face, his long, flaxen hair trimmed and tied back to fully reveal his narrow, youthful features, slightly elfin ears, and those blue-green, summer-sea eyes that momentarily stopped Korena's breath as they caught her own before another cough broke their hold.

"I take it he meets you approval?" asked Casselus.

Keeping her expression a controlled smile, Korena said, "Yes. Good work, as always, Casselus. I now won't have to worry how I will look having him accompany me. But tell me, did you not bring him anything to keep warm? He might freeze the moment we step outside."

Bowing, Casselus said, "I have a chlamys folded on the chair for him there. I thought you should be the one to bestow it, Miss, all things considered."

Korena nodded and approached the indicated chair. She took up the pin sitting atop the folded garment–gold stamped with her family's crest of wheat bound by an olive branch and carried in a shield, prosperity held together by the peace her family helped to ensure through victory in arms–and lifted the heavy wool chlamys, pleased by the simple, elegant design of the weave and Casselus's consideration of color and how his mistress would look in her own covering followed by the rendeilxue. Yes, the man knew how to present her House well, whatever the occasion.

Clearing her throat, she held up the pin, saying, "This is my family's crest, and I grant you the right to wear it. With it, though you should be an Asgradi alone in the middle of Thenika, none shall dare harm or bother you, knowing your connection with my House."

Restag watched her as she carried the chlamys to him and held it out to him. For some reason, she hesitated and blushed. There was no special meaning to the gesture beyond what she had said, and yet between Casselus's insistence that she perform this part and the way the thanesman was looking at her with curiosity and suspicion, why did it feel like there was? And why did this rendeilxue have such a strong gaze?

Behind her, she knew Casselus was flushed with pride. As long as she had been alive, he had taken more pride in her family's name and privileges than she did. She waited for Friathri to finish translating before reaching up to fasten the cloak with the pin. Before she could, however, Restag grabbed her wrist. It was a strong grip, though not the rough restraint from their initial meeting, and there was nothing preventing direct contact between them. Wide-eyed, she looked up at Restag's firm jaw and eyes.

He spoke in a measured voice, Friathri translating, "I will use my own."

"What?" Casselus snapped behind her. "Wha– how–You uncultured barbarian! Do you know whose favor you are rejecting? The honor? Why, you should be kneeling in humble gratitude at being given permission to bear such an emblem upon your breast!"

Despite the servant's outburst, Restag's gaze never left Korena's. It was to her he had spoken, her word alone to which he was heeding, as he said, "It is a token, a gift, from my master. I need no other."

Casselus's ranting continued, but Korena heard none of it. She only heard the words Friathri had made understandable to her, echoing in her mind in the rendeilxue's solid, steady voice. Not moving her eyes, she said, "Casselus." The servant's sputtering ceased, and she said, "Send someone to fetch his things. I believe Paskhalon has them stored somewhere."

"B-but, Miss!" cried Casselus, "the insult! He has spurned your generosity, and your family—"

Finally turning to face the servant, Korena hardened her voice, taking a tone that denied further argument, as she said, "It would be an even greater insult from me to deny him the token of his thane, as if I were claiming, even if only in appearance, the oath for myself that has been given to another. Now, if you will not send someone to retrieve his belongings, I shall do so myself."

Despondency overcame the manservant's face, but with a voice utterly drained of the will to fight, he ordered one of the servant boys to run off and ask after the rendeilxue's effects.

A bit to the side, Friathri smiled triumphantly at her mistress, the only one among House Iegam who understood the worth of what had just transpired. She, alone, saw the surprise flash across Restag's eyes as she quietly translated Korena's words and the subtle shift that played out within his gaze as Korena requested he release her so she could fetch her own shawl, his eyes for the first time containing something like respect.

Soon after, Korena was hiding a smile as Restag's eyes ran across the painted columns, vaulting ceiling, and tiled floor and walls of the main halls of the king's palace. Until then, he had remained in the area around the infirmary, which was part of the Old Palace surrounding the original and smallest of the palace's courtyards. Those walls were thicker, plainer, built for a fortress to withstand sieges and only slightly changed beyond routine renovation since their construction over a thousand years before. In contrast, the section of the New Palace through which they now walked had been added at the height of Ithaenian opulence a few centuries ago and used every inch to show it. He seemed especially impressed by the enormous double front doors—ones so thick and heavy they needed gears and cranks to open—commenting how not even a giant could break through them in one blow. Korena wished she had thought to ask the king to authorize the opening of the doors themselves, promising the rendeilxue a demonstration in the future.

Restag's amazement continued as they passed through the small door built into the larger ones for daily use out into the walled walkway that, in other times of the year, held a hanging garden that made the air smell sweet as it led to a round containing a large, multi-tiered fountain that had already been stopped for the winter. The walls of the round opened on four sides, the gardens continuing toward the main palace gates that could be seen ahead. To either side, narrower arches led to the barracks hidden by the walls and to the grounds that surrounded the palace proper. Taking one of these side arches, Korena brought Restag out into an enormous space occupied by sleeping orchards and walking paths, including one leading to the fifty-foot high palace walls. Restag gasped, his eyes tracing the walls' length and height and turning to see just how high the palace domes rested. If not for the clouds formed from their breath, Korena would have wondered if the man was breathing. He turned to her, motioning as Friathri translated, "The stories of King Aleukus's wealth have been but grains of a mountain! My thane's realm could fit two, no, three times over within his Mead Hall alone. The wall of his domain stretches beyond the reach of sight. He must, indeed, have enough shield-men to storm a dragon's lair!"

This time, Korena could not hold in the grin, her eyes dancing with excitement. She said, "I thank you, Thanesman, for your gracious praise and shall ensure my king hears of them. Only, you are mistaken on one account."

Restag frowned, and Korena beckoned him onward, toward the wall. She considered asking to take the lift, for the sake of the recovering man's strength, but her dramatic side won out, and she started up the spiral stairs in one of the wall's towers instead, moving fast enough that he did not get much chance to look through the periodic arrow slits, nearly pulling him the last few steps out onto the battlements. It had been a tiring climb for him, so he almost didn't mind the short silencing of his blood at the very end, the presence returning when Korena released him as they stepped back out into the sunlight, her eyes gazing outside the wall, his own following.

His breath stopped.

Stretched out before him were buildings upon buildings upon buildings, all crammed together for what looked to be miles. Here and there, chimneys tall as pine trees billowed out white smoke in between rows and layers of roofs and buildings of various sizes and shapes, like a riverbed covered in multicolored stones and, in the case of domes, the occasional shell. Beyond the wall on which he stood were four more lines of stone of similar height but greater and greater length, the final one looking like it ended the land itself as deep, blue water spread out to the right and left, running along a coast of cliffs and beaches out to the horizon. It was as if the world had transformed into stone and metal, mortar and water. But how could there be enough people to fill such a world? It was as if all the lives that had led to his were suddenly laid out before him in one place And if the men of such a place, such a country, were to take up their spears against another, how could any stand against it, magic or no? And what kind of thane could keep such a place alive? Such a thane must hold the deepest secrets of the gods within his hands.

Korena watched with immense satisfaction as the terror rose into the rendeilxue's eyes only to quickly morph in wonder. Based on stories she had heard from her family's rendeilxue servants, she could imagine what kinds of thoughts currently crossed his mind. She drew his attention, startling him out of his trance, to welcome him to Thenika, the greatest port city in the known world and political and religious capital of Ithaenia, and began pointing to different districts and buildings, naming them and giving a brief description of their purpose or character. He listened with rapt attention, only interrupting her once to marvel as she pointed to her own home not far beyond the palace walls, noting the woman's family grounds alone might contain his entire home town within its stuccoed walls. Korena observed Restag's focus, noticing his eyes drifting away back down to the city. Smiling proudly, she said, "Do you want to go down?"

The light gleaming in the man's eyes did not need words.

Chapter 8

They took a carriage from the palace through Central Thenika, where lived the ancient and esteemed nobles and families, beyond two more layers of walls, and out into the city's third "circle," known by most as the Market Ring. During the trip, Restag's eyes remained fixed on the world passing by. At several points, such as when they passed the Akegia Basilica, seat of the patriarch of Ithaenia and the eternal jewel of Ithaenian architecture, Korena expounded on already mentioned details, promising to visit in the future. On their first trip outside the palace walls, however, she wanted the rendeilxue to get a glimpse of Thenika beyond the nobility and had suggested they search for something to bring back for Witheric.

The Market Ring formed a transition area between the nobility and the common folk. Those with wealth but neither blood nor title lived there, and any merchant who could buy or rent a storefront, or even just a street booth, did so. While each of Thenika's seven districts within the bounds of the Outer Walls—save for the first district, where sat the houses of High Nobles, the Basilica, the King's Palace, and any other building of government or ancient origin—had its own smaller and even specialized markets, for a taste of everything one of the civilized world's premier port cities and international markets had to offer, the markets that took up the third district were the place to go.

They stepped out of the carriage into one of the Circle's many plazas to more people than Restag had ever seen in a single place except the battlefield. It was loud, voices shouting over each other and mixing with the conversations of passersby and the clack of horses' hooves on the cobbled streets. Just standing there, watching the faces change constantly, was exhausting. Upon most of the buildings, which were built of stone and plaster and tiles and paint of various colors and many of which possessed carved columns or eaves that made the city look almost like a living thing, hung sprigs or boughs of pine or cypress or other evergreens, apparently in preparation for what the humans called "The Twelve Days of Light," days of feasting following over a month of strict abstinence from various common foods. According to Friathri, it was the second largest religious holiday of the Ithaenian people, celebrating the coming of the "Divine Light God" into the darkness of the world along with the new year, a celebration second only to the fifty-day Pascha Feast that happened around spring after forty days of fasting. During those coming feast days, candles and oil lamps would sit upon the lintel of every house, the ornate, metal street lamps he saw all around him would be further adorned and strung with decorations, and there would be singing and dancing and many communal feasts throughout the city. Trying to imagine any addition to the overwhelming stimulus Restag saw before him suffocated him who had lived all his life in halls and homes of the warm brown of carved wood and the occasional shine of gilding accented by the vibrant, masterful weaves of the Asgradi's loom. To stand now in this alien world of wealth and layers upon layers of extravagance and the people passing and pressing him from all directions even as he simply stood there suddenly made him long for home as he had not since the first few days after leaving.

He tried to push the longing away, to accept that he had finished mourning, but try as he might, he could not but feel that the enormous world that now surrounded him, a city that he knew dwarfed giants and whose buildings soared like a mountain range above him, suddenly felt small and cramped, while the tiny village he had left behind held within its wooden walls and the surrounding land space for all the world. Even the loose garments covering him felt strange and constricting in their unfamiliar drape and texture. And he knew, as he always had but had never fully understood, that he was lost in a place that was not his and that he did not know.

Then he felt the familiar texture of wool press against his arm, and Korena led him away, taking him out of the thick crowd to a small street between buildings where few traveled. A short way in, she stopped and turned, asking, "Are you all right?"

Korena kept her hold on Restag's arm, her shawl and his own chlamys protecting him from her touch. After leaving the carriage, she had looked away only a moment, searching for the street she knew they must take to reach her planned destination, but when she looked back, her heart had jumped at the transformation in the rendeilxue's posture and expression. Though people kept bumping into him, it was as if he had not seen or felt them, his face completely closed off from the world. Even his expressive, ocean blue eyes had disappeared, replaced by a gaze as cold and dead and unfeeling as sapphires.

Thankfully, the eyes into which she now gazed were much more themselves, though still dimmed, drained of their usual energy. The rendeilxue man closed his eyes and took and released a deep breath, saying, "Yes. I fell through the Reinor's ice. But I am out again, if not yet warm."

"It's an idiom," explained Friathri. "It means he was caught off guard and overwhelmed but will be okay with time."

An ominous idiom, thought Korena as she nodded silently. "I apologize, Thanesman," she said at last. "Saint Paedia's is one of the Circle's major plazas. It's always busy during the day. Though it would have taken us longer, I should have asked to be dropped off somewhere quieter, but I didn't think…. Our destination does not see nearly the traffic of Saint Paedia's. Hopefully it will be better. Come."

She then looped her arm through his, still covered by her shawl, only for him to suddenly jerk his arm away, a distinctly uncomfortable look in his body language and on his face. "Is there something wrong?" Korena asked.

Rather than translate Korena's question, Friathri answered, "No, Miss. Not exactly. Asgradi are simply not so… physical as Ithaenians. We do not have a habit of touching or holding onto each other unless for practical purposes or necessity."

Creases formed between Korena's eyes. "But we have touched multiple times already, and he hasn't pulled back like that except in reaction to my ability. And you…."

An amused grin tugged at Friathri's lips. She asked, "I was your nursemaid, child. And how many of those touches with him were ordinary circumstances or without conflict?"

Korena thought back, and the closest she could think of was when she had pulled him out of the infirmary and the times she had grabbed onto him to help him walk or stand that first day, neither of which, come to think of it, could really be called "ordinary" or "without conflict" when examined in context. She blushed, and Friathri said something to Restag, probably an apology and explanation for her mistress, for the thanesman frowned but nodded. Friathri indicated for Korena to continue, so the young woman led the group through a few alleyways until, around ten minutes later, they emerged out into a small plaza lined with booths and shops, in the middle of which sat a little, dry fountain. There were quite a few people as well, but not nearly so many as before, most hurrying along, bundled in their cloaks and chlamyses and other layers, trying to ignore the calls of street vendors. On the far side of the plaza was a small church, its bell tolling the fifth hour after sunrise.

Motioning for the rendeilxue to wait, Korena ran over to one of the vendors and purchased some skewered shrimp and bread sweetened with honey, handing her companions a bit of each. She then went to sit on the side of the fountain, Restag following suit as she explained, "People like to use these streets as a shortcut to get to bigger market squares, so of course vendors decided to start putting up booths and other stores to take advantage of the foot traffic. Right now, they only have their seasonal market set up, and the streets are small and narrow, so you can't bring cabs or carriages through, which means it stays pretty quiet, too. It's almost a shame, since I have found some delightful shops around here, and Loushian there makes the best shrimp and crab. Oh, and squid."

Restag seemed intrigued by the last dish mentioned. Korena hurried back and purchased him a sample and then promptly laughed as his face contorted. "Is this your first time trying squid? The texture is different, isn't it?"

He nodded, swallowing but refusing more. As she finished the delicacy herself, she watched him taking in the scene, his gaze trailing slowly across the plaza, as if to commit every chip and crack to memory. "So," she asked, "have you any idea what you want to bring back? What does your thane like?"

Restag's focus turned inward, searching for the right words. He knew what he meant, but, Dar's ravens, he could not bring to mind the names Witheric had used. Finally, he said, "Maps. And scraps of strange leaf covered in curved runes, sewn together, and covered in leather."

It took Korena a moment to picture what he meant, after which she said, "Do you mean books? Books and maps? Then I know just the place!"

A few alleys over, Korena opened the door to a dim shop lit by only a few high windows. There were no candles or oil lamps besides the one on the counter where the shop keeper sat, the man doing a double take as two rendeilxue entered behind a young noble woman. Korena pointed to her pin, and the shopkeeper looked away, feigning loss of interest. As Dampeners, those at least resistant if not immune to magic, the Iegams were one of the few families that felt comfortable employing the magically-gift half-fae as servants or bodyguards, so while a single woman being accompanied by two rendeilxue was certainly an unusual sight to the average man, it was often written off as yet another example of her family's eccentricities rather than a cause for alarm.

Restag missed the exchange, his attention focused on the shelves of books lining the floor and running down the room, somehow fitting in a smaller space more books and paper than Witheric's study ever had. Restag could hardly believe such a place existed! How could they afford all these pages and ink, and who had the time to fill them? To which Korena smiled and said they were printed using a machine where someone could hand over a hand-written document, arrange letter-shaped metal in a tray, and then press or roll the paper over the metal wet with ink to make several copies of the exact same page. Some even contained pictures, the rare colored ones made from a similar process only with engraved plates rolled over multiple times, a different color applied each time. And they were all almost exact copies. The same books made again and again and again in so little time!

Once they returned to the palace, Korena promised to take Restag to the king's book-room, which, she claimed, contained over a thousand different books, not just copies of the same ones as it was here. Restag decided this human woman had moved on to tricking him for her own amusement, much like with the squid, and promptly dismissed her, walking down and between the shelves, eyes scanning the lines of unfamiliar letters. Here and there, he pulled off a book only to replace it after flipping through a few pages, his amazement turning to indecision. There were so many, and he couldn't bring them all back. He knew Witheric had read some of the Ithaenian histories and wise men, but not which ones, and beyond those, he didn't even know what kinds of books his friend liked. He had simply seen them cluttering the tables and floor, covered in script he couldn't read, their only value to him the identity of their owner. Would just anything do? As far as he knew, Witheric had not been particular about his collection, just buying whatever the human merchants happened to have, but with the ability to actually choose, Restag wanted to give his friend and master something he would enjoy, especially after so long a time spent sick and the pain they had endured to get here.

He was so consumed by these troublesome thoughts that he did not notice Korena approach him, a large tome in hand, such that when she spoke, he started, his instincts taking over. Sound vanished. He swung around, bringing his arm around in a back-handed strike, ready to follow up with his other hand only to stop as his first strike hit the book from her hands and sent it to the floor with a loud thud.

"Miss!" cried Friathri, glaring venomously at Restag as she pulled the young woman away. "Are you all right?"

"Yes, I'm–," began Korena before the store owner appeared at the end of the shelves, looking concerned and asking if anything was wrong.

He saw his book on the floor, a sour look coming over his face as he snapped, "What are you doing with my books? That one was hard to come by!"

Putting on a false smile, Korena said, "Yes, sir. I apologize. I tripped and dropped your book. I shall reimburse any damage, if necessary."

The shopkeeper looked doubtful, and Korena knew Friathri had noticed her shoulder where she'd hit the shelf jumping back from Restag's strike. Bending down, she reached out, in part for Friathri's benefit, and picked up the sizable book on the floor, saying to the shopkeeper, "Do you have any other items such as this, sir?"

Hesitant, he replied, "I have a couple more. You want to see them?"

"Yes, if you don't mind," said Korena.

Knowing when his customer's business stopped being his own, the shopkeeper nodded and went off into his shelves.

From his place behind the language barrier, Restag could not understand the exact phrasing of the exchange, but he understood the gist. With an apologetic nod to Friathri, he said, "I request pardon for my reaction."

Rubbing her shoulder, Korena said, "I apologize, as well. I should have made you aware of my presence. I must say, your strength is impressive for someone who looks barely fed."

"He is rendeilxue, Miss," replied Friathri with a hard look to the thanesman. "We may look delicate, but our bones and bodies and abilities are beyond that of a mere human's." In Asgradi, she then concluded, "It would be well for this guest of a human king to remember the fragility of his hosts in comparison to himself and the possible implications of harming foreign nobility."

Korena frowned as whatever her maid said caused Restag's posture to stiffen, glowering at the older woman. She wondered and feared what thoughts currently swam behind the warrior's eyes, but before either side could say more, she stepped between the two, saying, "In any case, I am quite fine, Friathri. It was my own fault as well, since I surprised him. Again, I am sorry Thanesman. I was excited to show you this book and did not give you proper notice."

She waited for Friathri to finish translating and for a touch of curiosity to push its way through the anger in Restag's face, his brows and jaw still tight but eyes attentive, before she opened the book. A moment later, Restag held out a hand for the tome and began flipping through the pages.

With a chuckle, she came beside him so she could see the book's contents. Maps. Pages and pages and pages of printed maps, with little boxes in each corner describing the topography or history of each image or noting the differences between the map on one page as compared to its updated edition on the next.

"Isn't it lovely?" she said, turning a few pages herself. "With the recent improvements to ships and carriages and the Holy Empire's campaign to repair and improve the ancient trade roads, more and more people are interested in pilgrimages and traveling to exotic locations. Atlases and travel books have been gaining popularity, along with anything about maps and their history and development. I knew there would be something in here and thought I'd take a look. When I saw that one, I knew I had to show you. Look. This one is my favorite!"

She stopped on a page covered in old script labeling a map of what looked like a large lake surrounding a peninsula, the land crowded with monsters and giants and other like terrors, the water home to sea dragons that, if to scale, could swallow a small island whole. "It's a copy, of course, of an ancient map of Ithaenia, back before there were as many towns and cities and the Fae had a stronger presence in the land. And this," she said, pointing to a mark on the peninsula's eastern coast, "is Thenika. Where we are."

Restag's intense focus on the pages, going right back to the beginning as he reached the end and taking more time with each page, gave Korena immense satisfaction. Knowing the answer but unable to hold in the question, she asked, "Do you think your master would like it?"

At last, Restag's eyes left the pages, their depths shimmering like the sea reflecting the sun. With breathless wonder, he said, "It is a thane's-gift!"

Korena only needed to see the surprise on Friathri's face to know he had given an unusually high compliment. Nodding to the book in the thanesman's hands, she said, "Good. Then we shall buy it. Are there others that caught your eye? Or anything for yourself?"

Almost without thinking, Restag scoffed and replied, "What use are scribbles to one who cannot read them?"

The human woman seemed taken aback by the answer. After a moment, she said, "I suppose that's true. Well, then would you like me to teach you?"

He stared wide-eyed at the young woman and then turned back to the book, tracing his fingers over the curving script running across mountains and forests and floating upon water. Over the past week or so, he had been so focused on Witheric's ongoing illness, few other things had come into consideration. That simple question, asked in innocence, had revealed to him yet another trial he had not wished to take on just yet but had, in fact, already pressed itself upon him: he did not know how long they would be here. He could neither speak nor read the language and had to rely on translators who, he had already witnessed, came in various levels of reliability and skill. Up until that moment, he had dismissed his master's years of self-study and secret practice in the red-blood's language. Now, if he was to be of use to that same master, he could not afford to throw any such help into the fire. Wordlessly, he nodded.

The effect on the human woman was minimal, but just that slight upturn of her lips, that merest crinkle at the corner of her eyes, that smallest softening of her already graceful posture, just that feather-weight dip in her head and the resultant ripple in her shawl gave her, for a hair-thin moment, an airy, eerily Asgradi-like beauty. That is, until he snapped the book closed, breaking that momentary spell and causing both human and Asgradi woman to start. He held out the book to the human, saying in a level tone, "My many thanks to you. You have my word-bond that I shall repay the boon you have given in obtaining this treasure."

The human named Korena appeared a bit confused at first until Friathri followed up with something else. The human smiled slightly before saying, "Consider this a gift, Thanesman, from our ring giver to yours. Please reserve your thanks for the master, rather than the servant."

This time, Restag watched in some confusion as Korena approached the counter to pay.

A few minutes later, they walked the streets again. There were more people than earlier, mostly clustering around the food vendors as the hour wore on. Korena led the way, confidently moving through the twisting streets that had Restag lost after only a few turns. He questioned how any could live in a land of snake-roads and carved stone where nothing grew or stood to speak of the hidden ways and right paths. To which Korena answered first with agreement, much to his surprise, and then began to show him how she way-found in such a place, the marks on buildings and occasional way-runes carved into the stone. She pointed to plates of iron nailed onto buildings, revealing the place-name, and explained how few actually traveled the roads as they did now, instead remaining within a small area of the city, following their mother's or father's steps till those steps became their own, and of other such matters. He was not sure how, but from there, they moved into his own life, his own ways of path-finding and the life he lived between the forest and fields and river. He spoke of harsh lands where every step beyond the walls contained the possibility to trip into Faerie or encounter a hero-trial.

"Is your scar from such a trial?" asked Korena, eyeing the dark and twisted skin upon his arm.

He grimaced, flushing a dark olive-green and saying, "No. This is... this is no such thing. As we journeyed here, my master and I crossed paths with a wudwyrm–"

"What? Really!" cried Korena after Friathri, her face a mask of disbelief, translated. "A tree wyvern? How did you– I've read stories of those monsters. How did you survive?"

The thanesman's hesitation and shame-filled blush only increased. He stopped in the road, hands clenched as he said, "We lived because we ran. Rather, I ran and brought my thane with me. It is... this mark is no sign of strength or courage but of my cowardice."

To his shock, Korena scoffed. She said, "I highly doubt you got a scar that bad on your arm because you were too afraid to fight a lesser dragon. Besides, from what I have heard, wyverns easily take a whole team of gunmen to kill. If the way you came to us is any indication, staying to fight it would have been suicide, which I would contend goes against your duty to protect your thane, correct? No, thanesman. Retreat was not cowardice. It was prudence."

It took Friathri some time to translate the concept of that named virtue. In the end, she settled for the unsatisfactory term "Dar's-choosing," in reference to the Asgradi king deity's patronage of wisdom and hidden knowledge. Restag disagreed with the analysis, and they continued to debate the point as they rounded the corner and one of the street vendors hailed the thanesman.

Korena likely would have simply waved and walked on, as she had with all the others trying to catch their attention, except that the vendor, a burly man with a full beard and mustache and dressed in articles from various regions that he somehow managed to coordinate, followed up his greeting with, "Oh, whatsyername–Restag! Restag, wasn't it? Survived, did you?"

"Excuse me, sir, do you know this man?" Korena asked.

The street vendor's eyes grew as they found the pin securing her shawl, and he gave her a deep, flourishing bow, the kind she had seen only from the more flamboyant foreign visitors to the king's court. The man's dark eyes gleamed as he said, "Apologies, child of the Blood Houses. Didn't think you were with him. Yes, I know the man. I brought him here, after all, him and a little man you'd think was no more than bones. Thallas is the name, Miss. I'm a shipper and merchant by trade. I was just on my way back down the northern river when these two appeared out of the snow like ghosts. Ha! Might as well have been ones, too, with how near death's door they were."

Korena nodded and curtsied. "Yes. I read the report. I am sure my king has already expressed his gratitude, but on behalf of King Aleukus, I thank you for rescuing his acquaintances and for all the care you gave them. I assume you were reimbursed the expense?"

"More than that, Miss, not that His Majesty needed to. I'm grateful, of course, but you know how it is. Wouldn't feel right to just leave the half-human bast–I mean, gentlemen–pardon the slip, Miss–to die in the snow like that. Just wouldn't be right," he said with a shy smile.

Friathri translated the conversation as it went, and when Thallas finished, Restag stepped up, bowing himself and saying, "I have been enlightened that you saved my thane and myself. Many thanks to you, ship-master. I owe you a life-debt twice over."

The man's shy smile was matched with a blush, and he said, "Nah. Nothin' for it, fae-man. As I said, twas only right. Although, if you want to pay me back, I wouldn't mind you lookin' through my stock here. Got back late this year, and with all the local grifters setting up shop, it's hard for a sailor to get a good spot to sell even a trinket. And I've got the real stuff, too, none of those imitations. All from far away places, anywhere you can reach from the waters of the Ostran Sea. I'm sure you can find something of interest for yourself, or maybe for your pretty lady-friend."

He winked, making Korena flush terribly. Thankfully, though, it seemed Friathri did not translate that last part. The Asgradi did, however, decide to take a look, eyes trailing over several odds and ends and items so bizarre he could not think of a kenning to describe them. Then, near one end of the table, he noticed a small, wood carving of a bird sitting on a branch. It was a delicate thing, crafted with skill and little details that spoke of the artist's intimate observations of its subject. It seemed almost a living thing, despite its warm, brown tone and dark, swirling wood grain. He lifted it, wondering why anyone would make a carving with no apparent use besides its beauty. Yet, at the same time, he felt his eyes drawn to the little bird, thinking how Witheric, who had piled up his study with seemingly useless scraps of paper, some of them just because of their beautiful pictures, would probably not mind having such a purposeless thing taking up space.

"What do you have there?" asked Korena.

"Olive wood," answered Thallas, nodding in approval. "Good eye for mastery you got there. Picked it up farther down south a couple years ago, but no one seems appreciative of simple skill anymore. All anyone wants is the fantastic and the strange, whatever will catch an odd look and give them a chance to yammer on to their friends and guests some bogus story made up by the merchant. But that, my friend, is a real piece of art, one of the last made by a homeless man who had been sitting outside an old monastery for decades, carving away at the branches the monks gave him. An odd sort of fellow, probably not all there in the head, but equaled by none with the whittling knife. Heard the last time I stopped by there that they had buried him in their own graveyard only a couple months after I picked it up, God rest his soul…. That reminds me, how's your friend doing, the waif-ish one. He all healed up, too?"

After a short pause, the little bird was gently placed back on the table, Restag's tone closed off as he said, "He's still ill. Even now, he has not truly woken up."

Thallas looked genuinely troubled. Leaning over his table, and smiling sympathetically, he said, "Sorry to hear that, friend. Truly sorry. I wouldn't worry too much, though. If his dragging you two out of that hellish blackness proves anything, he's a fighter. He'll pull through."

Restag quietly agreed, but he did not open up again. Beside him, Korena asked him something, her rhythmic words filled with concern. He shook his head, not wanting in that moment to understand. The human woman then said something to Friathri before bowing to the man named Thallas, who returned the bow and then gave one to Restag. The Asgradi had barely finished a curt nod before Korena guided him away. He had no idea where they were going. In a way, he didn't much care. He only knew that it felt good to walk, to push through crowds and move down one alley after another, to do something rather than speak of that which he could do nothing to fix. To speak again of the danger facing his thane against which any action on his part would be useless.

Compared to confronting treacherous relatives, murderers, water sprites, and wudwyrms, that was much worse. It had been the worst part of the witch's house, those minutes trapped behind that door, unable to do anything for his master on the other side, and it was the worst thing now, being awake and growing stronger every day while seeing his friend struggle in that place between wake and sleep, life and death, that plain through which only the gods could walk with will and purpose, and to be completely and utterly useless to him. Anything, even being dragged along by some mutt of human and Asgradi, whose very touch disturbed him, was a boon to such a bane.

She hurried him through several more twists and turns before, as if by some magic of Faerie, they emerged from the maze of stone to an open space, over which hung a cloudless sky as blue as forget-me-nots. Tree and bush-lined walking paths, much like at the palace, stood before him, and in this place grass was allowed to grow, brown and bristley on that winter afternoon. Here and there, a patch of green poked through the brown where some evergreen resisted its peers. It was as if he had stepped out of a grave and back into a world of life.

Korena spoke, pointing to a stone bench. He didn't know what she said, but he nodded, following her and sitting down, taking in the contrast of green, blue, and brown and feeling as if he were finally permitted to breathe again.

During the time waiting for Friathri, they sat in silence. It was an odd thing, in a way. Since the beginning, they had never been alone, and never in silence. There had usually been the chance of a stray comment or some conversation mediated by a translator. Now, there was none. Only the fact of another person's presence and the air around them. Strangely, he found Korena's air relaxing.

Friathri caught up with them a few minutes later, carrying Korena's shoulder bag. Restag let the two of them speak for a bit, his thoughts content to focus on the trees and the city's buzz that somehow sounded far away despite it, in truth, being just a few turns away.

"Do you like it?" came Friathri's voice following Korena's. The human smiled softly and gestured to the trees and bushes. She said, "There are small parks and gardens like this throughout the city. It's nothing like the real country, but it's often quiet this time of year. Very few want to be out walking in the cold.

Though, I suppose for you, it's hardly cold at all."

Her smile took on a playful tilt, but he simply replied, "No. It's not." and went back to watching the slight sway of cypress needles in a subtle breeze.

"Restag."

The name sounded strange with the Ithaenian accent, and when he turned again, Korena's cheek held a slight flush. She followed up with, "Are you ill?"

He did not know how to answer that. The answer should simply be "no," but the outer fact did not seem to match the inner feeling. After a long pause, she looked away, her dark eyes focusing on something beyond the trees around them, something beyond their vision, and she said, "Tell me about yourself, Restag Thanesman. Tell me about where you live and what you do. You said before that your home is dangerous, but that must not be all. What is it like? Is it beautiful?"

"Yes," came the word, like a sigh. Restag's own gaze turned away, traveling even farther than hers, far north—he wasn't sure how far—to a land always familiar yet strange. He had tried not to use his power. He knew it would be painful, perhaps make him regret his decision, to see it all again as if he were there. But he felt the brief burst of heat shoot through the veins in his back, spreading out through his body like a furnace, driving away any hints of cold, as he Saw. Eisensaet was quiet, draped in thick snow, smoke like little clouds puffing into the sky, wood slick with ice from where the sun had melted the piled up snow only for the water dripping down the posts to freeze before reaching the white-coated ground. It was a world encased in crystal, a glass kingdom seated upon stones like little mountains, overlooking hidden hills, shining hills, hills of light and steel-blue shadow. The bare, ice-covered trees broke apart the white like cracks, both black and shining, while glimpses of a silver-vein snuck through gaps in their branches. Near the horizon sat Dar's face, his few hours nearly spent in that dark time of year, when Dir's power grew and the howl of Halsk's hounds echoed across the sleeping earth, their soundless paws making no prints as they rushed across the land, seeking the prey for which their master called.

He pulled back a mere moment later, too quickly for either woman to notice anything had changed. With another sigh, he said, "Yes. It is beautiful."

And so Restag Thanesman began to speak of what he had seen, of the trees and rocks and hills and river, of the women at the loom and the men at the anvil and mothers and shield-men, of winter and spring and summer and autumn, to speak of all as memory. For that was all it was now. He knew he must not speak of it as if it still was. For to do so would be to summon regret, and he must not regret. For his master's sake, he must not.

Korena listened as if enchanted, smiling at small things and nodding at simple ones, but never speaking until, a while later, he drifted back into silence. With a breath filled with longing, she said, "Yes. It does sound beautiful. I would very much like to see it someday, this land you call home." She chuckled. "You have a fascinating way of describing things. I must admit, I never would have thought to call a river a 'fish-road,' a boat a 'water-plough,' or an oven a 'bread womb.'"

Restag nodded. "From Witheric I have learned how boneless is your speech and how hard it is to see."

"'Boneless'?" repeated Korena after Friathri finished translating and trying to figure out if her own language had just been insulted.

The older woman grinned and said, "He means abstract, rather than concrete. It is a common element, or rather what we would call a 'kinship,' among our dialects to use what's called a 'kenning,' bringing words together so as to describe the purpose or nature of the thing, rather than always naming the thing itself."

"That sounds… terribly complicated and imprecise," said Korena.

"It is poetry, song-speech," replied the older woman.

Eyeing the patiently waiting Restag, Korena said, "So… the 'thane' is the 'gift-giver' or 'bane-shield' or other such ideas, and the thanesman is…?"

"'Thanes-spear'," replied Restag readily. "'Thanes-shield', the 'third-eye' of the thane, or 'third hand.'"

"So basically someone who extends the thane's will," said Korena, receiving a nod in response. She pointed to the man's shoulder, which she knew held the far reaches of his Blood Mark. "The strength of your gift is an even greater blessing, then. It is not technically a secret, though families like mine rarely speak of it to those outside the Blood Houses, but among your people, that is Rendeilxue in general, you tend to react more when we touch you if you're strong, while the weaker you are the less you feel the loss of your power. I also saw your mark while taking care of you. It is quite impressive."

The open curiosity Restag showed as she spoke about her own power quickly pulled back behind a more reserved, thoughtful face. He said, quietly and deliberately, "The Mark speaks only of the presence of fairy blood. It speaks nothing of that blood's power."

Friathri made an exclamation, startling Korena. After apologizing to her mistress, she translated the thanesman's words, her own confusion giving the younger woman concern. Korena asked, "Would you explain?"

There was a long, tense silence, Restag's face a mask save for his eyes clouded with conflict. Eventually, he said, "My own Mark is lesser than some others in my family, but none hold our gift so strongly as I do."

Friathri looked unconvinced and still greatly disturbed, but she faithfully translated while Restag continued, "It is a common belief, however often it may prove false, and few wish to deny it. The strength of one's blood, as divined by one's Mark, affects many parts of our life. It is a key to sooth-saying, is used to determine marriages and alliances, to select heirs, and to choose children."

Korena noticed an uneasy pause before Friathri spoke that last phrase, which only added to the disturbance it caused her. Feeling dread creeping across her skin, she repeated, "To choose... children?"

Friathri did not tell him Korena's question, despite the look they both gave her, urging for answers the older woman did not want to give. She fidgeted with the edge of her shawl, feeling the stiffness in her fingers and wrists hidden by her youthful appearance. In a voice cracked with resignation, she said to her mistress, "When... when a child is born to the Asgradi, it is common practice to hand the newborn first to the family head, who then uses the child's Blood Mark as an indication of that child's potential strength... in order to decide whether or not to keep it or leave it to die."

As Korena's face turned a sickly shade. Friathri turned away, abandoning Restag to the young woman's horrified gaze as she whispered, "Is... that true? Do you really kill your babies?"

Friathri knew she had to translate the words even as she felt her fear confirmed by Restag's confusion at the question. In a dreadfully matter-of-fact tone, he said, "It is the family head's chief duty to keep alive the fae-gifts, chiefly his own line's. If doubt should seed for whether a gift shall reveal itself in a child, creating a weak-link in the family chain or prove the weak beam that shall topple the house, it is his right to uproot the seedling before it should root too deep."

"Children aren't plants to uproot!" Korena cried, startling both Asgradi. She shook her head, gripping her shawl close against an air that suddenly seemed much colder. In a quieter voice, she said, "That's awful. Just... just awful!"

Restag did not understand the words being spoken, and he could not understand the human's clear distress over something so normal. Even his own parents, he had been told, had seen several off-spring taken before he finally came to them, weak sprouts plucked and thrown out to provide and make room for the stronger. Time and again he had been present to hear the first cries of a would-be cousin that was also to be their last. It was simply what had to be done for the sake of the clan. To see this human woman's eyes shine with gathering tears and to see her turn away from him with something like anger as those tears began to spill over down her cheeks, baffled and troubled him.

Friathri then came beside him, her tall, slim, towheaded form a pillar of stone among the trees as she spoke quietly, gently, as if conscious not to disturb her grieving mistress, saying, "In her religion, all men, even half-men such as ourselves, are made by the Great God as his mirrors, created to reflect him on the Mid-Plain. To intentionally shatter one such mirror, other than for such reasons as just reparation for wickedness or in defense of home or another, this is judged a deed fitting only for the Halskrad."

Anger colored Restag's cheeks as he stood and glared at Korena's back, snapping, "You deal doom-speech against my forefathers and my people?"

The young woman did not face him immediately. After a few moments of silence, she took a deep breath, wiped her face upon her cloak, and turned. Her makeup was half-removed, the bruise on her cheek an ugly yellow and the kohl from around her eyes creating charcoal streaks down her face and chin. Tears continued to fall from her eyes, but her face, though neither angry nor hard, was firm as she said, "Yes. I do. It is wrong, barbaric, to murder someone, especially a child, just because you think he's weak or you don't want him."

Restag scoffed. "You have little knowledge of what you speak. Perhaps you, living in a place where winter is not but autumn, where the gods do not provide a ready-made tomb with every snowfall, you who have so many and such large walls to turn away the spears and swords of those who wish you dead, perhaps you can risk such foolishness. We cannot afford such waste."

A touch of anger returned to the young woman's eyes, and she said, "Don't blame your land or your circumstances for your people's wickedness! We have our own evils and troubles, and there are things that are wrong and evil no matter where they are done or by whom. Another's life belongs to God, not to us. It is not ours to take as we see fit. Even if you have reasons that make it more understandable, that doesn't make it right!"

"There is good and right that has come of it," countered Restag, his voice seething and his eyes daring her to challenge him.

Korena shook her head and shouted, "I don't care! Am I supposed to think it's fine to commit wicked acts because there might be good that comes of them? No! Some acts are wicked by their nature, regardless of the results."

As she finished and heard the thanesman respond, Korena realized this wouldn't work. They did not think the same way. He was thinking of his land, his family, his experience, concrete things from his own life. He would not hear such abstract arguments. She needed some other way, something more concrete, more personal, an example of equal strength to counter, and the only one that came to mind caused her pain at its cruelty. She waited for him to finish, but before Friathri could translate, Korena swallowed the lump in her throat and said, "Restag, what if that child thrown out had been Witheric?"

This time it was to Restag that Friathri hesitated to translate, her eyes wide, face pale, and voice unsteady. As she did, Korena braced herself, but even that did not prepare her for his response. She had asked the question as a hypothetical. She had seen Witheric's mark, knew how it stretched across his back in a thin, emerald web, knew that, despite a body that was slight even compared to other rendeilxue men, his Blood Mark spoke of power. With that knowledge, she had posed the question expecting indignation, perhaps anger, from the proud thanesman. She had not expected the bare-faced horror that overcame him.

The thought came that she had hurt him. Somehow, the blow had been more than intended, had struck a point she did not know or had not foreseen, and emotions of fear and pain that the thanesman had hitherto hidden were suddenly so clear to her that it was frightening and painful for herself. Then she realized what the scenario implied. Even if only imagined, she had placed in his hands the infant life of the man he served and loved and would die to protect, had placed in his hands a knife to slice that child's throat. It made her sick to think of, made her lose control of the tears that wanted to fall, but she did not take it back. Instead, she wiped her eyes again and said, her voice quiet even to her own ears, "A man's life does not become precious, Restag. It simply is."

She wasn't sure he understood, or if he did whether or not he agreed, for that final blow appeared to have been too harsh against him. Guilt pricked her as the silence hung over them like a cloud of smoke, polluting the air in her lungs, only lessening when Friathri came over and said in a low voice, "It is getting late, Miss, and there is a long ride back. Perhaps I should fetch a cab?"

Forcing a smile, Korena agreed, the older woman giving the younger a comforting touch on her arm before leaving. The silence returned. Korena glanced at the Asgradi man and shivered. He had completely closed himself off, even his teal eyes shut behind some barrier she would have been unable to climb even if she knew his language.

That silence continued to press on her heavily as the cab clattered back through the streets, all the way from the third district to the first, past the beautiful buildings and clean walls and streets, like some dead thing that could not be seen but was known to be nearby.

As they rode up to the front gate of the palace, Korena said to Friathri, "Could… could you take him back to the infirmary? My shift would have ended soon anyway and… and I'm not sure I…."

Friathri nodded. "Of course, Miss. I wouldn't want to be seen with my makeup in such disarray myself."

Korena smiled a little, the more shallow of her reasons unveiled.

The cab stopped a minute later, the driver opening the door. Friathri explained to Restag that she would take him back, as her mistress was tired and needed to rest. Restag's gaze wandered to the young woman for the first time that entire return. Her eyes were still a little red and her cheeks flushed. Her makeup was smeared, the unmasked bruise on her face looking gruesome between the dark streaks and the weakness in the human's face. He was still seething, and yet it disturbed him to see her looking almost like what the ruins of a once great hall might in human form. He looked away, willing the image to leave his mind as he followed Friathri out the cab door. Then, he heard his name, small and timid, and felt the chlamys tug against him. Turning, his eyes met hers. Regret shone plainly in those brown eyes. She tried to speak, but the words, it seemed, did not want to come, and after a pause, she simply reached beside her and pulled out from her bag the paper-wrapped book, as well as another small item wrapped in parchment.

Her voice was much smaller, more fragile, compared to Friathri's translation as she said, "Don't forget this. And here. You… you seemed to like it, so…."

With a wordless nod, he accepted the parcels, the shadows of a smile rising to the young woman's lips just before she pulled back and turned away. He, likewise, turned away, following Friathri absently through the palace halls. Before he knew it, they stood within the infirmary, Friathri saying something to the wound-mender before leaving with a curtsy. Paskhalon did not speak to him afterwards as Restag went to take his seat beside Witheric, whose state appeared unchanged from that morning. As he gazed into that suffering face, Korena's horrid question drifted around him, latched itself to him, like a shade come to haunt him, to whisper his greatest fears and pull out the darkest thoughts hidden in the shadows of his heart.

As much to push away the ghostly feeling settling around him as to satisfy his curiosity, he took the small, paper-wrapped item Korena had handed him along with the book, undid the string, and pushed away the paper to reveal the little olive-wood bird from Thallas's booth. He knew, based on the young woman's words, that he should have expected it, yet the gift surprised him, startled him out of his gloom. Slowly, he turned it over in his hand, tracing his fingers across the delicate details and graceful curves, the masterful choices in cut and carving, the warm, brown wood with its dark grain bringing to mind a pair of equally warm, brown eyes.

In order to pass the time before the next guards should arrive, when his words would no longer be secret, he set the bird aside, letting his fingers linger a little longer on the sculpture's texture before he unwrapped the book. Gently, he placed Witheric's bone-thin hand on the cover, saying, "I went into Thenika today, Witheric. It is… it is an amazing place. We found this in a little shop. One full of just books. Your precious books full of script and pictures. You would love it. Kor… the one who took me said there is an even larger book-room here, in the palace, though I think she only joked. But look, here, let me show you this."

He opened the pages, going one by one, describing each page as he placed his thane's hand on it, mentioning as it seemed fitting bits and pieces of what had happened that day, what he had seen and the city they now found themselves within. All the while, the little bird sat on its branch, watching them with its gentle, wood-grain gaze.

Chapter 9

They did not go out again that week, Korena deciding to focus more on the palace. Understandably, Restag showed the most interest in the training grounds. They met the arms master, who informed them that he had gotten the Asgradi's weapons cleaned up and sharpened. A quick test of the repaired sword led to high compliments from Restag, which the weapons master returned by commenting on the quality of the smith work, especially for one made of iron rather than steel, resulting in a discussion on the various pros and cons of weapon and armor materials in a land where the Fae dominated. Meanwhile, Korena found herself admiring Witheric's wheellock revolver, an antique in an age where rumors of cartridge weapons were beginning to cast doubts on the future of the flintlock market, but a piece of art among firearms nonetheless. She asked how he had obtained such a rare and expensive weapon, but Restag shrugged his shoulders, saying human traders were always willing to trade useful things for the oddest trinkets, a statement she couldn't deny.

However, the most satisfying visit was to the palace library. Korena had suspected Restag's disbelief in its existence, and to see his amazement, one only eclipsed so far by his first sight of Thenika proper, delighted her. When her comment that the public Central Library had an even larger collection, the honest wonder he expressed made her promise there and then that it would be the next place they visited outside the palace. She also promised to negotiate with the palace librarian to allow him to remove some of the collection to the infirmary.

To her surprised relief, most of their interactions that week were of a similar amiability. She had feared the conclusion to their outing would be a cause of distance or further conflict. On the contrary, the opposite seemed to have resulted, Restag's attitude toward her slowly cracking open, revealing more and more of his emotions and inner thoughts. He had always been honest and opinionated. However, there seemed to be something more… unguarded about them now. Why this should be the case she could not guess, and she was too afraid to ask. It felt like there was a delicacy to her situation now, like a glass vase that could be shattered by the slightest nudge in the wrong direction. She did not want to lose it, did not want to lose the glimpses she was catching of the man: his unveiled care for his friend and master, his frustrations at "bending runes and switchback speech" as she introduced him to the Ithaenian alphabet, his stubbornness to learn said runes and speech, and the muttered curses as they stumbled across the script's calligraphic form with all of its exaggerated swirls and curves and joined letters and flourishes. She liked seeing his working face, one full of constant thought and hard determination to somehow make the impossible work, as well as the concern and consideration he was not afraid to show. There was no stoicism in the man. Subtleness, yes, and restraint, particularly regarding those gentler emotions, but no denial. Everything in the man's face was honest, but without manipulation. He did not need her to agree with him. He knew how he felt and what he thought, and there was an irrelevancy to whether or not she felt and thought the same that was refreshing and oddly liberating, as if for the first time in years she spoke with someone around whom she could just be. And as she watched him, she felt she began to understand why he, of all men, should be the thane's right hand.

The thought still occupied her as she stepped out of the cab and walked up the steps of her family's mansion and handed her shawl to the doorman only for the spell to be broken when Karas called her from the sitting room as she passed down the hall, sending a maid to fetch another cup of coffee for his returned sister.

As she joined him on the cushioned bench, he asked, "How was today? Did the rendeilxue give you too much trouble?"

"No, not at all," said Korena, accepting a bowl of nuts from her brother. "Today went much the same as yesterday. He displayed general annoyance at our language and scoffed at a statement or two, but nothing worth specific comment. I am sure Witheric's slight improvements and Paskhalon's hopeful predictions have helped keep him in a good mood."

"Good," said Karas. "Yes. That's very good. So no… well… disagreements, I suppose?"

"Karas, stop expecting me to come home crying every day. I'm fine."

"Yes, yes, of course you are," said Karas, tapping his fingers against his coffee cup. "Only, it's just… Rena, can't we please see about getting someone else to take your shift? Surely the king doesn't need all of his strongest Dampeners staying with them. I just… you know, that first day, with the bruises, it's still bothering me. You could at least–and then you crying. Rena, you never cry. What if… I mean, they're still barbarians, you know. What if something…."

"If they were going to do anything to me, I am quite sure it would have been before they knew they were King Aleukus's guests," replied Korena, accepting the cup from the maid as she returned. "They, or at least Restag, appears determined to be a good guest."

"Only for now, while his thane's life is in the king's hands. Once he recovers, who knows what will happen! You know history. You know how the Asgradi refugees betrayed the Holy Emperor over a thousand years ago, betrayed their own rules of hospitality and nearly led to the collapse of the entire empire," countered Karas.

Korena couldn't help but grin. "I highly doubt two men can overthrow all of Ithaenia."

"Unless they're assassins!"

"If they are assassins," said Korena, looking seriously at her brother, "then that's all the more reason I cannot step aside. I am part of the king's guard. If there is any danger present, especially of a magical nature, it is my duty to remain. If you have a complaint in that regard, you can take it up with Father."

She knew it was unfair to invoke their father when his current position on the matter was obvious, and the guilt that came as she saw her brother deflate before her eyes prompted her to scoot closer, lean on his shoulder as she had when she was little, and say, "Thank you, though, for worrying. You're probably one of the few who does and definitely the only one who says so. I appreciate it."

Karas placed a hand over hers. "I just… there's so little I can do for you. Please, Rena, be careful, and even though there isn't much, if there's anything I can do for you, please, tell me."

"I will," she promised. Then grinning, she said, "Actually, there is one thing. What kinds of presents do men like?"

The young man's brow furrowed. "Why do you ask? You always do just fine with choosing presents. In fact, anything you choose will be perfect."

Sighing resignedly, Korena replied, "Never mind."

Restag paced the infirmary restlessly. More often than not, Korena's visits over the last week had kept him moving and given him plenty to focus on and process, but his other guards did not seem so comfortable with him leaving the room or wandering the palace. Most of the time, he did not mind quiet or stillness. He had certainly appreciated having plenty of time to think the day he returned from his first visit into the city, plenty of time to turn over the image Friathri had given him to explain Korena's distress. By the next day, he was still angry at the human and the insult she had levied, but he had also come to accept her view of what his people did as some form of blasphemy against her god, or perhaps some version among her people of thane-slaying, which made her reaction at least understandable. It still haunted him, though, especially that last question the human woman had asked, one which carried far more weight and had struck far deeper than she hopefully understood, and as the long hours of silence and lack of stimulation dragged on, he found the shade roused with a greater frequency and more persistent presence. He needed movement to satiate it, so he had begun pacing more while trying to focus his thoughts on other matters. Witheric had improved, as well, and the hope of his master's recovery combined with the business of the last week had reawakened his low tolerance for inaction.

Paskhalon irritably watched the Asgradi, his fountain pen paused over his page, wishing the man would go back to his moping at the window, or whatever it was he'd been doing, rather than remind him every couple minutes that the sanctuary of his infirmary was occupied by people who were far from in need of it. Practically invaded. Glaring at the guards, Paskhalon snapped, "Oh, for the love of—can't you two take him outside before he wears a rut through my floor?"

The Dampener of the pair, Tokolos, saluted sharply but said, "Yes, um… where would you…uh…."

Gesturing vaguely, Paskhalon replied, "Anywhere. Just. Not. Here. Bah! How meatheads like you get to run around His Majesty's halls without assistance is beyond even my ability to comprehend."

Tokolos flushed angrily, but as he was about to retort, the translator, a soldier from the City Guard named Leskinor, held him back, saying to the physician, "As you say, sir." Switching to one of the northern Asgradi dialects, he called out, "Hey, shield-man!"

Reacting to his own tongue, Restag looked up and responded with such seriousness it made the translator grin, "I am no shield-man. I lost it more than a month ago."

With an amused roll of his eyes, Leskinor said, "Alright. Then sword-man, or whatever you are now. Doc says we've got to go. We're rippling his pond."

Restag nodded and, after looking over Witheric one more time, he followed them out the door under a glare universally understood to mean "Don't come back soon." Once a few yards down the hall, Tokolos let out a string of curses, finishing with, "And what does he mean by 'meathead'? How does he get off being such a prick? And you, how can you stay so calm around him?"

Leskinor shrugged. "If you're translating for the a people who might literally slice or blow your head off with a look, it's pretty important to stay calm. And trust me, the Asgradi are much better at insults: hollow-skull, frog-faced, dragon's-leftovers (dragons apparently don't leave 'leftovers,' by the way, except from behind), and dung-ass are a few of my favorites so far."

"Hmph. Glad I'm not a city guard," said Tokolos.

"As am I," replied his coworker with a laugh.

A tap on Leskinor's shoulder brought his eyes around to the Asgradi tailing them. The half-fae's eyes darted to Tokolos, and he said, "Is this about the bone-mender?" After the translator nodded, Restag continued, "Then perhaps you can solve a riddle for me. When High Thane Aleukus came to see us, the bone-mender and he did not seem to fit well. Though it seemed strange to me, I had thought, perhaps, it was not so dishonoring among humans for a man to speak displeasingly to his master in the presence of others. Am I wrong in this?"

Leskinor was surprised by the question. The Asgradi had spoken so little to them, and he often seemed so unaware of the world around him. He replied, "Yes. You are mistaken. Among any people, I should think it ill-received to press against or insult your thane. Even more so before other eyes. But he is highly skilled in his craft, and he has many times shown his loyalty and desire to preserve the thane's line to be as rooted as a mountain. Much can be forgiven for such goods."

Restag thought through this answer, eventually giving his assent. Yes. Much could be forgiven for the sake of loyalty. Had it not been so with the Elders, whose word-stones were so often forgiven for the sake of their perceived loyalty and for respect of their place and skill? Of course, it had all proven false. The thanesman said, "It's still ill-advised to keep such men close. Many might feign love with one hand and hold a dagger with the other."

"True-speech that," said Leskinor. "And if he wanted the thane dead, Paskhalon has had plenty of chances. A lot of us have. Thane Aleukus is a very open man. However, he is no fool. He is careful in who he lets close to him. He knows to seek for a good man and to treasure him when he finds one, even if some parts are not so liked…. Or even if that man is only half-a-man."

Leskinor gave Restag a meaningful look, though before the Asgradi could discern that meaning, the translator said, "So, where do you want to go?"

The question took Restag back a pace. So far, Korena had decided where they went, and Restag had expected the same from these men. However, after only a moment's thought, the answer came.

The outside air was chill and echoed with the voices of men and wood and metal. Restag held a practice blade, testing out a craftsmanship and material that were different from his people's. The sword's balance felt unnatural. However, there was still a comfortable familiarity in the feel of a leather grip against his palm and the earth-drawn weight of a weapon, as well as with the cleaned and polished steel rings beneath his tunic. Tokolos had run off as they approached the grounds, eager to sweat out his annoyance.

Leskinor asked, "When did you visit the training grounds?"

"Korena showed them to me," he replied. Noticing the surprise on the translator's face, Restag said, "What?"

A slight flush came to the man's cheeks as he coughed, glanced quickly around the small assembly on the field, eyes turning toward them as they noticed their strange visitor, and said in a low voice, "Just a suggestion, but I wouldn't call Miss Iegam by her first name around the others. It's not… in Ithaenia, it's a word-sign of closeness between people, and she's the, how would you say it, the dragon's gold, in a way, among the palace guard. Every man wants her as a wife—the Blood Houses for her abilities and us ordinary men for her beauty—but few have the courage to try."

Restag looked in a mix of confusion and disbelief at the other man. "Why? She is a woman, and they are men, are they not? They desire the treasure, yet they stand by and do not act? What prevents their charge?"

Leskinor shrugged. "For a few years, we all thought Aristi would marry her. He used to be in the guard, a gift-sleeper like her and Tokolos. But he didn't. His little brother, Ortheus, has been pestering her ever since. A few others have asked, but she's turned them all away."

"Why would you need to approach her? Simply prove to her father you are a good match, and if he is a wise man, will he not give her to you?" asked Restag.

With a laugh, Leskinor said, "You speak a distant dream, Asgradi. No. Maybe that's still how it works among your people, but the Holy See, basically God's thanesman among the priests, and the other eparchs–that is, the head-priests over a group of priests–ruled hundreds of years ago that both the man and the woman must agree to the match. Even if her father tried to marry her off to Ortheus, for instance–not that he would, the man is too proud to wed his powerful daughter to a weak gift-sleeper like him–but even if he tried to, all she has to do is say no, and it won't happen."

Restag gaped at the man. He said, "With just a word? But how then can bonds between houses be formed? How can the line be ensured strength? The house be preserved?"

They approached the practice dummies as Leskinor said, "Oh, there are political matches all the time. It helps if each child is attracted to the other, but it's hardly necessary, only willing agreement to the match by both. What of you? Don't your people ever wed for attraction, for affection?"

Restag swung the dull, steel sword a few times in the air, letting his illness-weakened body adapt to the weight of the blade. He said, "Yes. I have seen such, but it is the parents who must agree, not the children. Marriage is for the preservation of our fae-gifts. This must be considered in choosing a good match, and if there is great concern, such as an imbalance coming from the one entering the other's house and of the outside gift being passed on at the cost of the house's, the house head can deny the joining, even if the parents agree."

Leskinor frowned. "That sounds so…."

As he searched for the right word in his own tongue, let alone how to express it in Restag's, Leskinor's eyes fell on the wooden dummy. He pointed to it and said, "It's like that," then pointing to Restag, "instead of like that."

The Asgradi frowned. "I do not see your meaning."

Shaking his head, Leskinor said, "Sorry. I'm no good at your Dar-speaking, or whatever you call it."

With a snort, Restag replied, "If most were, it would not be Dar's speech."

A slight grin tugged at the translator's mouth. He said, "All right, Thanesman. That's enough stalling from you. Show me what you have."

He was the one who needed to see that for himself, thought Restag. In fifteen years, he had not gone so long without holding a weapon, let alone wielding it. He felt an odd mixture of lightness and weight as his muscle's memory awoke from their month-long slumber, his feet shifting to stand solidly before the wooden frame wrapped in straw. With a sharp breath, he swung, matching the movement as the breath left his lungs, increasing his force. Again and again he repeated the motion, bringing his breath in line with his movements, strike with exhale, retract with inhale, the rhythmic sound of blunted blade hitting wood matching the rhythmic beating of the heart. He found himself pulled into that rhythm, his muscles straining to act on their memories against their atrophy. Then, mid-swing, another blade appeared, swinging up from the side to meet his and hitting with such force it broke his balance and made him step back. He used the momentum to pivot, bringing his sword arm in the same direction. There was a shout of surprise, and a form jumped away from the arc of Restag's sword.

"Who are you?" demanded Restag, leveling the sword against the smirking newcomer, his eyes quickly scanning the scene, which soon revealed Leskinor lying on the ground, pinned down by a few other men who also kept him gagged as he tried to break free.

Resorting to a bite finally got his voice free in time for Leskinor to shout to the other men, "Let me go you idio–Parchaes, front!"

The new man, Parchaes, who had looked away from the rendeilxue at the sound of his co-conspirator's yelp and subsequent curse, had just enough time to leap away again as the Asgradi charged him, sword first. The moment he did, the Asgradi changed course, barrelling into the men holding down Leskinor without warning, catching the whole crew by surprise, and soon had one unconscious from a blow to the head with the sword pommel, another kicked away, and the rest scrambling to crab-walk away as the swordsman lifted the translator up by the arm and returned to a defensive stance. "Are you hurt?" he said.

The man who had been struck in the head groaned as he returned to the waking world. Restag cursed. He thought he had hit him harder than that. Quick as a thought, he turned and knocked the recovering man to the ground again on his back, sword tip at the man's throat. Even blunted, such a blow could kill, and the captured man's trembling told Restag he knew it, too. In a firm voice, the Asgradi shouted, "Who are you? What is your purpose? Answer me, or–"

Suddenly, the captured man started screaming curses, followed up by, "Parchaes, you bastard! You never said I'd get killed for this! Idiot! Son of a–" From there, it descended into increasingly vile curses.

Parchaes began to laugh, doubling over from it as he tried to speak. "So-sorry, He-Hesten. I didn't think he'd-he'd-ha! Ha! Ha!"

Confusion heightened Restag's tension, and he prepared to use his Sight, ready to search out the hidden motives of these shouting men whose words he could not understand, when Leskinor's hand fell on his shoulder, and the translator said, "Stand down, Asgradi, or you'll kill your host's men."

Suspicion colored the tension now as Restag replied, "High Thane Aleukus's? But they—"

"—Are idiots who decided to play a bad joke on the newcomer to the training grounds, like they do to everyone, to size him up and see what he'll do," finished Leskinor with an irritated glare at Parchaes as he recovered from his laughing fit. Switching to Ithaenian, Leskinor snapped, "Hope it was worth it, Parchaes. Someone could have gotten killed for that prank!"

Hesten scrambled to his feet the moment Restag's foot lifted and made a dash for his companions, who had decided to keep a good several feet away while Parchaes took an easy posture and said, "Sorry, Leski. I really didn't expect him to do all… well, that."

Leskinor felt the beginnings of a migraine, and the jolt of pain gave his voice a dangerous edge as he said, "He's an Asgradi, idiot! And a warrior! Probably only a month or two off the literal bloody fields. How did you think he'd respond to the sudden appearance of an apparent threat?"

The other man only thought a moment before saying, "Not like that."

Leskinor felt a sudden and intense desire to pummel the guard, but before he could act on the impulse, Parchaes leapt past him, holding out a hand to Restag and saying, "Getir dar, Asgradi, sir! Sorry about all that. Just the usual greeting from us poor, bored palace bastards and all that. No harm, no hard feelings."

A reproving snort came from the group of guards, which Parchaes completely ignored, while Restag glared at the man and his outstretched hand suspiciously, hints of indecision flickering in his eyes before he finally lowered the sword, though without relaxing. Meanwhile, the rest of the men on the training field decided to investigate the sudden ruckus, Tokolos at their head as he joined Leskinor and asked what happened.

"Nothing you needed to be here for. Nothing, not even you Blood Houses, can stop a man that determined to be an idiot," said Leskinor, moving to place himself between the two parties as quite probably the only man among them with reasonable experience with Asgradi. He said, "By the way, Parchaes, it's 'getar dar,' not 'getir dar.' Words with 'a' endings are masculine, and 'i' endings are feminine, generally. So, 'getar dar' for the day, 'getir dir' for night, and you only mix them in the early morning, when the sun is still coming up, for 'getar dir.'"

"Really?" said Parchaes, shoving his hand out farther. "Well, then, getar dar, Sir Warrior."

Restag remained staring suspiciously at the man, weighing the potential insult to Aleukus's hospitality versus the advantage of insight if he used his Sight on the man. In the end, the responsibilities of his position won out, and he held out his own hand as he had seen others do while at the same trying to keep the guard's invasive energy from rousing his irritation. Said guard had begun rambling about something which, after another apology, Leskinor translated as, "He's asking if you want to spar with him instead of just hitting a wood pole all day."

Without needing much thought, Restag nodded. He needed to get a good idea of how far he had fallen behind from his usual abilities, and that was better done in combat with someone who could respond in kind. Meanwhile, Parchaes's eyes caught an eager glint, and he said, "Excellent! I've always wanted to try fighting a real rendeilxue barbarian, not just street thugs. Show me what it means to be a king's man, Asgradi."

Restag did not know the exact words spoken, but he recognized the challenge in the other man's eyes. How many times had he seen it in his fellow shield-men or from the champions of other tribes calling for a match? He followed the guard into a small, fenced in area, his ears already filled with the sound of pounding blood. They took their stances, Parchaes armed with a blunt sword much like his own, and without even waiting for a signal, they began.

Parchaes struck first, bringing his sword up in an easy swing that Restag just as easily blocked, though his arms did not move nearly so quickly as they should have. It was a testing strike, and the next series came faster, harder, and in patterns unfamiliar to Restag, who found himself in a frustratingly defensive position. His arms were tiring too quickly, as well, and it was far too short a time before Parchaes managed to get in behind his guard, and trip him with a swift ankle swipe, sending the Asgradi onto his back with a sword tip at his throat. Parchaes looked down the blade with bored disappointment.

"Is that it?" he said. "That's all you half-fairies have to offer? Bah! All that build up and stories about how terrible you guys are, and this is—Woah!"

The shout came after Restag dropped his own sword, grabbed his opponent's blunted sword blade with his freed hand halfway to the hilt, gave it a sudden twist, and soon had it out of the guard's relaxed grip and flung several feet away, giving him an opening to roll over and pick up his sword to swing it around as he rose to his knees. With real, sharpened blades, it would have been a stupid move, leaving his dominant hand sliced and badly bleeding, but they were not using sharpened blades, and Restag had learned many times to use the type of weapon as a weapon itself.

Despite the suddenness of the maneuver, Parchaes managed to avoid the blow, hurrying over to pick up his own sword while Restag got to his feet. Facing his opponent again, the human growled, "That was a dirty move there."

However, any other criticisms were soon swallowed as his eyes met the Asgradi's, and he saw a chilling hardness in those eyes, like blue stones set within the handle of a blade. From some deep cavern within him, the thin half-man's deep voice formed a single word, which Leskinor translated to, "Again!"

Excitement trilled through Parchaes as he resumed his stance, feeling himself being drawn into the hint of wilderness beyond the city, which he had only glimpsed during the storms that sent the sea waves pounding against the city where the walls reached the edge of the land. They began again, and again he felt himself only slightly pushed beyond the level needed to disarm most of his fellow guardsmen before he had the sword knocked out of the Asgradi's hand and his own sword pointed at his opponent's chest, this time making sure to have it firmly in both hands. However, as before, the barbarian took hold of the blade, though this time, rather than try to yank it away, he held it steady, his gaze focused, as he repeated that word, "Again!" before turning to pick up his dropped weapon.

A few more times, they repeated this, and each time after, Parchaes found himself pushed harder and harder. His opponent, he realized, had stopped trying to strike as often, focusing on parrying, sometimes not even holding a proper stance with a full guard, instead learning to read him and coming closer and closer each time to a successful counterstrike. Fear began to build. Shouldn't this man, who was allegedly only a couple weeks released from total bedrest, be getting tired? Parchaes was, the sword weighing more in his hands with each strike. Eventually, the inevitable happened, and Parchaes brought his sword around too slowly to block a strike to his padded side. The blow hit him with shocking force, knocking the wind out of him. Immediately after, he saw a sword tip mere centimeters from his face. He blinked, looking up the blade to the Asgradi at the other end. Then, the blade dropped, the barbarian took a few steps back, and, to the watching crowd and Parchaes's horror and amazement, said that dreaded word, "Again!"

This guy was crazy!

However, looking over him in that brief respite, Parchaes began to notice what had been hidden in the midst of the fighting. He saw how the Asgradi quickly switched his sword to his other hand, letting him shake out and stretch his main one before carefully taking it up again, how the sweat rolled down his face and his chest rose and fell with panting breath, how the position he took up required almost no effort to hold the sword until he raised it to block or strike, and he realized the Asgradi was just as drained as he was, if not more. And yet, he demanded another round.

"He isn't sparring," Parchaes realized with a shiver. "He's on a battlefield! He's seeing how long he can last, the bastard!"

Out loud, he said, "You're insane, you know that? But," he readied his sword again with a grim smile, "there's no way I'm sitting down before some skinny, half-dead, fairy-man."

A matching grin spread across the rendeilxue's face, and he charged again.

"You. Are. All. IDIOTS!" yelled Paskhalon as he roughly slapped a cloth slathered with salve to a cut on Parchaes's arm.

The guardsman winced and said, "Come on, Doc. It's not that big a deal. Don't you fix us up all the time?"

With a murderous glare, he pointed to the half-mummified form of Restag, once more sitting beside the sleeping Witheric. One arm hung in a sling after addressing the dislocated shoulder, and a large amount of bandage held a blood-stained compress to his face. Shrill-voiced, Paskhalon said, "You almost got a man killed! Why didn't you stop after popping out his shoulder?"

Parchaes shrugged. "He didn't want to. Besides, it's not my fault he cut his face on my sword when he fainted At least he missed his eye."

A blood vein appeared on the physicians forehead, and he generated another yelp from his patient as he forcefully placed another medicinal pad over an open wound. "Since when has 'manliness' become synonymous with 'stupid'?" He growled.

From his and Tokolos's position at a safe distance, Leskinor said, "Parchaes wasn't hired to be smart. And he is a special and very stubborn kind of stupid."

The glare turned in the pair's direction, making Tokolos flinch. "And why didn't you two do anything to stop this mess?" said the doctor.

"I refer back to my previous statement," replied the translator.

The dodge did not satisfy the doctor, who continued verbally dissecting all the ways all four men had displayed their idiocy. For not the first time, though perhaps never with such strength, Restag was grateful he could not understand the Ithaenian language and could instead lean back in his chair and mentally step away from this particular conflict. His body ached and complained terribly, telling him in ways he had forgotten it could that he had gone too far. Even just settling himself against the wall agitated his sore muscles. However, he did not regret it. Yes, he would likely be in pain to one level or another for the next week and so would not be returning to the training grounds during that time, but he understood now how far he had to climb to return to normal. It was not so far as he had initially feared. At that encouraging thought, weariness began to settle in. The Ithaenian words began to clatter together like stones rolling down a hill, creating an ambient noise that, despite the volume, worked with his body's exhaustion to begin pulling him toward sleep.

However, as his head began to nod, a different sound, a disturbed groan, reached him through the noise, striking his ears like a pin prick to the arm and jolting him awake. He looked down beside him to see Witheric stir and groan again. Then, as if it were painful to do so, his eyes slowly opened. Paskhalon's rant abruptly stopped as the four humans heard the sound of a chair overturned. All turned to see Restag, teeth clenched as he hissed in pain and leaned against the bed, suddenly shout his master's name in a plaintive voice discordant with his appearance and push himself up to look into the hooded, ice-blue gaze of the smaller rendeilxue.

Witheric kept his lips half-closed, his eyes adjusting to the sudden brightness before his friend's face and body provided the shadow necessary to ease the light-induced pain. Blinking slowly, he said, his mouth and lips dry and voice parched, "Res...tag? Where...?"

A jubilant cry caught in Restag's throat at the same time Paskhalon arrived at the bedside, a cup of water in hand. Gently, he eased the sick man up and held up the cup, coaxing him to drink. Meanwhile, Restag held onto his master's hand with his good one, willing his already weakened legs not to give out as Paskhalon commanded something to the others and Leskinor ran out of the room. After

Witheric had finished the cup, the physician slowly let him down again and began working with several items on his desk with fervored motion.

Half to himself, Restag said in a voice weakened by relief, "You're awake. You're alive."

Witheric's eyes still looked dazed as he stared at Restag, a slight wrinkle forming between his eyes as he said, "You're… hurt."

Restag shook his head. "Not from ill cause. There is no danger."

"I can't… move… well."

Squeezing his master's hand gently, Restag said, "You've been very ill for a very long time, much of it near Halsk's Gates."

Witheric's head moved with a nearly imperceptible nod. "Where? What?"

"Thenika," said Restag, smiling softly as his friend's dazed eyes widened in comprehension. He began recounting what he knew of their arrival and some of the events since. Witheric grew in awareness with every word so that while he was still too physically weak to take hold of the tonic held out to him when Paskhalon returned, he no longer looked on the boundary of sleep.

After Restag finished, Witheric said, "If any but you told me these things, I would think him false."

"Even if you disbelieved me, you would see it soon enough yourself," said Restag.

"And this Thallas, too, I hope," said Witheric. "I owe him a life-debt. I owe many life-debts, it would seem."

He let out a small, tired laugh. It was good to hear. It was all good to hear as Restag, his legs tired and body sore, bent to right his chair only to find it back under him as he was pulled back into it with a painful thud. An arm suddenly draped over his shoulder, and Parchaes's face appeared beside his, his free hand outstretched, as he practically yelled into Restag's ear, "Say, you're this guy's king, right? Huh. Pretty small compared to him. Never would have guessed. Anyway, nice to meet you, little king."

"Parchaes!" hissed Tokolos, staying a good distance from the physician who was staring blankly at the arm putting weight on an injured shoulder. "Don't– he's an Asgradi king! You can't just talk to him like that. Besides, he can't even understand you."

Parchaes frowned. "If he doesn't understand me, then why would you be upset about what I say?" earning a groan from Tokolos.

Witheric's eyes travelled from one man to the next as he spoke. Returning to

Parchaes, he cleared his throat and said, "Um… c-could you say again? More slow. It was fast."

A broad, elated smile stretched across Parchaes's face at the same time Tokolos's paled, and the cheery man said, "Hey! Look. He can understand! You heard him too, right, Doc?"

Still staring at Parchaes's arm as Restag tried, unsuccessfully, to remove it from his shoulder, Paskhalon said in a voice heavy with condescension, "Of course he can. If you read the king's report, you would know he has some capability with our language." Finally looking back to Witheric, he said steadily, "Apologies for this man. He is a fool. As you may have guessed, I am Paskhalon, your physician, or I suppose your people call those like myself things like 'bone-menders'."

"And I'm Parchaes!" jumped in the other man, pulling Restag forward with a bit-back grunt of pain. The human didn't seem to notice as he went on with a deliberate enunciation bordering on choppy, "I am a palace guard. And that is Tokolos. Leskinor went to get the king."

Witheric smiled. "Many greetings, and many thanks, bone-mender Paskhalon. And to Parchaes and Tokolos. Um… may I ask it to you to not to break my thanesman. He is much hurt, and it would be… it would be to climb heaven to find a new one as him."

Blinking blankly, Parchaes asked, "Why would you need to climb Heaven to get a new one?"

At that moment, the door opened, and as before, a collection of guards, though a smaller one than before, entered the infirmary, followed by Aleukus and Leskinor. Apparently he had been briefed on Restag's injuries, for he only stared for a moment, as if he had expected the report to be an exaggeration, before approaching the bed and giving a small bow to its occupant. With genuine warmth, he said, "Welcome, Witheric Iron-Brow, High Thane of the Eisenband, to Thenika, jewel of Ithaenia, and to my palace. I am pleased to see you awake."

Witheric was not sure what he had expected Aleukus, King of Ithaenia to be like, but as he looked at the broad-set man draped in layers of rich cloth outshone by the ruddy face and bright gray eyes framed in ebony curls and a chest-length beard, he doubted anything he had imagined quite fit the many words he had received for the past couple years as the man before him did now. He tried to sit up but was helped in the end by Restag, who propped him up with his bandaged arm. After an apologetic smile to the stone-like face hiding its owner's pain, Witheric said to the king, "Many greetings, Aleukus Jewel's-Thane, King of Ithaenia. Many regrets. My arms and legs. It is weak. I cannot give back your king's greeting."

Motioning for his guards to stand down, Aleukus, followed by Leskinor, came around to the other side of the bed and pulled over a chair. He said, "No need for regrets, friend. I am only glad to finally meet the man behind so many gracious letters."

The king reached into a pouch on his belt and pulled out Witheric's signet ring. The Asgradi thane lifted his hand as high as he could, and the human king gently placed the ring within that open palm. After a few moments' silence, Witheric spoke to Restag for a little in their own tongue. The thanesman lowered his master back down, and Witheric, with a sigh of relief, said in Asgradi to the translator standing beside the king, "You know our tongue? This is good. Please, give my regrets to your king. It is tiring to my mind and tongue to try to use your speech at the moment. I hope it is not thought ill if I speak mine."

Following the translation, Aleukus said, "Of course not. I only came to welcome you, and it would make me a poor host to not take heed of my guest's health and exhaustion. If you need, I will come back at a better time, when you are stronger, and then you can tell me how you came to my doorstep in your current state rather than with an escort and fanfare fit for a king."

Nodding, Witheric replied, "Yes, that would be best. I am very tired. But you have my word-bond, I shall give you the tale, though it is not a pleasing one."

"I should expect not," said Aleukus, rising. "Rest well, my friend. And rest easy. You are safe here."

"My thanks to you, your friendship, and your hall, High Thane Aleukus," said Witheric.

The king nodded his acknowledgement and then filed out the door, Paskhalon ordering one of the other guards to pull a protesting Parchaes out with them, leaving the room in peaceful silence. Restag watched them go and was preparing to settle into that silence when he noticed Witheric's triumphant expression. The thanesman gave him a questioning look, to which Witheric responded, "Did I not say Thane Aleukus is true of speech?"

Incredulity crossed Restag's face. "You're bringing that up now?"

"Of course," said Witheric with a slight chuckle. "It is always a victory to have my thanesman's doubts prove false after too many times proven right."

Still too relieved to be much irritated or formal, Restag simply sighed and said, "Get some rest, Witheric."

Sighing and turning to Leskinor, Witheric said in Ithaenian, "See you what I must face every day? I sleep Dar-knows how long, and he wants from me more. I hope he has not been much trouble for you, too."

"Actually," the translator replied in Asgradi with amusement, "As far as I have seen, he hasn't been until today. It seems he's been unusually submissive."

"Submissive?" said Witheric with such surprise it made Restag tense. Switching back to his thanesman, he said, "It seems you have saved your peace-keeping for all but your master."

Recognizing the familiar light in his friend's eyes, Restag relaxed and said, "Would you have me be otherwise?"

"If you were, I'd be dead," said Witheric without hesitation. "No, I will not request my stubborn, tinkering, troublesome thanesman ruined."

Face softening, Witheric addressed Leskinor again. "Many thanks for caring for him, and to your bone-mender for his craft. It seems you have borne our burden heroically."

Shaking his head, Leskinor replied, "No. I have had no part in your healing, and, as I said, your thanesman has been very quiet until today. If there has been any care of him, it would seem to be the work of Shield-Maiden Iegam."

"Shield-Maiden Iegam?" repeated Witheric. "Who's that?"

Restag snorted, startling both men, followed flatly by, "A troublesome person."

To which Leskinor added, "And the dragon's gold of the guards, most desired, but not yet by any obtained."

Witheric's eyes sparked with interest as he said, "I think I should most like to meet this 'troublesome dragon's gold.'"

"Well you won't today," said Restag with curious sharpness. "Now, get some sleep."

With a deep sigh, Witheric turned his gaze to the ceiling and closed his eyes, saying, "Very well, Restag-Thanesman. I shall try to grant this boon, but you must do the same. For a moment, when I first opened my eyes, I thought...."

Witheric's exact thoughts remained hidden, but his hands weakly clenched around the signet ring. Restag replied, "Very well, my thane."

"Good," said Witheric, the word released like a sigh, and soon after, his chest rose and fell again with the rhythm of sleep.

Chapter 10

Korena shivered as she stepped out of the carriage. With less than a week before the longest night of the year, the air was getting too cold for merely a cloak over her sleeveless dress. She had not made herself up quite so much as that first outing for the simple reason that her concerns delayed sleep, resulting in rising late that morning. Friathri had done her work well, however, quickly plaiting Korena's front locks around her head and away from her face and letting the rest of her dark curls drape over her shoulders, pinning a white scarf over the top of it all for warmth, and applying a quick bit of makeup to bring out the young woman's features. It was simple and practical, and if any of her fellow young women of the first district saw her, they would likely make some veiled slights while tittering behind their hands. Korena had long accepted being too high born to insult directly and yet too lowly to ever be above condescension.

It was often a strange feeling, then, to be greeted with respect the moment she entered the palace, a place few of her peers could enter so casually as she did, exchanging polite greetings and bits of idle chatter with the men at the front gate despite the cold. More than once, she had profited from this brief gossip about the hours after her previous day's shift. Such was the case that morning, and she didn't even think to stop to straighten her scarf as she burst through the infirmary door, generating a cry and accusation of attempted murder by heart attack from Paskhalon and drawing two pairs of blue eyes farther in the room from the pages of a large book.

At the sight of them, her mind and voice immediately jumped from "He really woke up!" to "What happened?" as her quick steps carried her over to the bandaged Restag and his frail master, unsure which should demand her immediate attention. Satisfying herself that Restag was still able to sit by himself, she focused on the recently awoken man, who sat propped up by pillows on the bed, blankets pulled up to his lap, and the large book lying flat beneath his thin fingers. Finally thinking to check her appearance, she quickly straightened herself up and gave a deep curtsy, saying, "Welcome to Thenika, Thane Witheric, and my happiness to your recovery. I am sorry that I was made aware of your waking only this morning. Had I known sooner, I should have come to greet you."

She had expected the translation to follow, as usual, only to realize that somewhere in her haste, she had left Friathri behind. Flushing, she said, "M-my apologies. It would seem my translator is… um…."

She looked around, hoping the translator from the previous shift was still present. However, when her eyes met Paskhalon's, he said, "I dismissed the fourth and first shifts. It's not like there's anything for them to do most of the time, and they only disturb my mornings with chitchat."

Frustration crossed Korena's thoughts she faced the rendeilxue again, replaced by surprise as she saw the bedridden man, who looked little more than a child with his youthful face, bright blue eyes, and small frame, smiling broadly. Motioning to Korena, the thane said, "You are the shield-maiden Iegam?"

Though she had read the report and knew of Witheric's correspondence with Aleukus, she still had not expected to hear her own tongue in his heavy accent. With another curtsy, she said, "I am, indeed. Korena Iegam at your service, sir thane. I am a guard in service to King Aleukus of Ithaenia."

A hint of gravity touched the emaciated man's thinned features as he said, "Yes. Restag tells me of your blood. It is true words to say it is a time for the old stories to live again. What it does mean, this I wonder."

The shadow passed from his face. "But, that is of no help to spin over now. It is much goodness to meet you, Korena Shield-Maiden. Hm? Why do you look to be… um… how do you say… of little understanding?"

Feeling a light flush as she cleared her throat, Korena said, "Pardon me, Thane Witheric. I had expected a… stronger reaction than this to knowledge of my bloodline."

"Should I have been stronger? And how to mean?" he replied, mirroring her confusion.

With a quick glance to Restag, she said, "Perhaps… horror, or maybe disgust. Thinking I am something from Halsk."

Witheric appeared shocked. "Why?" he said. "It is ill blood, yes, but even those of ill or lesser blood may prove of better word than the purest of your own line. And to the side, if you could be of Halsk, Restag would think no good of you. This I do not see."

Smiling self-disparagingly, Korena replied, "Forgive me, sire, but that may speak more of your thanesman's self-restraint than his true thoughts."

Witheric's brow furrowed, but as he began to respond, Friathri arrived in the doorway, panting heavily. Excusing herself, Korena went to her servant's side, supporting her and then pulling up a chair for the Asgradi woman. Friathri took a few moments longer to catch her breath before saying, "I apologize, Miss. It would seem old age is now above my pace and shall soon catch up to me."

Unlike Korena would have expected, it was not Friathri but Witheric who first gave a small, respectful bow of the two. In their own language, he said, "Greetings, Elder. For what reason am I honored by the presence of another's treasure-speaker."

"By fact of my mistress's thane's request for her to aid you, Thane Witheric of the northward Reinor-lands. For our shared speech, I, Friathri Tribeless, give her my service."

"Then your reaching us was well timed," he said. "I seem to have reached a wall in my understanding of your mistress."

Nodding, Friathri asked Korena what she had just said so she could translate it. Of course, that would mean Restag would understand it as well, and that fact made her hesitant. However, she gave a quick summary of the context and then her own words. The older woman gave Korena an odd look that made her uncomfortable and then said, "My mistress speaks lowly of herself, saying any good thoughts or lack of ill speech must be by virtue of your thanesman than herself."

Korena wished dreadfully she knew what Friathri had just said when Restag's eyes momentarily darted toward her own before returning to some kind of preoccupation with the book on Witheric's lap. In contrast, Witheric laughed amiably and said, "You speak too lowly, then. To speak truly, he does call you troublesome, and that is no small matter for he who may be called 'trouble's bane' with only little jest. However, it is no grave accusation, either, and that, too, is no small matter, with all considered. As for your own virtues," his hand brushed along the page open before him, and Korena noticed for the first time the detailed map his fingers traced, "I am told it was you who provided this of your own hospitality. It is a thane's gift, and no poor one at that. You reflect well upon your master with your judgment, care, and generosity."

Friathri flushed proudly as she translated the thane's words to her mistress. Korena, however, only felt disturbed. She had not meant for her actions to be representative of her king, and she felt afraid as every action and possible mistake she had made suddenly held more weight than she, a single citizen in a city of nearly a million, had ever thought to bear. Out loud, however, she put on her best, formal smile and said, "You speak very kindly, milord, far more than I, a mere servant of His Majesty, deserve, and I thank you for your generosity."

As Friathri translated, Korena felt another's eyes on her and found herself again looking toward Restag, who bore a crease between his sea-blue eyes that only seemed to deepen as she solidified that smile, so she looked away.

Witheric, too, had caught the exchange, just as he had caught notice of Restag's tension and feigned apathy. He had recognized the hints of irritation as he and Korena had spoken in Ithaenian, as well as the way his eyes had lost focus on the page the thanesman was supposedly studying as Friathri translated the young woman's words. Restag was wary of her, though not in the way of distrust or suspicion. This was a different kind, but he kept his curiosity to himself. Instead, he said, "I will admit, Friathri of Thenika, I had not expected to meet our own people here within the humans' walls."

"There are a few," replied the woman. "More and more, over my fifty years since coming here, most, like my family, having lost their tribes to the wars and seeking to prevent the complete draining of their bloodline. King Aleukus and his grandfather before him, both kind and wise, allowed those of us who do not bring our wars with us to live where he can watch us, though, again in his wisdom, he has kept the greater part of our people outside the walls, where any fights that do arise between those who refuse to leave them on the battlefield will not touch his people and can then be subdued.

"There have been horrors, as well, especially during the reign of the King Aleukus's father. More than once during his time, I stood on the wall top and witnessed soldiers drive Asgradi, even women and children, over the edge of the cliffs and into the sea, for the men refused to sheathe their swords stained with generations of blood, and there are many among the humans who are frightened of us and may kill one of us who have found peaceful work within the walls, lighting the fires of vengeance so that some of our own then go to collect the blood that is owed for the killing. In those moments, even should the king and the priests of the human god demand otherwise, many will side with their own rather than place true weights upon the scale, so that the human deaths are avenged but not the Asgradi. It is hard. Yes, it is hard. But not entirely unhappy.

"My family, mere beast-speakers of lesser power, has found a place as servants to one master or another and, at most times, does not need to fear as we walk the streets so long as we wear the sign of our masters on ourselves." She motioned to the pin on her clothing, one styled like the one Restag had refused to wear. "We have found masters who, though not true thanes of our own blood, nonetheless protect us as if they were and, indeed, treat us at times better than our own would. To them, we are not thralls, and they value our loyalty and abilities while also having no fear of our power due to their own. And so we still live, though we do dream, perhaps, to one day return to our true home."

Korena watched as the nursemaid she had known since infancy spoke words she could not understand but with feelings she could. As the older woman's voice faded into sorrowful silence, she reached out the place a gloved hand over the Asgradi woman's. Friathri smiled at the touch and said, "I am all right, Miss. Only speaking of the blood wars and the truth that man, whether full or half, cannot simply live in peace even with himself, let alone others."

Witheric nodded gravely. In his thick accent, he said, "It is much regretful to hear so much death does come from wars of ruling chasing a long-dead age."

A laugh sounded in Friathri's throat, and the old woman, continuing in Ithaenian for Korena's sake, said, "What an odd thing for an Asgradi thane to say. Are you not all warlords still? But, no. Perhaps... perhaps it is true. Perhaps there is hope for rest, at least for a time, among our people."

"Hope?" said Witheric, his tone catching Restag's attention.

"Yes," said Friathri, her voice and eyes growing hard. "Perhaps you have not heard, Thane Witheric, but there are rumors that arrived during your sleep. Whispers that say the direct line of the Eisenband has been cut."

Korena watched as Witheric's already pale face took a sickly shade. Kneeling beside her maid, she asked, "Eisenband? What's that?" Even in the reports, she had not encountered this term that appeared to hold great power.

A grim smile came over the old woman's face, and it disturbed Korena to see the woman she had long seen as an image of nurturing and comfort grow angry in gaze and tone as she said, "A spiteful, ruthless, poisonous line! A proud people who call themselves the Eisensaet, the Iron Seat, who have not blood but ice and iron in their veins. Long ago, they ruled many of our people. From the North Sea to the islands named the Dragon's Spine, to the borders of your human empire, they made thralls of free men and of free women whores. A wicked tribe who claimed the gods' favor and the right to rule all other tribes. For a thousand years they lorded over us, and for a thousand more if they'd had their way, for though their fall began now several centuries ago, and though they are by now stripped of their conquests, still they demand our submission, and still they feed and encourage and demand blood wars, setting tribe against tribe, brother against brother, reminding one tribe of another's unpaid debts, and always trying to regain their power and use our own fighting against each other for their gain.

"The last thane, Witheow Wolf's-Bane, was among the worst in our memory, a fierce warlord and slayer of foes, who called down the fire of the gods upon spear-man and household alike, even as they fled. At least, that is what I have heard, for, thankfully, my family was driven out by his father before him, who at least had some respect for our elders and children. Many feared Wolf's-Bane's second son would take the Eisenband, the symbol of their supposed claim to power, after him, and just as many rejoiced when father and spawn died in the same battle. However, the line was not yet drained, and it would seem the poison runs strong even in the weakest of their wicked line, for I have heard the thane who did follow dared claim for himself the title of Dar's-Mouth. Ha! Imagine, claiming for yourself the speech of a god, of the head of the gods. Further, despite stories of a weak body that forbade him from taking to the field himself, he still proved himself a warlord, winning battles and thwarting his enemies' attempts to finally free us of that tribe's yoke, aided by a warrior who had already earned the title Blood-Spear when he had barely entered manhood under Witheow's reign and who Dar's-Mouth named Thanesman after receiving the Band upon his brow. I cannot speak from my own witness, but I can say many times I have entered the servants' quarters late at night or spoken with my fellow Asgradi and heard fearful murmurings regarding these men and what might come of their joined strength."

Then, the anger turned to vengeful triumph. "But no longer. Word has reached us that the direct line of the Eisenband is now destroyed. Slain—and I hate to speak of it for its horror and its evil and unnatural nature—but the stories say the line of High Thane was cut by his own Thanesman."

"What!" Friathri and Korena both jumped at Witheric's outburst while Restag tensed and focused on his master, confusion and disturbance on his face. Even Paskhalon started from his work, his chair screeching on the tile floor, and Korena felt her breath catch at the blatant fury burning coldly in the young man's icy eyes. Witheric's boney fingers gripped his blanket as he said, "Say again. What do they say?"

Friathri paled as a dreadful possibility entered her mind. Trembling, she said, this time in Asgradi, "It… it is whispered that the High Thane of the Eisenband's direct bloodline has been ended by the hand of his own Thanesman in an attempt to claim the throne for himself. However, the evil was uncovered and condemned by the High Elders, who attempted to avenge the blood only for the thane-slayer to escape."

Based on the looks that came over both Restag and Friathri, Korena concluded that the outburst that followed from Witheric was beyond the pale. She even thought she saw sparks flash across the thane's fingers, followed by the smell of burnt wool, only for a coughing fit to hit the recovering man, summoning Paskhalon to the bedside with his own set of curses. In the next moment, before she could even ask what was wrong, the room spun around and she found herself pulled out the infirmary door, her wrist hurting from the strength of Friathri's grip. A good bit down the hall and several unheeded protests later, Korena managed to break free of the rendeilxue's hold. Holding her throbbing arm, she snapped, "What's wrong, Friathri? What happened? Why did you…?"

Rather than answer, the older woman tried to take hold of Korena again, but she backed away. "No! Explanation. Now. What happened?"

From between clenched teeth, the Asgradi replied, "I was reminded of the wisdom against fully believing rumors. I should have known it! From the start, I should have realized–a thanesman by name of Restag, hailing from the northlands–I should have drawn the lines, but I was a fool!

Exasperated, Korena cut in, "That's not helping. What should you have–"

"It's them!" Friathri snapped, the words venomous as an adder strike, making Korena flinch. "He, Witheric, is the High Thane of Eisensaet! Heir to the title Iron-Brow, and heir to the blood-debt of my people!"

It took several moments in the chill of that shadowed, stone corridor for the full meaning of Friathri's revelation to set in. "You mean… he's… and Restag is…."

"Yes. It would seem the truth is somewhat beside what has been told," said Friathri, a harsh laugh in her throat.

"But–but that would mean Restag was framed!" cried Korena.

"Worse than that," said Friathri, and as she spoke through her thoughts,

Korena watched an alien cruelty grow upon the woman's face. "Yes, much worse than that. He has been accused of the worst crime among our people–the murder of one's own master–and for the murderer to be the thanesman, the icon of loyalty among the tribe, makes the crime all the worse. Such slander makes him not only anathema to his own people but to all Asgradi, his name forever after a byword and a curse. Even those who would respect his skills and his virtues even as they hate his allegiance will have but contempt for him. Only honor could come from killing such a man on sight."

"That's horrible!" Korena gasped.

"It is justice!" countered Friathri. "For how could such a man ally himself with such wicked people and not meet anything but ruin. Yes. The scales of justice return to balance even if just a little. The treacherous, pure line of the Eisenband is assumed destroyed, and who should bear the blame but the man assumed to be the most virtuous of them all? It is poetry. The poetry of the gods written by the sins of man."

"But who would–"

Dismissively, Friathri said, "Oh, probably their Council of High Elders. Who else would frame the story with them as the heroes and could spread it with any authority?"

The more she heard, the more horrified Korena became. Feeling herself close to tears, she said, "How can you speak so coldly? How can you call this justice? They were betrayed, driven out, slandered! Restag, who anyone can tell just by watching him would never hurt his thane, let alone kill him, he's being accused of the worst murder in your laws. That's not justice! That's wicked!"

"It is both, for those who ally themselves with evil shall find themselves the prey to that very evil. Even your religion has examples of this," replied Friathri.

"But Witheric isn't evil! You were just talking with him. He was just sympathizing with you over the pointlessness of these wars and the death they've caused. That hardly seems like what you've been describing about his family," said Korena.

Scoffing, Friathri said, "It matters little. Likely, it was just a trick, a way to hide himself so that he, in his weakened state, would not be discovered. And even if those were his true thoughts, it does nothing to relieve the blood his predecessors have shed and what evil they have wrought. If he would insist on inheriting his father's crown and throne, he should inherit also his father's sins, the blood-debt owed to my family and the tribe he destroyed."

"But he wasn't the one who killed your family! Not even Restag, even fighting on the battlefield, he wasn't the one who–"

"Korena!"

Childhood reflexes reemerged, and Korena's mouth clamped shut. Friathri's bright eyes shone cold as she said, "They are murderers. Even if it was not their own hands that swung the sword, it was their father's or their father's father, and such a debt cannot be forgiven or repaid by pretty words and feigned feelings. This," she gestured back down the hall, "is the price of what they have done. They have ruined the houses of others, and now, their own houses lie in ruin. They have sown chaos and death, and now, chaos and death shall come to their people from both inside and out by wars of succession and those who recognize the time to strike. They have acted with disgrace, and now they are disgraced. Wallowing it in like the swine they are. And I shall be glad to let them."

Dread spread through Korena's veins. "This is wrong," it told her. "This, what I see before me, is wrong. Even if some of it is right, it's wrong. So very wrong!"

She shook her head. "No, Friathri. No. I won't listen to any more of this. I'm going back."

As she turned to go, however, Friathri took hold of her, hissing, "No! You will not! Do not join yourself to them, Korena. If the king insists on keeping them, let him. That is his business, but I shall not let your family be dragged down with them. When we return, I shall speak with your father, and you shall be removed."

Anger joined Korena's dread and revulsion, and she said, "You will do no such thing. You are neither my master nor my mistress, not even my mother. I have been given my duty by my king, and I shall do it, whether you like it or not."

Friathri's eyes narrowed till they resembled the edge of a knife. "You would bring ruin to your family?"

"I shall do what I believe is right," replied Korena. "And I will judge a man by his actions, not his pedigree. By his enemies, too, if they give any insight, and if this tribe is as evil as you say, then the fact that its elders have made themselves enemies of men who have so far shown themselves more virtuous than vicious, then I can hardly see that as a stain on their character."

Seeing the hurt and anger in the old woman's face dampened some of Korena's. With a sigh, she softened her voice. "I shall not demand you think the same way I do or that you forgive them. I shan't even ask you to stay, but I shall stay, even if it means you'll hate me. Release me, Friathri."

Another moment of angry silence cut between them. Then Friathri shoved away Korena's arm, causing the young woman to stumble back a few steps under the half-fae's strength. With a voice as cold and sharp as a steel blade, the woman said, "Very well. If that is your wish, then as a servant to your family, I shall respect it. However, know that I shall never support it. I shall only pray you come to your senses before it is too late."

Before Korena could respond, Friathri turned away and marched resolutely down the hall, disappearing without either a pause or the flicker of a glance back. Pain deeper and sharper than that in her wrist beat within Korena's chest, but she wiped away the tears gathering in her eyes and turned back the way she had come. When she again entered the room, this time in a much more subdued manner than before, she saw Witheric staring furiously at a cup in his hands. The book sat closed on a bedside table, and Paskhalon glared at her from his desk as she entered.

"Miss Iegam," he said, "it would be appreciated should you and your own not emotionally disturb my patient and cause him to nearly set my blankets on fire."

"I apologize, Paskhalon," she said. "I promise, it won't happen again."

The physician dismissed her then with the wave of a hand and went back to his work. Meanwhile, Korena gingerly approached the bed and took Friathri's vacated chair. Between his gaunt form, clenched jaw, and burning eyes, Witheric looked terrible, almost like some specter of death made flesh. Restag looked little better, in no small part from the bandages but also due to the emptiness of his expression, one which hurt the young woman more than she cared to admit. They both look like they wanted to cry but refused to do so. It showed in different ways, but she felt it to be the case.

"Are you okay?" she asked, though she knew the answer.

"No!" snapped Witheric with such violence it jerked Restag out from his daze as Korena flinched and flushed.

Korena fiddled with the tips of her glove's fingers. Quietly, she said, "I'm sorry. That was the wrong question. I apologize."

Witheric's skeletal fingers turned bone-white as he gripped the cup tighter, snarling "They are snakes! Vipers! Liars and oath-breakers and thane-slayers! Halskrad of Halskrad! Poison even to worms that should eat their flesh!"

As his voice tightened, Witheric began to tremble till the remaining contents of his cup began to swish against the vessel's inner wall. Wishing to prevent another coughing fit, or worse, another uncontrolled outburst of magic and whatever harm might come to his master, Restag firmly took hold of Witheric's shoulder and said, "Witheric, stop. You are not yet well. This will not–"

"They blamed you, Restag!" Witheric said, turning sharply to his friend. "They blamed you for their own crimes! And all because you did not betray me! Because you were loyal! For that they punish you, not only with exile but now with laying upon you the shame and vile stains of the darkest pits of Halsk while they claim for themselves your virtue! They are not fit even for the jaws of Halsk's hounds!"

"I know," said Restag, forcing his own voice to be level. "I know that, but… but we knew, Witheric. We knew what kind of creatures the Elders have become. We knew–I knew that to follow you would lead to no glory or honor, that I would be giving up everything. I knew that."

Witheric shook his head. "No, Restag. This is more. This is more than everything, at least in the way we understood. Restag, they have not even left you your name! Your honor, your respect! You… Restag, so long as they hold power, you can never go back! Never! They have even taken that from you. And all because… and it's all… all…."

Witheric blinked angrily, trying to rid himself of the sting in his eyes. Glaring at Restag and voice rising with each question, he said, "Why aren't you more angry? Why aren't you upset? You've been stripped of everything! Why? Why aren't you–why don't you…."

The questions, finished and unfinished, left Restag even more disturbed than before. Why wasn't he more angry? Of course he was angry. Why wasn't he upset? Of course he was upset. How could he not be? And yet, what was he to do about any of it? He knew he had not murdered his thane. But what of it? And what dreadful questions had Witheric dared not finish? The anxiety and uncertainty were beginning to lodge in his chest and throat, making it hard to breathe, when he suddenly felt a gentle touch on his arm that brought with it a startling silence that shocked him back into awareness. Korena had reached across the bed, her glove removed, and laid one hand on top of the arm resting in its sling while her other, still gloved, took Witheric's hand clenched around the cup. She caught Restag's eye with a lingering, worried look, before addressing Witheric. "Have you two eaten breakfast yet?"

"No solid food for the sick man," interjected Paskhalon. "His stomach is not ready for them and will not be for some weeks."

With a bright smile, Korena said, "Understood, sir. Is there anything you want me to bring back from the kitchens for you, Master Thane?"

"No," said Witheric.

Nodding, Korena stood and said, "All right, then, come along, Restag. Let's get something to eat. I'm quite hungry, and I'm sure you'll think and feel much better once you've eaten. Paskhalon, I shall leave Thane Witheric's care and sustenance to you."

While she spoke, Korena had come around the end of the bed and taken Restag's arm, aggravating his sore and bruised muscles from the day before as she pulled him to his feet. He yanked himself away, giving a questioning look to Witheric, who translated the exchange. At the thought of leaving his still upset friend and master, Restag began to protest only to be cut off by Witheric. "Go, Restag. She is probably right, and I… I need some time to think. Alone."

Even as he obeyed, Korena noticed Restag's irritation and kept a small distance from him as they walked down the hall, making their way to the dining area used by the castle guard. The three, room-length tables were nearly unoccupied, due to the late morning hour. Around this time, most anyone not on duty was either sleeping, as the late night-to-morning guards likely were, or training. Those lingering or wandering into the mess hall at this hour were usually either nursing a hangover or still waking up. The pattern appeared, at first, to hold true. However, then a voice called out to them, alerting every bleary-eyed guard in the room to Korena's presence. Several of the men appeared to suddenly become more alert and began hailing her only to pause as they noticed her companion. Only the original speaker continued waving, motioning for them to sit with him. Korena recognized him as one of the guards usually assigned to the late night shift, one Parchaes.

Korena approached the empty seats on the bench by Parchaes, taking note of the various bandages and bruises across his arms and the black and blue around one eye. As she spread her cloak on the seat, she said, "You're up earlier than usual. You look as though you lost a fight."

Laughing gaily, Parchaes replied, "Nope. Won most of them, actually. I did get suspended from duty, though, and got my pay docked, which was a bastardly thing to do. Not that I regret it. Did a good number on my opponent, too. Ain't that right, king's man?"

Restag took a seat and gave a respectful nod of greeting to Parchaes. Wide-eyed, Korena pointed to Restag's bandaged face and the arm in a sling, saying, "Did you do that?"

Parchaes grinned proudly.

"How are you still alive? Paskhalon must have been furious!"

After another laugh, Parchaes said, "Angry as the damned. But Restag's little king was nice enough to wake up before the doc could murder me. Came pretty close, too, with how long and loud he lectured us."

"I can imagine," said Korena. "By the way, could you keep him company while I get us some food? Make sure no one causes him any trouble?"

Winking, the guardsman replied, "Anything for you, Princess."

With an exaggerated roll of her eyes and poorly restrained smile, Korena turned to leave, only taking a moment more to tell Restag to wait there and hoping he understood. Restag did not watch her go, caught up in a mix of restlessness and irritation. He shouldn't be here. He should be by Witheric's side. Until then, their food had been brought to them. There was no reason for him to be here rather than by his distraught thane's side except that Witheric had told him to go. And that was the strangest part of all. Why had he been sent away? Surely anything Witheric had to think through he could share with him, as he had nearly every time before.

A conspiratorial noise made Restag flick his gaze across the table, where Parchaes whispered, "Lucky you, huh? Getting Princess Iegam all to yourself. She working her charm on you yet?"

The meaninglessness of Parchaes's chatter to his ears only made his irritation worse. He prepared to tune it out when, as if from the air, other men appeared around him and across the table. One even sat down beside him, throwing an uninvited arm over the Asgradi's shoulder.

The man's voice was tinged with envious teasing as he said, "Right there, Parchaes. How'd that happen? Eh? And why have you been hiding all this time in the sickbay when you could be sharing a welcome sight to us poor, hard-working soldiers? And all made up ladylike, too! I'd give up a month's wages to see her like that every day!"

Other voices chimed in, echoing similar sentiments. Restag understood none of it. He shoved off the man's arm, ignoring the annoyed response, and glared at Parchaes, figuring somehow what he had said had brought about this additional layer of frustration. Parchaes, however, seemed not only unrepentant but even amused by his response. And still the words pounded against him from every direction again and again and again.

He had left Witheric for this?

Concern for his thane pierced through his thinning patience, and Restag made all sight and sound of the dining room vanish as he used his magic, searching through halls and passing through walls till he finally found the familiar, dark stone of the old palace and from there the infirmary. He entered, and at once alarm heightened his attention as he heard the sound of sobbing from the room. Beside Witheric's bed sat Paskhalon, the closest Restag had ever seen to gentleness on the man's face, and curled up under the blanket lay the little thane. Between sobs occasionally came words, begging Restag's forgiveness.

Restag leapt to his feet, pushing the bench back and generating a round of surprised and angry exclamations from half a dozen men. Shame and fear and worry drained the blood from his face while the suddenness of his returned senses and his standing brought both pain and dizziness and made him lose his balance. He caught himself against the table, gasping in more than one kind of pain as his mind tried to understand what he had seen and where he was and what was happening.

"Restag!" came a familiar voice, followed by a loud clutter of clattering as Korena roughly placed a serving tray laden with food and a pair of cups on the table and rushed through the line of men that parted for her. She came up to his injured arm and helped steady him as he stared dumbly at the table. Glaring around her, she demanded, "What happened? What did you do?"

One of the men held up his arms in a gesture of innocence. "Nothing, Miss Iegam. Just some light teasing. Honest."

Korena looked to Parchaes, who nodded. Beneath her hands, she felt Restag trembling and his rapid pulse. She heard his breath grow ragged, and his eyes darted over the wooden surface in mounting distress. Taking a gentle hold on his injured arm, she said, "Restag? Restag, what's wrong?"

The Asgradi's eyes jumped toward her voice, and the anguish she saw within them made her breath catch. It was only by reflex that her grip on his arm tightened as he tried to dash away, nearly knocking her over while simultaneously jerking him back with a pain-filled cry from the force placed upon his injured arm. After several gasps, he stared furiously at her, snapping something that she guessed was a command to let him go. A sense of apprehension, similar to when facing Friathri earlier, filled Korena, and she shook her head.

Restag did not like that, and he gave his command again, trying to free himself from her, despite the pain it caused him. Korena held on tighter, shaking her head and saying, "No. You need to stay. Sit down."

"Let me go!" growled Restag. "I must–I have to–Witheric–"

"Restag-Thanesman, sit down!"

The force of the woman's tone stunned all those present. Blankly, Restag blinked down at the woman staring up at him with angry concern. Pointing firmly at the bench, she repeated, "Sit. Down."

He obeyed, more by habit than by will. Korena sat beside him, one arm still locked with his like a chain link. She spoke to one of the men around them, and the man brought over the tray she had left, placing it before her. Taking a roll of bread, she held it out to Restag. "Now, eat."

Restag stared at the food as if he did not know what it was or what to do with it. His mind was still tangled in on itself, trying to understand something he did not know how to deal with, something he knew he should not have seen. As he did, the cracks in his calm caused by the stress and distress widened and lengthened. Something he knew but had not let himself fully understand was beginning to sneak through. Witheric was upset, even more upset than he was. He was crying, sobbing like a child in pain, in a way Restag could not help him with. But why? From what? Why was he crying? And why did he ask forgiveness from one who was not there to give it?

Restag's eyes widened as the full weight wrapped itself around him, squeezing him like a snake. He looked at Korena, unable to hold back the trembling in his voice as he whispered, "I can't go home."

Though she could not understand the words, Korena understood the plaintive tone. Swallowing the lump forming in her own throat, she took Restag's good hand and placed the roll in it. "Eat," she said gently. "It'll help."

Restag glanced from the roll back to her and began, "Witheric–"

"Paskhalon will take care of Witheric," Korena said. Pointing again to the food, she said, "You need to take care of yourself. You've had a hard morning, and you're injured and, I suspect, tired. Eat, Thanesman. You need to become strong again, for both of you. And for that, you need food."

The thanesman followed the woman's pointing and hesitantly took a bite. It was tasteless, but the moment he began, his body remembered its needs and urged him on. Soon he finished the roll and moved on to slowly spooning some kind of porridge sweetened with fruit and honey into his mouth, washing it down with warm milk. A few times, the guardsmen tried speaking or asking something, but Korena quieted them.

As soon as he was finished, she helped him to his feet and led him from the room and out into the palace halls. They wandered a while in silence, Korena's arm now wrapped around his good one, going from what seemed endless hall to endless hall, the decorative walls and ceilings and architecture a blur to him. Eventually, he found himself outside in one of the many gardens, the cool air, open sky, and bright sun refreshing to his face and lungs. They had passed by a few trees with branches bending with fruit, a marvel to him for this time of year, when a small, ragged sigh brought his eyes down to his escort's face. At some point, quiet tears had fallen from Korena's eyes. The sight made him stop, and she looked up at him in surprise. She blinked and, as if noticing them for the first time, wiped the tears away with the corner of her scarf.

"I'm sorry," she whispered, even knowing that without Friathri she may as well be talking to herself. Yet she felt the need to speak. "I didn't mean to cry. It's just… it's so unfair! Why are you being blamed for everything? Friathri, the ones who betrayed you, why are they throwing all the blame on you? It's not… it's just…."

She finished with another angry sigh, and Restag watched her, the anger and sorrow she expressed somehow easing Restag's own suffering soul. Then he noticed a strange peace within himself, an unfamiliar quietness that somehow lent its own aid to the calming of his spirit, and he realized it was the quieting of his fairy blood, brought on by Korena's absent-minded hold on his arm. It was an odd thing to notice, to discover in that moment of agony what it meant that her gift was named not only Slayer but also Sleeper, and to experience the rest that could come from that same sense of absence that had so disturbed him many times before. He felt no need to see beyond himself or his present place, no drive to know what might stand beyond immediate sight or sound, no temptation to discover the secret workings of another's mind. It was quiet. The quiet of a moment suspended in solitude.

By the time they finished their round through the garden and made it back to the infirmary, Korena's tears had stopped, and she had tidied herself as well as she could using her reflection in a small pond such that she looked nearly as she had before they left the room. Witheric once again had his book open and was flipping through the pages too quickly for him to be reading them. He looked up, and, like Korena, most signs of crying had disappeared, though the exhaustion still showed. Smiling weakly, he welcomed them back as Korena released Restag to go to his master while she spoke with Paskhalon.

"You were gone a long time," said Witheric with feigned lightness.

"We went on a walk," replied Restag.

To which Witheric replied, "Yes, I guessed as much…. I would also guess that Friathri will not return. It seems my ambitions are truly greater than even our first fathers, or perhaps even the gods, could have dreamed."

He laughed in his throat, but that laughter soon died as he looked into Restag's guilt-weighted eyes. Quietly, ashamedly, Restag said, "I am sorry, Witheric. I was worried for you, and I… I saw. Forgive me."

It took a moment for Witheric to understand, and one more for the color to rise to his face. His own eyes dropped, and he let out a deep sigh. He said, "No, Restag, Forgive me. I… I truly have ruined you. Forgive me. Forgive me."

Restag shook his head. "There is nothing to forgive, Witheric. And if there were, it would be already given."

Witheric tried to thank his friend, but the words seemed too heavy for his tongue. A long quiet stretched between them, disturbed only by the quiet speaking between Korena and Paskhalon. Equally as quietly, Restag said, hesitantly, "She… knew, Witheric."

Meeting his master's questioning gaze, Restag continued, "She knew what you needed, what I needed. She recognized it when I could not."

A small smile pulled at the thane's lips, and his eyes drifted to the young woman still in conversation with the doctor, the one who had pulled the two of them apart at the border of collapse, giving them both a chance to grieve away from the other's sight. "Yes. It would seem so," he said. "It is a mysterious power women have, to recognize without words hidden meanings and secret signs we may not have said or even meant, for better or for worse."

Restag snorted. "Are you now claiming mastery of womanhood? Claiming for yourself experience and knowledge hidden to men?"

The smile turned mischievous as Witheric responded, "I have more experience and hidden knowledge than you, Restag-Thanesman, even with your Soul-Sight."

The comment made the swordsman flush, and at last Witheric's laugh was real and, even, a touch happy. It also caused Restag's eyes to drift thoughtfully toward the young woman, the kohl at the edges of her eyes slightly smudged, and her brown eyes looking intently over some note in Paskhalon's book as her lips responded to his prompting, speaking words whose incomprehensibility made him oddly irritated.

Witheric caught that momentary flash of frustration and followed his friend's gaze to its object. Suspicions began to form in the young thane's mind, but he was too tired to pursue them further. As Korena thanked Paskhalon and began making her way over, Witheric put away those thoughts for now and said, "By the way, Restag, you said something about a 'book room'?"

Chapter 11

Winter progressed. Compared to his companion, Witheric was slow to recover, perhaps because the sickness had been worse for him, perhaps because he had always been the physically weaker of the two, perhaps because of both. He developed fevers with enough frequency that Paskhalon still checked in every morning and evening to give him medication and track his health. Even so, the thane was able to climb out of bed with support before the new year began. Two months later, though he still couldn't walk by himself and there was little he could carry or hold due to the deterioration of his muscles, it was better than Paskhalon had expected of him by that time, and he banished the patient from the infirmary as soon as he could sit without support. He began to fill back out, as well, once given permission to eat full, solid meals, and though still unhealthily thin, he no longer looked like too much skin stretched over bones as he sat in bed, pretending to flip through a dictionary while actually listening to Restag struggling to read the last words of a passage Korena had written out for him.

The two sat at a work desk pulled from against the wall to near the bed. It was the same guest room Aleukus had prepared for Restag months before, only Restag had insisted Witheric be given the bed while he set up his own sleeping arrangements in the sitting room just next door. Their frugal belongings had been transferred into a single chest, though both Korena and Aleukus had provided a fuller wardrobe for the two men, who now wore the buttoned, high-necked vests and loose shirts that was the common fashion of the day more often than their own clothes. If not for their pointed ears and lithe bodies, they might have even passed for humans, albeit with uncommonly light hair and eyes for that region. That is, until they opened their mouths and their thick, rough accent wrapped itself around the light, clattering syllables of Ithaenian, turning them into a rock slide of words and phrases that grated against the unaccustomed ear. Korena, however, had come to rather like it from the days and weeks speaking with Witheric and helping Restag as she was now.

"'...and they weren otra—were not rain but r-rays of li-leeg-h-t....'"

"'Light,'" corrected Korena. "That word says 'light.'"

Restag looked distastefully at the script. "Not drawn to look as that," he said.

Laughing, Korena replied, "Well, what would you expect? Weren't you the one who said Ithaenian spelling is as bent as its letters?"

The edges of a restrained laugh escaped Witheric's throat, gaining him a long side-eye before Restag turned his eyes back to the paper. He sought out where he had left off and continued, "'Not rain but rays of light like stars fall-fall...falling to… to....'"

He pointed to the last word. "I know not that."

"That one says 'earth,' and you have seen it. It's just been a while. Sorry. I probably should have brought that one up again," said Korena. She took the paper from him, circling all the words and phrases he had struggled with, saying after she finished, "You're doing very well, though. Amazing, actually."

A scoff sounded in the rendeilxue's throat. He scowled and said, "It goes too slow."

Korena gave him a long, indignant look. "No, Restag," she said. "I have a hard time believing you never studied Ithaenian before with the progress you've made!"

True, he was nowhere near the self-taught Witheric (whose growth on his already impressive skills was a wonder in its own right), and Korena also knew how Restag spent much of his free time—outside physical exercise—in study and practice. However, while his speaking and reading skills were still very rough, and grammar did not seem to exist in his mind, his listening comprehension over the past couple months had grown incredibly, and he could usually slap together some chimera of words and gestures to get his thoughts across. Poking his forehead, which now bore a long scar that ran from his cheek to his hairline, Korena pouted and said, "In fact, I'd appreciate it if you'd be a little less competent. It's frustrating to see how far you've gotten and compare it to my lack of progress in Asgradi."

Restag looked at her with an expression that said either he didn't understand her or she had said something insane, or maybe both. On the other hand, Witheric dropped any pretence of reading to say, "I fear it is not possible to him.

When he knows his goal, he will not stop till it is his. Also, though he seems to be of humbleness, in truth, he loves to show off to certain people."

"Certain people?" said Korena. Witheric merely grinned in response, and further inquiry was interrupted when Restag took hold of her wrist to pull it and the pen in her hand away from his face. That was another thing. At some point during the past two months, he had stopped flinching from or avoiding her touch. Sometimes, she even wondered if he was, in fact, using circumstance to touch her, though she immediately chided herself for such ridiculous thoughts. And yet, the idea persisted, much to her secret embarrassment.

"You're making a joke of me again, aren't you," he asked Witheric.

"Maybe," replied Witheric, the grin still in place.

Narrowing his eyes, Restag said, "You seem well-pleased with yourself, Dar-Speech. But I shall soon enough unveil your secret runes."

A playful light flashed in Witheric's eyes, and he replied, "You would challenge the gods, then, Far-Sighted, to look upon their secrets? For what cause could such a hero's quest be taken on? Or for whose?"

Deep, olive green filled Restag's cheeks, and he cursed himself for giving Witheric such an easy opening. Ever since the day they had learned of the Elders' final treachery and Friathri had abandoned them—no, even before that, just more consciously so after—Restag had found his eyes wandering more and more to the young woman who had stayed behind. At first, he told himself that it was simply for practical reasons. After losing Friathri, Witheric had insisted on being translator during Korena's time with them, saying he wanted to improve his own skills. Overall, it had worked out well, but because of Witheric's weaknesses and lack of experience in actual conversation, Restag had found it helpful to watch Korena's body language in order to better understand what she was saying. He told himself that his attention was only for this reason. However, as his own understanding grew, and as she worked with him and began speaking with him, rather than through Witheric or someone else, telling him about Thenika or things she wanted to do once Witheric was well enough or about her own life and listening to him try to speak about his, he found it harder to keep telling himself the same. Especially when Witheric had noticed and decided to make the idea near impossible to uphold. A stray comment here, a tease there, the subtle lift of his brow and amused curve of his mouth, all chipped away at the mental barrier Restag was struggling to maintain.

He stared daggers at Witheric, who anyone else might have assumed to be the soul-sighted of the two with the expression he now wore. Just as a retort formed on his tongue, Witheric said, "You, of anyone, could make the journey faster, should you choose it."

The thane tapped his brow meaningfully. The idea had crossed Restag's mind many times before. More than once, he had felt the urge to use his power to touch another's mind, to see the meaning intended by a word or phrase, or to see the answer to a question. However....

He sighed and said, "No. I shall not. Should Wyrdi prompt necessity, that is the time for such a thing, but to touch upon another's soul and expose its hidden thoughts for such a reason... No. I will not do it."

Pride filled Witheric's eyes. Returning to his book, the bedridden thane said, "No. You would earn what you will have, even if it should cost years of seeming fruitlessness, of hopeless dedication. But, in the end, it shall be yours, whatever you seek." A grimness passed quickly over Witheric's face, and he said, "It's a good thing you hold pride in your restraint, Restag, and that your mind is quick but not crafty. Or else nothing would be safe from you."

Then, the shadow left, and Witheric said in Ithaenian, "Korena, could you tell me what is this meaning? It makes as little sense to its word."

Pushing aside the curiosity and frustration she had felt as the two men spoke Asgradi to each other, Korena approached the bed and looked at the dictionary lying open beside the book Witheric was reading. The dictionary had been Korena's gift to him, and she had been most pleased at his wonder that such a book, whose practicality even Restag could not dispute, should exist. She had been less satisfied with Restag's gift, which had been merely to request of the king permission for the thanesman to resume wearing his sword outside the training grounds, on account of his duty as Witheric's bodyguard, and to provide him a whet stone and blade oil recommended by the palace weapons' master. He had seemed far more grateful than such a small thing deserved, and Witheric insisted that Restag was, in fact, overjoyed by her actions and simply did not show it well, but she still wished she could have gotten a similar reaction from him as from his master. She did wonder, though, if she had given it to him now, with another two months of nearly daily watching him if she would catch those too often subtle signs of the swordsman's happiness.

"Which word are you wondering about?" she asked.

"This one," said Witheric, pointing it out.

"Philosopher?" she said, reading through the academic definition with a frown. She nodded. "Sometimes the people who make these books forget the wholeness of the word for the sake of exactness. Let's see. 'Philo' means 'love,' and 'sophie' means 'wisdom,' which in Asgradi might be what you mean by 'Dar's-Speech.' So, a 'philosopher,' at least a real one, is someone who loves wisdom and is trying to gain more by understanding the nature of the world."

"Oh! What a beautiful word this is, philosopher!" said Witheric. "But what do you mean by 'real' philosophers?"

"There are many people who claim that title and use the tools of philosophy not because they love wisdom but in order to have an excuse for their own ill deeds, or even to try to destroy wisdom herself by twisting words against their own meaning. This second group once called themselves sophists, and even there you can see the kinds of people they are. Even though they named themselves after 'sophie,' after wisdom, they are liars who will argue that an oath is not an oath and a bond is not a bond and yes means no, now means never, good means evil, and evil means good, just so long as it benefits them or lets them do what they want," she replied.

The thane's eyes flashed angrily, and he laughed harshly before saying, "Another useful word, this 'sophists.' Yes, perhaps I, as well, have to known such men. A true-word is not chained to the land of its birth-tongue."

A knock sounded on the outside door, and Korena quickly stepped aside as she opened the door to King Aleukus. He greeted her as he entered, as did Leskinor and another man, one with a similar stockiness to the king's and the same dark curls and gray eyes, who Korena recognized as Prince Aganectus. She had just enough time to get past her surprise at the royal party when they entered Witheric's room, the thane greeting them cheerily and Restag bowing.

After waving away the offer of a chair, Aleukus said, "I apologize for visiting so early. My brother here has been emphatically expressing his desire to meet you, and I'm afraid he has little time to spare."

Witheric gave an understanding nod before the king continued, "Then allow me to present to you my younger brother, Prince Aganectus, captain of the City Guard. It was his men who acted as translators before now, as part of the Guard's duties is mediating conflicts between the rendeilxue and Ithaenians, as well as keeping the peace between the different rendeilxue peoples living here."

Bowing as well as he could from the bed, Witheric said, "It is well-met, Lower Thane Aganectus. Your two-tongued soldiers have proved very much of help to my thanesman. For this, I have many thanks."

A pause came over the room, one that had just begun to reach an awkward length when Aganectus's eyes narrowed, and he said, "Did you just insult my men?"

Witheric blinked in confusion and said, "No. I did not think to be so." Looking to Korena, he said, "Did I?"

From beside the king, Leskinor struggled to hold back a grin as he said, "It's a misunderstanding, sir. The Asgradi use 'tongue' to mean 'language.' 'Two-tongued' means 'speaks two languages,' not double-tongued or deceptive. It was a compliment, not an insult."

"Oh," said Aganectus. Smiling broadly, he said to Witheric, "Sorry about that. Thought you might just be another little guy who likes throwing insults. You know how it is."

He released a series of bellowing laughs while both Witheric, this time joined by Restag, turned once again to Korena, eyes speaking confusion. Under her breath, she said to them, "It's just the kind of person he is. Just… pretend he's river rapids: you just have to go along with it and not hit the rocks."

"Ah," came Witheric's answer, while Restag simply nodded. What each meant exactly, Korena didn't know, nor did she get the chance to ask as Aleukus cleared his throat to say, "May I remind you, Aganectus, that we are in the presence of foreign royalty, and you are expected to act as such." He gave a glance to Korena, making her flinch and flush.

A confused look came over Aganectus, and then his eyes widened and he said, "You mean this little guy is the barbarian king?" He looked Witheric over. "Isn't he a little small?"

Korena quickly placed a warning hand over Restag's as it jumped up to rest on his scabbard, his face tinged olive green. Witheric, however, smiled amiably and replied, "I fear all our people should seem that way to you, King's Brother. We do not grow so thick as your people. It is not for the sword to resemble the shield in width, though they may still have their own strengths."

"Ha! True enough," said Aganectus. He motioned to Aleukus. "Like my brother and me. He's better at king stuff, so it's a good thing he was born first."

"Yes. It is good fortune that it was so," replied Witheric.

"I mean, can you imagine? Me? King? Ha!"

"It is a most frightful image to behold, indeed."

Stepping in before the line of conversation could progress further, Aleukus said, "Indeed. You are not, and, as I said before, you are very busy."

Nodding gravely, Aganectus said, "Yeah. Those 'Like Gard' bastards can't seem to stop taking insult over every little thing. Like a pot of angry bees, those guys."

The change that came over the two Asgradi was strong enough to both see and feel. Restag's grip tightened on the scabbard, and Witheric's face grew troubled as he said, "'Like Gard'? Are you meaning the Leikgaard tribe?"

Before Aganectus could say anything more, Aleukus silenced him with his hand and said, "You know them?"

Witheric nodded. "Very much. For many fathers and sons, my people have slain and been slain of them. They are a troublesome line, so see everything that gets in their way as a blood-debt, even if the beginning offence is their own."

"Yes, we have seen that ourselves," said Aleukus. "We have yet to actually see blood, at least on the scale you describe, but we have had to break up individual conflicts, and any push back against what they want is treated as an insult. Tell me, Asgradi High Thane, how would you deal with them?"

"Drive them out," Witheric replied immediately, earning raised brows. "Every one of them, to leave not a one in your land. Even if have not shed blood, man or woman or child, he is to be thrown out, and all who would not cut all ties with him."

Aganectus's brows furrowed, and he said, "That seems a little much, doesn't it? I mean, it's not like they're all troublemakers."

Witheric shook his head. "It is not understood. They are not... they are not philosophers. They do not think to know Dar-Speech. They do not care to be good guests, to make themselves as much like their hosts and cause as little problems. They do not think to know that another's home is not their own and to not have all they want as they want or even to remember a kindness when before them stands an injury. They think only of blood and vengeance. For to imagine, if they were to know of me and of Restag, they would tear down every stone of Thenika if it were to kill us. Even you, High Thane Aleukus. If you again and again stop them from claiming debts for insult or past bloodshed, they shall count your blood as debt, as well. No. They must be driven out till all are dead or disappeared from the land."

A chill settled over the room. Into that chill came Aganectus's confident laugh followed by, "Seems you're still a barbarian, huh? Only an idiot would try to destroy a city just to get one or two guys they don't like, especially Thenika. She's made of strong stones. Very strong, and my men wouldn't let it happen.

Speaking of, I need to go take a look at them. Who knows what trouble they'd get into without me."

Numerous retorts to this abrupt statement and departure went through several minds, none of which were spoken as the captain bowed and left the room. In contrast, Aleukus's face looked grave. "These are ill tidings you give, Witheric High-Thane. And not something that would be met well among the people here. We are not, by nature, lovers of war, and many still live who witnessed the bloodshed of my father's time. To see a whole people slaughtered or driven out, whether or not each individual has committed a crime is… distasteful, to say the least."

Witheric shook his head, saying, "Yes. It is regretful. Perhaps it is to keep me from being part of the glory of the Final Battle, and perhaps you may say it is strange of me, but I, too, do not seek war and wish all could be forgiven without bloodshed. And yet, Valaka shall come and go as he should wish. Even someone as myself can see that some do not listen to fine words but only to strong arms and the sword's edge. Some can only be kept in their own lands if there is to be peace."

A grim smile tugged at the king's lips. "This visit has become like all those books arguing political theories my teachers assigned in my youth." He let out a long sigh. "Very well. I shall take your words into consideration. However, I will say, to counter your point, this is not the first warlike people to be seen in history, and there are examples of such people turning from their ways, in time or with the right guidance. Even you, Witheric Iron-Brow, are an example of the potential of a people you admit yourself desires war and bloodshed."

Witheric sat in silence for a time before saying with another shake of his head, "I cannot say what it to be possible, for only Dar knows all such things. But if such things can be to happen, it is neither of human nor of fae nor of Asgradi to bring it to be."

The king's face softened, and he said, "On that, we are in agreement, little philosopher king. But enough of such heavy things. I did wish to see how you are doing. Have you both been treated well? I have heard… interesting complaints from the training grounds, about bruises and aches in places the men didn't even know could hurt so much."

A flash lit Witheric's eyes. "Yes, my thanesman proves himself to be quite recovered, I think. He is worthy of his name, is he not?"

"Indeed," said the king. "And what of you?"

"I am well cared for," Witheric replied. "There is much attention, and much to fill my time. And I am most grateful every day to be proven right about your friendship, even in the ill-nature of our exile."

Gesturing to Restag, Aleukus replied, "I'm glad you are comfortable. Though, I must say, I fear my own virtue is but a pale light compared to the one you have beside you."

"Yes," said Witheric, his eyes growing distant. "Yes. Next to him, the treasures hordes of every dragon be but worthless trinkets."

The king nodded and then shifted his attention. "And what of you, Miss Korena Iegam? Are you still sure you wish to remain at this post?"

With the two rendeilxue now familiar faces to the guards and their assigned servants, most of the soldiers and dampeners had chosen to return to their regular shifts. As Witheric's linguistic abilities increased, even the translators were no longer necessary. Only Korena and Leskinor insisted on remaining on a job that most had grown to regard as little better than babysitting.

Korena had not expected the question to a matter she considered closed. Fumbling with her thoughts, she said, "Yes, your Majesty. I'm quite occupied and busy and in no need to be given something else. It's quite interesting. And besides, if I left, who else would tutor Restag?"

Aleukus glanced at Leskinor, who was clearly holding back a smile, and said dubiously, "Yes. Who else, indeed." Turning to back to Witheric, the king said, "And what of you? Does my Nullifier's presence bother you? Or her... nature?"

Korena's heart caught in her throat. She hadn't even considered what it might mean, politically, for a king to keep someone with her powers near his guests, as if he did not trust them even after so many months. Witheric, however, replied cheerily, "Oh, Korena is good to have. It is more... less dragging of time, and she is very helpful. She just said to me just now of philosophers and sophists, and they are very good and useful words."

Hiding his own amusement, Aleukus turned next to Restag. "And you, Thanesman?"

Restag frowned irritably. He had not been able to keep up with the conversation for a while, and to be asked something when he didn't know what he was under discussion... However, once Leskinor quickly summarized the conversation for him, he gave a suspicious look to Witheric's interested gaze and said, "She is of much use and has much to say."

None of the humans knew how to take that, but Witheric nodded sagely and said, "Yes, and she has promised to show us many more things. It would not be good, then, for her to go yet, or it would not be true-speech."

The king watched as Restag picked up his papers and straightened them, despite their already crisply aligned edges. Curiosity, however, surrendered to the delicacy of politics, and he let any questions fall to the side for the time being. Nodding to the book on Witheric's lap, he said, "And I see–and hear–that you have been making good use of my library."

Proudly and carefully lifting up the volume from his lap, the thane replied, "Very so. Now, I near the last of this book, but Korena says it is only part one. Soon, I shall be in need of the next."

"Oh, I can–ah, that is, shall I pick that up for you, sir? I need to return a few volumes myself," said Korena, placing herself in parade rest before nodding to a small stack on Restag's desk. "If there are any others you wish for me to check for, I can do that, as well."

Witheric replied, "Yes, that would be helpful. Restag."

The thanesman pulled out a blank sheet of paper and took up Korena's pen, jotting down a few titles his master gave him. Despite Paskhalon's best efforts, the thane's dominant hand still shook terribly if he tried to grip a pen, and it seemed increasingly doubtful that he would ever again be able to use it for any dexterous or detailed tasks. It had been a deep enough blow to send the young man into shock for a whole morning. However, Restag had responded with additional effort to master the 'Ithaenian runes.' While his notes might not be technically correct in spelling, they usually conveyed the sounds close enough that Korena could decipher them. Except when, in moments of indecision or forgetfulness, he resorted to an equivalent-sounding symbol in Asgradi, making his writing an interesting code of firm, angular Asgradi and crisp, curving Ithaenian legible only to himself. The first time he saw it, Leskinor joked that if he wrote out a key, the City Guard would never have to worry about intercepted messages ever again. The other consequence of his writing style was that whenever Witheric wanted a book, he and Korena almost always went together, as only he could read his notes and only she, of the two of them, could read the spines to find the matching sounds.

Picking up the book Witheric currently had, Korena noted the translator and exact title. When she tried to hand it back, however, Witheric, only paying half attention, habitually reached out with his damaged hand and lost his grip. With mutual yelps, both reflexively grabbed at the book, both catching it mid-fall.

"I am sorry, Korena. I did not think...," Witheric flushed, angry and ashamed at the persistent weakness.

Korena began to excuse him, noticing in the middle, however, her bare hands touching his. She looked up to apologize, only for the words to catch in her throat as Witheric took the book from her and said, "Forgive me, High Thane Aleukus. I have come near to harming part of your word treasure."

"No offense and no apology required," said the king. "I know a near-accident when I see one, and if a book gets damaged, at least it's from use rather than sitting gathering dust on a shelf, however mad it might make the librarians."

Witheric let out a genuine, light-hearted laugh and said, "You are true generosity, King of Thenika. Though, perhaps I do now ask too much generosity of you, for I am wishing to speak of something, if there is time for you."

"I have a little more for my guest, if he should need it," said the king.

"Good," said the thane with a nod. To Restag he then turned and said, "Then that is enough to look for, if you will."

Restag gave a quick bow and turned to call Korena only to hesitate at the troubled expression on her face. How it came to be, he could not guess, but he disliked how she forced out her formal smile to reclaim a veneer of normalcy. As they closed the door to the guest room behind them, he half-expected her to begin speaking her thoughts, but she remained silent the entire walk to the library. She did not see the disgusted look the librarian gave them when he saw them and would have forgotten to return her own book to the room's guardian had Restag not reminded her. She appeared normal enough once they began searching through the collection, checking Restag's list and pulling and replacing books till they managed, after a good half hour, to locate nearly half the list within the large, and largely disorganized, collection. It had been an irritation of Restag's from the start how hard it was to find anything, but the king apparently kept his most referenced books in his study, and the librarians seemed more intent on keeping the books "safe" than making it easier for people to disturb the mess. The lack of order did have the small benefit that Korena found by accident a few tomes she had meant to read and one she even thought might be good for Restag to use for practice, such that when they left again under the even darker glare of the librarian, each carried a small armful of the volumes that, until recently, would have been seen as a luxury to the Asgradi but had now become almost an ordinary part of life. When he took the time to think of it, the sheer slope of change he had undergone felt nearly overwhelming.

As they came back out into the hall, Korena fell back into silence. It was not until they were once again within the nearly abandoned halls of the older palace that she stopped, silently drawing his attention. She looked at him, took a deep breath, made a false start, anything it seemed to keep from speaking her thoughts. Finally, however, she took another shaking breath, her eyes reflecting the dim, oil lamps in their troubled depths, and said in a voice small and alien to her, "Restag?"

The whole performance took the man aback, and all he could manage was a disturbed, "Yes?"

She hesitated again, as if about to say something that should not be said. Then, in that same small voice, she spoke in the Asgradi she so struggled with. "Witheric's gift… small?"

She flushed ashamedly, but Restag could not discern why. His confusion must have shown, as she went on, more rapidly than before, "I-I touch. I touch, but… but no see."

Korena held up her hand as if to illustrate, and as he stared at it, he remembered her own gift, including how she could discern with certainty the strength of his blood, the same blood that now drained from his face as he realized her meaning. Korena watched as the books dropped from Restag's arms and jumped with him as they slammed loudly against the stone floor. She, however, recovered before he did and quickly bent over to pick them up, using the motion to avoid his shocked expression. Trying to keep the trembling in check as she felt her own, terrible suspicions confirmed, she said, "S-sorry! I'm sorry. I shouldn't… that's, I mean, it's not really… just never–forget I–"

Her breath caught as Restag's hand suddenly settled on top of hers. She did not want to look up, knowing if she did there would no going back, no asking him to forget. However, when his voice whispered her name, she felt her eyes drawn up till they lay captured by his, those blue orbs filled with disquiet, like the very sea they resembled, and he said, "Say again."

She had meant to keep the idea a secret incase of passersby, but as she knelt there on the floor, her thoughts racing and trying to fit themselves together, all Asgradi fled from her chaotic mind. She said, "I… when I touched him, just now… he… he didn't seem to notice. At all. Restag, he didn't seem to feel anything at all!"

She had not considered the possibility before, when she had touched them both two months before in the scaling heights of emotion, doing the only thing she could think of to shock them enough to listen. The thane had seemed surprised enough, but perhaps that had just been the usual reaction of one caught off guard. Since then, she had not actually touched him, her bare skin to his, that she could remember. Had no way to counter the hypothesis that seemed to become closer to theory at every moment.

A heavy silence followed. Then Restag took the books from her and held out a hand to pull her up. Even after she stood, however, he held that grip a moment longer, as if to confirm something, and spoke in a voice both soft and serious, explaining as well as he could in her language how Witheric had been born sickly, often brushing against Halsk's Gates from the moment of his birth. Many in the High Council had argued that he was not worth keeping, that his flesh was too weak and would only be a danger to the tribe, the weak link that would break the chain. Some, however, noted the reach of his Blood Mark and the promise it showed for a gift of great power, one too great to lose. Days of debate had followed, and in the end, those who argued for his Mark won out. He was permitted life, and by the time the Mark proved a false sign, it was too late. He was too old, for to kill him would now be to kin-slay. All that those involved could do was rue the choice they had made that day.

The guest room had settled into such silence that Witheric could almost hear the dust fall around him. He wished he had not given his visitors the faces he had in their conversation, and he hoped what the arrangement they had discussed would not come into play. But it had been necessary. His fingers traced the imprints on the leather binding on the book on his lap as he stared at the ceiling, revisiting the conversation, turning over the contents and the king's and Leskinor's uneasiness at what he said. Yes. He wished he could have done otherwise, but....

"But I am Thane, and all must be accounted for, as much as can be," he said to himself. All accounted for, and all preparations made in case–

His thoughts were broken as the door to the bedroom opened, admitting Restag and Korena, their hands full of books. Putting aside his own troubles for now, he greeted them happily only for his thoughts to again stop prematurely as Korena rushed across the room, dropped her books on the bed, and suddenly wrapped her arms around him, sobbing into his shoulder.

After recovering from the shock, Witheric felt a confused flush fill his cheeks as he tried to ask her what was wrong only to be responded to with a shaking head and more tears. Bewildered, and not a little frightened, he turned to Restag, who had also just placed his own books on the desk and raised his gaze to meet his thane's. Though he did not cry as Korena did, Witheric saw the sharp sorrow in his thanesman's eyes and found it hard to speak the questions building up in his throat. Thankfully, Restag did not need to hear those questions to know to answer them. "During your long sleep, she learned of our Blood Marks and their use in choosing whether or not to keep a child. And earlier she… uncovered the truth of your gift. It has upset her, to think of the two beside each other and how it might—should have been, but for the mischief of the gods on account of your Mark."

The news shocked Witheric, though he wasn't sure if he was more surprised she hadn't known before now, as he would have thought the one time he used his gift would have revealed its weakness, or how else she should have come to know.

"Why should such a thing unravel her?" Witheric asked. "It is a bane, this is true, but is it not of Wyrdi's weaving that some should be of strength enough to face this daily battleground and others of a weaker stock should be sacrificed for the sake of his companions, as with any war?"

Restag did not meet his eyes, but Witheric saw them soften as he said, "To her people, such thinking is a greater bane than even thane-slaying. It is almost as if to slay a god, to slay Dar himself."

This only amazed Witheric further. Those of Midrad, to be like gods? Yes, the old stories spoke of a time to come, when those chosen of the Asgradi will leave their place beneath the Moon to join the Sun as the Asgrada on the Final Field, when the Great Ice Ring shall melt and the sea waters drain into the ether and the Old Gods emerge from their wyrm-guarded prisons to fight in the glory of the Last Destruction and the Ending of All Things, when even Wyrdi and her loom of fate shall find their end and all return to Chaos. Perhaps in such a time, it might be said that men had become as gods.

But this was different. This was now. And it was not of the chosen, who had proven their strength and power on the field of battle or in the war of life, shown themselves worthy to be granted that last, dying glimpse of glory. It was something else. Something frightening. Something that would say he and all those before him had been wrong, terribly, terribly wrong. That those who sang the praises of his long, noble line of blood sang in truth of a tainted stream, that those who came before him and cleaved the way to his own life had cleaved it with Halsk's hammer. It would mean his grandfather was wrong, for Witheric knew of aunts and uncles, brothers and sisters and cousins, that he had never met and whose cries had vanished beneath their mothers' wailing. His father would be wrong. His brother, his mother, the Elders, all his people and all their lines that had trickled, against the flow of time and through the crags of space and the violence that is life, had been wrong. And the idea horrified him.

Some time later, Korena's crying lessened, and the one who had once been High Thane pulled her away and tried to soothe her. He spoke of how he had been saved by Fate from what should have been by the mark on his back and the mistaken gamble of his people. He spoke of happiness, of a life free of being forced to attend to the arts of blood-spilling, of the absent eyes of his father and the Elders that had let him run away to learn the Ithaenian tongue and read their books and see their thoughts. He even spoke of Eathir, his love, who, perhaps had he been stronger, may not have been deemed worthy of his blood, and their brief time when all was happiness. Of all these and more he spoke, to fight against the cruelty and horror the young woman's tears had suddenly revealed to him and to comfort her.

But she would not be comforted. She shook her head against it, and said, "No, Witheric. No. Even if you see it as a mistake or a trick or mischief, that shouldn't even matter. It shouldn't matter if you're born strong or weak. To kill a child like that, to treat a child like he is just a thing that can be thrown away or abandoned when he is imperfect or inconvenient or unwanted, is evil. And I will not call what is evil by any other name. Especially not by anything good."

The young woman's words wrapped around the thane, summoning through the horror an image that could only be a dream. But it was a beautiful dream, one of what could be if these words were true, and though he had intended to soothe her crying, instead he found his own soul softened as that image brushed against it like the downy feathers of a newborn chick. He bent down and lightly kissed her brow, smiled gently, and said, "Thank you for your tears, Korena Shield-Maiden, though I do nothing to earn them."

A small smile finally broke through. "They're freely given, Thane Witheric, though I suppose they're a poor gift."

No. He did not think so and could not, in light of the value they held to him, though he did not say it, for with such things words could only lessen.

Chapter 12

Korena examined her surroundings as she unlocked the back gate to the family mansion. There were some servants tending the garden, and she noticed one maid straightening a window curtain, but there were few to witness her return or question the puffiness around her eyes. If she was careful, she might even avoid alerting Karas before she could sneak back to her room and make herself a bit more presentable and less likely to be questioned. She slipped inside and began approaching the front door by skirting the wall. As much as she wished to use the back or kitchen entrance, there was no way she could escape the outcry that would come if one of the cooks saw her, and her mother always spent mid-afternoon in one of the rooms facing the garden, doing whatever leisurely activity she felt like that day. Even if she hadn't noticed Korena's arrival through the servant's gate, she, or someone with her, most certainly would not miss the uniformed figure walking across the open garden to the back door. The front, at least, was guarded only by the butler, who was experienced enough in the care of nobility not to pry.

However, when she slipped through the front door a few minutes later, it was not Baredese who waited for her, but her father. Immediately, her thoughts turned to flight. She was too tired, both emotionally and physically, to fight, and Kairon never left his study during his work hours unless for business or when his mood prevented him from focusing. Korena did not for one moment dare hope those cold, granite gray eyes watched for anyone but herself.

Keeping her movement and tone as steady as possible, she said, "Did you need me, Father?"

He did not speak but simply turned and walked away, assuming, correctly, that she would follow. As soon as she closed the door to his study and he sat at his desk, he crossed his fingers on the wooden surface and looked her squarely in the face, saying, "I was sent compliments from the king for your dedication to your work. It seems you, alone, remain from among the Blood Houses in service to his majesty's peculiar guests."

"Yes, Father," she replied, not meeting those eyes. "I expressed a desire to remain on this task, and the king graciously permitted it."

Though he nodded in approval, the man noted the tired laxity of his daughter's posture and the signs of distress on her face and said, "Perhaps you are too committed, however. You look ill. Are you sure you feel well enough to continue?""

"How I feel is of little importance so long as it does not interfere with my work. I believe these words are you own, sir."

Kairon frowned deeply. "The meaning I had intended with those words are not the same as how you have just used them. Precision, Korena. Be precise with your words. Not all these vagaries. I will not have equivocation and sophistry."

Korena flinched, much to Kairon's surprise, and she finally looked up to him before swiftly diverting her eyes. He could not have missed the glimpse of tumultuous emotions she was holding in as she sighed and said, "Yes. I apologize, Father. I didn't… no. I apologize. Something upset me near the end of my shift, and I was venting. I ask your pardon."

The man's frown deepened, and his brow furrowed as he leaned in, saying, "This is the third time, is it not, for you to return with signs of emotional disturbance. Korena, I am proud of your dedication, but if your present position is going to continuously push you to lose your self control…."

Her heart beat within her ears. He wouldn't understand if she explained it, if she explained that it was not loss of self control but something else, a part of her that could never be a soldier and which rebelled against the hardness and stoicism he desired of her. He had never understood. Instead, she said, "I will be fine. It is nothing to be concerned about, and the king is confident enough in my work that he even sent you his compliments. As I said, it does not disrupt my work, and I shall not allow it to do so."

Though he remained unconvinced and showed as much in the grim lines on his face, Kairon only said, "Very well. However, do not forget that you are a professional, and the pride of House Iegam. You are our most direct representative to the king and his house. Do nothing to disgrace the family name. That is all. You are dismissed."

With a quick, military bow, Korena left the room. That parting shot had been the last thing she needed at that moment, and she had to chide herself for hoping for more sympathy and comfort before she could reign in the anger roiling inside. When she finally took a deep breath and could pull her shoulders back, she heard her name from behind her and turned to see Karas looking at her with the very sympathy she had hoped for from their father. He approached her and took her in a quick hug.

"Are you all right?" he asked.

"Yes," she lied, quickly followed up by, "No. I'm not. Sorry. It's been a long day. I'll be fine in a bit."

He took that moment to look over her face, his concern only growing as he saw the signs of crying, pulling her in for another hug. He said, "I'm sorry. If I had known, I wouldn't–sorry. I made Father furious, and he was just taking it out on you."

"You?" she asked, looking up from his embrace into his face. "What could you have done to make him that angry?"

A small smile pulled at the corners of his mouth.

Korena hardly believed his answer until she stood in the doorway to the sitting room, seeing the young man stretching languidly across the couch, feet propped up on the armrest, holding a thick book he had likely started that day but was already over halfway completed. Some of her weariness fell away, and she smiled broadly. "Aristi! You're back!"

Aristi Meathorsis glanced up from his book, swung his long legs from the couch to the floor, and stood to welcome Korena with a quick embrace. He said, "Korena, you look awful! The only thing that could make it worse would be lack of sleep and running kohl. What happened?"

Following his guidance to the couch, she said, "It's a long story, and one too much like others you've heard. But what about you? How was your trip? Where did you go? Are you staying long?"

Aristi lifted a brow at Karas. They had known each other since childhood. He knew as well as Karas when the young woman was dodging a conversation, but all he said was, "It was profitable. I had planned to be back months ago, but the sailors simply refused to leave port after winter set in, and I got stuck in Badarga. Ghastly place. Not worth it. Visit Agrima instead. Better architecture, nicer people, much more representative of Xersia as a whole. Anyway, I ended up having to take the land route. Land! Around a sea! What is the use of a large body of water if we can't cut across it? So, I had travel around nearly the entire Ostran Sea, which is far larger than you'd think from a boat, before I finally found someone in Epra who was willing to take me in his private boat the rest of the way. Took a few days at Father's to recover, and then came here. As for how long I'm staying, I haven't decided yet."

"Well," said Korena, "at least you got to see the countryside."

The young man laughed. "Yes. The most underrated treasure of Ithaenia by those who live here. I swear, Korena, I will never again lack appreciation for real trees after so many months staring at almost nothing but rock, dust, and the oversized bushes the Xersians call by that name."

"What were you doing tromping around in the desert?" she said.

"Hm, nothing illegal," said Aristi with a lazy shrug.

"But the less I know the better? That kind of thing?"

The young man grinned. "Yes. One of those."

"Will you never cease corrupting my sister's imagination?" laughed Karas as he took the seat on Korena's other side. "I'd prefer she retain some chance of a respectable marriage, but with those kinds of hints and the rumors surrounding you, I fear she'll instead end up chasing after some villain with wild stories of the great unknown and its alien wonders and promised adventures instead."

"Your own imagination continues to astound, Karas," replied Aristi. "And? What of you, Rena? I hear from Karas that you've been moving up in the world."

Korena motioned to her uniform. "You mean this? You know that Father would never give up the chance for House Iegam to retake the position of most powerful representative of the Houses among the palace guard. The moment you left, he sent me to fill the space."

"Is there some kind of value or award for being a powerful grunt in the palace ecosystem?" said Aristi. "If something like that mattered, he should have been pushing you that way for years, not letting you begin adapting to womanhood. Magic nullification is nullification. Your ability is just as great as mine."

The words stung in a way the young man couldn't have understood, but Korena channeled the pain into a bitter smile and said, "Not while you were there. Even the best trained woman is disadvantaged in combat when compared to a well-trained man, let alone one trained as you are. And I'm not as keen to win as you are. No, Aristi, I can't compete with you, and Father knows it. In fact, if you came back, I'm sure King Aleukus would forgive you and gladly welcome back someone with your talent and ability."

"Hm. Maybe. If events should work out in that way," said Aristi. "I rather doubt your father would be happy about it, though."

"No," admitted Korena. "He's still pretty upset that you left like you did."

Aristi laughed harshly. "No. He's more upset that I didn't marry you than about me leaving my post. If I had just taken up the offer, he couldn't have cared less if I'd stayed on or not."

Karas sucked in his breath sharply, and Korena felt herself go rigid as her heart skipped a beat. Clenching her hands within her lap, she said, "That's not...."

Aristi gave her a hard look that made her blush. "Don't try to deny it, Rena. I know it's true, and so do you," he said. "And at this point, my father is probably the only one who refuses to accept the truth and still hopes for the union. I wouldn't be surprised if that's the only reason he hasn't disavowed me yet."

Korena's heart pulsed painfully against her chest. Old memories and hopes raced across her mind, reviving old pains and longings. She felt the desire to cry forming in her throat–her already drained emotions were not ready for more of that–so she rushed out the first thing that came to mind, regretting it just a moment too late, "Do you have someone in mind, then?"

The young woman's mortification at herself was immediately interrupted by another laugh from Aristi, followed by him saying, "No. Not at all. Which is just as well, since I do not intend to marry."

Korena saw her brother's eyes widen as he exclaimed, "Are you thinking of becoming a monk, or maybe a priest?"

"Ha! No. Come now, Karas, let's not speak blasphemy," replied Aristi. "To be sure, it would be another way for me to return to my family's grace, but only at the expense of losing Divine Grace for what should be the excommunicable offense of a man like me donning the cloth. No. My current aims are more of an academic nature than religious, and while I don't know how far I will go, I do know my minimum is of a level which would necessitate the near abandonment of any marital duties. And so, with so much work to do and no current inclination towards that life and its pleasures, I have decided to set aside that particular pursuit."

"You would make many women, both eligible and ineligible, weep if they heard you, Aristi," said Korena. With a sad smile, she turned to look at her own calloused hands on her uniformed lap and said with a sigh, "Maybe I should do the same. Give up on marriage and just focus on my work."

If Karas showed any horror at the idea, Korena didn't know, for her attention was immediately pulled back to Aristi as he made a derisive sound. "Few," he said, "are called to the celibate state, and I can say with certainty that you, Rena, are not one of them."

She straightened, flushing and staring at him defiantly. "And how would you know that? How would you, Aristi Meathorsis, out of everyone else, know that?"

He held up fingers to count and said, "First, because of your phrasing. To 'give up' can mean sacrifice for a proper end, but to 'give up on' is the language of defeat. And second, intuition and many, many years of observation. Trust me, Rena. Someday, someone will come along who can hold your heart, and who will treat it better than I did."

A pair of blue eyes flashed across her mind, but she quickly shoved them away, pain stabbing her soul, though it did nothing to keep tears from stinging her eyes. She turned away, taking a deep breath to steady her shaking voice, and said in a subdued voice, "You did nothing wrong, Aristi."

She felt the young man's large hand on her head and saw her brother take her own. Her friend's deep voice said, "Maybe, but it hurt you all the same."

Then she gave a startled protest and small laugh as the large hand suddenly began tilting her back and forth, as if mussing her tightly braided hair, knocking her into her brother's shoulder. Aristi's smile was back as he released her and said, "But enough about all this. Actually, when I mentioned moving up earlier, I meant your current assignment. It sounds like you have an interesting situation on your hands and some rather... unique persons under your care?"

The reminder once again brought Restag's face to mind, which, this time, Korena could not dismiss so quickly, causing her to blush briefly before the memories of that day filled in the space around that figure, and she began to cry in earnest, her fortitude broken at last. Karas began comforting her immediately while Aristi watched the series of reactions in thoughtful silence. Thankfully, the lack of control passed quickly, and Korena soon dabbed her eyes with her brother's handkerchief, saying, "I'm sorry. It's—I just heard some terrible and cruel things today, and it's been... emotionally difficult to process it all."

Both men tensed, Aristi's eyes narrowing while Karas exclaimed, "I knew it! Rena, we have to get you out of there. What have they been saying to you? What did they do?"

"What? No!" she said. "No, no, no! Nothing about me! They've been very kind to me… well, Thane Witheric has been. Restag took a little time, but he's not cruel. No. I meant about their lives and their culture, and what they've gone through. I just… I don't know how people can just keep going through those kinds of things… let alone see someone you care about go through what you can't change as you try to support him through it."

The image came to mind of Restag, sitting seemingly alone by Witheric's bed during his thane's long sleep, and the thought of what he must have had to witness and hear and endure during their lives, of what it must have been like to see everything come together in that betrayal that had driven them here, and… and that final blow dealt by Friathri. So hard. So harsh. So horrible and evil and cruel, cruel enough to almost break those strong shoulders carrying so much weight.

Aristi watched the young woman, noting small movements of her fingers and the emotions in her eyes, processing the picture of a girl attached with what he recognized as more than just professional or common sympathy, though of what kind or level he could not yet conclude. Though other hints from earlier gave him some idea of what the answer might be. Slouching back against the couch, he said with practiced disinterest, "I think I'd like to meet these barbarian guests of the king."

Karas stared at his friend. "Aristi, you can't be serious!"

Jumping up from the couch, Aristi replied, "Of course I am. And don't pretend you don't, Karas. I'm sure both of us wish to see for ourselves what kind of men are making our Rena cry."

"Well, yes, but–"

A crossness came over Korena's face. "I already said it's not like that. I'm really fine."

"Well," countered Aristi, "if they're really so well-behaved, then there shouldn't be a problem with our meeting them, right?"

"B-but they're the king's guests!" said Karas. "In the palace! You can't–we can't just…."

"Why not? They're guests, not prisoners. I don't remember anyone ever saying a guest can't have guests just because they're the king's," said Aristi, his eyes already shining with the idea, a bad sign if they wanted to try arguing the point. "So, be up bright and early tomorrow, Karas. We're going to the palace!"

Witheric traced his finger along the defined roads of the map of Thenika Restag had copied for him. It had been a long night, sleep coming late and then fitfully interrupted by thoughts and memories and the occasional fever, though never of a bad enough level that he felt the need to wake Restag to fetch Paskhalon. Still, he felt too exhausted at that moment to read and instead satisfied himself with reviewing what Korena had told him so far of Thenika. Each section, or rather District of the city was labeled, as were the various gates, the ports, and a few landmarks. So far, he had only seen the city from the wall top, carried up there by Restag, Paskhalon having forbidden anything more strenuous until his fevers finally stopped and his muscle mass was recovered enough to walk for extended periods without assistance. It had been breathtaking, unbelievable except that he had seen it with his own eyes. There was so much! He only hoped….

Voices from the sitting room caught his attention moments before the door suddenly opened to a face he did not recognize: a lean, young man–though Witheric could not guess his age, humans all looked so much older than they were–with long, black hair pulled back from his bearded face, revealing intelligent, green eyes that quickly took in the room and then centered themselves on Witheric. Despite his lack of bulk, the man across the room dominated the doorframe, and Witheric instinctively stiffened his posture, matching the inquisitive gaze with his own.

Then Korena's voice came from behind him as she ducked around him, saying, "Aristi! You can't just barge into someone's bedroom!"

The man, Aristi, smiled brightly at Korena, but before he could respond, another voice, this one higher though clearly male, interjected, "Stop blocking the door. Do you have to be so rude and inconsiderate of others?"

In response, Aristi glared behind him, made as if to move aside, and then slammed his foot against the doorframe just as a third person, a man on the shorter side, tried to walk inside, causing the smaller man to slam his chest against the booted leg and stumbled back a step, nearly colliding with a fourth person, who Witheric guessed by resemblance to be related to Korena.

"What was that for?" cried the smaller man.

Aristi shrugged. "Felt like it."

The smaller man's face colored deeply, only worsening when he noticed Witheric watching the events play out. Trembling, he said, "Now look what you've done! You're making a fool of us!"

Aristi stared flatly at the other man, saying in a tone laced with irritation, "No one asked you to come, Ortheus. In fact, I'm pretty sure I declined your self-invitation, and you still came on your own anyway. Nor is anyone asking you to take credit for my actions. I'll worry about me, you worry about you."

"All right, all right, let's slow down," said the fourth man, placing himself between the other two glowering at each other. "After all, this really is not the time or place, or even the reason we came here, so…."

Puffing up his chest, the smaller man named Ortheus strutted into the room, smiling condescendingly at Aristi and saying, "Well put, Karas. Not as well as I could have, but to the point. Anyway, as for why I am here despite so rudely being left behind, well I just knew you would need me, Aristi. You can't be trusted with any real responsibilities, after all, so I decided to come and help, purely out of the goodness of my own heart, of course." He added the last phrase with a quick smile in Korena's direction, though he did not seem to notice her glazed expression. He went on, "So, just stand aside, Aristi. I'll show you how to be a proper representative of civilization."

Ignoring Korena's protests, Ortheus walked up to just a short distance from Witheric's bed, gave a theatrical bow, and said in oddly accented Asgradi, "How to do, oh Upper Thane. Better to be you, we seeing and much happy."

It took Witheric a few moments to process the small man's garble, to which he replied in Ithaenian with a polite nod of his head and stage-worthy false smile, "A goodful morning and many thanks to your greetings, Ortheus of Thenika."

Ortheus's already pasty skin turned sickly before flushing terribly as Aristi's deep laugh filled the room. Korena, her own face bright red, gave Aristi a backhanded slap on the arm and chided him for laughing before approaching Witheric, giving an irate glare to Ortheus as she passed him, as well. Standing at attention, she said, "I am dreadfully sorry, High Thane. I had intended to announce them first and ask if you were open for company, but…."

Folding up the map, Witheric replied, "It is of no stain to you. This I can see for myself, though your regrets are taken into hand. And? Is there something these others are needing?"

"O-oh, um… no, not exactly. They just wanted to meet you," she replied. Motioning to them in turn, she said, "If I may introduce everyone, this next to me is Sir Ortheus, heir presumptive of House Meathorsis of the Blood Houses, and his elder brother, Aristi. The last is Karas, first born and heir apparent of House Iegam, my brother."

Ortheus puffed back up in the mention of his title, and Karas nodded with respectful hesitation toward the Asgradi thane. Aristi, however, came up beside the bed and gave Witheric a quick look over, noting the other man's lean form and youthful, even child-like features. With a skeptical raise of his brow, he said, "Don't really fit the image of a barbarian king, do you?"

Witheric waved away any outcry from the other humans, looked Aristi in the eye, and said, "Yes, this I hear very much, though I am to note that even Ithaenia does not choose her next head of house by appearance only." He motioned to Ortheus. "But the question is understood. In my people, too, I am not of first thought for a thane, though I was of first birth. But my father and brother, they are dead of the battlefield, and the Eisenband fell to my head. Such is as Wyrdi has woven on the loom that marks the paths of living men."

"Fascinating," Aristi mumbled, his eyes alight. He fell into his own thoughts for a few moments and then said, "So this 'Wyrdi,' that's like your version of the Fates? Bit of a heavy card you got dealt there. Can't say I envy you."

The beginnings of a pained smile pulled at Witheric's lips only to be overtaken by a softer, more amused one as he noticed Korena staring absently toward the nearby desk. In an offhand way, he said, "If you wonder after Restag, he is to get us break-fast. He is to be back soon."

The sudden rigidity of Korena's posture and slight flush to her face spoke volumes to Aristi, as did the flash of anger and contempt in Ortheus's. Anticipating no little excitement, he said, "Speaking of, do you mind me asking a rather… not so much personal but perhaps you might call sensitive question?"

Witheric's eyes turned suspicious and wary, and Aristi could see the gears quickly turning in the barbarian's mind. Without any hint of uncertainty, he replied, "It is permitted to be asked, but if to answer is to depend."

"Fair enough. So, which of you two made Rena cry yesterday?"

"What?" cried Korena and Ortheus together, though the color of their cheeks had very different shades. Back by the door, Karas groaned into his hand.

"They made Miss Korena cry?" shouted Ortheus. Grabbing Korena's hand in both of his own, he said, "When? Where? How? I just knew it! I knew they couldn't be–"

"Th-that's none of your business!" she responded, yanking her hand free. "And it's certainly nothing to get upset about. Neither of them did anything wrong. And you," glaring at Aristi, "I already told you that. Don't start trouble just because you can!"

Karas Iegam watched despondently as Aristi responded with an impish smile. For all his virtues, Aristi could be hard to deal with, and whenever Ortheus shoved himself into the mix, usually in some vain attempt to win over Korena, the situation always became impossible to keep peaceful. And now Korena was angry, and they'd made complete fools of themselves in front of a foreign dignitary. If Father heard about any of this…. Karas felt nearly sick from the stress his imagination generated, so when he suddenly heard someone speak behind him, his tension hijacked him. He screamed and suddenly felt himself falling, having tripped over himself in his surprise. Then, just as suddenly, he was suspended in the air, his feet dangling almost a foot off the floor.

As a group, the other occupants in the room turned to the panicked sounds to see Restag holding up Karas by the back of his vest. While the others stared in stunned silence, Ortheus cried out, drew a dirk from his belt, and took a fencing stance while pointing the blade accusingly at the Asgradi warrior. "Fiend!" he cried. "Barbarian! You show your true colors once again! First, with Miss Korena by wounding both her face and her feelings, and now her esteemed brother. Attacking him unprovoked and now using him as a shield, are you? Ha! Northern terror, I shall avenge them, and you shall spread your ills no more!"

Restag stared unblinkingly at the small blade. His eyes then wandered up to the rest of the room, fixing themselves on the man standing by his thane, his instincts immediately picking up on the confidence and command the tall, lithe man exuded. Before he could address this real issue, however, it would seem the small man, whose high-pitched squeaks were irritatingly familiar–though Restag could not recall from where–seemed insistent on pointing a weapon in his direction with one of the worst sword grips the warrior had ever seen. He lowered the human he had in hand, letting the trembling figure find his feet before letting go and moving past him, and approached the armed man.

"Ha! So, the barbarian has some honor at least. Or perhaps you realize it is best that you surrender, fiend," cried Ortheus, not lowering the blade.

In response, Restag used his non-dominant hand to draw his iron sword in a reverse-grip, upward slash, knocking the long knife clean out of the astonished Ortheus's hand. The Asgradi then flicked the sword into a natural grip and swiftly swung it around till it rested on the small man's shoulder, the cold iron barely not biting into his neck. Moments later, Restag re-sheathed his blade as Ortheus's quivering legs gave out under him. Stepping around the collapsed form, he said in his native tongue, "Witheric, what by Dar's ravens is all this?"

"I'm rather unsure, myself," replied the thane. "That one you caught earlier is Korena's brother, and these two appear to be kin to each other, though it strains me to see it. As for their purpose, I rather wonder if most of them know themselves. By the way, where's our food?"

"On the table in the other room. I saw the door was open and heard noises. It seemed of greater purpose to investigate with free hands than full," he replied, his gaze settling squarely on Aristi.

Witheric nodded, looked at Karas, and said, "One who is spoken to be Korena's brother? My thanesman has left our food behind. Would you to please to get it, it is many thanks."

Karas straightened and, with a fearful and intrigued glance to Restag, gave a quick bow and started out the room, only for Ortheus to protest as he struggled back to his wobbling feet, "Y-you can't just tell us what to do! We aren't your servants!"

"Ah, yet I am your guest, am I not?" said Witheric, lifting his chin so as to look down sharply at Ortheus with icy eyes and using a tone Korena had never heard before. "And is it not to be believed 'civilized' to treat guests as if you are to serve them when no servant be present? Or perhaps it is of only barbarian ways to treat one taken beneath his own roof as such. Perhaps it is, rather, of the civilized to invade a guest's room, threaten his thanesman, throw to him accusings of the breaking of hospitality and so of the attacking of your king and his house, to speak as if the guest is a mere beast or a creature of the Halskrad. Or perhaps it is simply true-speech that a boneless tongue can birth only boneless men? But no, that is not so, for I see King Aleukus and some such of his men to be no such nature. Well, then, tell me, one who is to be head of his house, which is the case? It is, it seems, of hardness to me to know which, indeed, is of the civilized and which of the barbarian."

Ortheus stared blankly at the High Thane, confusion plain on his face. Taking advantage of the pause, Korena said, "I shall get your breakfast, Thane Witheric. I am the one assigned to help you, after all."

A strange smile came over Witheric's face, and he said, "Oh, no, that is of no need, Korena. I do not, you see, wish another claim that you are to be ill-treated under my care. If my thanesman and my own self are to be not trusted with such a thing, let those who would suspect prove to themselves if it is of truth or not."

He gave a quick nod to Karas, who immediately clicked his heels together, bowed, and rushed into the other room, coming back quickly with a tray clattering within his shaking hands. Both from pity and her own concern for the dishes, Korena did meet him partway across the room and relieve him of the tray, motioning with her eyes for him to take one of the room's chairs, a suggestion the rattled man took willingly.

By this time, Aristi was laughing quietly to himself. As Korena put out the food for both rendeilxue, he said to Witheric, "You've got a devious mind there, and, it appears, a liking for drawn-out speeches. I guess you can be kingly when you want to."

"I am High Thane, if you should wish it or not," replied Witheric before popping a piece of bread into his mouth. An idea then came to mind, and as he swallowed, his eyes shone mischievously as he said, "Korena, Aristi said before 'Rena,' and the one named Ortheus said this is Korena, correct? A nearness-name, perhaps?"

Neither he nor Aristi missed the slight pause in Restag's movements as he leaned against the desk, a biscuit in one hand and a few sheets of paper in the other. Korena also stood by the desk, sorting through papers, but she looked up at Witheric's question and prepared to answer only for Ortheus to cut in, muttering loudly, "It's 'Miss Iegam' to you. She is not some common-born or pub wench. She is a lady. She deserves respect, not to be spoken to like a maid!"

Flushing with anger, Korena said, "Ortheus, please! This is hardly the time or place for this. Besides, I do not mind, so neither should you."

A look of profound hurt and betrayal came over the little man. "B-but Miss Korena, I-I-I was only looking out for you."

Despite her own reason telling her to let the topic die there and then, the sparks of irritation from the last few years caught flame. "Well you can stop! You are not my brother, nor my father, nor my husband nor fiancè nor even my friend! You do not need to keep forcing yourself into my life and causing trouble. So just leave me—"

"Rena."

A small gasp sounded from Ortheus as Korena caught her breath and turned to Restag. She thought she caught a brief glimpse of olive green in his cheeks before he held out the papers to her, saying, "A question."

"O-oh, um, okay. Where?" she said, taking the papers from him and coming back around the desk to stand beside him so he could easily point out his issue. From his place on the other side of the bed, Aristi watched the two with confirmed suspicion. Over in the chair, he saw Karas's eyes widen in sudden and terrified realization while right in front of him, Witheric settled back into the pillows, a satisfied smile on his lips as he continued his breakfast. The gears of Aristi's mind turned swiftly. He cleared his throat and said, "So, Restag, you're a warrior?"

Restag looked up from Korena's interrupted explanation and, following a quick bit of speech from Witheric, nodded mutely, his eyes wary. It was, in the end, Witheric who responded, proudly saying, "Restag is my Thanesman. He is of a giant's height in battle, like as one with dragon's blood and Svanril's favor.

Aristi had no idea who 'Svanril' was, but Witheric's response sounded boastful enough, so he said, "Then, what do you say to a little contest between the two of us."

"It is accepted," said Witheric at once, to Aristi's surprise. If he had expected anything from the thane, it was simply a translation to let his warrior decide, but the translation only followed after the fact, resulting in another nod from Restag. Well, if the Asgradi king could decide these kinds of matters for his soldiers, it was none of his business. Continuing his casual tone, Aristi said, "How long do you need to prepare? One day? Three? I can't promise more than a week."

"Today," said Witheric, eyes shining. "There is no need of us to wait. Only let us to finish eating and finish some of work before. Is possible for you?"

Restag looked concernedly at Witheric. Though he did not know the entirety of what was being said, he understood the gist, and he could not help the unease he felt. Even with his best efforts to appear otherwise, Restag knew Witheric had not slept peacefully and was exhausted. However, the excited light in his master's eyes, one that was so rare these days, kept his objections chained within. Even so....

He glanced beside him to Korena, her own expression a mixture of emotions. Within a moment, he made his decision and whispered, "Rena."

Her eyes jumped to his, but thankfully no one else seemed to have heard him. Heat rose to his cheeks and ears, and he quickly muttered, "Something I much need of you."

She blinked at him in confusion. Then his eyes quickly shifted to the bed and its occupant, who now looked at the pair with curiosity, before jumping back to her gaze. After a few moments, Korena's eyes grew wide, and her breath stopped as the meaning of that look came over her, or she thought it was the meaning. It seemed too great a trust for him to give her, but acting on her reasoning, she nodded demurely, saying, "Okay. I'll take care of him."

Tension she had not noticed before left Restag's shoulders and expression. And though he then turned his attention to rebuff a teasing question from his master, the exchange left her feeling oddly warm and giddy and kept her mind distracted as the men worked out the details of their contest.

Korena knew more or less what to expect when they made it to the training grounds, but it was still surprising to see the excitement of the other men at Aristi's appearance. They would have known about his presence in the palace from the guards stationed at the entrance, and there were plenty of scowls and looks of remembered injuries among those gathered, but the prevailing sentiment was of respect. There were fewer who recognized Karas, but he was not so prone to make enemies as his friend, being of a generally accommodating temper, and was welcomed happily enough, as was Restag, though many of the group still appeared cautious of the barbarian, half-fae warrior.

Korena followed a little ways behind, pushing Witheric in a wheelchair. Though still relatively warm by the rendeilxues' standard, it was an unusually cold day for Thenika, and both Restag and Korena had insisted he bundle up, making him actually look like he weighed something as the wheels scraped across the cold, hard-packed earth in the direction of the fenced-in sparring ring.

"He is well-thought of by them," said Witheric, his breath visible as he motioned toward the soldiers gathered around Aristi.

Ortheus, who had followed sulkily behind everyone else, huffed. He muttered, "Only because, for some reason, they think bashing each other with your fists means you're a good guy. Even though he ran away from his post and left Korena at the altar, you guys still like him. Ridiculous!"

Witheric's eyes snapped toward Ortheus, making the other man flinch as the intense orbs latched onto him, the thane's thin fingers clenching the chair's armrests as he said, "Say again! What is this done?"

Memories of Witheric's reaction to the treachery of 'oath-breakers' and Friathri's mentions on the Asgradi's value of loyalty flashed through Korena's mind, and she quickly said, "He didn't leave me. There were talks between our parents, but that was all. We were never officially betrothed. Furthermore, he did not 'run away' from his post. He just… left it without telling anyone about it first. But the king has already forgiven him for it."

The Asgradi's gaze focused dubiously on Korena. However, the fire in his eyes dimmed to a smolder, and he nodded, though he did not look completely placated as he stared at Aristi. "It is a slight to High Thane Aleukus. It is his place, not mine, to judge and meet out justice," he said.

As she looked upon the thane's expression, Korena decided it best not to inform Restag of Aristi's past failures.

A cheery voice called their attention, and Parchaes burst from the group, hailing them and calling over two dozen mens' attention to the young woman and the 'Little King,' as Witheric had come to be called among the guards and soldiers over the past couple months. Though he rarely left his room, more than one man had met him on an infirmary guard shift, and Parchaes had stopped by enough times to see Restag that nearly every man in the guard had one opinion or another of the barbarian king who "held the thanesman's chain."

"Were you assigned a day shift, Parchaes? Or are you suspended again?" Korena asked.

"Nah, but the others said Aristi was back, so no way was I gonna stay in bed," Parchaes replied. Waving a gloved hand, he said, "Hello there, Little King, and… uh… oh. Why's he here?"

Ortheus blushed angrily and walked ahead of them, arms crossed and shouting behind him, "I go where I want! If I want to be here, then I will!"

Parchaes frowned after the smaller man, shrugged, and turned back to Korena and Witheric. "So," he said, as if his cheer had never been disrupted, "Restag and Aristi say they're gonna fight. Who do ya think will win?"

Puffing with pride, Witheric announced without hesitation, "It is no true question. Restag surely is to win."

Whichever guards had remained neutral to the thane after seeing him accompanied by Korena Iegam, princess of the palace guard, now found himself bristling with a shared sense of wounded pride. Aristi may not be part of their guard now, but he had been once, and the absolute confidence of the little thane's statement set most, excepting Aristi's enemies and the amiable Parchaes, against him. For his part, Parchaes grinned and said, "You're only sure 'cause you never saw Aristi fight. He plays to win. Every time. He's not gonna go easy on your guy."

"Perhaps. But Restag is Thanesman. And so, he is to win," replied Witheric.

From the crowd of men came Aristi's deep laugh. He looked to Restag and said, "Your little master has quite a lot of trust in you."

Nodding, Restag stated plainly, "He is Thane. I is Thanesman."

"Yeah, well, we'll see what that means for the battlefield in just a moment, won't we?" said Aristi, nodding his chin toward the sparring grounds. "As agreed: one round, fight till one of us either can't fight or yield, and since I'm the challenger, I'll even let you choose the weapon. Except guns. That would defeat the purpose."

Immediately after Witheric finished translating, Restag replied, "Spear and shield."

Aristi raised an eyebrow. He had fully expected the rendeilxue to choose his sword, but he agreed. It mattered little to him, and soon the two stood in the sparring grounds armed with wooden shields and blunt staves weighted on the end to the approximate weight of a spear. Restag's sword and scabbard sat on Witheric's lap within the crowd gathered around the ring.

From behind Witheric, Korena watched Restag give the practice weapon a few warm-up swings. Though Aristi was by no means bulky, he was the taller of the two and well-toned. The half-fae Restag appeared almost fragile by comparison.

"Do you wish Aristi's victory?"

Korena, startled, looked down to see Witheric's sharp eyes watching her. A knowing smile came across his face, and he said, "Or does the shield-maiden worry for another champion?"

The chill left her as her face colored. "I-that is-I-I don't… I'm not sure," she admitted in a lowered voice, one designed for only the man before her to hear. "Aristi is a close friend and… and I loved him for a long time. I still do. Not in the same way, but I do. Of course I want him to do well, but…."

Witheric's smile softened to an almost familial affection, and he placed a hand upon hers, saying, "Do not be worried. Restag is to win."

He looked back to the pair that had begun circling each other, saying in a whisper barely heard over the already cheering crowd, "He is Thanesman. He will not lose to an oath-breaker."

Any response Korena might have given was immediately stolen from her as a cry went up and her eyes darted back to the men within the arena. Aristi had struck first, sending a series of swift jabs and swings toward the rendeilxue only for Restag to block or avoid each one. Still, he was being pushed back against the quick blows without a chance to counter attack.

Then an opening came, and Restag made a sharp swipe that Aristi had to jump back to avoid, giving his opponent the chance to reclaim a stronger stance. Aristi smirked and said, "Not bad, Northman. Can't win if you keep running, though. Come on. Show me what a rendeilxue 'thanesman' can do. I don't even mind if you use your magic."

A murmur of interest rose from the crowd as they realized that none of them had, in fact, ever seen the rendeilxue's magic. There had been much speculation, of course, about what it might be, but so far the answer still lay hidden to them. Voices began calling out, urging, demanding the Asgradi show his power. From their spot in the crowd, Korena paled. "Oh, no! Restag!"

Korena tried again and again to catch the thanesman's attention, but the other voices drowned her out.

"What? What is the matter?" asked Witheric.

Pointing to them, Korena said, "I forgot to tell Restag. Aristi! He's a Nullifier, a strong gift-sleeper, like myself. If Restag uses his magic, Aristi's going to nullify it and use that moment of surprise to strike."

"Ah, then it is no matter," said Witheric, calmly. "Restag does not favor his magic in battle unless necessary. It is, he says, a distraction."

"What? But-but he's your thanesman! Isn't he supposed to be a strong warrior, an example of virtue? How can he be a better warrior than another rendeilxue if he can't use his magic to fight!"

"He can use it, but he does not need it in most times." Witheric hushed Korena's next objection and pointed to the arena, saying, "Watch."

Restag stalked in steady circles with his opponent. The crowd's shouting was annoying, but with all the unknown words and various voices crashing together, he could largely ignore it. He did, however, know that Aristi had tried to taunt him and that the shouting all around him had something to do with magic. He eyed the other man suspiciously, knowing he was trying to accomplish some trick. Therefore, he was ready when Aristi, seeing his bait had not caught, attacked again. This time, the human's quick, skilled blows were not a novelty, and Restag, adjusting more and more to the rhythm of the fight, found each blow easier to parry or dodge. Even so, he saw few chances to attack, and each one he took met with a skilled block or dodge from Aristi.

Had the match happened a couple months before, perhaps Aristi's skills would have been too much for the thanesman, but Aristi's delayed return, along with the many matches against Parchaes, had given Restag the time needed to recover much of the legendary stamina of an Asgradi warrior. Aristi realized his disadvantage quickly as his own breathing began to quicken and the staff and shield grew heavy. While skilled in the weapons he used, he had not spent years on the battlefield in drawn out combat, having to pace himself in order to endure that weight for so long. What he lacked in experience, however, he possessed in intellect and talent, and his initial, quick strikes soon stopped, replaced by a more measured approach much like the thanesman's. For the next several minutes, spears and shields clattering together, interspersed with attempts to use their legs or weight to gain an advantage that simply would not come.

Then, seeing an opening on the side of Aristi's shield arm, Restag struck, landing a glancing blow against the man's side, while Aristi, seeing an opening of his own, dropped his shield and grabbed at the bare skin of the rendeilxue's hand with his own. To any other Asgradi, the moment of shock at that touch would have been the end of him. However, Restag, though startled by the revelation of Aristi's ability, had grown familiar with the sudden quieting of his blood and reacted on reflex, bashing his shield against the other man with such force he released his grip, stumbled back several feet, and fell, losing his grip on his staff in the process.

Cursing, Aristi instantly turned to grab the staff rolling across the arena only to be stopped mid-motion as something flashed before his eyes and he found himself staring at the quivering shaft of Restag's "spear," the blunt end embedded firmly in the hard-packed ground. He stared, shocked, at the display of raw, physical strength mere inches from his face and hardly even noticed Restag come up to him until the Asgradi stood over him with Aristi's own staff pointed at his chest.

In a matter-of-fact voice more threatening than any war cry could be in that moment, the thanesman said, "You are dead."

Aristi blinked at the weight pressed against his heart and then looked up to Restag, saying as he raised his hands, "So I am. Very well, Thanesman. I yield."

A brief silence followed the surrender, suddenly breaking into cheers and yells as several men, Parchaes at their lead, rushed into the arena. Restag, withdrawing the weapon, held out a hand to help Aristi stand, and the man had to laugh lightly as he saw the bare, open palm, took it, and said, "I suppose it was too much to bet on someone who's spent so much time with Korena to be unfamiliar with a Nullifier."

Then the group that had jumped the fence reached them and began congratulating the men on the fight. Even Karas stood among them. He placed a hand on his friend's shoulder, shaking his head and saying, "It was well-fought, Aristi. Still amazing."

"Yeah," said Parchaes, slapping them both hard on the back with winding force. "Never a dull fight with you. You sure you don't wanna be a palace guard? Oh, but I guess since you lost to Restag and Restag's lost to me, that means I'm better than you now. Ha ha!"

A glint came to Aristi's eyes. "Wanna bet on that, Parchaes?"

The guardsman stared blankly a few seconds, gave a false start, and then nodded mutely when another man chimed in to say, "Best stop the yapper now, Par, or you might not have it much longer."

From back outside the arena, Korena smiled with flushed elation, both at Restag's victory and at the laughing cluster of men surrounding the combatants. She spied Ortheus watching them from the sidelines, his face the look of utter dejection as he saw the man he most admired and hated, his own brother, laugh at and celebrate his own loss. It utterly confounded the man, and he could only mutter to himself about his brother's lack of proper pride and self-esteem as he gazed in envy and longing before turning away to return home, back to the title he was soon to enjoy in his shameless brother's place. A small consolation, but a consolation nonetheless.

As Korena watched him go, she felt a pang of pity, knowing the kind of man he was and that she could not console him without inviting further misery upon them both. So she turned her attention back to happier things. Smiling broadly, she looked down to Witheric, saying, "Congratulations, High Thane! Your thanesman has proven himself!"

Her happiness, however, quickly turned to apprehension as Witheric returned her gaze and she saw him flushed and sweating, despite the cold air. His voice sounded labored, as well, as he said, "Yes. Did I not say it should be so?"

Korena suddenly felt afraid as she stared at his dazed eyes and damp face. "W-Witheric? Are you okay? You're sweating. Is it another fever?"

Witheric looked surprised by the question. However, he then said in an increasingly distant voice, "Oh. I suppose… perhaps it is so. I only thought… thought…."

Then he fainted, and Korena screamed for Restag.

Chapter 13

Aleukus was surprised when he entered the guest room and saw Aristi leaning against the wall just beside the bedroom entrance. Their eyes met. Pushing aside any other thoughts and their accompanying emotions, Aleukus approached, saying, "How is he?"

Aristi motioned to a figure on the couch. "Why don't you ask him."

The figure gave the king greater despair than anything else could have, for it was Paskhalon, sitting not with his patient or working furiously at one of his work tables but with head in hands. Only one other time had the king seen the physician so despondent, when his own, aged father had passed away several years ago. He nodded his thanks to Aristi, came up to the physician and placed a strong hand on his shoulder. Kneeling to the other man's level, he said calmly, "Tell me, Paskhalon."

Paskhalon shook his head, released a shuddering sigh, and then said with his face still buried, "I don't know what's wrong. I've tried everything. Everything! Every treatment I know, over months, looked through every book, every scrap of research I could find, and I just don't know. And every time I think I might have found it, it turns out wrong. There's too little we know about them, too little on how their bodies work, how they're different from ours, and they sure as hell don't have anything, since they rely on magic and basic herb lore without a shred of proper alchemy…. I thought… I thought maybe it was finally finished, that he was about to recover, but… I don't know the how or the why or the what. I don't know if it's the illness, if it's an ongoing issue or a new one, if it's the dosage, the mixtures, their purity, or if it's just their damned fairy blood! Dammit, Aleukus, I just don't know! It's beyond me. It's beyond what I know and what I can do, and I… I…."

Aleukus patted the man's shoulder and then stood without a word, turning to see Aristi watching them, his own calm facade breaking for a moment to reveal, despite the usual appearance to the contrary, a man of deep compassion before the mask went up again. The king placed a quick hand on the young man's shoulder as he passed into the bedroom.

The scene inside brought pain to the king's heart. Karas Iegam sat in a chair pulled up beside his sister's, holding her hands as she stared helplessly at the figure breathing painfully beneath the bed covers, his friend sitting beside him, his master's hand desperately clenched between his own. Aleukus approached the little group solemnly, coming up to the bed and saying in a low voice, "How are you, my friend?"

Witheric's hazy eyes fluttered open, and he said in a voice like a sigh, "Al...eukus? You... you are...."

"Yes, I'm here," he said.

A sad smile crawled across the rendeilxue's face. Releasing a weary laugh, he said, "I am sorry to... to see. Paskhalon, he is... not here."

"Yes. I spoke with him."

"Then... then you are to know... know...," Witheric's words disappeared beneath a miserable groan. Restag jumped up, crying his master's name while Korena hurried to change the cooling towel on the sick man's forehead and began dabbing his face, feeling tears form as she felt the heat of his skin. She swallowed back a sob, tending to the suffering man till he returned to steady, labored breath. He opened his eyes again, looking to Restag and forcing a smile in reply to the anguish that stared back. As lightly as he could, he said in Asgradi, "How great a boon that you refused the blood-oath when I offered it. You... would be duty-bound to wed for the sake of my line, not your own, bearing the weight of a crown you would not claim and a duty you could not meet. What a... a burden I so nearly chained to you, Restag."

Restag shook his head. However, he struggled to make words come. Eventually, he forced out, "It... it would be no burden, for it would have never become mine to bear. You'll see."

Tears appeared in Witheric's eyes, but he blinked them back and shook his head. "No... no my friend. This is the end of my place in Wyrdi's weaving. But... but it is still good. All... so far as I can see, all has been accounted for."

Fear, an emotion so foreign to his friend's face, filled Restag's eyes. "What do you mean? Witheric, don't use such empty-speech!"

Rather than continue the argument, one which he knew he had neither time nor energy to endure, Witheric turned back to Aleukus. "I am sorrowful to ask of you your word-bond, friend Aleukus. I had thought… hoped…."

Aleukus nodded. "I had hoped for better, as well. In truth, I had hoped to never make good on my promise."

Korena and Karas both looked to their king. "Promise? What promise?" said Korena, afraid to know the answer but also too afraid not to ask.

The king merely looked sadly upon Witheric, who said, "Yestermorn, when you were to get my books, I requested of Aleukus that… that if I… should not rise again one morn, if he would take on care for Restag."

"What?" came Restag, half-understanding. "Witheric! What are you saying?"

"Korena," said the thane, drawing her attention from the demanding voice of Restag. Witheric held out a hand to her, which she took, and he said, "My thanesman… you see, he is… he…," Witheric's voice broke, and he looked pleadingly to her, "Korena, he has gave all else for me, and I… I fear… I fear he will to be lost when… when I… please. Help him. Please."

Holding back her own sobs, Korena smiled gently and said, "Of course."

"Thank you. Thank you," he said, pulling her hand to his forehead before releasing it.

"Witheric, by Dar's Own Speech, answer me! What is going on?"

At last, Witheric returned to Restag and said, "My duty, Restag, my last duty, as your thane. You are all I have left as thane, Restag, the last of my people to… to protect and provide for. The very last."

"No!" said Restag, growing angry in his fear. "No! Not the last! Perhaps for now, but not the last for all. You… you still need to go back! We came to this place for help, to gain help to bring you back, and you must. You are High Thane. You are to end the blood wars between our tribes, to form a bond with the human king and then to use that bond to help end the blood wars. That is your duty. Not this. Not me. That!"

"Ah. Yes. I had… somewhere… I had forgotten," said Witheric. "It is such a distant thing now, a mere dream. I am sorry, Restag. I… I won't be able to fulfill that promise to you. I am sorry. Please, forgive your thane his weakness. I have failed our people. But this, at least, I can do. You, at least, I can protect, at the end of all."

"No! No, you… you said… you said…."

A weak laugh escaped Witheric's lips. "Restag, you, alone, have ever believed my ambitions to be possible. You alone, and for that, I thank you, or else I should not have believed them, either. But now, it is at an end. You must release them, just as you must release me. There are more important things than to cling to the dead and to chase dead dreams."

Witheric reached up and placed his free hand on Restag's head, saying, "And for the sake of that, I, Witheric, High Thane of the Eisenband relea–"

"Don't!" cried Restag, pulling the hand away. "Witheric, please, don't release me. Don't free me of my bond. Don't! You can't!"

Witheric stared at his friend, wide-eyed, realizing, in a foggy way, that something was wrong. This was not how it should be. This was not....

Another spasm of pain ran through him, and he doubled over, only half-hearing Restag's cries. He tried to piece together his thoughts through the pain and heat, tried to figure out what was wrong. Finally, he gasped out, "Restag... you... you must... let me go!"

"No!" came the answer. "No! I can't! I can't!"

And as he stared through pain-blurred eyes at the despair on his friend's face, he knew, at last, where he had made his mistake, and he saw with the clarity of one facing death itself the danger in those anguished eyes, and he realized he would fail. Restag, the one who had given up everything to protect him, the only person he had left to protect, he would fail. He would die, and Restag, who clung to those he loved with loyalty unto death, would follow him into Halsk. Just like his mother, when she decided to join his father and brother. He had to act. Had to break that hold. Had to make him let go. But... how....

Then, in the midst of pain and fever, a choice arose. A cruel choice, a desperate choice, and the only choice he could think of. Before he could reconsider, before his soul had a chance to reject it for its horror, he acted, freeing his hand and grabbing Restag's arm with a grip that startled him.

"Very... well," he said, pulling his fevered gaze to his friend's, his voice hoarse. "Very well, Restag. If... if you will not be free... you said before... that you will... will do whatever I ask... if only not to force a blood-bond. Anything else, yes?"

Dread chilled Restag's blood, but he could only say, "Yes."

With labored breath, Witheric continued, "And... and now you say... you will not be freed. Even... even if I should... should wish it. You will be bound by... by your oath to me."

"Y-yes," said Restag.

"Then, Restag-Thanesman who would remain Thanesman, heed your thane's command. Swear to me that, upon my death, you shall serve Aleukus of Thenika as you would me, until either of you shall die or he release you of your bond."

Restag stared in blanched horror at the man before him. He heard his own heartbeat and nothing else, the world drowned out by the desperate pumping of his own blood. At last, he managed to swallow, though his mouth was dry, and said in a small voice, "N-no… Witheric… what… I… I don't–"

"Don't pretend you do not understand, Restag," said Witheric, fiercely. "You heard me. Swear it. Swear by your oath-bond to me that you shall take Aleukus as your thane and serve him as you did me. Swear it!"

"N-no. No. No, Witheric, I won't!"

"Swear it! This is my command, Restag, my last command, as your thane," said Witheric, no longer angry but still firm. "It is my last, Restag, and if you will be true of speech and true to your oath, you will swear this to me."

The world around Restag seemed suddenly dark, his voice almost not his own as he whispered, "I… I swear it, Witheric. I swear upon my oath-bond to you, that I shall take Aleukus of Thenika as my thane and serve him as I would you, until either of us shall die or he release me from my bond. This I swear to you."

Suddenly, the fierceness left Witheric's eyes, and he seemed to lose all strength as he released his hold and sank into the pillows, sighing, "Thank you, my friend. Thank… yo…."

Restag stared at the suddenly speechless form and its shallow breaths. "With…eric?" He took the other man's shoulder and shook it gently, but though the man still breathed, he did not open his eyes.

"Witheric? Witheric? Wake up! Witheric, open your eyes! Witheric!"

But he did not wake. Outside, the sky grew dark, and white flakes began to fall for the first time in that city for several years. By morning, a thin layer of white coated Thenika, Jewel of Ithaenia, and Witheric, High Thane of the Eisenband, had passed beyond the reach of dawn.

Chapter 14

Spring came, as it always did, during the Great Fast. For all the years she could remember, that period of the year, where one grew weak from lack of many favored foods and meals restricted to one a day, had been a time of hard, uncomfortable, but overall rejuvenating reflection, followed by joy and city-wide celebrations as the fast ended and they began the Great Feast that was the largest celebration in the liturgical year. This year, however, those early days of spring, as the weather again returned to comfort and cloudless sunshine, the peaceful days of memory disappeared in a series of violent riots and strikes within the city's walls, resulting in many deaths and city-wide fear. Thankfully, the city guard managed to contain the violence, eventually putting down the attackers, who announced themselves to be of the Leikgaard Asgradi tribe. As Witheric had foretold, the tribe, who had proven hard to remove or subdue peacefully, had formed a long list of grievances, including many exaggerated to weigh more than they did in truth, but all of which must be avenged. For the sake of that vengeance, they had burned and looted shops, killed and harassed civilians, and sent fear throughout the entire city. And while most had been eventually either driven out or killed, a few had escaped capture and still sent a collective shiver throughout Thenika with the oaths of blood-debt they had left behind them. This threat could still be felt over a month later, in the midst of the Great Feast. With a heavy heart, Korena thought of all the innocent rendeilxue she had seen or heard of attacked from fear, including some from her own house. No deaths had resulted so far, but it felt like only a matter of time if the final leaders of the riots were not found and publicly tried and punished, and she realized how seemingly suddenly the Asgradi's long-lasting conflicts had entered and overwhelmed her city at a level unknown to her generation, reawakening past mistrust. How long man, full and half alike, remembered old injuries, and how easily they revived old fears. How easily the Fallen Soul cracked and dirtied its mirrored surface. Even if she had known this dogma from childhood, it was entirely different to see it play out in front of her.

Other things had changed as well during the past few months. The queen had given birth to her second child, a prince, to the elation of the city. The baby was healthy, but the pregnancy had been harder on her than her first, and she had become ill soon after. Her full recovery, however, was finally in sight. And the sooner the better, to remove one of the many burdens on the king's shoulders. Aristi had left again, before the riots began, though where to was anyone's guess. She would have to wait for him to arrive and send a letter, as usual. She also did not know the state of Ortheus, except for the general knowledge of the doings of House Meathorsis, as he had begun avoiding her after her pushing him away as harshly as she had that one day, months ago. It still brought her shame to think of losing control in that moment, and she felt some pity for him, but also relief to no longer have him trying to woo her.

As for her own house, Karas had wed, as planned, soon after the Great Fast had ended, their father insisting that chaos outside their walls would not disturb the order within. It was a token phrase, as the Asgradi attacks had, indeed, disturbed the order of the house, with more requests for anti-magic body and security guards piling on Kairon's desk daily, but she appreciated the decision and the resultant bit of happiness for her now paperwork-buried brother.

As a member of the palace guard, Korena had, thankfully, been able to avoid most of the craziness of the city and her family's life. Yes, there was much more tension and its own kind of chaotic busyness within the thick walls, but it was more contained, in a way, at least from the Guards' perspective. The biggest change had been the lengthening of shifts as a fourth of the palace soldiers were sent to reinforce the City Guard's search parties, including most of the Dampeners. However, as one of the only Nullifiers in the guard, she had been kept on duty to protect the king and his family. It meant an extra two hours to her shift, with the threatening of another four if even more were needed by Thenika at large, but in a way it was actually a relief to have more time away from the manor during those days.

No, the difficult part for Korena was the change in her assigned hours, and that had been her own doing.

Korena yawned deeply and blinked in the dim light of her oil lamp, searching the shadows for signs of intruders and finding, as usual, nothing but plaster and stone. She had always been a morning person. Never so early to rise as her father or brother, but a woman of the natural cycles of sun and moon. To suddenly invert a lifetime of sleeping habits was proving difficult, even a couple months in. It didn't help that she kept falling into old habits that were preventing her from obtaining any regularity in bed time or rising.

"You did not have need to be here. You can to return."

Korena tried to give Restag a side eye only to be foiled by another yawn. He was right, of course. She hadn't needed to join him on night patrol, but she had submitted the request anyway.

Since Witheric's death, Restag had changed. It was understandable and some of it positive. His language skills had grown extensively, and as a result he had grown increasingly comfortable with a select few, Korena included. He still spoke the most with Leskinor during their rare free time, the two of them switching between Asgradi and Ithaenian with infuriating ease and frequency, as if they weren't two entirely different languages. But she was still coming to know the rendeilxue better, hearing hints of his dry humor and personality now in his everyday speech. However, something was off, as well. More than just the natural grief or prevailing sense of absence that dampened one's spirit, that knowing loss of a piece of one's self that cannot be recovered and yet feels so strange to acknowledge as gone. Perhaps if she had not been there that day, she might not have thought so much of it. All deal with grief in a way his own.

But she had been there. She had seen the frightening change Witheric underwent, the fear and anger and almost manic emotion that seemed to possess him, the harshness of his voice, and the horror of Restag's. There was no other word for it. Something terrible had happened in those last moments of the High Thane's consciousness, but she was too afraid to ask what. Too afraid to know. And yet, every time she witnessed Restag sink into that impassive face with its silent, stony eyes that she now recognized as him grieving, that too frightened her, as if this time he would sink too far, go too deep, and never resurface, and she yearned to ask, to know, to have some hold from which to reach out her hand to him to pull him back. And then he would return, and all that would remain in her was the ache and fear of the unknown.

She was not alone in her worries. Aleukus, as well, quickly picked up that the rendeilxue's state was worse than the ordinary turns and cycles of mourning.

After the second week of checking in to see Restag sitting and staring emptily at one thing or another–his desk of papers, the untouched stack of books by the bed, or any of the things Witheric had left behind–the king, concerned for the man's mental state, had begun giving him work to do, halving the usual period given for sorrow. The most natural course, based on the previous months, had been to allow him to join the palace patrol with the guards, who already knew him well enough to not be frightened by his presence. However, for the sake of the rest of the servants, who were not so familiar with the man, he had assigned Restag to the night shift. An especially wise move in hindsight, with the recent chaos that had come to plague the rest of Thenika. Upon learning of the decision, Korena had requested a reassignment as well, one readily granted by the captain, who was more than willing to keep a powerful member of the Blood Houses right beside the Asgradi warrior who was now accompanying his men. That had been nine weeks prior, and still the change to going to bed in the middle of the night and waking up around the sixth bell after dawn felt wrong. So far, however, she did not regret the decision as she watched Restag, now with duties and work to perform, gradually emerge from his grief-induced stasis and return to something more like living.

She gave him a reassuring look, saying, "I'm fine, Restag. Just a little tired."

The Asgradi, who almost looked human in the palace's chain mail and helmeted guard uniform, squinted at her and said, "Is it not of every night you are a 'little' tired? And what of these?" He pointed to the area beneath his own eyes. "What of the darkness as of many nights' rest-thieving?"

Korena flushed. She had tried to use her cosmetics to hide the dark circles, but…. Changing tactics, she grinned and said, "That makes it sound like I'm going around stealing other people's sleep."

He gave the notion a few moments' thought and then said, "That is of beside the matter… But it is not so untrue."

"Really? Whose?" she said, ready to laugh only to catch hints of a flush to the forward-facing man's cheeks in the dim light of hallway's lamps, bringing sudden heat to her own face.

A spear shaft suddenly cut between them, followed quickly by Parchaes shoving himself in, saying, "All right. That's enough flirting on the job. This is patrol time. Got it?"

"We-we're not-I mean, that's…," Korena felt her protests die away under the man's gaze as he put his arm over Restag's shoulders.

"You two are reminding me that I don't got a lady of my own. That means you're flirting," said Parchaes with a pout.

"That's not what that word means," said Korena, unable to hold back a smile. All patrols were made in groups of two or three, and Korena being a Dampener, in her sleeveless, padded silk vest and calf-length leggings rather than a fully armored guard, didn't count. When Parchaes had volunteered to be the rendeilxue's regular patrol partner, the other guards had been happy to go along with the arrangement. They might have accepted their half-human colleague, but that didn't mean they wanted to be alone with him, and the captain was a man who recognized when to skirt the usual procedures for the sake of peace and efficiency. Despite his absurd energy so late at night, which only brought into further focus her own exhaustion, Korena was glad to have him there, not only for his familiarity with the palace at night, which seemed a very different place than during the day, but also because of moments like these, when she did not know how to feel about Restag's linguistic improvements. It was a clear case of one part of herself telling her one thing and another part, the one that sounded like her father, screaming another, and between them sat her reason, trying to understand the different arguments.

She let out a sigh and said, "You should probably let him go. He doesn't look too happy."

"Nah, if he was angry, he'd have kicked my ass by now, right, bud?" said Parchaes.

However, Restag was no longer paying attention. As there had been no one else to inherit them, Restag had been the recipient of Witheric's few possessions: the maps that currently lay rolled up in their case at the bottom of a drawer, quite possibly the only remaining pieces of the late thane's handwriting besides his letters to the king; the clothes yet to be repurposed or given to one small enough to wear them; the wheel-lock gun he hardly knew how to use that currently hung in its holster from his belt; the signet ring, now with none to signify; and the iron pin within Witheric's bag resting against Restag's chest beneath his clothes. He still wore his own pin, as well, clasped to the shirt beneath the padded doublet and chain mail of the guard uniform, and an eerie sensation irritated his skin around both pins as he stood in that long, dim hallway following the onset of night. He recognized the feeling, remembered the unease he had ultimately ignored as he and Witheric had stepped out of the trees and into the illusioned safety of the hag's cottage.

He quickly pulled himself free, ignoring Parchaes's surprised criticisms, and looked around urgently. Nothing. Only a hall as empty as any other, the tiled floor reflecting the lamplight and the plastered walls with their painted patterns leading up to a ceiling whose ornate carvings could not be distinguished for the deep shadows. Serenely quiet and empty. And yet, he could not ignore the prickling sensation running across his body, like being stuck with pins across his arms and chest.

Korena came up beside him and asked, "What's wrong?"

"Someone...," he paused and then ran his Sight down the hall, searching for the mind whose magic caused his unease. Somewhere farther down, he found it, a mind with fear pulsing through it like a heartbeat, fear and anticipation, waiting, knowing something was wrong but also that it had not been found, not yet. It could not be found. It couldn't–

"If you wish me harm, then show your face, foot-dragger," Restag barked to the shadows in Asgradi. Parchaes and Korena looked at him in confusion as silence followed, but the unease persisted. Restag readied his spear, his eyes searching the hall for any sign of wrongness. Then Parchaes cried out, and Restag felt the air forced from his chest as the other man tackled him, sending both to the ground just as a gunshot rang painfully down the hall, the bullet burying itself in the unseen ceiling. Korena gasped back a scream as she looked back the way they'd come, and the two men followed her eyes to see a form standing in the stonework, the mosaics rippling around him as if waist-deep in a pool of water, holding a still-smoking pistol. Restag lunged after him, but he was too far to reach before he disappeared again into the stones. A string of curses came from Parchaes, while Korena asked in a shaken voice, "What was that?"

Restag shook his head. "I am not knowing its name. It is a gift I have not met before. It is still here."

Both humans quickly drew and loaded their own pistols. Restag felt tempted to do the same with the wheellock, but though he had been introduced to the use of a gun over the past month, he could still barely remember how to hold it properly, let alone aim and fire. With his other combat skills, it had not seemed a high priority before now.

"Parchaes," he said, eyes scanning the walls and floor and ceiling, "if you see, hold on him so Korena can grab. Do not let go."

Parchaes nodded, as did Korena, though she barely heard him through the pounding in her ears. Though a palace guard, she had never actually been part of a real fight. Though trained at home in the martial arts, she had rarely used them out of a controlled environment, and never in one where the other person wanted her dead. She felt as if she couldn't breathe.

Then, she saw it, down the hall and coming out of the unnaturally fluid paintwork, the barrel of a gun followed by hands and a face. She screamed, aimed, and fired. Her shot missed, impacting on the wall a few inches above where she'd intended, but it startled the gunman long enough for Parchaes to charge at the form with remarkable speed. The attacker turned his pistol on the charging man and fired, but he had moved too quickly. The shot went wide. Too late the assassin realized the mistake in his choice to fire rather than retreat as the powerful human grabbed his arm, yanking him clean from the wall and flinging him halfway to the next. Moments later, Restag had him on the floor, fighting to get him in a firm lock before he could melt again into the stones.

"Rena!"

The shout woke Korena from her mental paralysis, and she dove to the floor, grabbing at the attacker's bare wrist. Once she took hold, she dug her nails into his skin as he cried out and thrashed, trying to release himself of this unknown thing clinging to him. However, between the panic caused by the unfamiliar silence of his fairy blood and the decreased strength that came with it, Restag soon had a strong hold on him. The would-be killer glared hatefully at them, still trying to free his arm from Korena's grasp and shouting curses and damnation upon them until Parchaes pointed his pistol at him. "Shut up," he said. "Now, you're gonna listen and answer my questions, or it'll hurt, got it?"

"Parchaes, no! We can't do that. That would be murder, and he needs to be taken to the captain and interrogated," said Korena.

"Not til I know what's going on. If we turn him in now, who knows how long it'll take to know, if we ever do," said Parchaes.

The gunman spat and growled, "I not say to gift-less and false-bloods."

"'False-bloods'? What the hell are you talking about?" said Parchaes.

"Those of 'false blood' are traitors," said Restag, matter-of-factly.

The captured rendeilxue snorted and said in Asgradi, "The human words do not uncover the true form of your poison. False-blood you are, for who of the true Asgradi could submit themselves to guard a king of dust, spawn of a blood-debtor and himself a debt-giver? We had not believed such stories to be sooth, but we are proven fools."

Korena gasped. "There's more than one of you?"

The attacker's eyes darted to her in surprise, and his face contorted into fury at the thought that a mere human had understood his words. However, he did not speak, his mouth clamping shut, as he recognized the blunder he had made.

Parchaes tapped his gun barrel against the Asgradi's brow, saying, "Well? Answer the princess." But the man's mouth remained shut.

"Parchaes, take him," said Restag, shifting enough to let Parchaes quickly take over his position on top of the man, pistol still in hand. During the transfer, there was a brief moment where the Asgradi assailant nearly broke free, but with Korena still hanging on to him, Parchaes managed to subdue him again. Parchaes looked up to Restag to ask what to do next only to see the man removing his armor down to his padded doublet.

"What are you doing?" he asked.

Restag removed the bag holding Witheric's ring and pin from his neck and dropped his own pin inside. He then placed it on the pile of chain mail and other metal garments, reclaiming only his belt holding the sword and Witheric's gun. Without it touching or resting so close to his skin, the distracting hum of iron quieted. He said, "There is doom in his words. I will take a look and want not so much noise."

Parchaes raised a brow. "Take a look? How? You know, Restag, sometimes you really don't–"

"Restag?" cried the Asgradi, his eyes bulging. "No… it can't…Restag Soul… he said you were–no! No! No!"

Parchaes yelped as the Asgradi bucked sharply beneath him, screaming Asgradi obscenities as he tried to escape, and in that moment, reflexes built from years of wrestling and fighting–both on an off the street–kicked in, and the surprised guardsman slammed the butt of his pistol into the hostage's head, leaving him unconscious.

"Parchaes! What did you do?" cried Korena, staring at the white of the rolled-back eyes.

Flushing, the guardsman replied, "S-sorry, it's just-I-I didn't… Hell! Now what do we do? We still don't know anything."

Restag knelt beside the man, saying, "It is of little matter."

He reached out and placed a hand on the unconscious man's face, and before either Korena or Parchaes could respond, he dove into the man's mind. Rivers stood before him, rivers of differing lengths and widths, as if filling in the spaces between sun-cracked earth. He followed one tributary to another, trying to follow the tangled mess of memories as one thing connected to another. Though he had downplayed it, Restag found himself wishing Parchaes had managed to keep from knocking out the assailant. Perhaps then, in his panic and desire to hide it, he might have shown Restag the river he needed. His instincts told him he did not have time to wander through this man's weals and woes. In one memory stream, he saw his man's eyes look over another's shoulder and stopped as he read the words on an unrolled page, listing both the king and an unnamed Asgradi guard and a rude diagram of the palace. Then the other man turned back, revealing a face familiar and impossible to mistake from its sheer malice.

Korena watched as Restag's eyes became unfocused. It much resembled the times when he closed off himself, but rather than become shut in, this gaze appeared to be far away, in a place beyond anyone's reach. She could almost feel his absence in that space. The silence stretched out down the hall, filling cracks and rounding corners for the next several minutes, creating a space cut off from all others till Restag's sharp intake of breath and dark creasing of his brow reminded her of their danger, and a few moments later the silence suddenly became a series of movements as the Asgradi jumped up and ran off, shouting over his shoulder, "Get Paskhalon! The queen, the king's-son! I go to Aleukus! Hurry!"

Before Korena could fully process what it all meant, she and Parchaes ran down the hall in the other direction, the unconscious captive bouncing against the man's shoulder as they hurried to find the captain.

Restag's feet echoed in the mostly empty halls as he periodically shot out his Sight, locating Aleukus in his study and finding himself both relieved and further driven each time he saw the man bent pensively over his work, worried but alive. He spent most nights there these days, poring over reports till his lamp ran low of oil, his daylight hours split between his usual duties as king and his concern for his recovering wife and newborn child. Everyone in the palace knew it, and anyone looking to find him at this hour would know where to look.

As he reached the study, the sentries at the door called him to identify himself, but he simply ignored them and threw his shoulder against the door, his supra-human strength knocking the unlocked barrier away immediately to the guards protests as they restrained him before the astonished and startled eyes of their king. "Restag?" he asked, putting his fountain pen in its holder as he studied the man's expression. "What's wrong?"

Restag, however, was not listening, his eyes instead searching the room for potential signs and areas of entry, settling on the doors leading out to the balcony overlooking the central courtyard three stories below. Using his Sight, he placed himself outside on the balcony, and he mentally maneuvered his vision to look down at the sheer, shadowed wall, seeing, as he expected, a figure stealthily moving up the side with unnatural ease. He came back to his own ears to gruff demands mere inches away. He tried to shove away their hold, but the contortion the guard had forced on his arms made it difficult even with his greater strength. Thankfully, Aleukus motioned for them to let him go, and he made a straight line for the double doors, saying in a low voice, "Get the king away. Now!"

The guards bristled at the order, but before their protests reached him, Restag had already opened the windowed door and used his Farsight to see the figure now crouched beneath the balcony, listening, startled by the ruckus from the room. Any moment, he could realize he was not so hidden or judge that the risks had increased to the point of a prudent retreat, so before he could reach that conclusion and escape, Restag moved. He charged to the edge of the balcony, vaulted over the side to the collected cries of the men in the room, and grabbed the railing, letting his hand slide till it nearly touched the floor so that he swung underneath, feet-first. Restag heard the assassin cry out and felt resistance that gave way beneath his foot, but either he had miscalculated his position or else the other man had reacted fast enough to decrease the impact and keep himself from being knocked off the wall. When Restag reached up with his other hand to begin pulling himself back up into the balcony, he saw the other man doing the same with much more speed as he darted, bare-footed, up the wall and onto the balcony, to the startled cries of the guards. In the light from the study, Restag finally saw the assassin's face clearly, immediately recognizing the cruel lines and gleeful malice of the Oathless who had escaped him at the human ruins outside of Eisensaet what now seemed so long ago.

The assassin did not waste time doing the same for him, instead charging at the group inside the study, his magic allowing him to scale one of the walls bare of wooden shelves and attack from the ceiling, sword drawn. The guards, though startled and terrified by this unnatural feat, were of the king's stock and managed to deflect the Asgradi's attempt on their master long enough for Restag to haul himself back over the side of the railing and out of open space. His arms hurt from the effort, reminding him of unfamiliar and untrained muscles, and he had to quickly catch his breath before he drew his own sword and followed the assailant back into the room.

With a quick note of regret that he had forgotten to grab a spear, Restag charged the hostile Asgradi, catching him off-guard and forcing him to retreat again up the wall in the face of the new attacker. The sentries took that moment to turn back to their primary duty and run, Aleukus escorted between them, shouting alarms down the hall. The assassin attempted to follow, but Restag moved to shove the damaged door closed and bar it with his body. It was then, as he cursed his fleeing quarry, that the assassin finally took the time to examine the interloper. His eyes widened and nostrils flared, and Restag did not need to see the other man's thoughts to read the hatred flooding over them as he recognized his former quarry. One who had escaped him and now resulted in the escape of another.

With a cry of animal rage, the Oathless leapt from the wall, swinging his sword. Restag blocked the blow, unwilling to move away from the door just yet and possibly expose the fleeing group to another assault. As they fought, Restag found himself hard-pressed to block the enraged swings, revealing his opponent to hold much more skill than he had demonstrated in their last bout, too much of a change for their previous match with its wide and clumsy strikes to have been anything but toying with his prey before the kill. However, Restag managed to keep himself braced against the door and block and parry till his enemy, ever more furious, attempted a thrust. Restag parried the blow, and the other's sword sank deep into the sturdy wood.

Restag struck, and the Oathless jumped back, reached into his tunic, pulled out a miniature pistol, and fired, finally forcing Restag to dive and roll away from the door, a motion made clumsy by the unfamiliar feel of the long pistol hanging from his belt and not quick enough to avoid the bullet ripping through his padded vest to clip his side. Furthermore, the moment he moved, the Oathless threw away the gun and pulled out a knife, hurling it at the thanesman so that it struck his right shoulder as he twisted out of his roll, only missing a more fatal area because of the practiced speed at which he had risen from the motion. Using Restag's moment of immobility from his double injuries, the assassin ran over to yank his sword from the thick wood.

Trying to ignore the pain in his dominant shoulder and his side, Restag stood and readied his own blade, growling, "Just showing your tricks now, Oath-breaker?"

Swinging his newly freed sword, the assassin replied flatly, "I'm not playing anymore, Thanesman."

Restag barely managed to avoid the next strike. Moving generated a new jolt of pain in both his side and shoulder, and he had to clench his teeth against the cry in his throat. In the face of that pain, he found himself relying more and more upon dodging than blocks. His enemy, recognizing this, pressed harder but still could not break through the other's defense. Both, however, knew who held the upper hand.

Confident in his position and eager to kill, the Oathless over-extended a strike, and Restag, using his longer reach, turned the attack aside and pivoted inside his opponent's defense, striking at his now-exposed enemy. Rather than flinch, however, the Oathless suddenly dropped his blade and dove at the charging thanesman, knocking them both to the ground. The impact was sudden and painful enough to the knife injury to finally wrest a vocal response from Restag, and he saw lights dancing across his vision as he grappled with and finally pushed away his enemy only to see the barrel of Witheric's gun aimed directly at him. Reflexively, he kicked up, sending the bullet to the ceiling, but by the time he managed to get back to his feet, the Oathless had run up the wall again and onto the ceiling, using Restag's inability to reach him due to the injury to the thanesman's shoulder to figure out how to rotate the cylinder, steadily pull back the hammer, and aim. Once again, Restag managed to dive out of the way, but he could not move fast enough to fully evade the third shot, the bullet embedding itself in his leg and making him collapse onto one knee.

Staring up at the black tunnel of the barrel as the Oathless rotated the chamber, Restag knew this must be his end, but the most he could feel was outrage at the cruelty of the gods that it should be by his dead master's arms. But then the shot went wide as a figure ran in from the hall and used the king's desk to leap up into reach of the assassin and take hold of him from behind. The two then crashed noisily to the floor as the Oathless felt his magic vanish, and with it his hold on the ceiling.

Restag watched as they both fell, unable to reach them before they hit the ground. Thankfully, the more robust Asgradi partially cushioned Korena's fall, though she did collapse on a sprained ankle after she rolled away and tried to stand. Restag also watched as the infuriated Oathless charged her and took her to the ground again, a death grip around her throat as he tried to crush her windpipe, all too far for Restag, with his limp leg, to reach and stop before it happened. Then he noticed Witheric's gun where it had fallen nearby. He dove for it, his fingers just reaching the butt of the weapon, and pulled it in, turned the chamber as he had seen his enemy do, and, barely taking the time to aim, fired.

The kickback was stronger than he'd expected, startling him and sending blinding pain through his injured shoulder. But as he had not bothered to aim for anywhere vital, only trying to hit the body of the killer not ten feet away, the shot that would have hit the assassin's side and might have left him incapacitated but alive instead struck him between the shoulder blades, killing him instantly. Restag did not know this until, using the long pistol for support, he managed to drag himself over and roll the body off of Korena's gasping and coughing form.

"Rena!" he gasped, dropping the gun to take her up by the shoulders. "Rena! You hear me? You are okay?"

She bobbed her head. Gradually, Korena's coughing stopped, turning into gasps, and then into violent sobs as she tried to speak. Restag had seen it before, when some of the young men under his care, virgins of war who had heard tales of the glory and bloodshed, first heard and tasted and smelled and saw the other side of war and then stared at their childhood friends' violated shells after their first battle, their only consolation those same promises of glory in the Final Battle at the End of All Things. However, though he had seen the reaction many times before, it had never hurt so much.

Unsure what else to do, he pulled her forward into his arms, and she responded likewise, wrapping her arms around his waist to cry against him. It was an unfamiliar thing, to comfort a woman. He did not want to speak to her the words he had used in times before to give courage to his own sex. It did not seem fitting. This young woman was, indeed, a shield-maiden, one who would stand guard against a dragon to defend her home, should necessity call her. But she was not a Valaki, charging before men with her gleeful war cries joining the hunting howls of her wolf. No. This woman was too gentle for chasing bloodshed, and he knew no way to console the gentle.

After their first debate, when he had been too angry to consider comfort, she had never reacted this way, and when she wept for Witheric's pains, he had only been able to watch from the side as his friend eased her sorrows. All others, it had been she, not he, who had been the consoler, and in that moment, all he could think was to hold her silently and wish and pray to any god that would listen to help her.

Help of a different kind did arrive a few minutes later as a small group of guards filed into the room, freezing one after another at the scene they saw. Restag, however, relieved for something familiar, reverted to habit as he said in a commanding voice, "Speak, spear-man. Of King Aleukus, he is of no harm?"

The guardsman, responding to the tone, clicked his heels together sharply as he said, "Yes, sir-uh… I mean… rendeil… sir. He has been placed under guard while a sweep is made of the palace for any other intruders. The same is the case for the queen and the crown prince. An attempt was made on her life, as well, but help arrived and the assailant killed before fatal injury could be inflicted, and a suspicious person was intercepted and shot approaching the nursery. Both the queen and the intruder are being treated, though Paskhalon has little hope for the suspected assassin."

Restag nodded. "Take me also to him. I am-we am both of need for help. My leg, it is shot, and I am to think her foot hurt, too."

"Understood," said the guard, entering the room, followed by his men. Nodding to Korena, he asked, cheeks coloring, "Is there any other injury to Miss Iegam?"

With one more quick tightening of her hold of him, Korena released Restag, still breathing raggedly, and said in a weak voice, "I'm… I'm f-fine. Just…."

She glanced over at the body of the assassin and shivered. The guard seemed to understand and did not press her further. Not long after, both she and Restag leaned against a soldier, walking the too-long journey across the palace from the king's study on the third floor of the New Palace toward the infirmary on the first floor of the Old. Before they had even made it down the first flight of stairs, however, they were met, or rather nearly collided into, by Parchaes, who on seeing them took a few moments to log their obvious injuries before saying, "No wonder you're taking so long. I just can't leave you two without you becoming a mess, can I? Nice timing, though, since I'm here to bring you to the infirmary, Restag. His Majesty is there. Says you need to talk."

Chapter 15

Despite the impatience clear in his pacing as they entered the infirmary, Aleukus stepped aside without comment to let Paskhalon and his assistants, called from their usual place in his office and laboratory a few doors down the hall to help, treat the two injured parties. Korena's injuries were quickly addressed, though not without a bit of waspishness from the doctor as she explained how she got them, but Restag's took longer. His leg was bandaged quickly enough, since the bullet had traveled straight through without shattering the bone, but Paskhalon insisted on taking extra time to check for any potential sliver of metal he could find under both magnifying glass and oil lamp before he would sign off on his assistants stitching up the wound. The guards—besides Parchaes and those assigned directly to the king—had been clear of the room for a couple hours and Korena had fallen asleep before Paskhalon allowed the king to debrief the patient.

Restag sat on the end of the operating table, dressed in only a clean shirt and a pair of loose, inpatient trousers. As the king's party entered, the rendeilxue winced and hissed involuntarily as he tried to bow at the waist before Aleukus dismissed the gesture while he took one of the available seats. He said, "How're you feeling?"

Restag grunted and said, "It is painful, but not most I have felt. Parchaes does worse."

The named individual beamed proudly, and even the grim-faced thanesman could not hold back the twitch of a smile. In a graver tone, he continued, "You have need to speak at me, King Aleukus?"

"No," said Aleukus with a wry smile. "No, if fact, I need the opposite. Parchaes told me what happened, or rather, what he saw. He said you touched a man and, a few minutes later, suddenly knew about assassins in the palace and their targets. I want to know how, Restag."

The rendeilxue nodded. "That is of my Far-Sight."

"Farsight?"

A confused wrinkle came to Restag's brow. "Friathri did never tell Korena? She… oh, but she is the age of my father's father, and it is not so willingly said of another's power even if asked. Yes, I am of the Far-Sighted clan. It is my blood-gift. I can see, and also hear, else than where I am."

"Elsewhere?" said the king. "Like where?"

"Anywhere," said Restag. "Or, so far as I know. I can see so near as past that door or to see Paskhalon's man or so far as Eisensaet yet from here."

"You can see through walls?" exclaimed Parchaes.

Restag thought for a moment and said, "No. Not so much as that. It is… it is more of that I am here, but I see as though there."

Nodding his understanding, Aleukus said, "I see. However, how does that become touching a man and knowing about an assassination?"

"To touch is not necessary. This is only to help focus. And it is as I said," said Restag."I am here, but I see as though there." He pointed first to himself and then to the king, or rather, to the king's forehead.

As the meaning dawned on Aleukus, his face paled. He swore under his breath. "You can read minds!" he gasped.

"It is perhaps mind, though to us, it is named Soul-Sight. If soul or only mind, this is a fight of many generations of the Dar-Speakers, bards, and elders."

"Seriously?" said Parchaes. "Hey, tell me. What am I thinking right now?"

Restag shook his head. "It is not of my preference to See into another man if there is no need. Such is poor for keeping trust, if a man cannot even keep his secrets, but if you should wish it…."

Holding up a hand to prevent Parchaes's reply, Aleukus said, "You can do this without the other man being awake?"

Restag nodded, and Aleukus stood, turning immediately toward the door and saying, "Can you walk? Good. I have a better task for your demonstration."

He took them to another room, this one with sentries posted both outside and inside the door. Within was a single bed guarded by additional soldiers, one of whom Restag recognized as one from the Blood Houses, all around a bed holding the unconscious form of another Asgradi, one Restag had not yet met and who he correctly concluded to be the last of the attackers.

"The man your patrol captured woke up and is being interrogated by my men," said Aleukus. "But this one... Paskhalon does not believe he will last the night, and he may have information his companion does not."

Restag nodded. "I shall look for what I can."

Aleukus had rather expected a more dramatic performance than what he saw as Restag's gaze lost focus, much as any man whose mind is elsewhere. However, there was no denying the veins visible from beneath his shirt collar suddenly shifting from black-ish green to shimmering gold, or the unsettling clarity and confidence in contrast to those unfocused eyes as Restag suddenly spoke a minute later, saying, "He is Oathless, payed by the Leikgaard to end the king's line as repayment for the injuries and insults to them by the Ithaenian people and the king stopping and arresting them when they tried to reclaim the injury. It is my thinking I, as well, was to be killed. For why was not known, and it mattered not. My shielding the blood-debtor human king was enough. He does not know if the man they met was of the rebels, for he covered himself well, but he does know where their contact is to wait for them to report tonight and the sign they are to give should they succeed."

"Tonight?" said Aleukus, some of the men around him perking up as they pieced together what was going on, their eyes widening in curiosity and fear at the rendeilxue. "Where? What sign? How long do we have to find him?"

However, Restag did not answer, his focus remaining distant and only his eyes occasionally shifting. Then, just as abruptly as it had started, his eyes refocused, and the visible bits of his Blood Mark dulled. He said, "I could find no name for the place, but I have tried to mark what details I could into my memory, if you should want to try to find it."

Aleukus hesitated a moment before he said, "Could you not hear me while you were... 'there'?"

"No," said Restag. "I had no eye or ear 'here' to see or hear. Why ask you?"

"Curiosity, and considerations for the future," replied Aleukus. "And yes, tell me the rest of what you saw."

One of the men jotted down Restag's descriptions, as well as the other images and bits of conversation he could summarize or remember, and then the soldier ran off to report the news to the City Guard and try to locate the rendezvous point before the contact realized the plan had failed and bolted. With that task done, Aleukus ordered Restag follow him out again, this time dismissing Parchaes as well, who left hesitantly, leaving just the two of them to walk, to Restag's surprise, to his own guest room. Aleukus seated himself on the chair across from the couch, fingers folded on his lap.

"Sit," he ordered, to which Restag readily obeyed. The king then leaned forward, elbows on his armrests and said, "I'm sure Paskhalon will have someone breaking down doors looking for his missing patient soon, and between the bedrest he's sure to impose on you and my own busyness, I'm not sure when we'll get the chance to sit and speak like this, but I wanted to talk with you privately, Restag Thanesman."

He paused for several moments, staring grimly at his own hands. Then, sighing deeply, he said, "Restag, let me speak with you not as guest and host but man to man. You know that Witheric left you in my care?"

Restag flinched, more so than Aleukus would have expected. His sea-blue eyes searched the king's gray ones, and a strange expression settled into the rendeilxue's face as he said softly, "Yes."

Taking a few moments to find the right words, Aleukus went on, "Good. Then, let me be clear with you. First, I thank you for what you have done for me this night. Your actions saved me and my family, and your–do your people call them gifts?–your gift may have just provided the information we need to finish addressing the current crisis and its instigators. For that, I am very grateful, more so than words can express.

"However, it is also the case that this news, the nature of your gift, will cause its own fear and suspicion. There are many implications to it, many dangers on both a personal and a state level. We didn't know, Restag, that such a power existed among your people, and no matter what we do, that will cause many to be afraid of you, to be afraid of what your people can do. Therefore, if I'm to protect you and protect them, I must request you to speak to me honestly. Tell me, Restag, can you really see anywhere, into any mind?"

"No," said Restag. However, before Aleukus could relax, the Asgradi said, "I cannot see Korena's mind. I do not know of those of her gift with less power. As I say, I do not wish to See unless for need. I, too, do not know if I could see her if I did not enter her soul but only looked to See her in another place, but to guess, I think yes. My magic is not bothered by her unless touching. All others, yes. I can See, if I am to try."

Nodding gravely, Aleukus said, "And? Is there any way to stop it? To stop you from Seeing into a place or a mind?"

This time, Restag hesitated, and there was no missing the conflict within him, one of such intensity that for a moment, Aleukus thought he recognized a passing look of despair before the Asgradi finally replied, "The… the Eisenband. That alone, I know. If there is others, I do not know."

"The Eisenband? You mentioned it before, and one of Witheric's titles was Iron-Brow, correct?"

"Yes," said Restag, his eyes growing sad and distant. "The Eisenband, it is the crown of the Asgradi, made of star-iron, a gift to Witheric's first father from Dar to mark his line as High Thane. To the one that wears it, all magic is of no use. He, too, cannot use magic, but so, too, none can touch him, not even my own. If I use my Sight, it is as if he does not exist, and I cannot enter his soul."

Conflict and helplessness played across the human king's face as he ran a hand through his hair. "'Star-iron,'" he said. "That sounds like the 'pure,' ethereal form of metals the alchemists have been chasing after for centuries. How can… is there nothing we can do? Could something else work? Perhaps alchemically purified iron? Could that help?"

Restag shrugged. "This is not known."

With an understanding nod, Aleukus continued, "We'll have to try. There are too many dangers an ability like yours presents. To think! A whole family of rendeilxue who can watch our every moves, see into our homes and councils, read our minds! And if anyone finds out…. How many, Restag? How many of your people are there like you?"

Once again, a heavy silence fell between them, and when Restag spoke again, Aleukus heard the strong emotion the man held back. "You tell me to speak of my family's hidden things."

At first, Aleukus thought perhaps Restag was angry at him, and a touch of fear snuck into his heart. Although the other man was injured, he had heard of the rendeilxue's bouts on the training field, how he could push himself and wield destructive force even with various injuries, as well as stories of the superhuman resilience of this people from his father's accounts and those of the City Guard. If the warrior decided to attack him, then even with those injuries, Aleukus knew he could not count on victory. However, then he realized the expression was not of anger but intense sorrow and resignation. A look of complete and total submission. So utterly hopeless was that look, it disturbed the human king. But despite the twisted feeling it gave him, he said, "Yes, Restag. Though I speak to you as a man, I am still a king. I have my own people I must protect, and for that, I must know what endangers them. Tell me, Restag."

At that point, Restag looked away, his face white with shame and despair that only drove the stake of guilt deeper into the king's heart. Even so, the rendeilxue took a deep breath and said, "None. I do not at once know the true-count of my clan, of that I would need more thought, or the true-count of all in Eisensaet with Sight, for not only those of the direct line hold the gift. But of this I can say. There is none other like as me. Soul-Sight, it is as Korena's gift. Not all of Sight can See of all things, and of my knowing, I only am of Soul-Sightedness."

Aleukus's eyes widened. He said, "Witheric has left me to guard a jewel from among his people!"

Restag flushed, but he did not speak.

Feeling pity for the man, Aleukus stood and approached to place a comforting hand on his shoulder, kneeling down to say, "Thank you, Restag-Thanesman, for telling me. Truly. I know it was hard for you, and I'm sorry I had to ask."

However, Restag pushed off the king's hand and spoke with a tone shockingly bitter or angry or some like emotion, saying, "Do not speak such. It is your right."

After recovering from his surprise, Aleukus replied, "What do you mean? Restag, I have no inherent right to your secrets, even if I am a king. I ask only because I must protect both you from my own men's fear and my people from a danger we never even knew existed. I only ask for that sake, and I will not force you to answer. If you thought otherwise, that was not my intention."

Restag's eyes widened, and his gaze jumped up to the king's. The anger drained away, replaced by realization and sorrow and pain.

"No," he said, almost desperately. "No, it is not understood. It is not...."

Restag's hands trembled, and his face fell into one of grief beyond the reach of words as he said, his voice on the brink of tears, "My thane now is you, Aleukus of Thenika. I swore to Witheric I would, swore on my oath-bond to him to take you as thane. To serve you as thanesman as if to him. It was... it was his last command to me. The very last."

A dreadful silence overwhelmed the air as Aleukus realized the full meaning of what he had just heard, leaving him unsure whether to be more horrified or amazed. Almost more to himself, he whispered, "Then your master left me a treasure so precious I cannot even imagine its worth."

Gently, he again put a hand on the other man, this time taking his arm not as one trying to comfort another but as two men sharing a battlefield against the same foe. Even knowing how little it was worth compared to what he had been given, the king of Ithaenia said to the once-thanesman of Eisensaet, "Restag, I solemnly swear to you that I shall strive to be a king worthy of such a promise. If I do not, may God justly repay me for so grave a trespass."

Restag searched the human king's eyes for any sign, any hint of deception, but Witheric's words proved true, for even should all others prove their promises as fragile as paper, the word of King Aleukus of Ithaenia was straight as a spear and binding as iron, and to so honest a gaze, Restag could only place his own hand atop the king's, bow his head, and say, "Thank you."

Smiling softly, the king released his hold and rose, heading toward the door. He said, "I must go let Paskhalon know your whereabouts and then see about following up on our lead. That you, also, were targeted, you who so few know to be here, and that they had a map of the palace, the implications are grave. Is there anything more you need from me?"

"No, my thane," said Restag, and the use of the title in his reply further realized the truth that had been revealed to him. The king had little time to ponder it, however, for he opened the door to see Korena standing in the hallway, her hand dropping away with the door and her face pale with fury.

Clearing his throat, Aleukus said, "Miss Iegam, it is unprofessional to eavesdrop, and borderline traitorous to eavesdrop on your king."

"Forgive me, Your Majesty," she replied, her voice hard. "I heard you two had headed in this direction, and I meant to knock, but… I apologize."

The king's face softened as the young woman wiped away the first set of tears. He said, "I shall send a guard to stand by the door, just in case."

"Yes, sir. That is very wise of you, sir," replied the woman, sniffing and letting out a shuddering breath.

Even after the king left and disappeared around the corner, Korena lingered in the threshold, trying to stop the tears already falling. Restag began to rise from the couch, but after his jaw tightened at putting weight on his leg, Korena finally limped into the room and sat down on the other side of the couch, fists clenched on her lap, staring with angled brows at the small table, letting herself cry as Restag looked on in confusion. He said, "Korena, you are still hurt? It is for better for you to sleep."

"I'm not tired!" she snapped, turning to glare at him. "I'm too angry to be tired! How could he do that to you? He used you! Used your loyalty against you! How could he? After all you did, how could he do something so horrible?"

Restag's eyes bulged and the blood drained from his face. "You are angry at Witheric!"

"Of course I am!" she said. "He forced you to serve another king against your will! And I know you didn't want to. You wouldn't have acted like you did that night or sound like you did just now if it hadn't been forced. It was a wretched thing for him to do, to manipulate you like that to force you to make a promise like that!"

As she spoke, Restag felt blood rush to his face and his hackles rise. He countered, "Witheric was a thane who look to care for his people even from after his death! He was a good master!"

Korena prepared to bite back, but a thought flashed across her conscience, a memory of the other time he had become so defensive so quickly, as well as the reason why she had later discovered, and the pity that overcame her cooled her anger, allowing her to see the fragility of the man before her and how easily she could break him if she were not careful. Saying a quick prayer of thanks and then a petition for guidance, she took a deep breath and, reigning in her tone as much as she could, she said, "I know, but he also used his authority as your master to command you to chain yourself to a new master you did not want. It was cruel, and it was wrong."

"No!" snapped Restag. "No, he wished only to protect me."

Swallowing the first response that came to mind, Korena said, "Even if that's the case, it was still an abuse of power, and it was wrong."

Restag shook his head and glowered at her. "That is also false. It is only my own doing. I would not let him free me of my oath. I would not be free, and so I am now bound to another. It is not of his doing. It is my own."

Korena's breath caught, and she could only gaze wide-eyed in both pity and horror at the young man before her for several moments before all remaining anger drained away, leaving only sorrow as she said, softly, "Oh, Restag. Restag, no, it's not. It's not your fault."

"Yes! It is!" he shouted, and Korena could hear the desperation in that cry as he went on. "It is not Witheric's! Witheric was kind, a gift-giver, strong!"

Korena nodded. "I know."

"He was a thane for his people, of much care to them and a wish to protect, not to kill for senseless things!"

"I know, Restag."

"He… he had desire to protect his people, to protect me. He was a good thane. A thane of a will of iron and blood of fire. A thane to wish for what not any before had dared."

"Yes. I know."

"And… and he was my friend," the man finished, his face still flushed as he stared defiantly at the young woman.

However, she did not flinch and instead said, "Restag, I know. I know all of that. Not so well as you, but enough to know it's true. And I also… I also know that he loved you. That he loved you so, so dearly. He loved you as his friend and as his thanesman, just as you loved him as your friend and as your thane. I know he was not a wicked man, that he was kind and gentle and wanted wisdom and to do right and to help you and protect you most of all. That he treasured you more than almost anything else. I know that he was, in many ways, a noble man, but he was also just a man, a man with weaknesses who hurt you."

Before Restag could counter her, she reached up and placed her hands against his cheeks, guiding his eyes to hers. "Restag, I know he hurt you. Deeply. You don't have to pretend he didn't. I know."

Restag glared into her eyes for a little while longer, but in the end, his defiance faded, and he looked away, saying so quietly it was almost without voice, "Yes."

Softly, Korena said, "He was so kind and supportive."

"Yes."

"He cared for his own and wanted to do whatever he could for you."

"Yes."

"He loved so much and so deeply."

"Yes."

"But," she said, moving her hands down to his and covering as much of his tight fists as she could with a soft caress. "But he also hurt you."

"...Yes."

"He forced you to take an oath you did not want, and it was wrong."

"Yes."

"Even if he had good motives, and I don't know if he did or did not, but it was wrong."

"Yes," came the chocked reply.

"He hurt you. He loved you, Restag. But it was wrong, and it hurt."

"Yes. Yes," he whispered and then broke into sobs.

Korena did not know how long they sat there, Restag's face buried in her shoulder and body shaking with quiet sobs, only occasionally releasing a short, sharp, creaking sound, like metal bending just before the breaking point, gripping her hands within his own like to an anchor. And all the while, she silently let him finally mourn. For what she had seen before, his closing off to all but his grief and his thoughts, she would never again call mourning. She let him mourn his loss of home, his loss of place and direction and common tongue, his loss of honor, his loss of family, his loss of friend, and most of all, his loss of master and the breach of trust that had come of it, and all the hurt and pain and anger and sorrow that had followed. She let him mourn it all, a still, quiet figure sitting stalwart beside him as he fought the waves and winds of grief.

And then the winds calmed and the waves died down, and all fell into exhausted stillness and the rhythm of his tired breaths. Extracting one of her hands, Korena reached into a pocket to pull out a handkerchief and began to wipe the remnants of his tears before giving it to him while she rose to fetch him some water. He took the cup gratefully and slowly sipped, running his fingers along the smooth surface.

"How are you feeling?" she asked.

"Terrible," he answered.

Korena couldn't hold back a small chuckle. "Sorry," she said. "I don't mean to laugh. I suppose I should expect nothing less blunt from you by now."

Restag's gaze settled on her once more, lingering on her brown eyes and lips gently smiling, and her cheeks glowing warmly in the dim lamp light, and he said, "No. It is better to see you smile."

The color in Korena's cheeks deepened, and she looked away, locking in on the door across the small room. Standing, she said, "Th-the guard and Paskhalon are taking a while. I should–"

"Korena."

The young woman stopped as Restag's fingers gently closed around her hand, and her eyes drew back down to his. He pulled her hand close, leaning his forehead against its back and saying, "Not yet."

"B-but they… they could be waiting outside right now," she said.

"Then let them wait a little longer," he replied, standing beside her and taking her other hand as well, pulling her closer.

She looked up to him, her eyes searching his. She whispered, "But they'll misunderstand."

"What is there to misunderstand?" he said, and he kissed her.

Her breath caught as his lips touched hers, and she let herself sink into the moment, time suspended with her breath. And then it was over, a brief moment that had shifted everything from then on, and she said, "Are you sure, Restag? I mean, you did just kiss a human."

The Asgradi looked pensive a moment and then replied, "You are not all human. It is tolerable."

For a few moments, Korena did not know whether to feel insulted or not. Then she saw the slight tug at corner of the rendeilxue's mouth, and she laughed. "It's a start," she said.

And in reply, he smiled, and with that smile, even more than the kiss, she knew there was no turning back. In the back of her mind, she knew her father would not be pleased, and she knew it would not be easy to deal with this half-fae Thanesman from the distant north, but there would be time to worry and face such challenges. For the moment, she let them slide away as he leaned in again and she looked up to meet him.

-To be continued in The Thanesman Chronicles Book 2-

234

Acknowledgements

In the proper order of things, my first thanks is to my Chieftain, the Champion of Mankind and Peace-Child of God, Jesus Christ, to the Holy Ghost, and to the All-Ruler Father, the echoes of whose cosmic song all artists attempt to carry to other's ears. Next, I thank my family, first my mother for her encouragement towards my creative pursuits from childhood till now, and then to my husband, who refuses to let me downplay the quality of my work. Next, I thank Dr. Rachel Fulton Brown for introducing me to *The Heliand*, specifically the G. Roland Murphy, S. J. translation, whose commentary gave the breath that brought the Asgradi to life. Finally, I thank the COVID lock downs for getting me working from home, which provided me the time and energy to write this story's first draft. Even that which is evil can be turned to good.

236

About the Author

V. A. Boston is a Catholic, wife, mother, the second of eight children, and a lover of language. She enjoys singing, rainy days, winter, and a cup of hot tea or cocoa by a cozy fire with a book. Her own storytelling career began with an unfinished manuscript about a knight on a mission to save a princess from a dragon written on scissor-cut paper bound with a shoelace between two pieces of cardboard. And her imagination hasn't stopped since.

237

More Books by V. A. Boston

Fairy Door